PRAISE FOR F. SIONIL JOSÉ

"The foremost Filipino novelist in English, his novels deserve a much wider readership than the Philippines can offer. His major work, the Rosales Saga, can be read as an allegory for the Filipino in search of an identity."
—IAN BURUMA, *The New York Review of Books*

"America has no counterpart . . . no one who is simultaneously a prolific novelist, a social and political organizer, an editor and journalist, and a small-scale entrepreneur. . . . As a writer, José is famous for two bodies of work. One is the Rosales sequence, a set of five novels published over a twenty-year span which has become a kind of national saga. . . . José Rizal's *Noli Me Tangere*, published in Spanish (despite its Latin title) in the late nineteenth century, was an influential *Uncle Tom's Cabin*–style polemic about Spanish rule. The Rosales books are a more literarily satisfying modern equivalent."
—JAMES FALLOWS, *The Atlantic*

"One of the [Philippines'] most distinguished men of letters."
—*Time*

"Marvelous."
—PETER BACHO, *The Christian Science Monitor*

"[José] never flattens his characters in the service of rhetoric. . . . Even more impressive is José's ability to tell important stories in lucid, but never merely simple prose. . . . It's refreshing to see a politically engaged writer who dares to reach for a broader audience."
—LAURA MILLER, *San Francisco Weekly*

"Tolstoy himself, not to mention Italo Svevo, would envy the author of this story. . . . This short . . . scorching work whets our appetite for Sionil José's masterpiece, the five-novel Rosales Saga."
—JOSEPH COATES, *Chicago Tribune*

"[José is] an outstanding saga writer. If ever a Nobel Prize in literature will be awarded to a Southeast Asian writer, it will be to F. Sionil José."
—*The Mainichi Shimbun* (Tokyo)

"Considered by many to be Asia's most likely candidate for the Nobel Prize for literature."
—*The Singapore Straits Times*

"F. Sionil José could become the first Filipino to win the Nobel Prize for literature . . . he's a fine writer and would be welcome recognition of cultural achievement in his troubled country. [He] is widely known and acclaimed in Asia."
—JOHN GRIFFIN, *The Honolulu Advertiser*

"[José] captures the spirit of his country's sullen and corrupt bureaucracy [and] tells the readers far more about Philippine society than many, far lengthier works of nonfiction."
—STEVE VINES, *South China Morning Post* (Hong Kong)

"The plot [of *Ermita*] is unfolded by concise, vividly picturesque, sometimes humorous, often tender prose. The candor with which Sionil fleshes out his sensuous earthy characters is balanced by his breathtakingly surgical dissection of their minds and souls."
—NINA ESTRADA, *Lifestyle Asia*

"José is one of Asia's most eminent writers and novelists. His passionate, sometimes transcendent writings illuminate contemporary Filipino life in graceful and historically anchored narratives of power brokers and the brokered, of landowners and the indentured."
—SCOTT RUTHERFORD, *Islands* Magazine

"He has achieved a unity in his writings such as that seen in William Faulkner in his stories relating to Yoknapatawpha County in Mississippi or in the Monterey stories of John Steinbeck."
—DOUGLAS LeCROY, *St. Louis University Research Journal*

Dusk

Dusk

A NOVEL

✛

F. Sionil José

San Francisco
Jan. 8, 2004

For Malu Engalla —
Maraming salamat!

THE MODERN LIBRARY

NEW YORK

Originally published, in English, as *Po-on* by Solidaridad Publishing House, in Manila, Philippines.

The first chapter originally appeared as the short story "The Cripples" in *The God Stealer* (Quezon City, Philippines: R. P. Garcia Publishing Company, 1968).

MODERN LIBRARY and colophon are registered trademarks of Random House, Inc

LIBRARY OF CONGRESS CATALOGING-IN-PUBLICATION DATA
José, F. Sionil (Francisco Sionil)
[Po-on]
Dusk: a novel / F. Sionil José.
p.   cm.
Originally published: Po-on. Manila, Philippines: Solidaridad Pub. House, [c1984]
ISBN 0-375-75144-0
1. Philippines—Fiction. I. Title.
PR9550.9.J67P6   1998
823—dc21   97-39435

Modern Library website address: www.modernlibrary.com

Printed in the United States of America
BVG 001

For Philip, Frederick,
Evelina, and Stephen Cichy

ACKNOWLEDGMENTS

I am grateful to the Rockefeller Foundation for its fellowship, which allowed me to write this novel in Bellagio, Italy.

I'd also like to thank R. P. Garcia Publishing Company, Quezon City, Philippines, where the first chapter of this book originally appeared as "The Cripples" in the collection *The God Stealer.*

NOTES ON THE WRITING OF *DUSK (PO-ON)*

WHEN people ask me which of my novels I like best, I always reply, you are asking me which of my seven children I love most.

My Japanese translator, Matsuyo Yamamoto, thinks *Tree* is the most evocative. The poet and critic Ricaredo Demetillo thinks *My Brother, My Executioner* is the most dramatic and *Tree* the dullest. It is really difficult for me to say which is what, but this I can say: *Mass* is the book I enjoyed writing most, because I wrote it straight from beginning to end in one creative spurt. Besides, I wrote it in Paris.

My daughter Jette, who is my editor, thinks *Dusk* (original title, *Po-on*) is the best. *Po-on*, which means "the beginning" or "tree trunk" in my native Ilokano, is the first in terms of chronology.

Of the five Rosales novels, *Dusk* took the longest to write—more than three decades. I had great difficulty, for it meant research into our past, the period from the early 1870s to 1898 and the Battle of Tirad Pass, the same period during which the Spanish regime was vanquished and the Americans took over. *Dusk* is simply the story of a family, or rather of a peace-loving man who led his clan in its flight from the narrow coastal plain of the Ilokos in Northern Luzon to the Central Plains. It is also a story of Spanish tyranny, and the Filipino response to it and to the American intrusion into our islands after the Spaniards left. The man who leads this hegira is the grandfather of Antonio Samson in *The Pretenders,* published in 1962, the first of the five Rosales novels. Four others followed: *Tree; My Brother, My Executioner; Mass;* and *Po-on (Dusk).*

All five novels may be read independently of one another, but all are linked, not so much by recurring characters as by their origins in a small Central Luzon town called Rosales. The name is incidental; Rosales can very well be any town in the Philippines. And running through all five novels are the basic themes that have always interested me as a writer: man's continuing search—often futile, often hopeless—for social justice and a moral order.

It is in *Dusk* where I define the patriot and hero. I do this at a time when heroes in the Philippines are movie stars and socialites turned politicians, soldiers who have betrayed the Constitution, and even returning widows with three thousand pairs of shoes.

The two major characters in *Dusk* are my fictional rendition of Apolinario Mabini, who in real life was the ideologue of the revolution against Spain, and Eustaquio Samson, the young acolyte who flees from the Ilokos with his whole clan.

Both heroes come from the lower classes. Mabini was lucky

enough to escape his rural origins and come to Manila to study law. He was very bright and morally upright. Aguinaldo, the president of the First Republic, picked him to be his first foreign minister. He was, however, ousted from his position by the wealthy *ilustrados* who surrounded Aguinaldo and betrayed the revolution. According to Ambeth Ocampo, a young, fastidious historian, they concocted a plan to milk the fledgling republic, but Mabini's ethical and ideological principles foiled them. They spread the gossip that Mabini was a cripple because he was syphilitic, an untruth that I had swallowed and presented as fact in this novel. In 1988, his bones were exhumed and it was discovered that he had had polio. The succeeding editions of *Po-on* bear this correction and my deepest apology.

How do we fight the traitors, the charlatans who use the nationalist guise and pontificate to us in the media?

I learned a lot about Mabini and the revolution from scholars. In 1958 I met historian Cesar Adib Majul shortly after his return from the United States, where he did his Ph.D. dissertation on Apolinario Mabini. When I told him that evening that I am from Rosales, he said that Mabini had stayed in my hometown for a few weeks for a rest cure before he fled to nearby Cuyapo, Nueva Ecija, where he was captured by the Americans.

I had already started writing the Rosales novels and had designed the sequence and the themes. I knew then that I had to use Mabini and his presence in my hometown as the core incident in *Dusk*.

Unfortunately, neither Professor Majul nor the other noted Philippine historian, Teodoro Agoncillo, knew the circumstances of Mabini's stay in Rosales. I went back to my hometown and tried to dig up records—they were either nonexistent to begin with or had been destroyed or lost. In the town *municipio* and the Catholic church, I couldn't find a trace of Mabini. I therefore deduced that he must have stayed with the leading *ilustrado* family at the time, the Pines, because they had the most imposing house.

The story of the Samsons who fled from the Ilokos bears personal meaning for me because I was also writing about my forebears, who came from a town called Cabugaw in Ilokos Sur. They settled in a village in Pangasinan that they named Cabugawan after the town from where they came.

I grew up in this village, listened to the stories of the elders about their flight from the north, the revolution against Spain. My forebears were very nationalistic and deeply religious as well. Most of all, I grew up with the knowledge of their suffering in the new land, their exploitation by the landlords, and the eventual dispossession of their lands. I also knew of the hardiness of their spirit, the dreams they shared, the angers that made them endure.

At the turn of the century, there were still no roads in much of Northern Luzon; there were a few stretches that were cobbled, remains of which may still be seen. Transport was usually on horseback, or on bull carts over rutted trails. The Ilokano carts had solid wooden wheels and were drawn either by bulls (there were many cattle ranches in the grassy foothills of the Cordilleras) or *carabaos*. The carts were covered with buri palm roofing. I saw some of these carts traveling the dirt roads of eastern Pangasinan in the thirties. As in the earlier part of this century, they usually carried Ilokano farmers from the north to eastern Pangasinan to glean the harvested fields or to help in the harvest. Land shortage in the Ilokos was basically responsible for this annual hegira.

The Ilokanos brought with them raw cotton, handwoven cloth, smoking and chewing tobacco, jars of cane wine, sugar, furniture, and in some instances, jewelry. They were prey to *tulisanes*, and this was one reason they traveled in groups.

Sometimes they returned to the Central Plains to settle. They would then usually carry all their worldly goods, the uprooted posts of their houses in the Ilokos, their santos and wooden chests, the weaving looms, all their farm implements and work animals.

These caravans often went all the way to Cagayan Valley, on the Santa Fe Trail (now Dalton Pass). Many of the settlers were not just land hungry; they were also fleeing Spanish tyranny. They were the pioneers who cleared much of eastern Pangasinan, Nueva Ecija, and the Cagayan Valley. These settlers were called the *mal vivir* or the *agraviados*. It should be remembered that as late as 1899, part of the big town of San Carlos, Pangasinan, was still jungle.

The merchants who took to the road, however, were different from the farmers. Most of them were Pangasiñenses, and carried provisions and produce they sold or bartered for grain. These were sugar cakes, sometimes made out of the sap of the buri palm, sweet preserves from pomelo rind, *alamang* (shrimp paste), salted and dried fish, twine, plowshares, bolos. There was much blacksmithing in Pangasinan then.

There was a lot of intermarriage between the Pangasinan traders and their Ilokano customers. The Pangasinan merchants did not come in long caravans; sometimes they came in just two or three bull carts. A merchant with a couple of bull carts would simply park in a village or town square until he was able to dispose of his goods. Much of this traffic was in the dry season, during harvest, and it ended before the rains started in May.

Another group of traders plied the byways of Northern Luzon. They were the Igorots, who came down from the Cordillera and Caraballo ranges to sell rattan baskets. Their presence was announced by the howling of dogs in the neighborhood because they brought with them packs of dogs tied by their necks to rigid bamboo poles so that it would be easier to manage them. They usually accepted dogs in exchange for their goods. Even then, we knew the dogs would be eaten. In my boyhood, dog meat was not very popular, the way it is today. The Igorots were called Bagos and they were always in G-strings. Seldom were they accompanied by their women.

In re-creating these people I have also tried to illustrate how little the times and the people have changed.

The last chapter is a rendering of the Battle of Tirad Pass. By the time I was ready to write this chapter, I had already read a lot not just on the battle itself but on the Americans and the *insurrectos* they fought. I was, for instance, surprised to see in pictures that most of the Filipino soldiers were barefoot. They were farmers, laborers, just as the enlisted men in our armed forces today come from the lower classes. It was difficult getting exact information on how the soldiers lived, their supplies, their arms. I also decided early in the gestation of the novel to visit Mount Tirad, in the Cordilleras in Northern Luzon. The opportunity came soon enough when I learned that the mother of Ambassador Delia Albert, a friend in our foreign service, lived in the town of Salcedo, which is in the foothills of Mount Tirad.

In the novel, Eustaquio Samson goes to Tirad from Rosales to guide President Aguinaldo and his men through the Cordillera range into the Cagayan Valley. They are pursued by the Texas Rangers. That battle high up in the clouds resembles Thermopylae, how a band of sixty Filipinos—all of them from Bulacan—delayed the American pursuers. In the battle, the boy general Gregorio del Pilar and forty-eight of his men are killed.

I went to Mount Tirad in early January. The time was ideal; the weather was cool—Siberian headwinds in the atmosphere. My wife, Teresita, was with me. Before Candon, a big town in Ilokos Sur, we turned right toward the mountains, on a dirt road that was quite manageable in the beginning but turned tortuous as we ascended the low hills. It was easy to imagine how horrible it must be to maneuver along the road during the rainy season, when it becomes a rivulet of mud. Mrs. Domingo, Delia's mother, said she had managed to get the Ministry of Public Works to release some funds to improve the road way back, but when she returned from a long trip, expecting that the road had been repaired, she was surprised to find it was the same, that the money was lost somewhere along the way, perhaps in the pockets of officials either in the Ilokos or in Manila.

We reached Salcedo in about forty-five minutes—a small town, really, apparently untouched by business and pollution. The main street ran through the usual conglomerate of Ilokano homes. Some of the roads had been paved through the efforts of the people themselves. The municipal building was a humble wooden edifice, as was the small market by its side. The town, unlike most Filipino towns, had electricity, and there was running water from the springs that gushed out of the hillsides.

We rented a jeep with which we forded the many turns of the Buaya River; it was the dry season, so the river was shallow. We entered narrow valleys and went up mountain trails until the jeep could go no farther because the ascent was too steep. I am sure that some of the young men we met along the way were members of the New People's Army, for this part of the Cordilleras was their domain.

We finally reached a settlement at the foot of the trail that led to the pass, and I asked the villagers what they remembered of the battle. There was a very old man who said he was a child then, and all he could recall was the sound of guns.

The trail actually had been widened to allow carts and horses. It was a shortcut from the Ilokos to the Cagayan Valley, and the Spaniards kept it open through the years that the priests preached in the Cordilleras. It was almost noon when my wife and I stopped climbing. A sedentary city man, I was dizzy from exhaustion. In any case, I already knew what the pass looked like, as I could see it plainly from below where we had stopped.

The first draft took a month to write. I was invited to attend a seminar at the Bellagio Conference Center in northern Italy, and after the conference, I was permitted to stay on to write the novel. Bellagio used to be the property of an Italian nobleman, but the Rockefellers bought it and converted it into a conference center, with quarters for the participants, a beautiful library, and one of the most scenic locales in all Europe. The villa itself sits on a promontory; on one side, to the right, is Lake Leggo, and to the left, the larger Lake Como. I used to take the hydrofoil from the village of Bellagio to Como, and from there, the train to Milan—a two-hour trip.

To reach Bellagio, you take a car from the airport closest to Milan and drive through a scenic route, the road hugging the sides of the mountain, and on the left, through turns and dappled foliage, the shimmering Lake Como. I got to the villa before noon, and there at the entrance was the entire staff lined up—as if I were royalty coming for a visit. Never before had a welcome been as formal and as impressive as this one.

A Japanese friend who had been a guest at the villa asked if I liked wine, and I said, frankly, I did not drink much because of my diabetes, and he said, "Bellagio will be wasted on you because the lunches and the dinners are served with an unending flow of wine!"

It was my first experience of northern Italian cooking, and I got to know more than the pizza and the spaghetti that we in Manila usually consider as Italian food.

It was also the first time I used an electric typewriter; in all the years that I have been writing, I had always used a manual portable. I was assured there would be a typewriter for me, so I did not bother bringing my old faithful. But they no longer had manual machines, so I had to learn how to use an electric machine. I then realized how much more productive I could be with it, and it is with this assumption that I have now shifted to a computer.

The manuscript was revised eight times and is still undergoing some minor corrections.

In the late sixties and early seventies when I was lecturing in the United States before the committees of the Council on Foreign Relations, I said that if the Americans did not suffer from historical amnesia, they would never have gone to Vietnam. In the Spanish-American War, 250,000 Filipinos (whom the American soldiers called "niggers")—mostly civilians—were killed, and thousands of Americans—many of them veterans of the Indian campaigns—were also casualties. As in the Philippines, in Vietnam the United States came face-to-face with that indomitable force, Asian nationalism.

The Spanish-American War was objected to vehemently by many Americans, including Mark Twain. On my first visit to the United States, in 1955, I met Robert Frost in Ripton, Vermont. He related how he, too, was against the war, believing that a nation that won its freedom in revolution must not, *cannot,* impose its hegemony on a people waging a revolution for freedom.

I have had all sorts of reactions from readers: one, a scholar, asked me where I got the letter from the priest in the beginning of the novel; he said it read like a historical document. I had to tell him that I wrote it myself, patterned after letters written in the 1880s.

In re-creating Mabini, and endowing the peasant Eustaquio Samson with the habiliments of a hero, what I had intended to show was that nameless thousands of Filipinos then, and now, are capable of epic heroism. All too often, our history is adorned with heroes of high station; there is nothing written about the common people, the foot soldiers who die in the hundreds so that their generals may live.

In writing this novel, I have also tried to look at our history not with the mind-set of historians and scholars who focus on major events and participants. I have focused instead on the "little people," to give them a nobler image of themselves.

I will perhaps be accused of being a revisionist, of creating new myths by edifying what is common. I understand only too well how myths become enshrined in a people's psyche, how Olympian heroes become role models.

But in presenting my hero in Mabini and the peasant Eustaquio Samson, I am presenting an ancient truth that many historians have overlooked.

A WORD
TO THE READER

This novel contains expressions and words—some Spanish, some specific to the Philippines—that may be unfamiliar to the reader. A glossary has been included at the end of the book.

Part
ONE

✠

My Very Beloved in Christ,
Reverend Father Superior:

Once again, I will acquaint Your Reverence with what has transpired in this distant post where I served for more than forty years, and once again I will summarize my activities during my last year there and beg your indulgence for what I will relate, knowing full well that you have grown tired of listening to me, particularly my insistence that we need more young people in the missions and, therefore, more of the Indios in the seminaries.

As evidenced by these figures from the mission, you will note moreover that the baptisms and marriages have increased while the deaths—barring another epidemic of cholera or smallpox—have decreased.

From these records, Your Reverence will also see, perhaps with some satisfaction, that there has been an increase in the population, not just in Cabugaw but in other towns, sometimes as much as double, during the last ten years. This makes it really necessary for us to build more churches—an activity for which we have always been known, attesting to our capabilities as builders, and for which I am justly proud.

The entire region is showing commercial importance. While it is true that indigo has been our best crop, now we are also har-

3

*vesting more cotton. The woven cotton sent to other regions of Fil-
ipinas has increased. The raising of draft animals continues and
our horses are sold all the way to Manila, where they often win
at the races. I hear that even the Archbishop keeps some of these
beautiful animals. As a matter of fact, when I was transferred
here from Cabugaw because, as Your Reverence said, of old age
and infirmity, I had hoped to be sent to Manila instead so that I
could see how these horses run in the races. Having cared for
them, I know their breed has improved. As for their endurance, I
have ridden them across the Cordilleras several times. They have
been reliable, and sturdy as well.*

*As for tobacco, it is true that the crop has increased the rev-
enues and pleased the* principalia, *but the monopoly has created
for us many problems. It has transformed honest men into thieves.
We have had this monopoly for decades and I am glad that it will
soon end.*

*Early next year, I will celebrate my fiftieth year in the priest-
hood, most of these years in Filipinas. Half a century! That I have
served this long, still read without glasses, and write with an even
hand as you can see, proves that I am still capable and should not
be shut up in retirement. I should be ministering to the people or
actively teaching in the seminary across the river.*

But the wishes of Your Reverence must be served.

*I must now reiterate my thinking about the conditions, not
only in our province, as I know them and as gleaned from travelers.*

*The people have not forgotten the execution of the three mes-
tizo priests in Cavite eight years ago. They were from distinguished families noted for their urbanity, education, and of*

course, loyalty to Mother Spain. It is not for me to recall the ec-clesiastical arguments concerning this tragic event; people of greater experience and wisdom have already commented on it. I am merely looking back and reexamining the arguments or the circumstances from which we can learn so that we may continue to build the Church as strongly as we have done during the last three centuries.

I say this knowing that in other parts of the world, particularly in America Sur, our influence is no longer what it used to be. Even here in Nueva Segovia this demonic English organization, this Masonry, has already reached out with its evil tentacles under alluring guises and seduced some ilustrados.

But before I proceed, may I describe what I consider to be the Ilokano character. I will make generalizations and, of course, there are exceptions, for in any community there will be those who do not conform.

The half century I have lived here has convinced me that the Ilokano is trustworthy; he knows gratitude and regards it as a paramount virtue. If we were to look for friends, they should be Ilokanos because I cannot think of a more loyal people than they. They are also hardworking, persevering, and frugal. Their indus-try is such that they work from early dawn to late at night, par-ticularly if there is moonlight, unlike the Tagalog and the Bisaya. And they have enduring patience. The women sit at the loom all day long. They harvest their rice stalk by stalk, and not with the sickle. They are not only patient, for after the harvest there is not a single grain in the field that has not been gleaned.

They do not waste anything—everything is useful. The trees around their homes, the plants in their gardens—all bear fruit or can be eaten. But beware; the water buffalo is a patient, friendly, and docile animal, but when it is angered, it is also the most vicious of creatures. Run away from it for your life is in danger—this we must always remember. Our tragic experience with the rebel Diego Silang has shown that such madness can spread like the plague.

The Ilokanos are true Catholics and nowhere else have they built churches as industriously and as devotedly as they have in this province. They are truly devout and they observe all the holy days of obligation.

I say all this, Your Reverence, because I feel deeply about what is happening in this part of the country, the growing discontent that is not yet expressed but will soon be. We could do so much as men of God to show to our flock that we not only mean well, but that it is only under the protection of Mother Spain that this land can be with God and progress.

Your Reverence, we have often prided ourselves on our sense of history. Indeed, history should be kind to us, for we have not been remiss in our tasks. But our service was not always tempered with wisdom. We know that we are not going to be here forever, that the institutions we are building can only last for as long as they are cared for by Indios themselves. For them we have already given our time, our sweat, and even our lives. And I worry that they will not care for these nor will they bother to strengthen what we leave them if they don't see these—our ministrations and the Church—as theirs. It cannot be otherwise; these institutions are in their land although we transferred them from a distant peninsula.

It is not for me, Your Reverence, to blunder into a realm about which I know little. But I have lived here so long, I can feel the passions which, I know, are seething in the hearts of many in my flock. This is not our country and these people are not related to *us by blood. A wide and cruel ocean separates us and, try as we may to impart to them what we know, they will always be Indios and we, Spaniards. They will imitate us and we flatter ourselves hoping that it is the best side of our nature that they will copy—the dignity, the pride that we have in ourselves. But this will not be so; they will instead inherit our vices, and as I look around me, I can already see what those are—the greed and the corruption that exist in the highest reaches of the* principalia *here as it had existed, too, in Valladolid.*

This is not what we want. When the time comes, I pray that we will go peacefully.

For the first time, some of their young men are now in Europe, learning what we ourselves have learned. Surely, they will return, their minds enlightened, their thinking broadened, in a way perhaps that ours would never be because we wear the cloth. While we have a spiritual depth which they cannot equal, they will also be more familiar with the secular world, which we sometimes do not fully understand.

It is inevitable, I think, that they should be prepared not just for the duties which all citizens of Filipinas should shoulder, but more than this, they should be equal partners in the leadership. The world is changing; we have already seen what happened to our provinces in the Americas. The time approaches when they should sit side by side with us in our highest councils not because this is what they want but because this is what we ourselves desire.

This means that there should be more Indios selected not just from the principalia *and the mestizo families, but from the peasantry, who will have to go beyond the* cartilla. *In the seminary, I should be teaching not just a dozen pupils but three or five dozen so that our strength and our influence will be permanent.*

Forgive me, Reverend Father, for what I now have to say. For-

give these thoughts of an old man who has been touched, perhaps
by fever, but just the same, please listen.

Eventually, we may have to admit into our Order the native
priests we have trained and train them further in our Houses in
Spain, not because we believe they are equal to us—which is
sometimes difficult for me to believe because I have always regarded them as children—but because they should be able to manage their own house eventually as all children must when they
grow up.

Your Reverence, I know that there are loud dissenting voices
in our fraternity, that our military grumbles, and many of the officers find the idea abhorrent. In your last visit to the mission, for
instance, I am sure that you remember Capitán Gualberto of the
Lawag garrison, how trenchant his views. But Your Reverence
knows as well as I do that where the sword is used, the cross is
cursed. Capitán Gualberto's objections are not really insur-
mountable, as can be seen by the effectiveness of our ministrations where we have persevered.

In the Ilokos, Your Reverence, we have succeeded because we
have remained and worked with the people, who showered us
with goodwill and sincerity. These cannot but be reciprocated.

I have mentioned how bright some of our wards have been,
and it is very sad to see that they cannot go beyond the schooling
now permitted them. Some ten years ago, for instance, I brought
into the mission in Cabugaw a farm boy of ten whom I had confirmed. There was something in the boy's face which proclaimed
not just his intelligence but qualities of leadership. I taught him
Latin, too, gave him the books those studying for the priesthood
read. I also taught him the little I know of physics, astronomy,
botany, and explained to him the native plants of medicinal

value. *I taught him what I knew of anatomy. I let him read* The Confessions. *He was full of questions.*

He showed great intelligence, for which his race is not particularly noted. I am aware of the advice against someone from the lowest ranks eventually joining the priesthood. He is still in Cabugaw and I mention him only to show how capable they are in learning and, perhaps, in administering their own affairs, so that those of us in the Order can attend to the more important duties at hand—the eradication, for instance, of Masonry.

We have been here so long. This alone convinces me of our God-given obligation to the Indios. I expect to spend my last days here in Bantay just as so many of us have done and I am happy that my life is my contribution to Mother Spain and to God.

We will be reviled, as, indeed, this is already being done by envious men of dark intent, but it is only because they do not appreciate the legacy that Catholic Spain has bestowed upon them, a legacy which assures them, even if they don't believe it, of one foot in heaven.

I remain, your devoted servant.

Jose Leon, S.A.

The concerns of Eustaquio Salvador, the sacristan about whom I have spoken with much praise in this letter, matter to me very much, Your Reverence. May I seek your permission that he be allowed to enter the seminary in Vigan? I ask this knowing that he will fulfill his duties with loyalty and devotion, and that he will serve his people and Mother Spain.

CHAPTER

1

D USK IS THE DAY's most blessed hour; it is the time when
the spirits of darkness drift slowly down the bright domain. The acacia leaves droop, the fowl stop their cackling and
fly to the boughs of the guava trees to roost, and as the light
starts to fade and the shapes of trees and houses and even the
motions of people seem shrouded, the essence of time, of
change, and the brevity of life itself is realized at last.

Istak often felt like this about the day's end. If he were still
in Cabugaw, where he had served as acolyte for the last ten
years, he would now be going up the musty flight of adobe to
the belfry. There, in the murk of early evening, he would toll the
Angelus, stirring the bats that hung in the rotting eaves. It would
be dark when he would go down the flight, the clap of bells still
humming in his ears. In the past, he sometimes bumped into a
protruding abutment, but he had learned to avoid the traps in

the corners. Down the dim hollow, he would hurry, hurry to the convent where old Padre Jose had already said the Vespers and would be waiting to impart his blessings to Istak first because he was the oldest and the best, and then to the younger acolytes.

Now, it was dusk again. He hurried up the path to their house at the other end of the village. A lightness of spirit lifted him; he would have the first good meal ever since he left the convent. In the late afternoon, before he went to the fields, he had watched his mother dress the chicken; told her he must have the gizzard and the liver. Mayang had humored him with the promise, then sent him back to the field to help fill the gaps in the dikes before the rains came and ripped them apart.

The low eating table was set and around it sat his mother and father and Bit-tik, his youngest brother. Only An-no was not present, for he had gone to Cabugaw to give the new priest their gift. Istak bade his parents good evening, but only his mother returned his greeting. The old man's silence worried Istak; his father was moody again. In the orange glow of the oil lamp, his face was lined. His front teeth had been knocked out by a civil guard's rifle butt and as Ba-ac chewed, the depression in his right cheek deepened.

Istak dipped his hand into the shallow bowl of water. Mayang had prepared a tasty broth; she had chopped fresh ginger together with green papayas, and now the scent of chicken and spice came to his nostrils.

"Here is the gizzard," his mother said. She picked the piece from the still-steaming pot which she had placed in the middle of the low eating table and, as in a ceremony, placed it on Istak's plate. Bit-tik, the youngest of her three sons, took the pot by its narrow rim. He was fifteen and hungry. He, too, had his favorite piece and he held the pot obliquely to the light and, shaking it, examined its contents.

"Enough of that!" Mayang whacked her son's hand. She got

the pot back, and with the ladle scooped out a leg and served her husband next.

Ba-ac picked up the leg and dropped it on Bit-tik's plate. He turned to his wife. "Let him eat the best. There is no use fattening chicken if we only give it away to the priest." He dipped his left hand—his good hand—into the pot and drew out the other leg. Shaking it before his wife's face, he continued, "How many did An-no bring to town? How many did we give for the salvation of our souls?"

Mayang was worried. Her husband was talking loudly. The neighbors might hear; they were all relatives, but still, what he said was almost blasphemy. She feared moments like this. It was as if in the caves, in the corners among the torn fish traps and under the house, gnomes listened. She had known him all her life, even when she was still a child and he was already a man. She was just forty, almost thirty years younger than her husband—and the first touch of gray had come to her hair. She wore the drab gray cloth which she herself wove for the family and had suffered the weaving, sitting for hours before the wooden loom under the house until it was too shadowed to see the shuttle and yarn, and now she seemed to have developed a stoop as well. Her head bowed, Mayang cupped with her fingers a small ball of rice from her plate.

"I am speaking to you, Old Woman," Ba-ac said, his voice rising. "I ask again, how many chickens and eggs have we sent to the new priest while you let your sons starve?"

"Ay, Old Man, you haven't learned."

She turned to her two boys as if she wanted them to agree with her. At her right, Istak was hunched before the table. If he stood straight, he was taller than his father. His brow was high, implying to her a keenness of mind. He had, after all, stayed in the convent for ten years, teaching catechism not just to the children of Capitán Berong—Cabugaw's wealthiest citizen—but to the offspring of other mestizos. Padre Jose had opened to him not just what he knew of philosophy but also practical knowledge that had enabled him and the other Augustinians to thrive in another land, often inhospitable, often alien to their own customs. Istak's hair, though cropped short, was not bristly like a pig's, but soft and pressed flat and shiny with coconut oil which made not only his hair but his skin shine in the sallow light.

Ay! He was indeed the marked one, and on his face—once pale like a banana stalk—Mayang's eyes lingered.

The oil lamp started to flicker and Istak pushed out the reed-marrow wick. He reached out to the corner and took a small jar filled with fresh coconut oil and let a few drops trickle onto his plate. Then he filled the earthen hollow of the lamp. It burned brighter and showed clearly what hung from the palm-leaf wall—the squash headgear, the fish nets.

"Old Woman!" Ba-ac was insistent.

Mayang braved her husband's baleful stare. "I want to eat, Old Man. Eat, too, and receive God's grace."

Her husband would not be mollified. He waved his stump of a hand. "It is not God's grace but ours," he said hotly. "Ours which you sent to town today. How many chickens did you give that young priest so that he will save our souls?"

Mayang turned to her eldest son, as if in apology. "Your father does not know what he is saying—"

"I know," Ba-ac interrupted her. "You answer my question."

"You will know when An-no returns with our indulgences," she said, trying to humor him, for her tone became light. She went to the jar by the stove. When she returned, she had a large coconut shell filled with drinking water.

"I will not wait for An-no," Ba-ac said. He turned to his eldest son. "You helped catch the chickens, didn't you? How many were there?"

"Five, Father," Istak said softly. He dropped the ball of rice he had just lifted to his mouth. He had lost his appetite as the old and nagging futility of it all started to ride him again. He could not understand why he felt weak like this every time his father, in his blabbering rage, shook his stump of a hand as if it were some proud emblem.

"Five chickens for his birthday. Multiply that by a thousand because there are a thousand households in Cabugaw. How many then will he get on his birthday? Think—then look at us. How many times do we have chicken on our table? Istak did live well when he was in town! He should go back there so we can be sure that when we send food to the convent, our son will benefit from it."

"I am no longer wanted there, Father. You know it."

"Be it that way then," Ba-ac said. The old man leaned forward, clenched his one good hand, and brought it down viciously on the table. The plates shook and the light—almost drowned by the oil—sputtered and dimmed.

"Stop this foolishness, you one-handed fool!" Mayang screamed. It was her time to be angry. Bit-tik continued eating, unmindful of what was happening. He straightened the pot and stirred the broth to see if there was some special piece he might yet pick.

"So I am one-handed," Ba-ac said, his voice quivering. "They should have killed me instead of lopping off just one hand."

"Be glad that you have one left; be glad you are alive, that you have sons who tend the field and look after you." She was no longer eating. The night had become grim.

Istak stood up and, without a word, walked away from the table. The slats creaked under him and the bamboo ladder, too, as he stepped down into the yard, where even the fleas must be asleep at this hour. He passed the bull cart parked in the shadow of the house. Tears burned in his eyes and he tried to hold them back but could not; so, too, the shame and the rage that had become a noose around his throat. He sat down on the tamarind stump by the bull cart and sobbed quietly. Let me not think ill of my father, for he has suffered. I never had and if at all, it is but here in the mind. I was never tied to a post and lashed, nor hung by one hand till the arm rotted off. But I have known pain just as keen because it lashed at the mind and heart. If only I were in Cabugaw again. . . .

ONLY A MONTH AGO, he had lived fully, complacently, serving the kindly priest. But Padre Jose had grown old and had to be retired in Bantay. And one morning, in the motionless clarity of April, a carriage drawn by two Abra horses rolled into the churchyard and disgorged a young priest. His black cassock, unlike Padre Jose's, which was always soiled and frayed, was neat and pressed. His eyes were sky blue and his hair was the color of honey. His mouth was large and sensuous, and his voice when he summoned Istak brimmed with authority. Istak kissed the white hand, and as he looked up, the blue eyes regarded him, "You must be Eustaquio," the young priest said, and Istak replied in polite Spanish.

"Padre Jose thinks you should study in the seminary in Vigan. I have heard you are quite learned, you even know Latin."

But of what use was all this knowledge now? Around him was the night, total and vast, the cold sparkle of stars. The lamps of the other houses had all been snuffed out, but the crown of the dalipawen tree was ablaze with a thousand fireflies, and on a night like this, the spirits would be there, in harmony with the world in a way he was not.

To the west, rockets swished up the black bowl of sky, then burst among the stars, and moments later, the hollow whumps of their explosions came. It was like this, too, when the birthday of Padre Jose was marked as the birthday of the new priest was now being celebrated. Istak recalled how mountains of food and fruit from as far away as Manila would be set in the hall of the convent and the crowds would spill beyond the church doors into the yard. And shortly after the High Mass, in the heat of day, the old priest would sit on his carved, broad-backed chair in the shadow of the convent door and there the long line would begin—the *principalia* first, the village leaders, then the people—all would come to kiss the old man's hand and present their tokens of respect and indebtedness.

Ten years he was witness to this ritual of homage and obedience; ten years, too, he pondered and recited Virgil and Cicero, taught the children of Cabugaw's nobility, Capitán Berong's mischievous daughters—Carmencita, most of all. He had served in the Mass for so long, he could be a priest if it were just the liturgy that had to be mastered. Ten years and he saw his palms slowly shed their coarseness just as a serpent discards its skin in molting. What have I brought back with me from the house where God breathed? What have I done to myself and to this puerile mind? *Nunc dimittis servum tuum, Domine*—he remembered the lines and found in them neither solace nor meaning. And yet, thinking of Cabugaw again, remembering how difficult it would have been for Padre Jose to live alone, Istak felt a sense of achievement. As the oldest of the acolytes, he had helped Padre Jose in keeping the records, in going to the Igorote country, and in running the affairs of the church. It was perhaps out of gratitude that the old man called him to his room one afternoon and said, "Eustaquio, I will send you to the seminary in Vigan if you want to be a priest. You are now twenty."

The letter was written but Vigan was a full day away on horseback and the old priest was taken ill. A week later, he was ordered to live out his last years in Bantay and teach in the Vigan seminary across the river, an hour or so a day if he could.

THE FATHER'S footfall was soft and slow; and, in a while, Istak could hear the old man's heavy breathing. But he did not speak for some time.

Ba-ac spoke finally, the anger gone from him. "Do you want to return to Cabugaw?"

Without turning, "No, Father. I am not wanted there anymore."

"But you are! You are!" Ba-ac cried. "Oh, my son, you don't know your worth. Here, nothing. But there, everything."

Istak let his father continue.

"Sometimes, I pray my strength will return so I would be able to take you away from this dark pit where we have all been flung. But I don't have the hand to do it and so I say words I never really mean. I am not cruel. Does any one of my children think I am? Yet, I sometimes sound like I am and only because of this arm . . ."

Istak turned to his father. In the darkness, he could see the wasted face, the stoop, the shabby clothes that clung to the shriveled frame.

"Go to town tomorrow," Ba-ac repeated. "You are needed there. The sacristans must have a place for you, even in the kitchen. Padre Zarraga should take you back. Beg him. Your place is there."

"My place is here, too," Istak said quickly. "You know I can handle the plow as well as An-no."

"That is not to your liking." Ba-ac was insistent. "I have known it since that day Padre Jose selected you. I still remember what he said, that you will go far because your mind is sharp. But what can I teach you?"

His father was going to start the ancient miserere again.

"How does a one-armed fool feel? Do you know what the priest did to me, Istak? Do you know how it is to be like this? He had no mercy, son. And he was a man of the cloth, a friar, a Spaniard!"

Istak had heard the story a hundred times, but he never stopped the old man, for every time he told the story, it seemed that the searing pain was eased a little.

"They hung me by the wrist of my right hand. How could I go to work on the new church when I was with fever? But they did not believe me and a week it was—a week and maybe longer. And when they brought me down, this arm was dead. I felt nothing but a rage as large as a house. And my arm—it was bloated and red. They cut it off—I watched them do it and I did not wince. I wrapped what they had cut off with banana leaves and buried it by the trail. They hung me by the right hand—and this stump—I swear to God, I stole nothing, not even time. Am I really a thief the way I am now marked? I stole not a single grain to feed you. You are the eldest, you know that. When I took you to town—a small boy then, barely up to my waist you were—but you were old enough then and you knew. Tell me, my son, that you believe me."

"Yes, Father," Istak said and within him he cried, Yes! I believe you. He rose, wrapped an arm around his father's shoulder. "There is nothing we can do but understand that we have to live, to know that we die when the time comes. As for the priests, not all of them are bad. Padre Jose—he would have helped if he had known. But he did not . . ."

"Still, you cannot rot here. Even Capitán Berong—he said you should be in Vigan, Lawag—or even Manila, where there are schools."

"They are not for us, Father, and you know that," Istak said. "But with Padre Jose's help, I could have gotten in."

"You will not return to Cabugaw, then, if the new priest asks you?"

Istak turned away and did not answer. He would not take me back because he is young and so am I. But more than this, he will not take me back because I know what he has done; he cannot share a roof with a witness to his mortal sin.

Across the black maw beyond the cluster of houses, a steady barking of dogs broke out. "Must be An-no," Ba-ac said tentatively.

Istak grunted and sat on the tree stump again. The whirr of crickets diminished, the barking of the dogs ceased, and the night became quiet once more. A breeze stirred and wafted to them the smell of dead leaves and the dung of animals. The sky above Cabugaw was slashed by the trail of a rocket. The thin line exploded, then came the distant whump. A dog barked again as a bull cart strained up the incline of the irrigation ditch before the village. Istak and Ba-ac turned to where the sound of creaking wheels came from.

The bull cart rolled past the other houses and headed for them. A couple sat on the bar before its bamboo canopy. As the cart stopped, An-no jumped down and went to Ba-ac at once, held his father's good hand and pressed it to his brow in salutation.

"You went to town on foot," Ba-ac said.

In the dark, the woman greeted them. Istak could not see her face, but her voice was warm and accented. The cart had a canopy; the visitor must have come from afar. She got down after An-no. Even in the dimness, although her face was indistinct, Istak could see that she was young. She did not have the stoop of an old woman. "She is Dalin," An-no said, introducing her. He was younger than Istak by two years, but though younger, he was bigger; the work on the farm had made him stronger, too. "They came from the land of salt," An-no announced.

"They?" Ba-ac asked.

"Her husband is in the cart," An-no continued. "Sick. He did not even speak all the way from the fork of the road where I saw them."

"He is dying," the woman said. Istak could make out her face now—a young face, with a full mouth and eyes that were large and bright.

"I am grateful to your son, Apo," she told Ba-ac. "I could not find the way. We have to hurry to anyone who knows how to care for the sick. My husband—since yesterday, he has been talking without reason and is very hot with fever. I must hurry."

Ba-ac ordered An-no to unhitch the bull cart and invited the woman up to the house, where a bowl of chicken broth awaited her. Having heard the voices, Mayang came down and joined them. She held a burning pine splinter and in its smoky glow, her face was serene. Now, Istak could see Dalin's handsome face, her shapeless cotton blouse, the full breasts underneath. In a glance Istak knew, too, that she had not yet known childbirth. She looked around her, at the family that welcomed her, and her voice quavered. "Thank God, I am with good people."

"You are very young," Istak said, amazed he had spoken the thought aloud at all, and when he turned away in embarrassment, his younger brother was glaring at him.

Istak took the torch from his mother and went to the cart. In its red glow, he saw what was inside—the sacks at one end, the figure stretched motionless on the bamboo floor—an old man with a pinched face and eyes closed.

"He is asleep," Istak said, peering briefly at them from the opening of the canopy. In that instant, a gust of wind snuffed out the light. Istak bent low to feel the man's pulse. In the last few years that he had worked in Cabugaw, Padre Jose had taught him what he knew of sicknesses, how to look at a person and from the feel of his pulse, his warmth, deduce what ails him. Istak's hand rested on the man's arm and he found no wrist or hand—just a stump that had grown cold. Like his father, the man did not have a right hand!

I have seen men die as Padre Jose recited the last unction and I stood beside him, holding aloft the cross before the eyes that sometimes could no longer see. I have seen the dead in repose, in wooden coffins, or just wrapped up in old blankets, buri mats, or even bamboo slats from fish traps. I have stared at their sallow faces even as the holy water was splashed on their ashen skins like rain upon stone. I have seen them, but touched them, never.

A chill came over Istak and he pitched out of the cart, the splinter smoking in his hand. "Your husband is dead," he said.

Dalin sank slowly to the ground. She did not speak. Moans were ripped from her—animal sounds that were not a wail, but the horrible nameless sound of grief.

BEFORE the cocks crowed, the neighbors already knew. An-no had gone to them asking for old bamboo that could be made into a pallet for the corpse.

Dalin had objected. "We can just wrap him in a blanket and let the earth claim him," she said.

"We have to bury him correctly," An-no said.

After Dalin had changed the rags of the corpse, they brought it down and laid it on the woven slats which they had tied together to make a coffin. Beside it burned a candle which Istak had given her. Their job done, the men and their women dispersed. Only Dalin stayed near the improvised coffin.

Istak dozed in the house. When he awoke, he peered out the

door and saw Dalin sitting alone on the stump. He went down to her.

"It is not for you to keep the wake," she said. "I have already been a burden to all of you."

"God sent you here," Istak said. "We have to accept God's will."

"No, not God," Dalin said. Her voice carried with it a challenge, but Istak did not want to argue with her. Besides—the thought came quickly—she was in mourning and she did not even have a black dress.

"It will soon be light," Istak said. "How far have you traveled? Where did you come from?" He sat on the fork of the cart behind her.

She bowed and cupped her chin in her hand. "It does not matter anymore where I came from or where I will be going."

The fine contours of her face, her straight back; she looked at him then and for the second time, their eyes locked.

"I am impolite," she said. "You have all been helpful, you particularly. You really want to know where we came from?"

Istak nodded.

She turned away and cupped her chin in her palms again. "My parents were traders," she said. "We had a boat—a fine boat—and we sailed up and down the coast twice a year. When its sails were full, its prow could slice the water with the ease of a blade. Then came a storm and one evening, off the coast of Bawang, we were wrecked. Many things happened to me. I clung to the mast for two days. My husband—it was he who rescued me. He was going south to look for land and had found what he wanted there. We were going back to his people so that he could tell them the news—to Lawag. He was old enough to be my father, you know that. But I was grateful and I had nothing to give."

Istak understood, but was curious just the same about how the old man had lost his hand.

She turned to him abruptly. "You don't know?" she asked. "Isn't your father without a hand, too?"

Istak was miserable and he regretted having asked the question at all.

"They called him a thief." Her voice was almost a whisper. "It is the simplest crime and it could mean anything, from stealing time or a sack of grain for which you have slaved a week. They hung him by the hand. Now, does it really matter where I come from or where I am going?"

What was there to say? Istak closed his eyes and tried to blot out the vision flowing to the narrow pit of his brain—the old man with eyes closed, the stump for a hand.

"But don't pity me," she said with that brightness that steered him away from his thoughts. "It is fate. Now I have no more home."

"Then stay with us," Istak said. "You are safe here and there is food—not much, but you will not be hungry. And there is always work and we will not bother you with your memories. Let the scabs harden and fall without our prodding."

"I would rather keep moving," she said. "Return to my home if there is a boat that will take me back, or to that plain which my husband saw, farther down Pangasinan, up the mountains, and then below—"

"Did you see it?"

She nodded. "I have been there," she said, and then was silent as if remembering all the bitterness that was banished. She spoke again, this time in quiet joy. "You can smell the land. Its freshness is in the air, in the light—all through the day. You can taste it in the water from the spring, in the flavor of the three-month grain. The plain is all around you, vast as the world, and without hills. It melts, hazy and blue with the sky, as far as you can see. The forest is there, too, alive with wild boar, deer, and pythons as big as coconut trunks, they say, and just as long. But it is a forest that is kind. It belongs to no one and anyone who goes into it soon loses fear of the dark. You become part of the forest, they say, your veins grow out of you like roots seeking the soil. In the forest, you can live even if you do not hunt. A new life awaits you there."

Istak listened, intoxicated and believing every word. He had heard of the new land, too, not just from the traders who had gone to the coast then backtracked through Pangasinan but from the Igorots whom he had met when he and Padre Jose had gone all the way to Natonin, and there, at the top of the mountain, they had looked down at God's country.

"If we could only leave," he said. "Here, we are fortunate if we own a farm as big as the palm of our hands. All the land we till is not ours."

He stood up and walked to the tamarind stump where she sat. The fireflies that had ignited the dalipawen tree had taken flight and disappeared in the bowels of the night. The air had become crisper and it filled his lungs with sweetness. Soon it would be light. "But what does the future hold for us? We are tied here forever," he said, rubbing his palms; they had begun to harden. They were soft once, almost like a woman's, because he had not held a plow for years and what he held were books, pens, and an occasional broom. And Dalin's hands—were they also as rough as his mother's? He took her hand. It was rough, as he knew it would be, and she did not draw it away.

"Do not worry," he told her, freeing her hand. "Although a widow, you are still very young."

"It was not my wish to be one," she said. "He knew I cared for him, that I tried to give him back his health. I wanted to make him happy."

"He is a handsome corpse," Istak said. "When we bury him in the morning, you will know what I mean. I was a sacristan and a teacher, too." He wanted to tell her more but he held back. He did not want to sound boastful. "Even if we do not take the body to church for the priest to bless—I know all the prayers. Do you believe that?"

She nodded.

"I could beg the new priest," Istak continued. "Maybe he will not let us pay."

She suddenly stood up. "I will not take him to the church," she said stiffly.

"That will be a sin."

"It is his wish, not mine," Dalin said shrilly, walking away. He followed her.

"I am only suggesting what is right," he said.

She turned to him. "But we must respect the wishes of the dead. Even before he became sick, this was what he told me, that there should be no church ritual for him, that it was enough that either the sea or the earth claimed him back. If God is everywhere, we don't have to go to church, do we? He knows where we are, and if He is a just God, He will also forgive."

He would have to believe her. For the poor, there is only God's bounty to pray for. He had long known that God's ministers could usurp the Word and twist it for their gain and comfort or, as it was clear to him now, for their merest whim. All of them in Po-on and in the other villages of Cabugaw—they could all be banished from the land they had claimed from the forest and farmed all their lives—all of them who were dark of skin, who were not adorned with titles of power, who did not wear the cloth.

In the grass that surrounded the yard, crickets started again and a gecko in the buri palm announced itself, its *tek-ka* keen as a whip in the still air. "He knew he was going to die," Dalin continued. "He had this wish and I promised I would fulfill it."

The east had paled and the cocks that roosted in the guava trees and among the fish traps under the house started to crow. The narrow cracks of the split-bamboo wall framed strips of light. In a while, he heard his mother stirring in the kitchen. Breakfast would be ready soon—fried rice, perhaps, and coffee brewed from roasted corn and flavored with molasses.

Dalin walked back to the cart, Istak behind her. "You must get some sleep," he told her. "My mat has not been rolled yet. You can go up to the house."

Gratitude shone in her face. She went toward the house and disappeared within. He heard his mother call out to him to go to the woodshed and bring up an armful of firewood.

The candle at the foot of the coffin had burned out and Istak lighted another and stuck it in the soft warm wax. As he turned for the woodshed, An-no came down and followed him. Istak was about to draw wood from the stack when An-no gripped him on the shoulder and spun him around. Surprised, Istak dropped the dry acacia branches and turned to his younger brother, who now confronted him, brawny as a bull and just as headstrong.

"I don't like the way you move about in this house," An-no said, throwing away the respect a younger brother should always give to an elder.

Istak was stunned. "You act like you are the best man here," An-no continued. "Not just in the house, but in the entire village. That is perhaps correct—you are the learned one. But don't forget, it is now we who feed you."

Istak recovered from his shock. "What nonsense are you talking about?" he asked sternly. "Have you forgotten I am the eldest?"

"I have not forgotten that," An-no said quietly. He was eighteen but farm work had made him appear older. "But there is no younger or older when it concerns a woman."

"What are you talking about?" Istak asked. Anger had coiled in him.

"You know what I mean," An-no said. "I found her, I brought her here. We made her husband's coffin. Bit-tik and I. You did nothing but snore . . ."

Istak moved away from his brother. "She is a widow, have you forgotten?"

"Does it matter?"

"And she is much older than you. A full five years!"

"And you say that she is about your age and just the woman for you? I found her first," An-no reiterated sharply. "And she will be mine. You must not stop me. I will take her and if she won't come, I will make her." He turned and marched away.

For some time Istak stood immobile, unable to think, unable to respond to his brother's sudden anger. It was not real, it did not happen at all—this aberration. Slowly, he stooped and groped for the branches that had fallen and, finding them, placed them one by one in the crook of his arm. His hands started to feel numb and he paused and stood up with but three branches. An-no would do what he threatened and he would not be able to stop him. He would never be able to be firm, to be a rock before anyone because his hands were like the dead branches he carried. He was like his father, and even more like the dead man they were to bury, a cripple to himself and to all the creatures in this miasma called Po-on.

CHAPTER

2

THE DARKNESS began to lift and the eastern rim of the world was tinted with silver. In a while, the cocks dropped from their roosts in the guava trees with a noisy flapping of wings and chased the cackling hens, and the sun burst upon the land in a flood of dazzling light, flowed over the foothills, and its rays impaled the mists upon the kapok trees.

They sat down to a breakfast of corn coffee and bowls of rice fried in fresh coconut oil. Dalin sat at one end of the low eating table, taking sips from the coconut bowl which Mayang had passed to her.

Istak could see her clearly now, the brooding eyes, the thick eyebrows. Even in her gray, shapeless blouse of hand-woven Iloko cloth, the contours of her body—her bosom, her shoulders—were as lovely as those of Carmencita, the eldest of

Capitán Berong's daughters, whom he had taught the *cartilla*. His brother stared at him, bothering him with his unspoken enmity. Istak left the table quickly and went down the yard to make a hearse of the bull cart. His mother followed him. Some of the neighbors who had come in the night—mostly relatives, cousins, and second cousins—had returned. Istak scraped off the candle smudge on the tamarind stump and put the half-burned candle in his pocket.

"Are you thinking of her, son?" Mayang asked.

The question surprised him. "Of whom, Mother?"

"The beautiful stranger," she said simply.

He did not know what to make of his mother's question. He decided to be evasive. "It is very sad that at her age," he said, "she is already a widow."

"She has not cried that much."

"Not all those who shed tears really grieve."

"Still, we do not know anything about her. We help because she needs it."

"I know that, Mother," Istak said. "Why are you telling me this?"

Mayang smiled. "My son, it is about time you had a woman, I know. But Dalin—do not let her and her misfortune mislead you into believing that she is helpless, that you should rush into helping her, then loving her." She turned toward the brown fields beyond the arbor of bamboo which served as a gateway to the village. Beyond, in the far distance, loomed the dome of Cabugaw Church like a woman's breast pressed to the sky. Her voice became soft, almost a whisper. "I can feel it—this omen creeping into our lives. Something is hounding her. Once we have done what is Christian, we should let her seek her fate."

Istak smiled. Omens. It was as if he were in Cabugaw again,

listening to Padre Jose after a break in his Latin lessons. The old priest had decided to teach him Latin when he was twelve or thirteen, and him alone, there in the sacristy itself, after he had dusted the shelves and seen to it that all the ledgers were in place. "Eustaquio, there are many things in this world that we cannot see, spirits that move about us, things we cannot explain, not even with the faith that we possess."

The old priest said he knew things which he was utterly ignorant of when he arrived in the Ilokos. Past seventy and too old to care, he could now say what he never dared whisper when he was young, the mystery of this land, the beliefs rooted in an experience that only a pagan past could have engendered.

Istak held his mother by the shoulder as if to assure her that he knew what he was doing, that no harm would befall them. "Evil is often a creation of our minds, Mother," he said. "It starts as a spark, then it is fanned into a fire, self-willed and self-sustaining. No, Mother, if we do not think about it, if we do not let it bother us, it will not be there. This is not to say that there are no evil men, but our best protection against them is our innocence and our truth." This was real Christian virtue, but even as he said this, his thoughts were about his younger brother. Did his mother know what An-no had told him in the woodshed? Had she seen his younger brother's face—the unbridled desire for Dalin which had now warped his mind?

He found himself saying, "It is An-no, Mother, that I am worried about, not Dalin."

"What has he told you?" Mayang asked. "Fool sons of mine—I could see him following her all the time with his eyes the way you do. And she had just been widowed. It is a sin!"

Istak shook his head. "You see more than what is there, Mother."

But Mayang did not hear, for she had turned to leave, mumbling, "My sons, my fool sons."

THEY WERE set to leave. Dalin came down the bamboo stairs, wearing a well-starched skirt. An-no walked behind her, a dark scowl on his face. Together they went to Istak, who had, by then, removed the palm-leaf canopy of the cart.

An-no told him: "I want to go to the cemetery to help dig the grave. It is better if there are two of us."

"What is this now?" Istak turned to Dalin, perplexed. She had washed her face and her skin shone.

"I tried to explain," Dalin said, "that I don't want anyone but the two of us to go to the cemetery—you because you can say the prayers and help me dig the grave. Just the two of us—it is best that way. I don't want to be a bother to people the way I already am. And the cemetery is far." She turned to An-no. "How can I repay you? You made the coffin, you brought me here. I will have a lifetime paying you for all you have done. But it is my wish that you stay . . ."

An-no dug his toe into the ground and mumbled something unintelligible.

"Help me carry the coffin," Istak asked his brother, and together they brought it to the cart. The few neighbors who had gathered in the yard had heard her wish, and to them she said, "God be with you, thank you for coming."

They drove out of the yard. Istak whacked the reins on the broad back of the bull and the cart dipped down the low incline onto the dusty path lined with dying weeds. The trip would take the whole morning and it would almost certainly be high noon before they would reach the cemetery. The brown fields spread around them. To their right, the Cordilleras seemed so near though they were at a far distance. Since he went to Cabugaw ten years ago, he had gone up these ranges every year during the dry season when the rivers were no longer bloated. Padre Jose always brought with them four of the best horses in the church stable. The old priest did not ride the best one; he reserved it for the tortuous trails to the land of the Igorots that lay beyond the narrow pass called Tirad. Istak had looked forward to these trips, to the rambling discourses of the old priest, to the meetings with the Igorots whom he finally got to know—and yes, to see them again—the bare-breasted girls who worked the narrow valleys and mountainsides, their arms tattooed, their bodies glistening with sweat in the sunlight.

He carried the Iloko missal, the holy water, and candles; on their two-pack horses were their ration of water, some salt, sugar, hand-rolled cigars (which the old priest was addicted to), salted meat, rice, and their iron cooking pot. He soon learned the way so well, it seemed he had lived in this forbidden land all his life. He knew them, too, the Igorots, who did not harm them although his own people expected otherwise; the Igorots were savages—did they not kill strangers or one another when their tribal laws were violated?

Now the mountains beckoned to him—if he could only flee this withered plain and lose himself up there close to the clouds where the air is so pure it made breathing such a pleasure. Maybe someday he would be able to go there again and forget what had happened, break out of the mountains into the valleys beyond. Dalin was beside him, and though he did not believe what his mother had said, she seemed to have cast a spell over him.

The bull loped down the trail and the wheels hit a bump—a root of a tree. Briefly their arms touched.

"Why did you not want them to come along?" he asked afterward. The village was well behind them, just a line of madre de cacao trees.

She turned to him, her face determined. "I told you I would bury him anywhere. That is why it is just the two of us. Over there, at the bend of the river where An-no came upon us, beyond the clump of bamboo—no one can see us dig the grave there."

"But why there?" Istak asked, surprised. "It is not done that way, you know that."

"It was what he wanted. He knew he was going to die. Bury me, he said, where there's water—the river, the sea. Any place where there is water, for water is life, too. Do you understand? And when we have buried him, then I will go. Far away to where his people are so that I can tell them. You will not even remember me then."

"But I will remember you," Istak said. He wanted to add, "always," but he held back. "You cannot travel by yourself now. You know how it is—by land, even by sea—the way is very dangerous. Unless you have companions. You know what I mean."

She nodded, not as if to acknowledge the truth of what he said but as if to accept the sorrow which she must bear. "But what can they steal from me?" she asked, expecting no answer.

Istak did not reply. "You can stay with us," he said much later. If she left, there would be peace in their household; the ill wind that his mother had prophesied would not blow their way. And yet, he needed to see her again. Banish the omens then. Why should he believe them? Did he not trust in Someone who bestowed grace on men and saw them safely through their journeys?

They rode in silence. The sun edged up the sky and dust swirled around them as the bull continued its even pace. In a while, the trail dropped into the wide delta of the river, and all around them, the sprouts of cogon grew lush and tall, and farther down, the earth had become sandy. Stones littered the way—some of them boulders that had slid down from the mountains together with dead, uprooted trees when the heavy rains fell in July. Dalin looked around her.

"This will do," she said, pointing to a spot surrounded by tall grass. Istak drew the reins and the bull stopped. They got down and Dalin unhitched the cart, then tethered the animal to a sprout of cogon and gave it some hay. She got a spade and a hoe from the cart and started digging. Istak took a spade and worked at the other end, the blade sinking quickly into the sandy loam. Soon, the hole was deep, up to their waists, and Istak clambered up, his body dripping with sweat. Dalin, too, was tired and her face was damp with sweat. They had worked in silence.

Questions cluttered his mind. Did she really love the old man? Why should she condemn him to hell? It was so easy to ignore a dying man's wish and do what was right. Could it be that she herself did not believe in God? And why should she? If God was just, the suffering she had gone through would not have happened. But to such questions, of course, Padre Jose had an explanation—the nature of suffering, the necessity for it, for faith was founded on it, and man would suffer as Christ did. In pain was man's redemption.

He offered her his hand and helped her out of the narrow pit. Her grasp was firm and warm and her hands were callused like a farmer's. "You are very tired; you have worked very hard," he told her.

She smiled, and in the sunlight her teeth were white and even; she did not chew betel nut or smoke, as did many village women, even when they were still young. They hauled the pallet

out of the cart; it was heavy and Istak marveled at her strength.
He sharpened two lengths of bamboo, then drove the stakes into
the ground on both sides of the pit. He tied two lengths of rope
then laid the ropes over the grave. They eased the pallet over the
ropes and lowered it slowly till it rested snugly at the bottom.
Istak intoned the ritual prayer: *Tibi Domine commendamus ani-*
mam famuli, tui, ut defunctum saeculo, tibi vivat . . .

Beyond the river, from the direction of the sea, the wind careened toward them with the smell of burnt fields. Istak started
shoveling back the earth. This was the end, this was the end, and
Dalin crumpled on her knees and cried silently at first, then she
took a deep breath, and softly, as if in a whisper so that her voice
would not travel, she started the wail of the widow.

Ay, I am now alone,
cover to the pot,
useless without you.
What have you left,
salt on my lips,
darkness in my mind.
Why now should I live,
with no blood in my veins,
no breath in my lungs.
Ay, I am now alone.

Istak continued shoveling the earth till a mound formed
over the grave. Dalin finally rose. Her eyes were clear; she had
no more tears. With her hands, she helped smooth the mound.
And the rest of the earth they spread out to mix with the sand
so that it would look level, not a grave but some spot where, perhaps, someone had dug up an old pine tree trunk to bring home
as kindling wood. The tall grass was not disturbed; it would only

be by accident that some boy would stray here, adventuring in this wasteland, and even then, he would not bother wondering what lay beneath this mound. The rains would soon come, grass would sprout even taller, and the flesh of the dead would feed those new roots.

If he returned home, he would have to wash his feet with warm water in the earthen pot laid at the foot of the stairs to cleanse his body and protect the house from the wandering ghost. There might be no such water waiting for him, so Istak said he would go to the river to bathe himself instead. He asked if she wanted to join him and she nodded. He sought privacy behind a screen of grass, where he stripped. Cupping his genitals with his hand he waded into the water and immersed himself quickly. The water was waist-deep, a soothing coolness in the heat. Somewhere, behind some tall reeds, Dalin was splashing. Like all the women who bathed in the river, she did not take off her clothes. Her wet chemise would now be clinging to her body, outlining her shoulders, her breasts. He had reproached himself for such lascivious thoughts—very disturbing but pleasurable—many times in the past, particularly when he conducted those lessons for Capitán Berong's pretty daughters. The delicious yet forbidden urge would ride down his whole being and flood him with warmth. He was past twenty and still a virgin. For how much longer? When would he finally know a woman?

He let the feeling subside, and after a while, he rose from the water, and cupping his limp manhood in his palm again, he hurried to the tall grass and, still dripping, put on his clothes, which were damp with sweat. He waited till Dalin called out to him that she was ready.

When he returned to the cart, it was still unhitched. In the shade of a camachile tree, Dalin had already laid on the stubby grass a palm-leaf mat with their food—chunks of leftover rice that she had cooked the night before, scraps of salted meat cooked in vinegar, salt, and oil, and small peanut cakes. Her hair was loose and wet and she looked even younger.

"Will you pray the nine-day novena by yourself and keep the year of mourning?" he asked.

She nodded. "Everything else that must be done I will do."

WHEN THEY were through eating, she gathered the leftovers carefully and placed the pots back in the cart. "Please," she reminded him. "If they ask . . ."

He nodded. He did not want to lie but he had to.

"I will leave you at the fork of the road," she said. "I will travel only in the day. At night, I will try to find a place where I can be safe. Then when I reach the sea, I will sell this cart and bull and return home by boat."

"You are very brave."

"I wish I had more knowledge," she said. "Not just writing my name and counting. I wish I had a little of what you know."

"Who told you about me? I am just a farmer."

"Your brother," she said. "On the way to your village last night he spoke about you, how learned you are and how you should be in Vigan, or even Manila."

"There are people who cannot even write their names," Istak said. "But they are wiser than most who can read." He turned to her; her skin, freshly scrubbed, was smooth and clear. She was really no more than eighteen—he could see that clearly now.

She bowed and said softly, "I am ignorant, I know." Then she turned to him, pride in her eyes. "But at least I can write my name."

"That is good, a beginning," Istak said quickly. "I was thinking, here in our village many cannot read. I can be a teacher. The *catón*. And the neighbors will pay not with money but with grain."

"Is that what you are planning to do?"

"Yes, but I'll farm, too."

"What was it like living with a priest?" she asked.

"It was not easy," he explained. "My time was well divided between my chores and my efforts to improve myself. The work was tiring, too—cleaning the *kumbento,* chopping firewood, looking after the horses, six of them. The easier tasks, keeping the files, the registry of births, marriages, deaths. And after that, the lessons the old priest gave—science, some botany . . ." He realized quickly that she did not understand.

Istak turned away as they came creeping back—memories of all those years, wasted now. When he entered Padre Jose's room for the first time, he was awed by the old books all over the place, leather bound, some of them with gilt edges. Before the old priest had selected him to be a sacristan, all that he knew was the church itself—how massive it was, its walls thick and impregnable, the wood in the sacristy and the *kumbento* the best that could be dragged from the mountains. Portions of the *kumbento* were roofed with tile, but the church itself was roofed with galvanized iron, which had rusted in parts.

As a child, he had believed that when huge buildings or churches were built, a fearsome creature called *Komaw* would kidnap children, kill them, and spill their blood into the foundation diggings so that the buildings would be so blessed they would last a thousand years and those constructing them would not be injured. Surely, it must have taken pails of blood to make this church endure. He had wanted to ask the priest but never dared, for Padre Jose, Istak learned later, was skeptical about the many miracles the other churches claimed and had a surfeit of, a skepticism which the old priest did not voice but which Istak knew was there—in the shaking of the venerable head, in the lift of the thick eyebrows when such topics were brought to him.

The church was more than a hundred years old; he had often imagined the multitude of workers hauling those big rocks and cutting them in perfect shapes to make arches that could withstand earthquakes. He wondered why the church was built on a rise of ground on the fringes of the town—not in the middle as it was with the other churches. The church was like a fort; indeed, it was a sanctuary from Moro raids along the coast— self-sustained, with granaries, wells.

When he was new in the church, one of his chores was to toll the bells. He had delighted in climbing up to the belfry and once up there, past the dim stairway, the wind whistling through, he would scan the vista around him, and look to the far distance, to Po-on, where he came from, where time began— just a smudge of brown hidden by bamboo groves, the river that emerged out of the low hills like a trough of silver and disappeared in the narrow plain, and all around the town, the fields ready for the seed, or—as it was in November and December— a sea of shimmering gold. He would hurry down after the Angelus, the tolling of the bells still humming in his ears, and in the sacristy join the singing: *Tantum ergo, tantum ergo.* Then to the kitchen where, with the other boys, he helped with the cooking and setting of the table in the dining room, above it a broadcloth which was swung continuously to stir a breeze when it was warm or to drive away the flies. Here was the chipped china, the polished candelabra, the frayed gray napkins, and Padre Jose's simple dinner of chicken broth, some vegetables, and rice that was cooked soft.

All the rooms in the *kumbento* and the sacristy were no longer secret; he had grown up cleaning them, learning in them the *cartilla* and all that Padre Jose had imparted to him—knowledge and a sense of right as well. The old priest was patient; sometimes he would surrender himself to reverie. His bushy eyebrows would lift, his gray eyes glazed, and he would then start those soliloquies—about his sister and brothers, his parents, and that sparkling whitewashed village in Andalucía where he came from, the skies that were always blue, grapes as big as chicos, the golden oranges, the sherry, and most of all, the bread his mother baked. Mail took so long, and sometimes he read to all the acolytes letters that described Spain. Once it was a mighty nation, possessing an empire that stretched across the oceans; but in the decades past, this empire had dwindled. Though Padre Jose never told him, Istak came to realize, too, that the old man joined the priesthood not so much in service to God and country, but to escape the poverty of his own village. And this was what Istak wanted to do, too, what his father and mother had hoped would happen—that he would be a priest, not just so he could flee the drudgery of the village, but because he was the eldest, he could help his brothers and all his relatives who were mired in Po-on.

But the priestly life was not one of ease; even in his old age, Padre Jose worked hard, tending to the people, reaching those *sitios* where the Ilokanos seldom went, across Tirad to the land of the Bagos where they could be killed, their heads chopped off to decorate some heathen's house. Padre Jose had prided himself on his order. "We are builders, Eustaquio; above all else, not just of buildings and churches, but of men. We will go wherever there are souls to rescue." He would tell them then of Saint Augustine, of the first Augustinian in the country, Padre Rada. Padre Jose, without any family, had taken on a bigger one, not

just the order to which he belonged, but the Ilokanos, whom he
had grown to love.

CAN ONE really love a people? And why not a village? A
family—or even a woman? It had all become so remote, Istak's
discovery of his manhood and the desires that had shamed him
once and at the same time warmed him to the pleasure that he
would surely forgo if he became a priest. She was the eldest of
Capitán Berong's daughters—Carmencita, sixteen and already
full-breasted, with flesh aching to be caressed beneath her long
skirt. Just looking at her made him feel that all the beauty there
was to behold in the world was in those red lips, the pert nose,
and the cheeks that shone. Her two younger sisters—Filomena,
fifteen, and Angela, fourteen—they were beautiful, too, but not
as Carmencita was. They were not bright but they were all clever,
and it was not difficult teaching them what he knew, a bit of history, arithmetic—and none of the homemaking arts that all
women of high birth such as they would learn in the school in
Vigan. It would all be wasted, of course, for Carmencita was just
waiting for the right suitor to come to her father's door so she
could be married off to settle in some Ilokano town as mistress
of a big stone house.

The sisters came to the convent in the afternoon, and stayed
till the Angelus, when they went down the wide churchyard and
the street, bringing with them their nubile laughter, and with
Carmencita a presence that often was a challenge and a tease,
for at sixteen, she knew she was desirable and if she wanted to,
she could command men to do her bidding. He would have
done so if only he had not been just a farm boy from Po-on. He
believed then—as the old priest had taught him to believe—that
with knowledge, righteousness, and faith in the Almighty, he

would open the gates of Heaven to his countrymen, benighted as they were. But probing his thoughts, his own being, he had felt so small and worthless, for he reached the conclusion that, above all, with the priesthood, he would be able to rise from Po-on, and, perhaps, bring up with him his parents and brothers as well.

"YOU WILL NOT HAVE a woman then," Carmencita had told him pointedly. They were in the room behind the sacristy, a wide room with walls of thick coral stone and a floor of earthen tile. Outside, in the shaded patio, her younger sisters were playing *patintero*, while upstairs, Padre Jose was fast asleep, one of the younger acolytes—his arms perhaps already aching—pulling at the huge cloth fan that dangled from the ceiling to ward off the strangling heat of a March afternoon.

What would it matter if he would never know a woman? "If I become a priest, señorita," he said diffidently, "but that is not for me to say."

She pouted.

He started the lesson again: "There are really only so many elements on earth. Some are metals—"

"I don't want to know about elements," Carmencita said, bending down again to examine her right foot, visible below the hem of her white cotton skirt. Again, he could see the white mounds of her breasts and yes, his heart thumped—the small pink nipples. She straightened up immediately and caught him, and now, the knowing smile.

"Am I beautiful, Eustaquio?"

He could not answer; the blood rushed to his head, to his limbs, burning him, imprinting in his mind that image of her bosom. How shapely were the legs beneath that skirt? The hips?

"Well, are you not going to tell me?"

His throat was parched, "Yes, señorita," he croaked. "You are beautiful."

"My foot," she said gazing at him, witch eyes beckoning while he seemed to sway. "Will you do me a favor? I twisted it this morning. Do you know how to massage a sprain? Weren't you taught something like that, too?"

He shook his head.

"Please massage it," she said, suddenly thrusting her right foot forward, baring a white, smooth leg up to the knee.

When he did not move, she repeated, "Please . . ."

He moved toward her as if in a daze, and then knelt. With trembling hands, he held her right foot and slowly started to massage it.

"Higher up the leg," she said, her voice bright with pleasure. The touch of her flesh kindled in him this want so intense, so deep, it stirred him immediately. When she finally said enough, he still knelt, ashamed to rise knowing that she would see what she had done to him, the proclamation of his manhood.

HE COULD NOT sleep that night. Carmencita had actually invited him, teased him, and he was shocked and at the same time ashamed of his feelings—he was a teacher and he had betrayed Padre Jose's trust. He need not have worried more about temptation and lust and his own willful proclivity for sin. The following day, the young priest arrived, and upon seeing the three sisters that afternoon, he forbade Istak to teach them—he would do that himself now, and when the old priest was transferred to Bantay, the young priest moved the classroom for Capitán Berong's daughters to the room upstairs, beside his quarters.

And it was there one afternoon that Istak had gone, and as

was his custom with the old priest, he did not knock on the door; it was there that he saw just the legs—the white, creamy legs and between them, the hirsute legs of the young priest. They were behind the high cabinets where many of the records were filed. Istak did not close the door—he ran down the stairs and on to the church, where he knelt and prayed, telling himself that he did not see anything. And that evening, the young priest called him after the Angelus. He asked no questions, he merely told Istak his services were no longer needed.

THE WHEELS of the cart, built of solid wood, were not oiled and they squeaked at every indentation in the path. Here was a woman, here was temptation again, and yet it was no longer the old temptation. It seemed as if he had known Dalin for a long time. Here was kinship, as strong as any that could bind two people together. She had listened passively at first, but now she seemed engrossed with everything he had to say. He told her of that inscrutable world whose fringes he had reached, the darkness—or was it light?—that had enticed him, the compulsion to know more, not just about faith and God, but of men, what made them what they were. He told her of his numbing sense of frustration when he was driven out of the *kumbento*, and how he would live in Po-on, to which he had become a stranger.

He marveled at how easily and quickly he had revealed himself to her, but this new kinship would surely go to waste, for very soon they would part.

The river was far behind them. They neared the fork of the trail, where she was to leave him. Clouds of dust whirled ahead and a man on horseback was cantering toward them.

Istak reined in the bull and pulled the cart to the side of the path. It was only the wealthy or Guardia Civil officers who rode on horses, and as the rider drew near, Istak recognized Capitán Berong in his finery, white coat and silver-studded squash hat. The mestizo stopped.

"Good afternoon, Apo," Istak said, bowing in greeting. Capitán Berong's father, a Peninsular, had settled in Cabugaw after serving in the Spanish army and acquired large tracts of land which he had passed on to his children from a union with a mestiza from Vigan.

"So it is you, Eustaquio," the capitán said, recognizing the teacher of his daughters. "How fortunate that I should meet you on my way to your village. Now I don't have to ride that far . . ." He wiped his face, burnt to a reddish pink. His leather boots were dusty. "I have been riding since morning, visiting barrios— not just yours. I don't like going around with the bad news, telling people of the misfortune that has befallen them . . ."

So what his mother had prophesied was coming true. But how could he believe in auguries after the many years during which he had learned from Padre Jose that much of the suffering in this world was man's own doing?

Capitán Berong appreciated beauty whether it was in horses or in women, even if they were the lowly daughters of his tenants. His eyes were on the young widow. "I have not seen you before," he said. "Who are you?"

Istak answered for Dalin. "She has just been widowed, Señor. She is staying with us . . ."

"It does not concern her then." The mestizo dismissed her, although his eyes were still on her. "It is about you, your family—and that *sitio* where you live."

"Yes, Apo."

Capitán Berong stroked his wisp of a beard and turned away as if he could not tell the young man the bad news to his face. "You have to leave the *sitio*, Eustaquio, you and your whole family. The new priest has been studying his books. He thinks the yield of the land is very low. He wants to give the land, in fact, all the land in your *sitio*, to a new set of tenants. Tenants he likes."

The words sank deep. "You are sure that this is what he wants, Apo? I cannot believe that this is so," Istak said, his throat gone dry.

Capitán Berong turned to him and nodded. "Yes, Eustaquio. These were his words. If it may comfort you—you are not the only ones. In the other villages—there will be changes, too. Some families he does not want . . ."

Istak wanted to say more, but Capitán Berong looked at him with great severity. "I do not speak rashly. You can stay in your village the rest of your life. You can keep the accounts for me and teach my children and the children of my children. It is better this way. Your fate is still yours to change."

"What should I do then, Apo?"

"Go see Padre Zarraga. Perhaps you can dissuade him."

"And if he refuses to see me?"

Capitán Berong seemed vexed with him. He pulled at the reins of his horse and wheeled around. "Tell the others in your village. Their fate is the same, only your family goes first. The rest can go after the next harvest season." In a while the chestnut horse and its rider had disappeared in a swirl of dust.

The sun was hot. Istak steered the cart to the shade of a camachile tree. This was where he would leave her and he would then walk back to his village to bring the news.

"But why should the priest send you away?" Dalin asked.

"For many reasons," Istak said. "Maybe he does not like us."

"But why now?" She was persistent.

Istak did not reply. Yes, there was reason for the priest to send him away from the church and though he was never told, Istak knew it was because he had seen. But to banish all of them, there must be a more stringent reason other than guilt, for Istak was an unerring witness to a mortal sin the new priest had committed; he was a debaucher, the way Padre Jose could never be. He recalled again his mother's warning that Dalin was a foreboding. He coveted the oval face, the dark, inquiring eyes. She was truth, she was life—but she had been cast adrift, without moorings, as he, too, had been. If only they could go together wherever the wind would blow them.

CHAPTER

3

"ARE YOU really going to leave Po-on? Where will you go?" Dalin asked as Istak got off the cart. It would be the last time he would see her.

"If this is what God wills . . ."

"It is not God's will," Dalin said.

"There is always land for those who want to clear it," he said.

"Is that what you will do? Look for new land? I have told you what I have seen."

"And it is so far away," Istak said, but quickly there flashed in his mind the vast valley well beyond Tirad and across many ranges. What Dalin had seen would not be much different. Would he have the will to leave Po-on or Cabugaw itself? And how would he tell his father, who had poured his sweat into the little plot he did not even own?

Dalin continued evenly, "I can go with you. Part of the way. Then I won't have to travel alone."

Istak turned to her—dark eyes beseeching. He smiled, and in a leap, he was beside her on the cart again. Yes, it was the right thing to do, the kindly thing to do—she would go with them since she had nowhere else to go. Where would it lead? There seemed to be no way he could elude what he himself had wanted to escape, this Po-on to which, like most of his people, he had been chained. But she was here, flower to the eye, and this was not good-bye.

He told her then how it was more than ten years ago. It was as if he were on the same cart, only he was not returning to Po-on, but leaving it instead. Padre Jose had come to say Mass, as he had done twice a year for many years, and after the Mass he had performed the rituals of confirmation on the children—many of them well into adulthood. The old priest had picked him out because he was the smartest, the most alert. That was the beginning and Istak did not disappoint his benefactor, although afterward, when he was older, Istak knew that the barriers to his ambition were higher than the Cordilleras. He had heard of what had happened in Cavite, and Padre Jose was not one to deny or gloss over it—how three native priests were executed "for leading a revolt" and one of them was from Vigan, an Ilokano like him. The disturbing knowledge had lodged deep in his mind, grown with him, merged with his flesh, and become an oppressive afterthought; he knew his place, he had accepted it. Perhaps it was possible . . . but he did not let the thought consume him. The ways of the world were set; he was not going to be a thorn. He was a man of peace and would turn the other cheek as Christ had done, to teach people to love others if they cannot even love themselves. He could have gone to the seminary in Vigan; he had visited there with Padre Jose, had seen the classrooms, the library shelves with so many books he would have loved to touch, but it was all over now—and it was God's will, perhaps, that he was not meant to be a priest, that he and his family would always be with the land. If this was so, then he should not fret too much. Thoughts of Dalin beside him, sometimes their arms touching, lulled him. He would have someone like her, and again, the shame and wonder—how it was with Capitán Berong's daughters, how they teased him, always leaning forward at the table so that he could peer down into their white blouses to the rise of their breasts.

When they reached the village, only Ba-ac was at home. Istak's mother was in the creek washing and his brothers were out in the fields. They waited at the foot of the stairs till Ba-ac came down with a large wooden basin filled with warm water. He strained down the flight, his left hand pressing the heavy basin against his waist.

When they were through washing, Istak told him what Capitán Berong had said. The old man listened calmly; he was easily given to anger, but now there was stoic patience in the shrunken face. After a while, Ba-ac said dully, "I will go to town and beg the new priest to let us stay for another year. If we move out now, how will we live? We have but little grain left. If it could be the next harvesttime, we might prepare."

"He wants us to leave immediately, Father."

"One more year will not make a difference." Ba-ac said. "We will be able to bring along some chickens and we will be able to uproot this house properly. And your mother can weave some lengths of cloth. Don't tell your brothers, or your mother."

"Let me come with you," Istak said. I can speak his language—he wanted to add, but did not.

"You stay here," Ba-ac said. "I do not think the new priest likes you, else he would have retained you, is that not so?"

Istak did not reply. His father had confirmed what had long

lain in his mind. And yet it was so obvious in the manner with which the priest spoke to him, as if he were a mindless child good only for kitchen chores. As the new priest had said, he had had his fill of "*la sopa boba.*"

The old man hurried to the house, and when he emerged he wore his white starched pants and white collarless shirt. He even seemed to be in good humor. "I will also ask him to take you back," he said brightly.

"He will not permit it, Father."

"I will beg," Ba-ac said. "Beggars cannot be proud. I will get on my knees . . ." His voice trailed off.

IT WAS a long walk to town—a full three miles of April dust and a sun which bore down on everything. The catuday and marung-gay trees along the trail were powdered with dust. At this time of the year, the frogs found refuge in the deep cracks in the earth, where they were sought and speared with barbed hooks.

Ba-ac reached the town shortly before dusk had settled. Soon they would be indistinct—the grass-roofed houses in yards enclosed by bamboo fences, the old houses of stone with tiled, high-pitched roofs and sash windows—the homes of Cabugaw's rich—and at the edge of town, the big church, its limestone walls painted creamy yellow, its belfry higher than any tree in the village. The streets were empty, save for a few stray goats and pigs. Near the church, across the wide plaza scraggly with dying grass, was Capitán Berong's big brick house. His daughters were seated in the iron chairs on the wide lawn over which stood an old acacia tree, its trunk huge. The sisters would probably grow into spinsters unless they went to Vigan, or unless some rich trader came and saw them, for there were no young men in Cabugaw rich enough or intelligent enough for them.

The churchyard was not yet cleared of the litter of the revelry which marked the new priest's birthday, the palm leaf and banana wrappers of rice cakes, the orange peels and frayed paper wrappings of candies, the blackened remnants of rockets and firecrackers. At the door of the *kumbento,* a young acolyte was scrubbing the tile floor. He recognized the old man, so he let him in.

How many times had he been here when Istak still served in the sacristy and yet had never set foot beyond the tile porch into the sanctum within. This massive building—his grandfather and his father had helped build it; they had fired the brick for its walls, and the lime that set the mortar, they had gathered it from the sea. He had seen the scars on his father's back, what the bullwhip had etched permanently there, like harsh lines drawn by the harrow on the land, and though he was very young then, he could never forget, and remembering it, Ba-ac felt a loathing for the building slowly coil in him. He pushed the heavy wooden door and stepped into an alcove, dimly lighted by an oil lamp. In a while, night would engulf the town and soon, one of the acolytes would climb the belfry to toll the Angelus.

Beyond the alcove, as the boy at the door had told him, were the stairs, and up the stairs of huge solid planks were the priest's quarters, forbidden to all of them unless they were called. He went up the flight, apprehensive that no one had announced his coming. The walls were lined with heavy velvet drapes, broken only where a sash window was open to the oncoming evening. He was in a *sala* with some cane furniture, and beyond it, another door. In a voice which quavered, Ba-ac announced himself. "There is a man, Apo. There's a humble servant entreating you for an audience . . ."

No reply. He wavered, wanting to return downstairs to the porch to ask the boy to announce him, or wait there till the priest made his appearance. But gathering more courage, he pushed the door ajar; it opened to still another room, better lighted than the alcove below. The last light of day shone on the mahogany floor and washed the walls with tawny light. A tall cabinet of shining wood with a glass front stood in a corner, a monumental piece of carpentry, exquisitely carved. On the walls were huge pictures of priests in various postures of supplication, their faces upturned and swathed with holy light. This is where my son lived, he told himself; he saw this every day, this splendor, and for a moment, he wondered if Christ would be comfortable here. He felt smaller now, and when he rapped on the door, he did it quietly lest he disturb the opulent silence. Barely above a whisper, he spoke in Ilokano, knowing that all the Augustinians could speak the language. "Señor, one of your lowly servants is here to beg a favor from you . . ."

No stirring beyond the heavy door. Then a voice called from within. "Come in—since you have already gotten this far."

Ba-ac pushed the door ajar and peeped in: another room except that the floor seemed shinier. Statues of saints—he recognized San Lazaro immediately—stood on pedestals. Barefoot, he barely lifted his feet so that he would not make any noise. A chandelier dangled from the rose-colored ceiling adorned with cherubs in pink, and as a slight breeze blew in from the open window, the many-faceted glass prisms tinkled.

The young priest was kneeling before a low cabinet; he was not wearing his soutane but was dressed only in long-sleeved underwear. On the floor were a silver crucifix and the chalice which he was cleaning with a stained piece of cloth. Ba-ac knelt before the priest, grasped his hand, and kissed it. He did not rise, he could not rise until the young priest commanded him to.

"Who are you and what do you want?" the young priest

asked in heavily accented Ilokano. He was muscular; his hirsute arms and his neck were pale, as were his hands; his face, which was exposed to the sun at times, was ruddy; there was a quality of malevolence in his eyes, and as he stood up, he lifted the big crucifix and appraised it in the fading light. The silver gleamed.

"I am the father of Eustaquio, Apo," Ba-ac said, still kneeling, his voice quavering as recognition came swiftly. His old eyes were not mistaken. This was the same young priest who had condemned him to his fate, who had—although he did not wield the knife—cut off his hand. It was the same face, deceptively young and kind in countenance; in the past five years—had it really been that long?—he had not aged one bit. There was something youthful about him, perhaps eternal as Satan is eternal, and now Ba-ac was face-to-face with him again, and this time he was again begging as he had done in the past, proclaiming his innocence in a frightened and distraught voice which was not heard. Yet it was possible that a man could change, as men everywhere have changed when confronted with the evil of their ways or a superior moral force. Perhaps, this was a new man—a vain wish, knowing it was he who had sent Istak away—his poor, patient, ever-forgiving son.

"And who is Eustaquio?"

"Your acolyte, Apo," the old man said. "He tried to serve you as well as he could, but . . ."

The young priest turned to him. "I know. And I suppose that you think he has become a Christian because he served here, don't you? And that you are one, too?"

"I am, Apo," Ba-ac said, bowing. "By Mary's breath, and Joseph's and Jesus', too."

"How gratifying! And your son Eustaquio. He is in your house now, among his *carabaos*. Did he really think he was bright enough to be a priest?"

"It was Padre Jose, Apo," Ba-ac said. "The old priest, he told me he wanted Eustaquio to be a priest . . ."

The young priest paced the floor. It was now nearly dark, but Ba-ac could still see everything clearly, the white underwear, the brute hands.

"Soon, they will be aspiring for membership in the order. Then they will want to be bishops—vicars of Christ. Soon, they will grab the habiliments not just of the Church but of temporal power. There is no ending to that. Soon—" He sighed and turned to the old man who was still kneeling before him. "Do you really think that you Indios are educated enough to understand the meaning of government or of God?"

Ba-ac did not answer; he had not come here to be told that his brain held only so much. He did not have the education of this priest, or of his son, but this he knew, that Eustaquio was asked by Capitán Berong to teach his daughters, that Padre Jose—and he was old and wise—wanted Eustaquio to be more than just a sacristan.

"I do not ask that you pity Eustaquio, Apo," he said. "I came here for the land—to beg you to allow us to stay one more harvesttime. We have lived in Po-on all our lives, Apo. My father, my grandfather. And the last harvest was not good, as you know. That was why your share, Apo, was not as much as it should have been. The drought—that was the reason. We did not keep anything you did not know about. We did not steal."

The priest looked at him, at the right hand that was missing. "I did not know Eustaquio came from a family of thieves. Padre Jose—he was too old to be sound of mind. He should not have trusted your son too much, given him ideas that made him feel important. It should not be difficult for you to survive—with your special talents, you will not starve. The land should then go to a farmer better equipped—with two hands. But tell me truthfully, do you people really have two hands? No, you have four feet like the water buffalo."

Ba-ac, still kneeling, let the words sink; they were lies, they were poison, and it was a holy man uttering them.

"All of you," the priest said softly, "you were born to be like the *carabao*, to serve us. The little knowledge you got from us— it is dangerous. You will soon imagine yourselves as Spaniards, and because you know it cannot be, you will soon be thinking like those robbers who want the country for themselves, fili- busters, rebels."

"No, Apo," Ba-ac said, knowing what the priest was leading to. "My son, he is a true Catholic. You cannot find a more loyal servant than him."

The priest glowered at him. "So you see why you must leave this place. I don't want contagion here."

There was no use arguing; perhaps, if he appealed to his sense of mercy. "All our lives, Apo," Ba-ac said in desperation, raising his left hand. "We have lived in Po-on, working faithfully for you. Please, until the next harvesttime is over. We have very little food, Apo. In God's name—"

The blow that blazed across his face did not really hurt the old man, although it knocked him to the floor.

"Don't blaspheme, you wretch," the priest said evenly. Ba-ac was prostrate at the feet of the young priest and when he opened his mouth to continue with his pleading, he tasted salt. He brought his palm to his lips, and in the shadowy light, the blot of bright and living red was distinct. He shook his head and rose slowly, leaning on the side of the cabinet behind him. His left hand touched something solid and in the corner of his eye, he saw it was the crucifix. The moment of truth, of revelation, and he grasped it.

The young priest was too stunned to react; what could this

armless old man possibly do, this ignorant Indio with fire in his eyes? He did not back away, although he easily could have done so, so that when the silver instrument crashed into his face, he did not even raise his hands to defend himself. He fell, not noisily like a tree, but just as slowly, and even when he was already slipping, Ba-ac raised the instrument again, and when he finally stopped to look at it, silver had turned to red. The young priest was unconscious, prostrate on the floor, and Ba-ac bent over him and struck again and again at the Castilian brow, the blue eyes, till the whole face was pulped.

Ba-ac stood over the man, not quite believing that he was dead. Blood still oozed from the wound in the face and neck. He glanced at the hairy arms which were nerveless, the powerful torso that seemed to dissolve into a black blur as the night encompassed everything. The Angelus must have already tolled, but he had not heard it. He must flee, not just this church, not just Po-on, but Cabugaw. But to where? He breathed deeply, and felt very light, as if the crushing weight upon his chest which had long oppressed him had finally been lifted by this single act.

The sense of elation stayed, but it was soon compounded with fear, not just for himself but for his poor, sinless family, and his younger brothers as well. He did not try hiding the dead priest under the bed, although it did cross his mind to do so— anything to delay the discovery, anything to give him time. But did he or Po-on really have this precious time? They had all been doomed from the very beginning, their fate foreordained because they had dark skins, because their noses were flat.

He breathed deeply again and tried to calm the trembling of his hand, the strangling in his throat, the earthquake within. Then he walked calmly to the huge wooden door, down the black stairway to the alcove. The young acolyte who had sent him upstairs was still there.

The acolyte was perhaps only twelve, or eleven even. "Did you see him, Tatang?" he asked.

Ba-ac nodded. "He did not want to see me—he said he was going to sleep . . ." He wanted to say more, but was afraid lest the tremor in his voice betray him.

At last, he reached the door and outside, in the wide yard, he could pick out the goats still tied to their stakes and grazing grass. He walked slowly, as if on a Sunday stroll; it suddenly seemed as if the churchyard were without limit, like the river delta he would have to cross. When he got to the fringes of the town where the houses were made of bamboo and buri palm and not of hardwood and stone, he walked faster, but without seeming to run. It was when he reached the open field that he began to run out of the reaches of Cabugaw. He was surprised at his stamina. He was consumed by only one thought: to flee as fast as he could, alone if that was possible. He was a dead man and it was a dead man who would return to Po-on, to Mayang and her quibbling, to the boisterous boys who bore his name.

As he crossed the river, he slipped on a moss-covered stone. But he rose quickly, then ran again, his lungs close to bursting, his throat rasping dry. Across the river finally, he paused on the bank. Was that the tolling of bells? He keened—yes, the church bells of Cabugaw were tolling as they often did when there was a fire, a calamity that must be announced, a Moro raid, although it had been ages since there was one. The tolling was long, insistent. They had found the body! Did the boy tell them that he was the last man to see the young priest? And did not the boy recognize him? Indeed, who would fail to recognize him since there were not all that many one-armed men in the entire Ilokos.

As he neared Po-on, Ba-ac consoled himself. They had a little time, as the Guardia and their Spanish officers did not like pursuing their quarry at night. They were afraid of the *bandidos* who hid in the villages and ambushed them on the trails to get their Mausers and their revolvers. This had become increasingly common, particularly because there had grown to be so much uneasiness and discontent all over the Ilokos. The bells had proclaimed to the whole town what he had done; he was marked, convicted, but they did not have him yet.

Ba-ac fled down the fields, over the rough, uneven earth the plows had gone through, the soft, ash-brown scars where the torches had seared. He was thirsty but amazed at his own strength, that he could reach Po-on so fast, not on a spirited mount but on his feet.

Even as he hurried, walking fast when running squeezed his lungs, there came lucidly to mind as if it had happened only days ago, how the same young priest had ordered him confined in Vigan and there, in the fortresslike *kumbento*, his inquisition had started, the memory ever present now like a branding iron scorching the flesh. He was an ever-loyal and obedient Christian. Did he not know that there were roads to be built, to lace the country so that progress would come to each town and village? These were, after all, what the *ilustrados*, the *filibusteros*, were asking for in Europe, where, like frightened dogs with their tails between their legs, they had fled? Ba-ac had tried to explain that he was with fever during those two weeks when his contribution to the well-being of the patria was demanded. He had sent word through his youngest son, Bit-tik. He did not mean to refuse service. Why should he when he knew what the punishment was? Had he not given up his eldest son to work for the church in Cabugaw and this dearly beloved son had seldom visited his parents in the last ten years? True, he had not given work for two weeks, but let him pay for that with four weeks' labor if it had to be paid double, for that is how long the rice which he brought with him would last.

The young priest was unmoved. Ba-ac, past sixty, was taken to a cell of the *municipio*, a dank and perpetually dark enclosure smelling of urine, and was hanged there by the right hand.

Now the hand was gone, but not the anger that blazed in his mind and the venom that had inflamed his being. He could still see the young priest as he saw him then—the ivory face, the sensuous smile—even as he pronounced Ba-ac's fate. Maybe he had not really been killed. Maybe everything was an aberration. But the image in his mind was clear, and in the muffled night, the bells which tolled confirmed only too well what he had done.

The camachile trees at last, the edge of the village, the growling of dogs. He stumbled once more at the margin of the field which they had planted to mongo beans, and bits of hard earth dug into his palm. As he rose, he glanced up to a sky sprinkled with stars.

An-no was in the yard, talking with Dalin, whose bull cart had already been unhitched. To him, Ba-ac shouted: "Hurry, hitch all the bull carts. We are leaving—all of us, we are leaving!"

An-no followed him as he rushed up the stairs to the kitchen where Mayang, her eyes red from blowing at the earthen stove, was letting a pot of rice simmer.

He drew a full pitcher from the water jar and drank, his throat making gurgling sounds, then he faced his wife, waving his left hand. "Old Woman, we must flee Po-on! Do you know what I have done? You have no time to serve that meal. Listen—all of us, your children, we have to flee . . ."

"You are drunk again," Mayang said, not minding him.

"I am not!" Ba-ac shouted at her. He brandished his left arm as if it were a precious ornament he wanted her to see. "With this hand, I smashed his face till it could not be recognized. I killed him!" Triumph, pride! "The young priest who sent your son away, who made me what I am. I killed him!"

His wife looked at him, disbelieving; then she saw his trousers grazed by dust, the white shirt specked with red. She peered at them, touched them, then withdrew her hand in horror, for the blood had clung to her fingers.

"Yes, it is blood, Old Woman," Ba-ac said. "I could not stop. I struck again and again."

Mayang crumpled on her knees, wrung her hands, and animal sounds escaped her. Her wailing brought Bit-tik to the house. "Old Man, you have decreed death for yourself and shame and punishment on all of us!"

"Shame? Punishment? Disgrace?" It had filled him quickly, this courage which lifted him as well. Mayang had grown old. He looked evenly at her as she struggled to hold back her tears. "It is not disgrace I bring you, my beloved half"— he rarely used the words—"it is honor. Don't you know what this means? I am not a servant anymore. So we must run away and hurry. Else they will find us here in the morning."

Mayang stood up sobbing and went to their wooden trunk in a corner. Their few clothes were inside, most of which she had woven herself, her skirts, her starched *pañuelo*. An-no and Bit-tik were now in the house, silent and tense, and Ba-ac told them what to do. They listened, understood, and in an instant they were down the yard herding the animals. The neighbors—they had committed no crime other than to live in Po-on and be related to him—they must be told, then they could elect to stay and suffer, or to flee.

"It is not your sons who should tell your brothers and cousins," Mayang told Ba-ac with derision in her voice. "Go tell them yourself. Are you not proud of what you have done? When the Guardia come, will they make distinctions?"

He needed Istak now. He would know the right words to bring the truth to them not as a bludgeon but as light. Where could that son be at this time? At the edge of the village again, thinking, dreaming? He went out and at the wall of blackness he shouted: "Istaaakkk—Istaaakk!"

ISTAK CAME running from the direction of the dalipawen tree, his white shirt distinct in the dark.

"My son, we have no time . . ." Then quietly, solemnly, Ba-ac told him. Istak listened, the words cutting deeply; when it was over, he embraced the old man and wept; his father's breath told him the deed was not the handiwork of *basi*. His father smelled of tobacco, the earth, and harsh living.

"It is my fault, Father," Istak said bitterly. "This happened because of me. So leave then—all of you. I will stay."

Istak knew the Guardia Civil. They were Indios like himself and yet they were different—the uniform and the gun had transformed them. What would he tell them when they came? Padre Jose had said that a father's success could be measured only by how well he had made his children able to stand on their own. The old priest was thinking, of course, of that time when Istak would be a priest, cast adrift by the ways of the world, but strengthened by faith. To the real father who would be hunted like a mad dog, how would Istak be to him?

"Help me tell our relatives," Ba-ac said. "I have brought disaster to them—"

He had not spoken too soon. From the houses across the mud-packed yard, his cousins, their wives, and their children came running, An-no and Bit-tik behind them, then Kardo, Ba-ac's youngest brother, Simang—Mayang's sister—and still others, the neighbors in the six-house village: they gathered in knots, their inquiries and anxieties a continuous murmur punctuated by exclamations—"Ay, fate!"

Ba-ac was the eldest, he was the leader, and they knew of the agony he had gone through. He did not speak of the young priest; he told the older people equably, without justification, and they listened intently, knowing that now they would share his punishment.

"So we must seek new land beyond the mountains," Ba-ac said to the hushed gathering. Above, the stars were out in all their splendor and the night around them was thick with the smell of earth, of sweat, of living. "We will go beyond the land of the Bagos; if need be, we can learn to live with them, start a new village, as others have already done—the many who also ran away. They cannot follow us there. They will not dare unless they come in droves and we will not be alone. Haven't others done this?"

Ba-ac turned to Istak beside him. "Tell them, son. Tell them it is not hopeless."

Istak turned to faces eager for solutions, for peace. He must tell them what he had always been told by Padre Jose—to have faith. As for patience and industry, they were Ilokanos born to these virtues—it was in their blood, in the very air they breathed.

"Since we have been ordered to leave anyway, we should not wait—we should look at this as a challenge. But in doing so, let us not forget the Almighty, that we go in peace although we be threatened, persecuted. This is the way of the Lord. I know some of you may want to stay . . ." From the older people, an immediate sound: one said, "No, we are all related, we will stay together."

"How will we live with little grain? Will we eat the seed rice?" his uncle Kardo asked.

"We will live as we have always lived—frugally. We will eat bamboo shoots, the green leaves of the mango and butterfly trees. And the forest provides—we can trap deer, wild fowl. We have known difficult times—remember when we had so little food we ate the pith of the big palm?"

They murmured approval. They were Ilokanos—they would

not starve anywhere. And they also believed Istak because he was the most learned, the most skilled in a language none of them could understand. Ever since his return, they had flocked around him, urging him to set up a school so that they, too, would know how to read and write—not just the rich mestizos and favorites of the friars. They would sustain him, weave his clothes, cut his hair, and give him enough grain to fill his granary so that he would not have to hold the handle of a plow and coarsen his palms. He had, of course, become enthusiastic about it, how much he could do—those years in Cabugaw were not to be wasted. He had already fashioned a series of lessons from the elementary *cartilla* to the higher form that would include philosophy and some science—he was going to impart to the young people of Po-on all that Padre Jose had given him.

He must tell them that there would be no school, and worse—that they really had to leave Po-on. This was all that the new priest wanted them to know. Now he would tell them that they had only the night to prepare, that sunrise must not catch them here. He remembered what Padre Jose had once told him of history, how the bearer of bad news was himself dispatched with the sword although the bad news that he brought was not of his own making.

To the right, across the level patch of ground, was the house of Kardo, his father's youngest brother. Istak felt closest to him, perhaps because Kardo was more like an older brother. What mattered were his wife and his five children. He must leave, and not in peace but in fear. They had been welded together, not just by blood or marriage, but by work, for they had always shared what could not be done by just one man or one family—the planting of rice, the harvesting, the repair of the dikes, of the irrigation canals, and of their homes.

Before the clump of bamboo which formed an arbor, a gateway to the village, was the house of his mother's sister, Simang. Her husband and children were before him, repeating, "Must we leave now?"

"But I will stay behind," Istak said quietly. He had decided on this, to stay and to beg with them who ruled, that what Baac did was on impulse. He would take whatever punishment they would mete out because it was for him that his father went to see the new priest. He spoke their language, he had proven his loyalty; they would understand. Yet he recoiled at the thought of what might happen; the Guardia did not care about justice; they knew only how to exact punishment.

Kardo told Istak there was no sense in being left behind, but Istak was adamant. If it was a guide they needed, Dalin knew the way.

He got an armful of firewood in the woodpile and tied it underneath the carriage of the cart. From below the houses, they gathered the chickens in bamboo coops. The pigs were trussed up. They did not have too many clothes—for each family just one wooden trunk and no more.

Tears in her eyes, Mayang dismantled the ancient loom under the house and carefully bundled the levers, the shuttles. The loom was her grandmother's. Would there be cotton in the new land? They would build new homes and there was no time to uproot the posts, the sturdy sagat and parunapin which their fathers had dragged from the mountain. There were a few old posts, however, from the old house—as strong as ever—and these they tied underneath the carts.

They worked strenuously, loading what little food there was, even the green papayas in the yard. Daylight was nearing and stars glimmered in the bowl of sky; they would fade soon and the feared sunlight would be upon them.

Six carts—thirty people, including the children—that was all of Po-on. They would join the many others, the *mal vivir* who had fled the Ilokos whenever there was a revolt or a crime against the Spaniards.

An-no was finished with his chores and went to Istak. "Why don't you want to come with us?"

Istak held his brother by the shoulder; An-no was taller and bigger of build. "This is what you want, is it not, my brother?"

An-no shook his arm off and his voice was no longer rimmed with bluster. "We need you, Manong," he said. "No one among us can speak their tongue. This is a journey where wisdom is needed."

"I have to stay," Istak said simply. "I must speak to them, beg them."

The dogs started to howl. Among the children roused from sleep and uncomfortable in the bull carts, one started to cry.

"This is one time we should stay together," An-no said. "Can you not see that Father needs help? What have you really learned in Cabugaw?"

"What does one need to know?" Istak asked, holding up his hands to show the raw blisters, but in the dark, An-no could not see.

He could make out An-no's angry face. "Stay behind, then," his brother said, "and recite your Latin. Maybe the fruits of the trees will fall at your feet." Then he wheeled and headed toward the line of carts being readied.

Alone, covered by the night which he sometimes wished was permanent, Istak cried softly. He was not going to be a martyr, he was not going to be heroic. It was they who were leaving who would be more than brave: the *tulisanes* preyed along the coast and the roads that led out of the Ilokos. If they went by sea, they would probably be safer, and if bad weather came, they could always head for some cove. But by sea, they could also be easily tracked and caught by the Spanish steamboats. If only Padre Jose were here to plead for him, for them.

IN THE HOUSE, Mayang had finished putting everything of value into the trunk. She had also gathered the woven bamboo crowns for the pots to sit on, the pine splinters for kindling wood, and lengths of rope. From a peg that stuck out of the bamboo wall, she took her most precious possession, a tortoiseshell comb inlaid with a thin veneer of gold. In the flicker of the oil lamp, Ba-ac recognized its gleam. "You are not wearing that," he said.

"If I will die running," Mayang said, "I might just as well die with this on my head."

Their most precious possession, however, was not their good clothes or, for the women, their tortoiseshell combs. It was the *carabao* which they treasured most, because without this docile animal, they would not be able to farm; they would go hungry. Its skin had no pores and had to be cooled with a daily bath in the creek or with water from the well.

From under the house, Ba-ac gathered the golden sheaves of tobacco hung to dry. They had been harvested two weeks before and some of the leaves were still greenish and not ready for smoking. The *municipio* was going to buy it all, but he would not give them that privilege now; he would need a lot to smoke, to chew, and to barter.

Then they were ready; a big pot of rice had been cooked and coffee had been brewed from roasted corn and flavored with thick molasses. Toward the east, still no glimmer of sunrise. They would not wait for daylight.

WHY should we be rooted here, in a land which is not ours? All over the north, in the past, men had fled to the forest. Free men, they cleared the land and started anew, well beyond the claws of the Guardia Civil, the friars and their fawning acolytes. No less a man than old Padre Jose had spoken about them when they had pressed beyond Tirad, down the fertile valley of Nueva Segovia. They were everywhere, with new names, new lives. They could start anew, too.

Not me, Istak told himself. If he stayed he could perhaps explain—hold back the storm that would descend and engulf them all. Explain he would, not with words but with his faith in the justness of God.

"I will be safe, Mother," he assured Mayang, standing by the lead cart which An-no would drive. Behind them, tethered with maguey twine, were the work animals, a *carabao* with a calf and two cows. In Po-on, they had the most, but where they were going they would all be equal. Six carts altogether, with children wrapped in coarse blankets, for it was cool. Underneath the carts and behind them stoves and cooking pots were carefully tied. Six carts, six families—how could they travel without being seen? If they went singly, they would fall prey to robbers who ambushed in the foothills and isolated distances. If they went together, they could easily be tracked, questioned, found out; now, more than ever, they needed cunning, which, perhaps, Istak would be able to give them.

"I will follow, Mother," he reiterated. "It will not be difficult to trace you. I just want to be sure, to know what will happen to Po-on."

"Don't look back, then," Mayang said, her voice sad. "Keep us in your mind."

Istak walked with them to the edge of the village, well beyond the bamboo grove, down the gully to the open fields, the carts in single file, their solid wooden wheels creaking. They must be oiled, Istak reminded his brother. In the darkness, he could make out the familiar faces, the nephews and nieces, the cousins he had grown up with. And as Dalin's cart passed—the seventh and last, she reached out and held his hand briefly. A dull ache coursed through him, the warmth of her hand filling him with warmth as well; so young and already a widow. Would she be able to show them the way? And what would happen to her? To them?

CHAPTER

4

THE ROAD to Vigan was well traveled. Ba-ac and his brothers had gone to the capital when they were conscripted to work on the governor's mansion and on the road to the south. They would not take that road—in every town they would be stopped by the Guardia, who would have been warned by telegraph. If they were not detained, their chickens, even their work animals would be taken.

But time was in their favor. The rivers were dry and the trails would no longer be rivulets of mud. They would skirt the foothills of the Cordilleras through land which they were familiar with. In the day, they would rest while the men scouted what lay ahead and when night came, they would be on their way again. There were enough hollows, folds in the hills and bamboo groves to hide them. They had bows and arrows tipped with iron, and their bolos were sharp. If they were lucky, they could even have wild boar or deer meat.

Daylight now. The sun rode the heavens and banished the dew that had covered the grass, glistening like many jewels. They were near the Cabugaw foothills, where the tall grass still grew lush and green on the dikes. They had traveled slowly on trails not often used. The *carabao* hooves had also dug a rhythm of hollows on the ground, and in places where the runners of sleds had cut, the ridges were high and it was difficult for the carts to roll smoothly and straight.

Ba-ac in the lead cart saw it behind, the cloud of dust in the first flush of morning far down to the horizon—the Guardia finally coming to Po-on.

The bend of the river was to their left—actually an expanse of sandy loam, boulders, and more scraggly growths of grass and stunted camachile trees no taller than a man. It was an act of God, Istak would have said, that they were there at that very moment. "Hurry! Hurry!" the old man shouted at the carts behind him. "Down the gully, all of you. Behind the grass, hide where you cannot be seen. And the animals—keep them quiet. Unhitch the carts!"

He was a leader, the repository of wisdom, though he had but one arm. They were all afraid even if they had done nothing. They would protect Ba-ac, too, because they were together, related by blood. Now, the morning sun poured on them. They waited, the mothers shushing their children, the men silently looking at one another. The dust cloud raised by the horses drew nearer and though they could not hear them, they could see the cloud disappear; they were crossing farther up the river and in a while, the dust cloud appeared again, a wraith on the horizon.

The animals did not make a sound. A long, long wait—then

it came, the crack of a gun echoing across the fields. Ba-ac went up the incline and peered at the distance.

Toward the east, beyond the thin line of bamboo and trees, a wisp of smoke plumed up. The smoke thickened and soon the trail of dust again, going back toward them. In the distance, the flames shot up with spirals of gray smoke. Po-on was burning! They did not even leave the houses for the next tenants to move into. Years of sweat had been poured into that village, the roofs they shaped, the posts they dragged from the forests. Everything was in that pillar of smoke reaching up to the cloudless sky. The men cursed, the women wept silently.

"I will go back," Dalin said resolutely after some time. "They are not after me, they have nothing to blame me for or accuse me of. I am not from Po-on . . ."

"What can you do even if you went back?" An-no asked. "If they burned Po-on, surely, they must have killed Istak, too, or taken him. They will catch you, torture you, and then they will know where we are . . . and where we are going."

"You don't know what I have gone through to be alive," the young woman said, looking straight at the man who, she knew, wanted her to stay, not just for her safety, but for himself. She hitched her cart. "Do not go away. I will return here," she told Ba-ac.

THEY ARE GONE. Istak turned over the words, feeling their bite. He glanced around at the houses, empty now and shrouded by night. How would it all look when daylight came— this ghost of a village, without the voices of children, the grunt of animals? Even now, he could imagine his mother's voice summoning the pigs to the trough, "Riii—say, Riii—say"; Ba-ac calling for the young calf to come home. "Ooooowah-ngek . . .

Ooooowah-ngek . . ." In their hurry, they must have left behind many precious things. Not all the chickens were in the coops, the firewood, the sheaves of tobacco were still under the house, the old pots, the seeds of mango, of tomato, and eggplant were still hanging in the eaves to dry. Even this wooden mortar on which he sat, its smooth hollow recessed deep by the constant pounding of pestles. As a boy he had helped his mother pound rice in it after the stalks were first threshed in a long wooden trough hewn from solid wood. The pestle had callused his hand. He had loved the rhythmic sound of the pounding if there were three of them at the mortar, the thuds following one another and echoing in the quiet. It was not the grain which he had enjoyed pounding, though; it was the boiled bananas mixed with young coconut meat and cakes of cane sugar. The bananas became pulpy and sticky, they sucked at the pestle, and part of the skill in pounding was in the ability to withdraw the pestle quickly before the next came crashing down.

An-no had argued against bringing the mortar, for it was heavy, so they brought only the pestles. He wondered if they would be able to find another trunk as solid and as hardy as this.

From its perch on the guava tree near the house a rooster crowed. Istak looked up at the sky, at the stars that still studded it like gems. The east had started to pale; he could hope for the morrow—this was what Padre Jose had always said, although his father had long since given up the fervent prayer. Padre Jose—a rock of virtue, of kindness, maybe because he had spent more than forty years in Filipinas. After dinner, in the early evenings, he would indulge in his only vice—a glass of *tinto dulce*, which Istak served. He had once caught Istak tasting the wine and he had roared with his only expletive: "*¡Carajo!*" But he had, perhaps, immediately felt so miserable at having to scold his favorite acolyte that he gave the young man instead one glass—one full glass—to sip in his presence.

Istak had gotten drunk, but Padre Jose was drunker and started to sing of his youth in a voice out of tune and loud.

And on Istak's twenty-first birthday, he was summoned to the musty room where the old priest slept. And from an ancient cabinet he brought out a ledger bordered with gold and gave it to Istak. It was handsomer than the ledgers he used for the registry of births, deaths, and marriages. Istak was dumbstruck by the richness of the gift. The old priest said, "Here, Eustaquio— write down your thoughts. In Latin because you know it well now . . ."

He had expected that year to enter the Vigan seminary and take the ledger with him, but when he left Cabugaw he also left it behind. The young priest would inspect his things and it would seem as if he had pilfered expensive church property. He left it in the sacristy among the other ledgers. It all came to mind, what he had written one early dawn like this when visions of the future were sunny, even in that dreary room behind the sacristy where the acolytes slept.

He wrote:

We go from one darkness to another and in between, the hidden light of the world, of knowledge. We open our eyes and in this circle of light, we see not just ourselves but others who are our likenesses. This light tells us all men are brothers, but even brothers kill one another, and it is in this light where all this happens. But living in this dazzling light does not blind us to what lies beyond the darkness from where we emerged and where we are going. It is faith which makes our journey possible though it be marred by the unkindness of men, their eternal faulting, before we pass on to another darkness.

SO THEY ARE GONE and, as he promised, he would follow them to Solana, to the valley, which Dalin said would be their haven. He would take the shortest route, cross the Cordilleras in Tirad, which he already knew, then risk the journey through Igorot country, hoping the friends he had made there would remember him.

Would he be able to leave? He had decided to suffer in his father's stead—so stay he must so that they could leave without being hounded. He would explain, he would beg, he would tell them his forfeited life was just as good. And perhaps there would be compassion for him; perhaps Padre Jose would intercede, tell them what a good and loyal subject he was. After what his father had done, there was no more hope—ever—of his going to Vigan. Of what use was this plodding, then? He was not a farmer; he must learn how to become one, to leave behind the intoxicating world of books. It had occurred to him how he had often felt a pang of guilt when he was still in Cabugaw, remembering his brothers and parents immersed in the drudgery of Po-on. He had been untrue to them, he could not pay back even a *kusing* of the debt he owed them all. Now was his chance to redeem himself. These were the thoughts badgering him when his eyes became heavy with sleep, and he lowered himself onto the polished floor of the threshing trough.

He woke up to the thunder of horses' hooves on the hardened earth. He rose quickly and recognized Capitán Gualberto of the Lawag garrison, a shock of blue-and-black uniform in the morning light, his golden epaulets gleaming. He had come to the convent so many times, always carefully groomed, his boots shiny, his uniform well pressed, his short-cropped hair trimmed so that the white of his scalp just above the nape and the ears shone. On these occasions Istak had served him hot chocolate and rice cakes, and the Guardia officer had always thanked him in a raspy, effeminate voice belying the anger that burned in him, anger at the recalcitrant Igorots whose domain was denied him, anger at the secret enemies of Spain, the masons. Maybe Capitán Gualberto would remember, maybe he would consider his plea.

With the officer was Capitán Berong and six Indio Guardia. Capitán Berong's white shirt was drenched with sweat and dirtied.

Istak rushed to meet them. To Capitán Berong, first, then to the Spanish officer, his eyes beseeching, in polite Spanish, as was expected of him, his good morning, then: "I beg for mercy, Apo . . ."

It was as if Capitán Berong, who had asked him to teach his daughters, had never known him. "He is the son," the capitán said to the Spaniard, his voice rimmed with derision. "Evil is in him as well." Was this the same man who had said he, Eustaquio Salvador, was needed in Cabugaw?

Capitán Gualberto drew the revolver from his holster. "And where are they? And your father with one arm?"

He did not want to lie, but God forgive me, I must protect them, I must be worthy of the blood that flows in me, and it came out quickly, the words carefully chosen, "Apo, when Capitán Berong said that we must leave Po-on where we were all born, we followed what we were ordered to do. Except for me, they all left yesterday, Apo. I chose to remain, to watch over this village in the hope that I—I may be allowed to stay"—he glanced at Capitán Berong—"perhaps to teach . . . but if by leaving they have committed a crime, then take me in their stead . . ."

"That is easy," Capitán Gualberto said, taking aim with his revolver. "Spanish justice triumphs again."

How does Death come? Dalin, *Ave Maria, purísima*—a rod of black catching a glint of sun, the hole—the big, black hole, Dalin, *Ama mi adda ca sadi langit*, the spark of fire, the thunder and the massive hammer, oh, the black, black pain, the blackness, Dalin, Dalin . . .

THE LIGHT came first as a ruddy glimmer which grew larger, brighter, then took shape, hazy but real, an arc of sunlight and above the arc, what seemed like a roof, yes, a roof of matted palm leaves. I am alive, I am seeing something real. I am alive, I can feel the throbbing in my head.

He stirred and a sudden pain exploded in his chest, seared his entire being, so sharp, so intense he screamed, the sound erupting from the depths, confirming that, indeed, he was alive. It all came back, the gun pointed at him, the burst of orange flame, the massive hammer that struck him. Now he tried to raise his right hand, but there was no right hand at all. Have I lost it? Have I become a man with just one arm like my father? He tried to turn to his side; the arm was there but it no longer followed his command.

It was not the voice of an angel which he heard, although it might just as well have been. No sound was more sweet, more well remembered afterward, than "I am here," she said. "Don't move, else you will start bleeding again . . ."

He turned to the voice; Dalin was silhouetted against the arc of light and though he could not see her distinctly, her presence touched him with its promise, her hand upon his left arm, like some magic balm that eased all the fears that possessed him. I can go to sleep now. This is not true, this is not true; this is some blissful dream and I don't want to wake up!

The pain crept back but no longer as sharp as when he moved for the first time, a dull weight against his shoulder and his chest. Though the air smelled clean, he had difficulty sucking it. Were his lungs punctured? He listened to his breathing—there was no whistling, no rasping, but the ache was there, deep and permanent.

"Be still," Dalin again, oh that beautiful, soothing voice; "You have lost a lot of blood. It is a miracle that you are alive. A miracle. There is a hole below your shoulder and behind your back where the bullet went through . . ."

His lung must be punctured and he must be bleeding inside. He was so weak, it seemed he had no body anymore and he was just a hollow man, his bones and innards taken out. He was dying, he was now sure of that. Our Father Who Art in Heaven . . . oh, dear God! Dalin, don't leave me, don't leave me . . . Above him, the design of bamboo slats which held the woven fronds in place—was this the last thing he would see? Dalin, Holy Mary, Mother of God . . . then darkness again . . .

And again, too, the arc of light, brighter now. It was no illusion, he was alive, his lungs were intact, he was breathing. He could even bring his head up a little, and in doing so, he realized that his chest was bandaged with strips of cloth.

"Dalin . . . Dalin . . ."

"I am here," she said behind him. He could hear her move toward him, then her hand rested on his arm. Her calm, lovely face, a finger pressed to her lips. "Do not talk," she said, squatting beside him so that he could see her, feel her leg pressed against his side, her whole wonderful presence banishing the lie of his passing. "I will tell you everything. Your father, your family—they are all in the delta waiting for us. We will not leave till it is dark so that we will not be followed . . ."

"And where are we?" His voice sounded weak.

"We are within a ring of bamboo at the foot of a hill, away from Po-on. It is no more. They burned it all. Nothing there but ashes and posts still smoldering. They left you in the yard. Thank

God, after they shot you, they did not drag you into the fire. Perhaps they thought you were dead. And why not? We were in the delta when we heard the shot, we saw the fire, and after they had left, I came after you . . ."

Sweet, beautiful stranger.

"I thought you were dead, but I looked closer. You were breathing. The blood had clotted and stopped the flow. I unhitched the bull cart, tilted it, and lifted you into the back."

Sweet, beautiful stranger.

"My bull is tethered and grazing. If you are hungry, or if you are thirsty?"

Sweet, beautiful stranger, my guardian angel, may you be always near.

"It will be dark soon, we will join them . . ."

Slowly, almost imperceptibly, the joy of being alive waned and a great, formless weariness dropped over him, the weariness not of the wound throbbing in his chest. Another wound festered deeper than the laceration in his flesh, the thought that they showed no mercy to him, ever loyal servant of the Church, of Mother Spain. He closed his eyes as the tiredness suffused him and now he really wanted release, the comfort of sleep, anything to dull the mind, to keep him from thinking. They were only men, doing what would prove them stronger, more powerful, and therefore, fit to rule. There is still a just God who will pass judgment. Or could this be but part of that suffering he must endure, condemned as he was to believe in a God who decreed that salvation lay in suffering?

BIT-TIK'S VOICE woke him, "Will he live?" The rustling of people, heavy breathing, murmurs indistinct and incessant, and blackness heavy and portentous all around.

"Let us pray," Dalin said.

Now he could feel the cart lurch a bit. They were moving, moving away from Po-on. A still, moonless night, the dark mass of the range their only guide; they would follow the foothills all the way down to La Union, then to Pangasinan.

They had onions and garlic; the two pigs that had squealed when they were still in the riverbed were quickly butchered, their meat salted. Not all the meat could be salted, however, so they feasted in the evening and for a moment forgot that they were fugitives. The chickens were quiet in their bamboo cages under the carts—it was the roosters and their crowing that could give them away, but there were roosters all over the land, many of them wild, their crowing everywhere.

There was room in Dalin's cart, so he stayed there, in her care. She had really joined them.

That night, Mayang gave him a piece of roasted pork. It should have given him pleasure; it had been a long time since he had had pork, not since he left Cabugaw. But it tasted bitter and he had no appetite. He was weak, he could hardly move, and his right arm was without feeling still. He touched his fingers with his left hand but could feel nothing. He was really like his father now.

Soft footsteps alongside the cart, the *carabaos* straining at their yoke. Moving along on uneven ground, the cart sometimes dipped or yawed, and each fall brought a bolt of pain. He felt the bandage again and again to make sure that he was not bleeding, and was relieved to find it was not wet.

Dalin sat out front and he could make out her shape, her turning to him occasionally. He slept fitfully and had disjointed dreams: Padre Jose in his black cassock drinking not his wine but *basi* in a coconut bowl; Carmencita—yes, he had dreamed of her many times—dressed in the white gown of a bride, baring her breasts to him, and he had grabbed at them, sucked them, and when the warm milk filled his mouth, he spat it out and found it red, the dark living red of blood. He woke up, then drifted back to sleep. This time he dreamed he had entered the seminary in Vigan; he was no longer a novice—he was wearing the soutane of a priest, and he was teaching—yes, he was teaching and his students were not Indios—they were all old and venerable friars, among them Padre Jose. They were all listening to him, rapture on their Castilian faces, as he spoke not about theology, but about the mind as healer, about the capacity of man to free himself from the bondage of his own carnal limitations. And he showed them how it was possible for someone of earthly shape like him to do what was not possible—he willed himself off the floor, and he rose till his head almost touched the ceiling, then he looked down at them, smiling benignly at their amazement.

"WHAT does it all mean?" he asked Dalin in the morning when they stopped in the hollow of a hill, surrounded by a flourish of butterfly trees. Children splashed naked in the stream behind the cart and the women were cooking the morning meal. The rich smell of roasting pork drifted into the cart.

"I do not know," Dalin said, lifting his head a little so he could drink the bittersweet coffee Mayang had brewed. His chest throbbed with a dull blob of pain. "My dreams are so simple . . . nothing as interesting as yours," Dalin continued, "although once I flew over the sea and could look down into the depths and see where the schools of fish were."

As they waited for the dark to come, she kept him company. Mayang drifted in and out, feeling his brow and bringing to him bowls of broth. Outside, the women prepared the meals, pounded rice, and the men mended their fish nets, or wove baskets out of the young bamboo which they cut from the thickets along the streams.

Istak grew weaker and his right arm was still numb no matter how much Dalin massaged it. The wound throbbed even more. He prayed, tears streaming down his face, asking that his life be spared, not because he wanted vengeance, but because he wanted to prove he could surmount this personal anguish to do service to his God still.

He thanked God, too, for Dalin beside him, comforting him, telling him now about herself. Who was this angel, whose touch was elixir, whose presence was light? Where had she come from? Lingayen: that was where she was born, a small town at the rim of the sea. Her people were fisherfolk and salt makers. They had a house surrounded by coconuts. Lingayen— a beach with white sand and a gentle surf. There was this tall and ancient tree at the fork of the road which led to their town and when people passed by, they always looked back. Lingayen— looking back—and that was how the town got its name. She knew enough of his language and she spoke it with an accent; she had learned it as a child when her parents sailed up and down the coast, selling coconut sweets, salt, and shrimp paste which they made from the tiny shrimps they caught in fine mesh nets in the gulf.

Long afterward, he remembered what Dalin said through his bouts with pain.

"I'll tell you what really happened. We were not ship-wrecked. All of us in our family, we worked very hard."

During the dry season, they gathered the dry leaves of co-conuts and heated the huge iron vats which had earlier been filled with salt water and then left out in the sun until the water had evaporated. Her mother bought the shrimp from the fisher-men and then stored them in earthen jars. And once they had enough to fill their boat, they sailed up the coast. In the next year, they journeyed by cart to the new towns of Nueva Ecija onward to Cagayan. They either sold the salt and shrimp paste or exchanged these for rice, which was abundant in the western plain. If they sailed up the Ilokos coast, they bartered for tobacco, handwoven cloth, and cotton twine, which the Pangasinan fishermen wove into fishnets.

On this particular trip to the north, a freak wind tossed them a distance from the shore. Toward late afternoon, they were overtaken by a boat with giant sails and six men aboard. They maneuvered their craft close to the frail boat for some time, bantering with them. Then toward sunset, the big boat edged alongside and the six men jumped into their boat. They killed her father; her brother and her mother, who were at the other end, were able to get their bolos but they, too, were overwhelmed. Her brother was able to wound one before he, too, was killed. Their bodies were flung into the sea. They tied her arms to a beam and leered at her. Soon it was dark; they loosened her bonds.

Through the daze and terror of the night, in those moments when she was left alone, she prayed that she would be allowed to live, although life would no longer be the same. Toward midnight, they gave her cold chunks of rice and salted fish which were like rocks in her throat. They let her drink a bowl of coconut water—but only so that she would have strength, for the six of them never let her rest.

"They did things to me," Dalin said simply.

When the dawn limned the east, they were some distance from the shore, and the mountains were a blue wall beyond the waters. Their boat was fast—its sails bloated with wind, its prow cutting the water like a blade. Except for one who was at the stern, manning the rudder, all were asleep on the broad deck, sprawled between the earthen jars of shrimp paste and bales of cloth which they must have taken from other hapless traders. They did not even bother to wash the knives with which they had slain her brother and parents. The blood had caked, and seeing it she retched and threw up all that she had eaten in the night.

In the morning, they transferred the salt, the shrimp paste, and the husked coconuts from her father's boat, which they had tied to their big sailboat. She was left on board. She could not make out where they came from, although they spoke both Pangasinan and Iloko. In the daylight their skin seemed darker, even shiny, perhaps from too long a punishment from sun and sea. For a time, she thought they were Moros, but those stories of their raids on the coast were of the past. Her parents were always aware of the dangers of travel by sea, but it was much safer than going over land that was infested with robbers, too.

The man who was at the rudder left his post, came over to her, and untied her hands. She would not dare jump into the sea, prowled by sharks and too distant from land. They did not touch her the whole day; they let her sit alone weeping, looking senselessly at the heaving waters around her, listening to the wind whip the gray sails above her. She feared the night, for they would surely come to her again.

They had a jar of *basi* and they took long draughts from it after they had supped on rice and salted fish. The helmsman often turned skyward, to a sky studded with stars. He pointed the prow to one of them. Perhaps, they never expected her to jump—she would not be able to swim that far to land and they no longer watched her. Drowning or being devoured by sharks was a better fate; if she stayed, they would eventually kill her anyway.

They circled many times, shouting, and at one turn, the prow of the boat almost bashed her head, but she always stayed under when their craft loomed near. They could not see her in the dark. They lighted a torch but that did not help. They gave up after a while and soon the high sails vanished in the dark altogether. She was finally alone, the awesome immensity of the sea around her.

As a child in Lingayen, she was no stranger to the moods of the sea; she knew how to keep afloat and her father had warned her and the other children about the undertow in the gulf that often dragged unwary swimmers to their death. They should not fight it and thereby lose their strength; they should just keep afloat and after the undertow had spent itself, then and only then should they attempt to swim back to shore.

God in His Heaven, where was the shore? Then she remembered the helmsman looking at the stars and guiding his boat by them. She recalled how it was on those nights when her father also turned to the stars and identified landfall.

The evening star—if she swam toward it, she would reach land. She could float—that was easy—but how could she defend herself from the marauders of the deep? Once, she felt something rough like an is-is leaf brush against her leg and her whole being trembled. A shark! The fishermen in their village had often caught baby sharks in their nets and fish traps and their skins were rough and could cut. For a long while, she waited for the snap of those razor jaws. But if it had been a shark, it did not return. She prayed again that she would not fall asleep, that the sea would not grow rough again and that she could continue to float without tiring too much. Already she had drunk mouthfuls of water and her stomach turned.

Dawn came stealthily shimmering on the waters and with sunrise, she was now sure where land was. Through bleary eyes, she could see the high outline of mountains—so near but really far. She paddled slowly toward the vision, doubting that she would be able to reach the shore.

Toward midday, a plume of smoke rose hazily in the distance. Soon it came into view—a black steamboat, one of those which must have come from the Ilokos or from other lands, headed for Manila—a place she had never seen but which she had heard about as the final destination of these giant boats that could go against the wind or sail on even when the seas were rough. It came closer and she could see shapes moving on the deck. She shouted till her throat ached and her lungs seemed ready to burst—but the big black boat did not lose speed—it glided on until it became just a speck in the distance, and then its plume of black smoke disappeared altogether.

In her worst moments of fear and hopelessness she thought she would just sink. But she kept on floating, marking time with her breathing, gulping the air painfully, her mouth now bitter and dry. Then, something glinted in the sun, and for a while she thought it must be a huge fish but it was not. She swam toward it for what seemed like forever and near it at last, she cried—it was a huge banana trunk and she embraced it, clung to it, and thanked God and all the spirits of the departed for this raft.

She paddled slowly. The sun rode the heavens and lashed down at her, blistered her skin, which hurt so much she would scream. Darkness finally came. It was cold. Her eyes closed and she would struggle to keep them open. The searing blisters, the aching in her throat were now dulled, even bearable, as sleep threatened to engulf her. Once, her grip on the trunk loosened and she seemed to have drifted off into sleep; she woke up in time, fear giving strength to her body and she gripped the trunk even tighter. Then, to her dismay, a skein broke off and now she was afraid that the whole trunk would fall apart before she reached the shore. Worse, it seemed as if the sea itself now wanted to claim her. The waves seemed bigger, and she could not see what was ahead as the sea heaved. Thoughts of death flashed through her mind once more, of fish feasting on her flesh as she sank to the bottom. Her legs were already numb and her arms were heavy as logs. It was then that she made the vow: that if she lived, she would serve whoever saved her for as long as she was needed and she would do anything, anything demanded of her . . .

Morning again; the shore seemed much nearer. A wave lifted her, and through eyes that smarted she was overjoyed to see the line of trees on the shore. But her arms were no longer hers, her throat was being scraped by thorns. With no food in her belly for two days, it seemed as if it were being gnawed by sharp fangs. The banana trunk seemed so enormous, she could no longer hold on to it, and all around her, the turbulence of waves, the sound of crashing surf, of thunder.

"I was very surprised to find out later that I was alive," she said. The man who rescued her had seen her from the shore clinging to the banana trunk. There were no houses in this part of the coast—surely she was not out there for a swim. He was not a good swimmer but he had four large coconuts whose husks were ripped partially then tied together. He used them as floats when he swam out to her. She was hardly conscious when he reached her, her arms like a vise on the trunk; he towed her to the shore and carried her to his cart, watched her sleep till early evening, when she finally woke up.

"It was dark," Dalin said, "but there was this cooking fire at my feet, and this man with one hand tending the pot. I cried again and again with happiness. My body ached all over—the blisters on my skin—and I realized that I was naked, that he had removed my wet clothes and covered me with a blanket. More than that, I realized, too, that he had bathed me with fresh water—there was no salt water on me. Even my hair had been combed. I remembered my vow."

He was more than twice her age. He had taken the seaside

route and was carrying back to the Ilokos three sacks of grain and a jar of salted fish. He had gone to eastern Pangasinan and had gleaned the newly harvested fields there. He would tell his people of the virgin lands where they could still settle, the mountains they had to cross.

That night she ate for the first time and never before had rice and green tomatoes dipped in salted fish tasted so good. But he forbade her to eat or drink too much. He made soup with marunggay leaves which scalded her insides and warmed her all over. He was right in warning her, for hardly had the food settled in her belly than she started to vomit.

She could not make out his face too well in the light of the cooking fire, but she could see the ridges on his forehead and his only hand. Before she went to sleep naked under the coarse Iloko blanket, the uneven earth covered with grass mat, she wondered what his thoughts had been when he undressed her.

She woke up very late, the sun a glaze upon the land and sparkling on the sea to her right. The blanket had slipped and her breasts and her belly were exposed. Nearby on the grass, her skirt and blouse were already dry and she stood up weakly and put them on. Her benefactor was nowhere in sight, the cart still unhitched beside her. He was not inside. Down to the left, his white bull was tethered to an ipil sapling and was grazing on the stubbly grass. Beyond the growth of ipil trees and scrub was a wooded hill; on the trail farther on, two carts were straining up the incline. He emerged from the screen of trees slumbering in the heat, on his shoulder a bundle of dry twigs for firewood.

He had a dark kindly face, a small nub of a nose. "There is food in the pot," he said with a faded smile. "You vomited everything you ate last night . . ."

She wanted to rush to him, to kiss his hand, but she could only stumble forward. He helped her to climb up on the cart, which was loaded with grain, coconuts, and the jar of salted fish, then he hitched it. He wanted to take her back to Lingayen, but there was no one there to whom she could return; besides (she did not tell him) there was this vow she had made. If she was going back at all, it would be on a pilgrimage of gratitude to the Virgin in Manaoag. Would he take her there? Yes, but first he must go back to his people in the north—they needed the grain he was bringing back.

That day, her dead skin started to peel and in time the blemishes disappeared. She gathered catuday flowers and marunggay leaves along the way, and cooked them flavored with young tamarind leaves.

He told her she could leave him anytime, particularly after she had regained her strength. After all, she was no stranger to this route but she said she would go wherever he would go. She was his servant and would ask for no money, just the food she ate. She drove the cart at night, and while they rested in the daytime, she gathered grass for the bull. It was a big beautiful animal—and patient.

On the seventh night on the seaside road they stopped by a river which they would cross in the morning. It was dry along the bank and on the opposite side other travelers had also stopped for the night. Her strength was fully restored, but sleep was often fitful and, as he told her, she often screamed in the night. She always slept in the cart, atop the sacks of grain, while he slept on the ground, sometimes beside the cart, but always close to the bull. They had eaten and she had washed the pots. Cicadas were lost in the grass as the darkness came quickly. Somewhere in the distance, a dog howled. All the cooking fires of the other travelers arrayed farther up the bank had long been extinguished. Below them, the river had become but a thin and shallow stream, gurgling now as it coursed through boulders and their catch of weeds. As the night deepened, she went down from the cart and lay beside him. He told her she was like a daughter to him. He was a widower; there was no reason for him to refuse other than his feelings of shame, if not of inadequacy. He had grown-up children and the grain he was bringing home was for them. I have not had a woman for many years, he told her, but in a while, he responded and quietly she accepted him. Gratefully she kept her pledge.

Years afterward, Istak would always remember not just this story but how he, too, had made his vow. That night she unfolded her past to him, he told her, "I will also do whatever you bid me."

Her touch upon his chest was soft and warm. "You are not well yet," she said.

CHAPTER

5

I T SEEMED as if an eternity passed before the second day
came. The pain—continuous and dull—the loss of blood, the
anxiety, all these had weakened him. His mind remained clear
and he could hear the quiet talk of his kin, the things they forgot to bring in their hurry, the scouting for the direction they
must take. He had not eaten anything except several spoonfuls
of broth his mother had prepared from marunggay leaves. They
stopped and when Mayang bent over to give him another spoonful, he asked in a whisper: "Where are we now?"

"You know how Bit-tik likes to wander. He says we are close
to Vigan. From here, we can see the bell tower of Bantay . . ."

Through mists and the throbbing pain, he could imagine
Vigan again, Ciudad Fernandina—regal city of the north, the
repository of wealth as only Ilokano industry and commerce

could amass it; Vigan, anointed domain of power and learning, of grace and beauty and all the plenitude of blessings that are bestowed on those who commanded in the name of God and of the Spanish realm. He first saw it as a boy of fifteen when Padre Jose took him to the seminary there. He had followed the old priest silently and in awe of the resplendent appointments, the convent with its huge oil portraits of beatified priests, and within the vast masonry, the august halls glowing with the luster of piety and age, as if wisdom were impregnated in the gray walls forever.

Then to dinner in one of the pretentious houses nearby, and from the kitchen where he was sent to eat with the other servants, he had glimpsed the wide living room ablaze with crystal chandeliers, the finely crafted furniture, the porcelain vases that stood serene in solemn corners. The kitchen itself was floored with tile. And beyond it, the dining room with its giant fan overhead, a table laden with sweet ham and other exotic meats, and under the table, two young girls with fans stirred a breeze and drove away the mosquitoes from those legs encased in black woolen trousers or billowy satin skirts and pointed shoes. Here they were, the men and women of noble bearing, educated in Manila and well traveled in Europe, the wealthy mestizos, Europeans, and, of course, the Spanish prelates who ruled. And after the dinner, Spanish brandy, preserved sweets, and the elegant music of a string quartet. They glided with ease, these elegant women in embroidered blouses, their fingers sheathed in diamonds, complaining of their peasant servants and how far they were from Manila, where they could be pampered with the latest gossip, fashions, and imports from the continent; the men in tight suits rambling on about the sinking price of indigo, the new profits to be made in ranching, and yes, their uneasiness and disdain for the heathen English

scourge of Freemasonry, which seemed to reach out to Ciudad
Fernandina.

ON THE THIRD DAY, the fever finally came. Slowly, almost imperceptibly, it spread all over him like a flood of hot mud flowing from the wound in his breast. His head seemed wedged
between two tree trunks and now the trunks began to press and
grind against each other. He shook with chills no matter how
many layers of blanket Mayang and Dalin covered him with. His
mind was fogged and in those few moments of lucidity and
wakefulness, he could see inchoate shapes of people, of children,
peering at him through the open archway of the cart, overhear
their conversations—the coffin which should be readied, but
there was none, how they would have to bury him not in a cemetery but on some desolate mountainside, in the shade of a great
tree so they could at least place a marker where he lay. Images
formed, the faces blurred and soon flitted away, and then from
the smoky chaos Padre Jose emerged, wraithlike, his eyes pierc-
ing, his mouth moving, though no words came forth. After some
anxious waiting, the words, though almost in a whisper, took
shape. The priest was speaking in Latin: "The ways of the world
are devious and the trials through which we must go to earn
God's grace come in many forms. Do not despair, do not
despair—we are men of peace, and we are destined to bring life
to the sick, happiness to those who grieve—this is our burden."

They were not in the sacristy or in the convent in Cabugaw but
on a mountainside, surrounded by Igorots whose arms and
breasts were tattooed. Again, Padre Jose spoke to him: "My God is
the God of all men, and it was He who gave this land to all of you."

"Look at yourself," the old priest commanded, and Istak
looked down at his belly, at his chest and arms. They were tat-

tooed. In his hand a spear—and his hair was long. He was an Igorot, too, and he was telling Padre Jose harshly: "Your God is not mine. He is not in the seminary in Vigan, he is not in you, and if he is in all men, then he wears the uniform of the Guardia, he has a gun pointed at us. I was baptized in the river and the river is cold and it is my brother An-no who carried me there, and it is Dalin and my mother who cared for me. It is they and my people whom I will serve, not you and your god. And as for you—and the likes of you—I will kill you! Death to all Kastilas!"

And with one mighty heave, he flung his spear at the old priest. But the spear bounced off the old man's chest and fell broken to the ground. Padre Jose was no longer flesh—he was stone!

The old priest smiled. "You are mistaken, Eustaquio. And I forgive you as I always have because deep in your heart, you are an honorable man, a man of peace . . ."

Istak picked up the broken spear, detached the blunted spearhead, and rushed at the old priest. He struck him in the chest again and again, but stone was harder than metal and with every blow, the ache in his arm increased until, exhausted, he cast the useless spearhead away.

Padre Jose spoke calmly: "My child, I am beyond touching or hurting. Still I would like you to know that like me, you have a mission. You will lead your people to the new land. You will undergo great suffering as you do now. You will cross many rivers and you will be filled with sorrow. But you will reach your destiny. Though you are not a priest, you will serve your people and your God as well, and you will do this because you have faith. You will do what I have never done, because you are from this land, because God has chosen you . . ."

ON THE SEVENTH DAY, the fever left him and he slept well and without screaming. Sometime in the night, he woke briefly to find Dalin by his side, wiping his brow. The solid wheels of the cart were creaking—they were relentlessly moving, moving. He slept on through the yaw and jerk of the cart. When he woke up, the cart no longer jerked; they were now on the plain, on a trail, or on the beach.

Soon it was daylight and they stopped traveling. No one was in the cart—they were all outside. Mayang was saying there should not be too much salt in the chicken broth. How sweet her voice sounded! Then she was saying how sad it was that she was not able to bring all the yarn she needed so that once they had arrived in the new land she could start weaving.

Beyond the door spread an obscure forest. Birds twittered outside, and the delicious scent of meat roasting over an open fire drifted to his nostrils, lifting him, and for the first time, he craved food. It came to him then, the dream about Padre Jose and for an instant, a chill coursed through him.

Inang! Inang!—he called but only a gurgling sound escaped his lips as if pebbles filled his throat. He coughed then repeated, "Inang! Inang!" and now the words took shape but were a mere whisper.

"My God, thank you," his mother said at the door. "He is alive."

In a moment, Dalin was in the cart, too.

They brought him newly cooked rice and roasted pork and sliced tomatoes; aroma flooding his senses. He had not eaten for days except broth; now was the time to practice self-restraint. Padre Jose had always dinned it into him, to restrain himself, to avoid temptation, for to surrender to it was to invite perdition.

He took just a mouthful of rice, a tiny piece of pork, savoring the meat fully, letting it linger in his mouth, and a cup of the chicken broth. He was weak; he could not even raise his head from the coverless pillow without Dalin holding him up. Then he realized that he could feel with his right arm the ridges in the split bamboo mat which walled the cart; the arm was no longer numb. Slowly he raised it, moved the thumb first, then all the fingers. They were all responding. He tried to raise the entire arm, flex it, and it was then that this lacerating pain lashed at him and he screamed.

They crowded around the cart. His brow was damp and cold. He asked Dalin to examine the wound to see if there was pus. She lifted the bandage carefully and smiled. "It is beginning to heal. The wound is closed and there is no swelling," she said happily.

The worst was over.

"You did not know what was happening," Dalin told him afterward. "We all thought you would die."

He smiled, remembering quickly the bits of conversation he had overheard, the dream.

Dalin said, "We were frightened. And when you became very hot, thank God, you told us what we should do."

"And what was that?"

"We took you to a stream and your father and An-no, they soaked you in the water, up to your neck, till your body cooled. On the fourth day, when your fever became worse and there was no stream, you told them again what to do. They cut a wild banana stalk, took off the skins, wrapped you in them, till the fever subsided again . . ."

He had not forgotten his lessons, not from the books that he had read, but what Padre Jose had told him.

"You know so many things," Dalin said, wonder in her eyes.

"I had a very good teacher," he said. "An old, kindly priest."

"A priest?" Dalin asked. Istak nodded.

After a while: "You were talking in your sleep," Dalin said, "Now I find it difficult to understand why you said those things."

"What did I say?"

"You were shouting, 'Kill the priest! Kill all Kastilas!' "

Istak became silent. It was An-no who took him to the creek, the brother who loathed him, who coveted Dalin for himself. It was Padre Jose whom he had always respected and loved—yes, he had really loved the old priest not so much in return for the many kindnesses that had been shown him, but for the light that Padre Jose had cast upon the path Istak had taken. And yet, in the deeper wilderness of his mind, in this dream, he had wished his benefactor harm. In wine, truth; in dreams, the soul?

If these thoughts were hidden in the fastness of his mind, if he did not recognize them, would they surface someday as evil deeds?

It was true then what Padre Jose had said, that there is evil in all of us, that only with faith and its capacity for exorcism can we master this evil.

"Where are we now? And how long have we been traveling?" he asked.

"A week," she said. "We are still close to the mountains, but in a day we will be down by the shore. We have been harvesting wild bananas and green papayas."

"How long before we get to the sea?"

"Tomorrow," she said.

He went back to sleep and dreamed that he was flying, floating over the caravan, scouting far ahead of it the plain beyond the hills. He floated above the treetops and waved at those below; he soared with ease in any direction he wished; it was such a natural thing for him to fly. Then he saw the narrow road which cut the mountainside and skirted the coast, and ahead were hundreds of Guardia waiting. They would all pass through this dreaded funnel, they could not hurdle the mountain.

He woke up at noon and remembered the dream. He called

for Ba-ac, who came to the cart immediately. They propped him up on a sack of grain. Beyond the line of carts, a dense growth of scrub, butterfly trees browned by the dry season.

"Father, we will soon reach the Spanish road and we will all be searched there."

"I know," Ba-ac said sadly. In the light, his father seemed much older. "But there is no other way."

"We must cross singly," Istak said. "They will not think of stopping or searching just one cart. One at night, one in the daytime. And we should all then meet . . . but where?"

Dalin, who knew the road, was ready with a suggestion. "Before we reach the Abra River," she said, "we cannot miss that, we will wait till everyone is there."

Istak had passed the road many times when he and Padre Jose traveled to Abra. The people were forced into building it, just as, even now, the *ilustrados* were forcing the people to work for nothing, exacting punishment if they refused. It was a narrow dirt road flanked by brick embankments, gently sloping with the descent of the hills, clinging to the strip of land before it plunged into a rocky coast. There were battering waves during the typhoon season, but the sea this time of the year should be blue and calm.

"If you look long enough," Dalin said, "you can see the bottom."

That night, Istak could not sleep. He lay, waiting for each lurch as the cart dipped into ruts or went over stones, the swish of tall grass as they cut through outgrowths.

"Where are we?" he asked. Dalin was in front, holding on to the reins of the bull. She turned briefly and shushed him. They must be passing again through dreaded territory and the wheels had been greased anew with coconut oil so they would not creak.

Istak closed his eyes but could not sleep. The pit in his stomach deepened. He would endure the hunger till morning. What was it compared to what awaited them in this dark maw of night? Even the Guardia were not safe here. But the cocks—they would give them away by their crowing. He was alarmed.

"They have all been killed," Dalin assured him.

MORNING again; the sky lightened slowly and the stars winked out. Istak could raise half his body now. They were on a rise of ground and close by the forest, with the mountain rising behind the tall trees. On one side, through the curtain of tall grass, the land plummeted to the sea, and there, like a brown line on the coast, was the Spanish road.

Even at this time of the year, when the land was scorched, the forest was a deep green, throbbing with secret life. Farther up the mountain, the green turned into a purplish black that cloaked the foothills all the way up to the peaks.

The forest was hostile, with unseen threats, but every year before the rains started he and the old priest had ventured without fear into it and beyond to the land of the Bagos—the Igorots, the ancient enemies of his people. He had listened, entranced, to the *dal-lot* and the life of Lam-ang, the epic hero whose courage and strength were tested in battles with them.

In times of peace, the Bagos came down, half-naked, their torsos caked with dirt, their spears glinting and awe-inspiring. But they did not come to fight, merely to trade their baskets, their dried deer meat for dogs, tobacco, and fibers for their looms. He could recognize them even if they dressed like Christians because they were short and squat, their backs broad, their legs muscular. They chewed betel nut continuously and their teeth were blacker than those of his own people. As a boy in

Po-on he did not fear them; it was the *Komaw* that frightened him, that huge and ugly kidnapper of children who would take him away if he did not behave as his mother instructed him.

Only the Bagos lived in these mountains, kindred to the wild boar and the python. They were hunters who could merge with the foliage, become one with the bush until they assumed the mystery of the forest as well, sharing its darkness and its sensuous promise. But there was no promise in the forest now. It was a black redoubt to be sundered so that its soil would bear the seed. It cannot be, it must not be the haven of those who fear the light—and Istak recalled again the dim sacristy of the church in Cabugaw and how secure he felt there with the ghosts of the past, of the nameless and innumerable dead in all those records that he had kept, his fear melting in the air he breathed. It was a far more mysterious forest which they would now face, and perhaps—he shuddered at the thought—they would not be able to go beyond it.

IT WAS the fourth day since the first two carts had left carrying Bit-tik and his aunt Simang. All the departures from the hollow of the hill were timed so that the carts would be on the coastal road late in the night or in the deep, deep dawn. It was Ba-ac who went first on foot and alone, balancing on his shoulder a small sack of rice, his stub of an arm on a sling of coarse Ilokano cloth. He was carrying this sack of rice as a wedding present to a niece in Candon; he was walking all the way even at night, hoping he would not miss the wedding. Istak had been to Candon, of course—it was a very prosperous town, one of the stations where Padre Jose used to stop for additional provisions before they turned left toward Tirad and the perpetual challenge of the Cordilleras.

Four days, and Istak wondered if all that he had taught them would be remembered, if they would be able to pretend that their destinations were not the same.

Now it was his turn and Dalin's. They had spent the last three days waiting. Dalin was never idle; she had tended the bull, done some sewing and cooking. There was always something a woman could do while a man mused and pondered his fate. The day comes different from all others, night quickly falls, and sometimes it is best to be silent, to be alone with one's thoughts. But for her I would be dead—but for her—there must be some purpose for this long journey other than shredding the soles, just as life is one journey from one night to another. So it must be, *exitus* and *reditus*, leaving and coming, and in between, the uncertainty which numbs the heart and lacerates the soul. But perhaps, though it is broken now, the body will be reborn— just as a tree might be ravaged by all forms of blight, yet in spite of its frailty, its fruit can be sweet because the tree itself comes from a good seed.

Dalin had calculated the distance very well; they left the hollow after they had supped on green papayas with pieces of chicken. She had cooked the food before sundown when the cooking fire would not reveal their presence. For a while, Dalin walked the bull through thickets of bamboo and shallow gullies; inside the cart, Istak remained still, braced as he was between two sacks so that the wound would not reopen.

Then, after a while, the cart stopped. From the rear of the cart, Dalin took the oil lamp out. It had not been used for a long time and the wick was dry, but soon it sputtered into a flame. She brought the lamp to the front.

Istak lay down. The light cast patterns on the canopy. The ride was smooth; they were no longer on rough ground or fallow fields but on the cobbled Spanish road, a light proclaiming their presence—persons of peace on a long journey. They were moving slowly, steadily, the wheels creaking, Dalin before him framed by the doorway of the cart, and beyond, the night dangerous and vast; Dalin near him, comforting him with her presence, easing the knot in his heart.

They had rehearsed what they would say—they were newlyweds going to settle with relatives in Pangasinan. As for their being married, "I hope it will be true someday," Istak told her.

He slept fitfully and though he often asked Dalin to lie down while he kept watch, she had refused. Once, he woke up to find that the cart was not moving, that the shadows the lamp cast were still. The bull was chewing its cud but Dalin was nowhere. He half rose in fright and saw that they were by the roadside, and Dalin was seated on a rock, resting the bull, while below them, the waves murmured on the rocks and the air was salty and clean.

"Please come and sleep now, and I will watch," he said. Dalin mounted the cart again.

"We have passed the two posts where we should have been checked," she said softly. "There"— she pointed to the distance where a lighthouse beam shone—"that was the last one."

"And they did not stop you?"

"Who would bother with a cart at this time of night? The sentries were probably all asleep."

He was right, then. The other carts must have passed the sieve.

MORNING comes to the Ilokos quickly, the sun rising from beyond the mountains and flooding the land with amber light. They were still on the Spanish road, for in this part of the country the mountains and the sea often meet, and the narrow road followed the coastline through narrow plains and villages that had begun to stir.

To their right, a few fishing boats sat motionless in the water, while beyond, a ship with smoke trailing long and black from its funnel headed toward the north. Perhaps it was one of the Spanish boats headed for Aparri, or even to Hong Kong. Toward midmorning, six horsemen followed by four carriages came thundering down the highway. One of the horsemen roared at them to get off the road and, for an instant, fear gripped Istak. But the man merely wanted the road to be cleared, for soon after Dalin had dismounted and led the bull aside, the four carriages rolled on, their well-dressed passengers chatting, among them a priest—perhaps a bishop, in his resplendent finery, on his way to officiate at some festivity.

Where possible, Dalin took the cart away from the main road and then ventured through seaside hamlets. This was what traders often did and in each she asked if there was any dried fish she could buy. For traveling, it was much better than dried meat, as it was not likely to spoil quickly.

By nightfall, they had to be on the road again. They were near the Abra River now. Istak knew this almost by instinct, and if it had been the rainy season, they would have had to cross the river by ferry. The river would be dry in parts and where the water was still running it would be shallow. There would be many travelers along the stretch of riverbed, for there they paused to cook their meals and do their washing before journeying onward to La Union and Pangasinan.

They stopped for the night in a village far from the road, their presence known to the villagers who on occasion would receive travelers seeking company and perhaps protection from the highwaymen who roamed these parts. And in the early dawn, long before daybreak, Dalin hitched the cart again.

They reached the river before noon. Bit-tik, who had waited along the road, rushed to them breathless with the good news: they had all managed to get through the eye of the needle—they were together again, farther along, down the wide arc of the riverbed, hidden by tall grass.

Dalin took the cart down a well-traveled gully. Along the way, close to the narrow stream of water, were the ashes of cooking fires, traces of a night's habitation, laundry spread out in the sun to bleach on the stones, women washing their hair, and children splashing about.

There were a few Igorots in loincloths. It would be a long way back across the mountains to their villages and for the moment, they were here in peace, although once in their own domain, they could be the fiercest hunters of heads. They could be Tinguianes, Istak told Dalin, who cringed when one of them approached the cart, baring teeth stained by betel nut, and asked in Ilokano if they had any sugar to sell.

They had none, of course, and after he had left and joined his companion, Istak assured Dalin she was in no danger, not while Bit-tik was with them. "Toward that turn of hill, that is where they are waiting," Bit-tik told them, pointing. They would get there by noon.

ALL OF THEM had bathed and their faces shone. But no one lived here, they said; who would be able to grow anything on this desert of pebble and sand? Even the camachile trees remained stunted.

Ba-ac would tell them again and again afterward how he had fooled the Guardia, how everyone was asleep at the first station except for one sentry. He had approached the sentry and asked first if he could have a drink, and after that, if he could just rest his tired legs and, perhaps, go to sleep nearby till daybreak, for here he felt completely safe—what with the rice and, perhaps, his only good shirt in the sack—he, a defenseless old man. He would relate many times till everyone knew it by heart, how the sentry did not even bother asking him where he came from, but had, instead, complained about the mosquitoes that infested the air, while below, the waves slapped sonorously and soon lulled him to sleep. In the early dawn, Ba-ac had asked if there were more sentries down the road where he could possibly rest again, and he was told there were a couple more, but who would travel on foot at this time except a crazy old man worrying about something as trifling as a few *gantas* of rice?

In the evening when they made ready to leave the riverbed, Ba-ac came to see him again. "You are much better, son," he said. "You are no longer as pale as a banana stalk. It is good that you have Dalin to take care of you. Now, at least, you can sit up and show us the way. You know it better than any of us, at least all the way to Candon. And from there, Dalin will be our guide." Ba-ac turned to the woman who was leading the bull to the yoke. "You are one of us now, young woman," Ba-ac told her warmly.

"Thank you, Apo," she said.

"Where is An-no, Father?" Istak asked. He could not forget how his younger brother had railed against him, how he wanted Dalin for himself.

"You are brothers," Ba-ac said. "There is no distance between you that cannot be bridged."

It was a cryptic reply. Did the old man know of the rift between the brothers that Dalin was the center of? Did he know how Mayang had looked at his relationship with Dalin to be as ominous as sin?

They would no longer use the Spanish road; again, they would take the circuitous route close to the foothills, away from the towns. They still had a long way to go before they reached Candon, where Ba-ac had second cousins who would probably give them shelter for a day. A long journey ahead still, and no peace with An-no in sight, only this silence and this distance that could widen if he did not move wisely.

It was all routine now, the women cooking the meals, the men walking ahead and behind the carts, particularly where the grass was dense and the farms far between, places where brigands could lie in wait.

Then, the plain narrowed again as the mountain dropped to the sea. An-no had gone miles out in front to check if there was any outpost where they could be challenged. He had returned with the glad news that the road was free. They waited till dark and only then did they come down from a fold in the hill.

The mountains gave way to fields, the plain unfurled. Beyond the bamboo brakes, Istak recognized it at once—Mount Tirad, stabbing the sky like a spearhead. He knew the way not just to Tirad but beyond, and if it had just been the menfolk with him, he would have suggested that they cross over to the valley through the pass. But there were women and children, and a venture into the land of the Igorots without Padre Jose was always dangerous.

Before the day would be over, they would reach Candon.

IT WAS ONE of the richest towns in the southern portion of the Ilokos. Even from a distance the spires of its magnificent church could be seen in the sunlight. The plains around it swelled with green, and to the left, up the foothills of the Cordilleras, were the ranches. From here, some of the best cattle and horses from the Ilokos were raised. Market days, as in most Ilokano towns, were festive as well. From the villages, the people came to buy their weekly ration of salt, oil, thread, matches, even books—cheap novels in Iloko. Istak loved the days when they sojourned in Candon, particularly the marketplace, where he saw so many goods on display, sometimes even better than those in the market in Vigan.

But the people they were going to see were not in town; they lived close to the foothills. Like Ba-ac, they did not know how to read and write, and they worked the land with diligence, for that was the only thing they knew.

They had been traveling slowly, determinedly, for ten days. The wound in Istak's chest had completely closed, but it was still painfully sensitive, its edges now hardened with pus which had turned to a scab that would soon fall off.

Every day, at his instruction, Dalin washed the wound with warm water that had been boiled with guava leaves, and her hands were ever gentle. He was still weak. Though he could sit with her in the front of the cart, he could not walk around as much as he wanted to.

They had paused in the shade of a lomboy tree and across the expanse of fallow land were the houses of a *sitio* where, Ba-ac said, his cousins lived. They had settled in this part of Sur some twenty years ago after one of them married a local girl.

"Do we have to see them, Father?" Istak asked. "And what will we tell them? And how do we explain to them why we do not have with us our house posts?"

"They are relatives, son," Ba-ac said. "They will understand our silence. They may even help us with provisions that we do not have."

"Why don't you go first by yourself, Father?" Istak suggested. "They know you—and then, when everything is clear, we can follow . . ."

Bit-tik went with his father to the *sitio* while the men unhitched the bull carts and the women started to prepare the noonday meal.

They would not venture into town, they would never go to places where there were people and, therefore, the Guardia and the priests. Not till they were far, far away from the Ilokos and all its encumbrances.

Ba-ac and Bit-tik returned while they were about to eat a meal of catuday flowers, eggplants, and tomatoes scrounged from the marginal farms they had passed.

"Blas and the others—they are all gone," Ba-ac said softly. "The houses are there, but they are empty—all three of them. Not one chick, not one piglet left—they must have left within the last two days—there were still fresh ashes in the stoves, and there is no dust on the floors . . ."

Could they have been ordered away, too? The thought hovered in Istak's mind. Could they have left because they could no longer endure the harshness of living in the Ilokos?

An-no, who had scouted the way farther ahead, returned in time for lunch. The way was clear and good, and there were no houses close by. Now it was Dalin's turn to be the guide, to stay in the lead cart—it was she who knew the way, for Candon was the southernmost point that Istak had ever reached.

By nightfall, they were crossing the Tagudin River, and though it was wide, a child could wade through the deepest part. The bull strained over stones. Across the bank, behind a screen of camachile trees, they stopped for the night. They would bathe again, do their washing, and in the morning they would be on their way. They slept well, except for the two men who stood guard quietly, ears alert to every sound; but there were none which presaged danger—just the wind soughing in the grass, the grunt of animals, the stirring of dogs, the murmur of the river as it coursed through, and the distant crowing of cocks.

In the morning, they were surprised to find that three carts had stopped nearby. Istak woke up to Ba-ac's happy shouts: his cousins were in the carts, and to them he ran, waving his one good hand. It was years since he had seen them last, but memory holds on to images, to joys that were shared.

Ba-ac's cousins and their wives came to them soon after with their daughters and sons. They were going to the valley, they had left Candon forever, and like those who came from Po-on, they, too, had been ordered to leave their farms.

Now there were ten carts. Istak had his doubts but he kept them to himself; he did not want to hurt his father, to suspect their distant relatives of some future perfidy. Did Ba-ac tell them everything? The reason why they were taking such a tortuous way to the new land? They would soon know, and they would then be afraid. If threatened by the Guardia, they would probably betray Ba-ac.

In afterthought, he need not have worried. He should have simply relied on the Ilokano iron sense of loyalty to friend and family. Istak was particularly happy with his new uncle, Blas, who was a man of words. A big, bluff man, he had been and still was the poet capable of stringing the honeyed phrases that could waylay the most aloof of women. But he was unable to bend to his will a girl from Candon who had come to Po-on to visit. He had followed her to Candon some twenty years or so earlier and in the custom of those who were not favored by either the parents or the object of desire herself, he had served in her household, working the land as a farmhand with no pay at all, except for his meals. He slept below the granary, apart from the house and close to the work animals—for he was almost treated as one—and for a year ingratiated himself with the girl's family, returning on occasion to Po-on to be the object of jokes from Ba-ac and all his relatives, why with his silver tongue he was not able to convince a simple girl to accept him after a few days.

His uncle's tenacity surprised Istak no end, but he knew also that he would have done this for Dalin if she were still the same unfeeling creature she had been in the beginning.

Just the two of them, Blas with big, handsome words rolling out of his mouth without effort, and Istak full of questions. It was one of those early evenings when the meal was done, the animals fed and safely herded, and the women had long since extinguished the cooking fires.

"I have known how it is to snatch a field from the forest," Blas said quietly. They had left the riverbed and were up the brow of a hill beyond which the narrow plain would unroll again. "That was what surrounded Candon when I first went there. It was hard work which drained the body of its juices and numbed the mind to dreams. Dreams that what we had carved out of the wilderness would be ours—but it would not be. Always, wherever we, the little people, will go, there will be those with more strength than us who will wrest away what we thought was our own."

"And you are willing to go with us and suffer the same fate?"

"My son," Blas said, spitting out the wad of tobacco he had been chewing, and turning to his nephew with melancholy in his eyes, "this is the relentless destiny of the poor."

"And you will go with us all the way to the valley?"

"We will journey with you to the farthest corner of the earth," Blas said, lifting his eyes to the grandeur of a full moon. "We have relatives now, people we know who will make our suffering endurable."

It did not matter then that they were his father's mere second cousins, *capidua*, as they were called, and perhaps it was just as well. For if they were first cousins, it would not have been possible to even think that in the certitude of the valley, in some future time, Blas's elder daughter, Leonora, also known as Orang, could be the wife of An-no, and that his younger daughter, Sabel, could be Bit-tik's.

CHAPTER

6

B Y THE END of the second week, they were close to the
mountains again, and the forest was now encroaching like a
green flood upon the sliver of plain. Dalin had never traveled
this far from the coastal road and all she knew was that they
were now close to the land of the Bagos.

In a few more days, moving slowly as they did, they would
come to where the divide would widen and become another
plain. In so short a time, the three families who had joined them
were no longer strangers—their faces took on names, particularly Orang and Sabel, who were often with An-no and Bit-tik.
Istak was glad. Perhaps Dalin would now be banished from
An-no's attention.

Istak desired her, as he once had desired Carmencita, although he had tried to subdue that longing, denied it to himself
as something beyond fulfillment. But not with Dalin, who was

with him every day, speaking with him, touching him. The wound was healed now, the pain completely gone, but at times there was some numbness in his arm, which he still could not move freely.

If Dalin had an inkling of how much Istak wanted her, she did not show it. There was the day's work, the gathering of grass for the bull, the preparation of food or the search for it—green papayas, wild bananas, and the edible leaves of trees.

They had stopped for the day, and the men had cleared the crest of a hill on which stood a giant tree. They were at the edge of the forest and to their right the land undulated in a series of low hills into the sea.

The women were cooking within the semicircle of the carts which had been unhitched around the tree and the men had returned from the shallow creek at the bottom of the hill where they had bathed the *carabaos*. The dogs, with their snouts encased in woven rattan so that they would not be able to bark, were leashed to the carts.

Istak had ventured down the hill, the afternoon sun warm on his face, and he had returned, worried. "There is not a single house nearby," he told Dalin quietly, not wanting her to be more apprehensive than she already was.

He wondered how really safe they were, and if the uncles who joined them knew how well the Bagos tracked their prey. The Bagos came to Cabugaw in the dry season with their cargo of baskets and colorfully woven cloth. They exchanged these for rice and a pack of scrawny dogs, which they then tied to a leash, the rope extending to the animal's necks through a small hollow bamboo, so that they would not get entangled. Their approach was always announced by the yammering of the dogs as they marched down the dusty streets.

Padre Jose allowed them to leave their dogs in the churchyard and to sleep under the acacia trees. He even gave them rice for their meals and *galletas* to eat with their coffee. They spoke Ilokano, of course, but Padre Jose chose to speak to them in their own language, which he had learned tediously through the years.

Istak had gone up to their villages for the first time when he was a boy. They had crossed over Mount Tirad, Padre Jose on a horse and he walking behind or leading the two other pack-horses. He had always regarded the Bagos as ferocious savages who chopped off the heads of their enemies and stuck them on the eaves of their houses. This was true, Padre Jose had said, but we are not their enemies—we are their friends, and we are bringing God to them.

Istak now wondered how they could defend themselves should the Bagos decide to attack.

"While you were ill, that is what they made," Dalin said. On the cart beside her lay two coconut bowls filled with very fine sand and salt. Thrown at the eyes of an intruder, the mixture could blind him for a while. From the side of the cart she picked up a bamboo pole which he had not noticed—there were four of them there. It was sharp, the point tempered and hardened in the fire. One had a spearhead—a knife that his mother used in the kitchen, thrust into the hollow of the bamboo, then woven neatly into place with rattan as only his brothers could do so that it was secure and would not be dislodged if it was thrown.

"They have made bows and arrows, too," Dalin said.

These were not allowed by the Guardia Civil—such weapons were confiscated, and depending on the mood of the Guardia at the time, the offenders were taken to prison or simply lashed.

Istak was still weak; so this is how one returns from the river from which usually there is no return. He could move his hand and he prayed that soon he would be able to move his arm at will. Would he end up like his father, who sat in a corner silently cursing the powerful men who had condemned him to a life that was maimed? More than ever he understood now how it was to have but one arm, not just the physical loss, but something deeper and more disturbing.

The shade of the great narra tree was cool. The white plumes of grass around the carts waved in the breeze. It was he who first saw beyond the curtain of grass that the caravan had been surrounded. The young boys who were their lookouts did not have his eyes. He saw them moving quietly beyond the grass, the brief glint of a battle-ax in the morning sun alerting him. He shouted the warning: "Bagos—we are surrounded!"

The men stood transfixed for a moment, then rushed to their carts. The children clung to the skirts of their mothers. The men crouched behind the carts holding on to their bolos and the stakes they had shaped from bamboo.

The lookouts had seen the Bagos and they rushed to the dubious protection of the carts huddled together, their faces pale with fear.

A voice from beyond the grass boomed. Although it was in Ilokano, from the intonation Istak was now sure that the warriors waiting there were Bagos.

"O countrymen, why did you trespass into our land? Did you not see the signs? Can you not read them? We do not enter your towns without asking your honorable permission. Why do you not respect us the way we respect you?"

Ba-ac shouted back. "Brothers—we did not see your signs. Forgive us. We did not use the road below and you have been here for a long time so you know the reason why. Permit us, brothers, to stay here till dark because we travel at night. We fear not just the Guardia who still steal our rice, but also the bandits who trouble defenseless farmers like us. We left the farms we were born on, brothers, because we were driven away. No one pities the poor. We beg your pity, your forgiveness . . ."

Silence descended upon everything, marred only by the rustle of the wind in the grass and birdcalls from the mountain.

"Brothers—will you forgive us? We will give you tobacco, rice, for having trespassed into your honorable country . . ." Baac shouted again. Still no reply.

Then Istak saw from beyond the tall grass a wisp of gray rising. Smoke! The Bagos were burning the dry grass. They would roast alive on the crest of this hill even if they had made a clearing around them.

"Fire, Father! They are burning the grass!" he shouted. His voice could carry only so far but Ba-ac and the others had already seen the smoke. The fire leaped now in crackling flames, kindling the dry grass as if it were paper. They hurriedly hitched the carts, the children screaming, the women rushing them into the carts even before they were hitched, scooping up their pots, everything, urging, shouting.

"To the sea," Ba-ac shouted, "Keep inside. Do not show yourselves. Lie down on the floor," he kept screaming at everyone, then they rushed down the hill through a chasm in the wall of fire, and when they passed through, it seemed the fire was eating into their lungs and they could not breathe, but the animals surged on blindly. They had just cleared the swath of fire when spears rained on them, some striking the hapless animals, some thudding on the woodwork and going through the roof. There were screams in the other carts. "God—they will kill all of us," Istak said, as a spear dug into the side where Dalin was crouched. It quivered, then was still. A little lower and Dalin would have been hit. The carts raced onward through a narrow valley.

"Do not stop!" Ba-ac shouted. The spears no longer fell but

still the carts raced, the *carabaos* straining. Panting, angry, and afraid, Ba-ac, who was in the lead, finally stopped. They were at the end of the narrow valley which formed a gully to the plain. The hills had dropped behind them.

They gathered the carts again. They were all there—ten of them. The men poured out with spears and their bolos. They would fight here, on level ground, where they could see the Bagos from where they might emerge. The tufts of grass were sparse and not as tall as the grass on the hill.

From one of the carts a wailing erupted. Dalin went to it. When she returned, she told Istak simply. "It is the boy—the youngest—of your aunt Simang. He is dead, a spear through his neck. She told him to lie down but he stuck his head out because he wanted to see."

They dug a hole in the center of the circle of carts and buried the boy there. Istak led the prayers and though not empowered to bless, he recited the prayer for the dead: *Tibi Domine commendamus animam famuli tui . . .*

But the Bagos did not pursue them. The family plucked a dozen spears from the sides of the carts, and from a *carabao* hit in the rump and bleeding.

"Now we have more weapons," Ba-ac said.

They did not tarry. For as long as they were on the fringes of the land of the Bagos, they would have to travel in the daytime and risk whatever attack might come rather than be ambushed at night or lulled into the kind of trap they had just escaped.

Dalin pointed to the mountain ahead that dropped into the sea. "Beyond that," she said, "is Pangasinan. And a week beyond that mountain, we will cross another range. Then it will be the valley."

Destiny was near, to be reached in one leap or by stretching out a hand. Dalin tried to ease Istak's mind. There were still

forests to pierce and rivers to cross, and death could still lurk behind each shrub, each tree.

AN-NO'S aloofness and silence bothered Istak. Dalin made it all
too clear, like daylight upon the plain, that she preferred Istak.
How could he tell his brother that he did not plan this, that it
had happened as so many inexplicable things do, because he
had stayed behind in Po-on to bear whatever punishment the
Spaniards would mete out? Perhaps, since Istak had climbed
out of the grave, An-no had controlled his passion and given up
his claim as well. Blood, after all, should be thicker than water.

There were times when he envied his younger brother, taller
and stronger of build. He wanted An-no to be happy. He could
give up Dalin; she was not his property, he had no claim on her.
In fact, it was he who must now serve her the rest of his life; he
owed her a debt which could never be repaid.

When the caravan had paused for the night and the dogs
had quieted down and the children had been put to bed, he
would lie awake, listening to her breathing. The silence was always thick—a steady ringing silence as if his ears were hollow
and he could clearly hear the whirr of insects, the distant sounds
of night. He would turn onto his side and touch her breast, worrying lest he disturb her, for she needed sleep. Sometimes she
turned to him, her breath smelling of life and sun warm upon
his face. She did not smoke or chew betel nut like the other
women. Always she was scrubbing her teeth with twigs crushed
into a brush. She was clean and not at all what the men had expected of the girls from Pangasinan. He suspected that she
wanted to be touched, but she always said, "Not yet, not yet. You
are not ready yet."

And once, when he was very insistent, she said, "I don't
want you to strain yourself. If you persist, I will sleep outside."

She was right; there was enough time in the coming days. He could wait. He prayed that the way to the new land would not be difficult. It should not be, not only because Dalin knew the way, but also because she was beside him. In the late afternoon, the clouds boiled in the horizon, then pushed up and hid the sun. The land smelled of heat and dead leaves. April was ending. Soon it would be May, and with it, the rains.

ISTAK was finally almost completely well; he could climb out of the cart and walk about. But his pallor was the continuing object of curiosity and pity. His hair had thinned and it seemed as if he had been ravaged by those dreaded diseases—typhoid and tuberculosis—which had afflicted so many in Cabugaw, their spittle scattered in the churchyard to be avoided and swept over with dirt.

Again, they traveled by night. To use the road, they would have to circle around the towns where the Guardia would be.

"We must change our names now, Father," Istak said. "If they ask where we come from, we must be truthful and say we come from Cabugaw. And our names will begin with *S* just the same. They can't know all the barrios there, so we won't say we came from Po-on . . ."

Ba-ac was seated on the side of the cart, his crumpled face somber in thought. His striped shirt, which Mayang had woven, had not been washed for days and was lined with dirt and sweat. They must stop by a stream soon, to wash and bathe.

"What should we call ourselves now?" Ba-ac asked sadly. "Salvador has always been our name. Yes, the Spaniards gave it to us, but we grew up with it."

"To survive, Father, we have to change," Istak said solemnly. He turned to his brothers, Bit-tik and An-no; they were talking with the daughters of Blas, who had joined them in Tagudin. Like his, their hair was long now and they needed a haircut. He remembered the stories of the Bible. "Samson, Father—it begins with *S*, too, but there is not a single Samson in the registry in Cabugaw—I know, because I wrote in it for the last five years every time there was a birth or a death."

"And how about our *cédulas*?"

"We will throw them away—and we will say that they were burned in our house when we left. We will have new ones when we reach the valley, and we will have our new name on them ..."

NEW LAND, new name. They had always been Ilokano, with all the faults, the vices, that had shaped them, the habits which the narrow and infertile plain had etched in them. This is the way you are, Padre Jose had told him, but you are also a loyal people who know how to return a trust, to stake your life for a friendship that had withstood storm, earthquake, and fire.

He had wanted to ask the old priest what precisely he had meant. Was this the hell he had been talking about? Why was it impossible for the three priests who were executed in Cavite to serve God as they saw fit? Was this the Guardia Civil marauding the countryside and forcing tribute from people who did not even have enough to eat? He was not going to live with the people in their wretched villages—he was going to be a priest, and he would have a new name, just as the high and the mighty had new names, the Don, the *gobernadorcillo*, the Apo. He would not be just Eustaquio Salvador, the peasant from Po-on. He had suffered through Latin, gotten up every morning at five to clean the sacristy, to toll the bells. He was going to be near God, said Padre Jose, and to be so, he must have a good name. It is what one really owns in the end, a name. If it were silver, you would have to polish it every so often with deeds. Even in isolation, silver tarnishes. Look at the candelabra, the crucifix, the chalice—aren't they streaked with tarnish if we don't polish them? But someday an earthquake or some heavenly fire will destroy everything and ashes will be blown in the wind. What then? There are names which will live forever, and he had read them, in Latin, in Spanish. And would Eustaquio Salvador—or Samson—endure? Would he engrave his name on the land that he would clear, in the children he would sire?

As these thoughts came, the image of Dalin—her quiet face, her long tresses—swooped into his mind. He dreamed of that day in another country when he would finally be strong and able to clear and plant, and after the first harvest, he would ask her. His name would then be written down in the registry—*Registro de Casamientos*—as he himself had written so many times in Cabugaw. Now they flitted across his mind, the pages with carefully written names, among them, Salvador. His father knew his grandfather—but that was as far as Ba-ac could go. It was now too late, but he should have looked it up in the ledgers when he was still in Cabugaw—found out who they were, for there had been Salvadors in Po-on before them, and in that dim past, they must have suffered, too, as all Ilokanos had done. Why did they take punishment without question? Did they really believe that man was made to suffer so that he could receive the final reward that only God could bestow? Be patient, his mother had dinned into his ears. And be industrious. Blessed are the meek, for they shall inherit the kingdom of God. And the meek are many and nameless.

TIIEY NOW traveled in the daytime, following the dusty road, just like the other carts leaving the Ilokos, carrying settlers like themselves, looking for land, free land. Land! What a melancholy and elusive word!

Sometimes they would come across a telegraph pole that had leaned and the wires were within reach. If there was no one to witness it, Ba-ac lashed at the wires with his bolo till they were sundered. "Don't tell them about us," he would say hoarsely.

In many places, the road was nothing but a swath of dust which swirled up like a funnel when the day was hot. These funnels sometimes loomed ahead, and once they were caught in one and could see nothing as dust enveloped them, and with it, this hot wind that seemed to suck everything. What a sea of mud the road would be in the rainy season! In some places, however, were cobbles of brick, but these only covered brief stretches of the road. Before the approaches of a town, they would head toward the nearest village instead to spend the night there, using the wells and the stoves of kindly Ilokanos.

It finally rained a week after they had raced down that hilltop. Every afternoon, the clouds had gathered and darkened but no rain fell. Now, gusts of wind tore down upon them and the clouds that had thickened on the rim of the sky loomed—a black and massive wave about to engulf them. Raindrops, big as pebbles, thudded on the dust and shook the grass. Then it came in slanting sheets, covering everything, and they could no longer see what lay ahead, the shapes of trees, the paths that now turned into rivulets of brown.

They had stopped to put up the detached palm frond doors of the carts, but the wind lashed against the doors, against the walls of the carts, and sent the rain through the tiny slits of bamboo siding, through cracks in the disheveled roofs. The children asked if they could go outside and bathe, and were quickly given permission.

It was May at last, and the first rain had a special magic.

They must bathe in it, wash their clothes in it, drink it. Mayang laid her pots outside till they were full, and after the children had bathed, the older folk went out, too. Istak went out without his shirt, his ribs protruding. An-no and Bit-tik were with the girls who had joined them and he could see them through the rain, laughing and joking. Maybe An-no had already forgotten Dalin.

Dalin was close by, bathing the bull, scrubbing its white hide. She was wet and her hair came down behind her in dripping strands. Her wet blouse clung to her body and in the rain he saw her breasts, the nipples dark and distinct. She turned to him briefly and smiled.

He gazed at her, at the skirt that clung to her legs. He admired her, seeing for the first time the fullness of her body. A pleasant sensation coursed through him—desire, just as he had once desired the daughters of Capitán Berong when they would bend before him so that he could see their breasts. Then they would face him while the blood rushed to his face, smile at him, and he would stammer, unable to continue with his teaching.

But the daughters of Capitán Berong were beyond the compass of his imagination. He was from Po-on and they were fair of skin, unreachable; the men who could claim them would not be brown like him.

Dalin was brown.

They stopped that night in a mango grove close to the road and a village where the women went to cook. The firewood that they had strapped behind the carts was drenched and would not kindle. It stopped raining shortly after sunset and the smell of earth blessed with rain, the leaves still dripping, was about them. The whole world was alive and breathing.

They gathered the carts in a semicircle and put the *carabaos* and the bull within the arc, and while the men talked the women prepared their meal or hung their wet clothes on the maguey twine which they strung from cart to cart. They cooked rice and vegetables for the next day's breakfast as well so that all they would have to cook in the morning would be the coffee to warm their stomachs before they started out again. They had one more mountain to cross and the trails through the forest would be tortuous and slippery, but thank God, they were now free from the land of the Bagos.

Earlier in the evening, An-no had found a *kutibeng* in one of the carts and was strumming it. Ever since Dalin had taken Istak into her cart, An-no must have concluded it was no longer possible for him to possess her. It was just as well, for there was this girl Orang. She had a younger sister, but Orang was more mature, although flat-chested, and her eyes were always bright. Now, in the dark, Istak could hear his younger brother singing an old ballad, and the words were meant for Orang.

Since his recovery, Istak no longer slept in the cart but beneath it. Tonight, however, the ground was wet and Dalin told him to come up. He had demurred. "They are already saying many things about us, how I have been taking care of you," she said. "Would it matter if we slept together now?"

He did not go to sleep at once. She sat before the cart looking out into the night, listening to the laughter in some of the carts, the mooing of *carabaos*. Cicadas called from the black shroud of trees around them, and beyond the shroud, in the open field, fireflies winked at them. The cooking fires of the houses beyond the grass kept them company as well.

It was cool, not like in the past when he was forced to take off his shirt, and this he had done with great difficulty because the wound, though healed, did not allow him easy movement. He needed a blanket now. Dalin faced him and their legs touched.

"Soon you will get back all the strength that you lost. I am happy," she said.

"You will really go with us wherever we go?"

She did not speak; he could not see her eyes but knew she was looking at him. Then she turned and lay down beside him. She had turned on her side and so did he.

"I will decide when we get there," she said.

"Suppose I asked you to stay with me . . ."

"You are not a farmer," she said quietly. "I knew that from the very beginning. I do not think you can stay long on a farm. Not that you will not work."

"I cannot be anything now but a farmer."

"You can teach. You know many things we don't know."

"There is no place for people like us except the farm, Dalin," he said. "Or the road, or the sea."

She asked him how his arm was. He lay on his back and extended it to her. He could move it but the shoulder reminded him of a greater pain each time he lifted his arm.

She felt the scar with her hand. He liked the feel of that hand on his shoulder and impulsively, he turned and held it.

She understood. "You are not yet strong," she said. "There are still many things you cannot do."

He could feel himself stirring, the blood rushing to the tips of his fingers.

"I am not a virgin anymore," she said with some sadness.

"You will be my first," he said.

He kissed her, but she pushed him away tenderly.

He could not leash the animal stirring, he could not stop. His hands groped for her, found her warm and trembling, but she would not let him. "You are not yet strong," she whispered into his ear as she half rose, looming so close, her face almost touching his. Then she kissed him and he tasted her lips, felt her tongue probe into his mouth.

"Don't move then," she told him. "I will do everything for you. And then, when you are strong . . ."

"You are the first," Istak said again, then there were no more words.

So this is how two bodies melt into one, a communion, a celebration. This is what he had longed for and would have missed had he entered the seminary. He was a weakling after all, unable to withstand the devil call of the flesh. They were not even married—this was what he was taught, this was what he knew. Yet, within his deepest conscience, this was not wrong. It was bound to be, not temptation, but fate that brought them together, not just her stumbling into Po-on but her going back to the village to take him away from the avid clutch of death. She had given him life, now she was giving herself to him as well.

HE slept well afterward, then woke up to the twitter of birds and the scurrying all around him, the boys hitching the carts, the women collecting children, animals, and clothes, getting ready to move. The pots had all been washed and he had slept through it all. He pretended sleep when Dalin went inside the cart and looked at him. The cart started to move, the solid wooden wheels squeaking. The children were talking about the falling star that night. Think of your birthday—and your wish will come true.

The air had a freshness to it; clean and washed, it flowed inside the cart. Dalin's back was before him and he remembered how he had embraced her, felt the smooth fall of her shoulders, the softness of her breasts.

"Dalin," he whispered.

She turned to him, her face radiant as morning.

"Thank you," he said gratefully.

"Are you hungry?"

He nodded.

"There is rice in the pot—it is still warm and the coffee is still hot. There is also a piece of dried meat on top of the rice."

He rose, squatted behind her, and ate. Occasionally, she turned to him, still holding the bull's lead, and watched him. They were in the middle of the caravan and his mother was walking up ahead. The grass was wet and the ground was still solid, but in many places mud had already formed and the prints of *carabao* hooves on the mud were indistinct now. One more caravan like theirs and the road would turn into a quagmire.

He got off the cart when he was through eating and caught up with his mother, who had lifted her skirt to her knees so that it would not be soiled.

He wanted to tell her about Dalin. She must have expected it. Before he could speak, she asked, "How is Dalin?"

"Why do you ask, Inang?"

She turned to him briefly, her face burned by sun and lined by years of work, the eyes sharp and sad at the same time, streaks of white on the hair knotted at her nape.

"She is good," she said quietly. "This I must say—in spite of all my forebodings. You cannot find a better woman. She works very hard. She has done so much for you at a time when I could not look after you. Your father, he is old and tired and very angry. Do you know what I am trying to say?"

He nodded slowly.

"Dalin is good for you. Take care of her," his mother said, "and she will reward you."

IT rained every afternoon and they stopped in the villages until the rain passed. Ba-ac was often seized by fits of anger, and as if he were mad, he would shout his curses to the wind: Cunts of your mothers, you are evil like lightning. What have I done to you? Why are you doing this to us? You will have your time, you will pay! And not just with your blood. We will chop you bit by

bit, your balls and your penises, we will throw them to the dogs.
Cunts of your mothers!

Mayang did not stop his ranting anymore. She would just
wait until he quieted down, his breathing heavy and tired, his
eyes wet with tears. Seeing him like this, Mayang often cried. The
children were too young to understand, but the other farmers
and their wives understood. They were silent, for the old man's
anger was also theirs; he was just giving shape to the emotions
that flamed in their hearts but could not burst out—neither
words nor deeds nor yet light in their minds to show them how
they could truly be themselves and not be hounded—helpless
creatures that they were.

There were more towns now and every time they approached one, they would circle away from it. An-no, Bit-tik,
or their uncles and the older boys walked ahead of the caravan.
The road had become muddier as the days lengthened into a
week.

Then, one morning, the Guardia came upon them—eight
mounted soldiers with a Spanish officer, their rifles slung on
their shoulders. They descended upon them from the rear so
quickly they seemed to have appeared like phantoms from the
grass. The men were brown like them, except for their officer.

Ba-ac, who was in the lead cart, happened to be asleep; he
had stood guard the night before and was about to rise at the
shout of "¡Alto! ¡Alto!" but Mayang quickly pushed him back and
covered him with a blanket.

Istak was holding the leash of the bull out front when the
Spanish officer rode past him and, briefly, their eyes locked.
Capitán Gualberto did not recognize Istak, although Istak knew
him at once. Who could miss his short-cropped hair, that
aquiline nose, and those eyes that seemed to burn with perpetual hate? But Istak was no longer the acolyte who had served

him in the *kumbento* in Cabugaw; he was now emaciated and pale as if he had just been snatched from the grave.

The Guardia had apparently been riding for some time; their blue uniforms were dirty and their horses were panting and wet with sweat. In his heavily accented Ilokano, Capitán Gualberto asked Blas, who was nearest to him, where they came from. Ba-ac's cousin meekly told the truth, "Candon."

And where were they going? "To the valley."

"Your *cédula*, your *cédula*," the Spanish officer barked.

From the wall of the cart, Blas took a small pouch and within was a piece of paper carefully wrapped with cloth; he presented it with trembling hands to the Spaniard, who glanced at it, then handed it back.

Istak felt his chest caving in, his knees giving out. Now the officer would ask for the *cédulas* of the others, now they would be found out and most probably killed right there.

But Capitán Gualberto did no such thing; one *cédula* seemed enough. He ordered them to dismount—all of them— and when they had dismounted, he rode to each cart and peered within. At the lead cart, he paused briefly to look at Ba-ac covered with a rough blanket, the face haggard, the eyes closed in sleep. "He is very ill," Mayang, who stood by, told him.

Not one of the Guardia had dismounted; they formed a line beside the caravan while Capitán Gualberto continued his inspection. There was nothing of value in the carts, just the usual provisions of poor farmers, until his eyes rested on Blas's two girls, first at the younger, then the older; his eyes widened and a grin crossed his face.

He asked Orang to step out of the line, and when she did, he looked at her again, her youth, her good limbs. The soldiers knew what to expect next and they were laughing boisterously. Blas was now livid with fear and anger, but a soldier drew a gun on him. His wife started to cry, and so did the younger sister. An-no, who stood by, knew what was going to happen, too, and though the darkest thoughts rushed to his mind, if he as much as moved a hand he would be shot, as Istak had been.

Dismounting, the Spaniard took the frightened girl's hand while the other soldiers kept guard over the caravan. He led her across the empty field stubbled with grass to where a patch of cogon sprouted. The soldiers joked and laughed and made obscene remarks; they were Ilokanos, too, but to Istak, they were no longer men but beasts; it was they who had burned Po-on, who had left him for dead. He heard himself repeating his father's curses.

CHAPTER

THEY WERE at the dusky rim of the jungle again. The tall razor grass was greener now and would no longer ignite as easily as it did during the height of the dry season. This portion of the road was rarely used, for in the last town most of the travelers stopped and from there they boarded the boats to the coast of Pangasinan, its towns rich with coconuts, fish, and salt.

The girl, Orang, did not want to join them anymore. She was sixteen and could read the alphabet and write her name, Leonora, that was all. All of them, they were going to learn to read and write with Istak teaching them. But now she wanted to kill herself, to drown in the first river they would cross, or to stay behind and work in any village as a servant, but not to go with them with her shame. The women—Mayang more than the rest—stayed with her through the night, soothing her, telling her it was not her doing, that no one among them could have stopped the dastardly deed.

When they started out the following morning, she was gone. She had slipped away in the night and they searched for her in the gullies, behind the mounds and the tall grass, shouting her name, their shouts echoing in the morning stillness. Orannggg . . . but the only answer was the sighing of the wind.

They could not leave without her.

It was An-no who found her weeping bitterly in the shade of a culibambang tree up the rise of ground where the foothills lifted. He had heard her and when he appeared, her weeping turned into a loud sobbing. He put his hand on her shoulder to comfort her. She shuddered and stiffened.

An-no rushed back to the caravan and told them she was all right, that he would bring her back. When he returned she was no longer weeping, but tears still streamed down her face and her eyes were swollen. She wore a shapeless skirt and blouse which her mother had woven.

"You must leave with us," An-no said, kneeling before her but not touching her.

She looked away. "And you will all regard me as if I were dirty and you would not want me among you. All of you . . ."

"Why do you say this, Orang? Haven't we suffered enough? Look at me, don't you think I feel so small because I could not help you? And if I did would I be here today? Begging you to come back? Manong Istak—he did not even raise a hand against them and they shot him. He can speak Spanish, I told you. He pleaded with them. Did they show him any mercy?"

"I cannot face anyone."

"Look at me, Orang," An-no told her. "Look at me or I will hold your face and force you to look at me."

She turned to him slowly, sorrow in her eyes.

"You are a woman now," An-no said. "If I ask that you live with me when we reach the valley, will you do that? I will protect you and pray that no evil will happen to you again."

"You will not take a soiled rag," she said. "You will want something clean."

"You are not soiled."

"I am now."

"Not to me. Not to me. You are pure and you are going to be my wife . . ."

She turned away again, but this time she was no longer crying.

THEY camped that night in a shallow field flanked by bald hills. Not long ago the field was planted to rice—they could see that in the strands that stubbled the land, in the broken dikes that bordered each plot. Close by, madre de cacao trees had started to bloom and there was even a sprout of banana trees without fruit. Istak wondered what had happened to the village nearby, why the people had gone. In the lead cart, he approached the hamlet, intoning loudly, *¡Bari-bari!*—the ritual incantation with which an intruder sought permission to pass unknown precincts guarded perhaps by inhospitable spirits. The houses were falling apart and weeds clambered over the bamboo fences and up the walls right onto the thinning roofs. The windows were wide open, gaping at them like sightless eyes. There was nothing inside but rotting bamboo and disheveled walls with the sun streaming in. The people did not leave anything, not even a broken pot. The houses had been abandoned for more than a year and houses with no people in them die like humans.

Ba-ac did not want to sleep in the abandoned village; it smelled of disaster, of hoary gloom, and so they moved on, farther up the valley before they would ascend the mountain.

The narrow road that slit through the jungle was slippery; grass and saplings grew wild on both sides and big trees arched above them and shut off the sun, so that although it was morning it seemed as if in this face of the mountain it was early evening. There were sudden breaks of sunlight among the trees, and birds flitted through the small frame of sky. Orchids dangled from branches, some of them in bloom, bouquets of purple and white, but they were high up and only monkeys could climb after them.

One of the children walking out front screamed in horror; he had felt an itch on his calf and when he looked, there was this black abominable thing as big as his thumb, slimy and fat, and he could not remove it.

"Leeches!" Ba-ac said. He went to the child and scraped it off with his bolo. The leech was bloody and full.

Although it had not rained that afternoon, water dripped from the trees. Around their trunks, up to the lofty branches, vines coiled like huge snakes.

It would take more than a day before they would break out into the open country again and know the sun. Istak pointed out to Dalin what they could eat, the tops of ferns which could be cleaned like bamboo shoots and cooked. No one need starve in the forest, he told her.

She asked him how he came to know so much and he said he had been in the forest beyond Tirad. Padre Jose had pointed these out to him and all the other plants that could sustain life. He showed her the fruit of the rattan vine which they could eat and that she already knew. There were other wild fruits and berries—they could all be eaten.

They stopped for their meal in a white patch of sunlight, but did not tarry. They moved on. Bit-tik and An-no were now in the front and Ba-ac was in the rear immediately behind Dalin's cart. The last cart carried their seed rice and was heavy, so no one rode in it except Ba-ac.

The big solid wheels of wood were creaking noisily, for they had not been oiled for days. It was no longer necessary—they were not going to hide anymore or travel in the night. They had passed the Guardia Civil. Ba-ac felt safer now. A few more miles, then they would break out from the low saddle of the mountain into the plains of eastern Pangasinan.

It was Dalin who first noticed it when she looked back; the cart was following them, but Ba-ac was not in the driver's seat. Istak called for all of them to stop. He peered inside the cart but the old man was not there either.

"Tatang! Tataaang!" he shouted. The forest echoed his voice.

"Maybe," Dalin said, "he stopped to defecate."

"He would have told us," Istak said. "And he would not let the cart go ahead without him."

He retraced the trail, shouting his father's name. Maybe Ba-ac had slipped, or had fallen asleep and toppled off the cart. But he would have awakened and called.

The forest seemed to close inexorably on Istak; he was far from the carts and could no longer see them nor could they hear him, for he had run part of the way.

Birdcalls shrilled from his right. There would be wild boar and deer here—if only he had a chance to hunt, but he could do that only with a gun. "Tatang!" he continued screaming. Still no reply.

He should work out a system by which every man would have to look back occasionally to find out if the carts behind him were secure. He must tell them that at the next stop.

At the turn of the trail, he saw it—this python dangling from a tree, as thick as his own thigh, and it was coiled around the old man, who was no longer moving, his eyes closed as if in sleep. The reptile was tightening its coil, squeezing the life, the blood, out of Ba-ac. For a moment, Istak stood transfixed with fear. Like his brothers and all the menfolk in the caravan, he always had a bolo slung on his waist. He knew what had happened; the reptile had swung down from its coil around one of the low-hanging branches where it had waited, struck his father, then quickly strangled him. As soon as all the bones were crushed, it would swallow its victim slowly.

The python had seen him, but it did not move or relax its tenacious grip. With all the force in his weakened body and praying that he would not miss—God give this wounded arm strength!—Istak struck at the python's body with his two hands. Immediately the coil loosened but the reptile was not dead; now it lashed around and again Istak struck at it. The shiny skin was now gashed with a deep wound, the white flesh opened, the blood started to spurt. The reptile fell on the ground in a heap, helpless, its great, slick body twisting, weaving. Again and again, with two hands Istak lashed at it, not caring where he hit it. Again and again, from each new and open wound blood spurted out. The reptile was now quivering, a dozen cuts on its long body, its head almost severed. Istak did not stop until it was still. Then he went to his father.

Ba-ac's body was completely crushed. His bones sticking out of the shapeless shirt wet with blood. Istak sank on his knees and cried. A massive wave of weariness swept over him, drowning him.

AN-NO and the others found him staring blankly, the python dismembered at his feet, its innards spilled on the wet ground. They carried Ba-ac back to the cart, his body wrapped with the leaves of the anahau palm, which grew along the trail, and tied carefully with twine. They also brought back one of the carts and loaded the python onto it. Its meat was good—like chicken, the

Ilokanos always said—and the women cut it up and salted it, for it would not do to dry it; the sun no longer shone regularly as in the season past. The rains were really upon them.

They buried Ba-ac at the edge of the forest. Ahead—perhaps a day or so, past the cogon-covered hills—were the plains of eastern Pangasinan at last. That night, after the prayer which he led, Istak asked his mother if they should go back to Cabugaw. "Father is gone, we need not flee from the Guardia anymore."

"And if we returned, what will greet us? The ashes of our former homes? A land which we cannot till because it never belonged to us? I am old, my sons; it is you for whom I must live. I will go wherever you want to go."

"I will go on," An-no said. "Orang cannot go back. We can start a new life."

"And you, Istak?"

Somehow, his mind was still cluttered with what Padre Jose had said, a tenuous hope that he could return to the *kumbento,* to the seminary in Vigan. Dalin had said that he was not a farmer and would never be one, but that he could help the farmer even if he himself never touched the handle of a plow.

"I don't know, Mother," he said.

"Ask Dalin," his mother told him.

It was dusk and on a dry patch of ground they had already placed the stones which they used as stoves, and lighted the firewood. Dalin had gone to the creek down the clearing to fill the water jar. He followed her. She was crouched on the bank and had put sand inside the earthen jar and was scrubbing the insides to remove whatever moss had gathered there. Watching her, he knew that he would not leave her, that he would go with her wherever she wanted to go.

When she was through, she filled the jar with water and rolled a piece of cloth which she placed on her head. Istak helped her raise the jar and lift it to her head. Neatly balanced, she carried the jar without holding it although the path was slippery.

They walked up the low incline.

"Will you tell me where you want to go?" he asked.

She did not turn to him; it was difficult to do that with the jar so. "Wherever you want to," she said.

"You must make the choice and I will follow."

He could not see her smiling. "It is you, my husband, whom I will follow. Wherever you want to go," she murmured.

"Tell me then, the valley?"

"I pray that we reach it with nothing setting us apart . . ."

"Nothing can set us apart now," he assured her. "Tell me, what is it like there?"

"A plain as far as you can see," she said solemnly. "And all the land you can clear. I will help you. I will work very hard beside you."

8

THEY DID NOT linger in the towns in the great plain. They kept to the narrow muddy roads. In places, the constant rain had washed away the roadbed and the foundations of stone jutted out, jolting the carts as the caravan labored over them. The new towns looked scraggly and unkempt, and they did not have the stone churches or the big houses of brick that lined the main streets of the Ilokos. It also seemed to them that the Guardia were far away. Among these poor settlers, there was not much booty.

In the near horizon, the Caraballos were a wall of deep blue. They would still have three days of travel before they reached those mountains.

They brought out the salted python meat to dry whenever there was sun; the white strips were laid on flat bamboo baskets

balanced atop the carts. They continued to worry about food—
they had barely enough to last them through one planting season. But there was always the tobacco they could sell freely now
that the monopoly had been lifted.

They met other caravans, Pangasiñenses with woven baskets
and salted fish to sell. They overtook farmers who were also
looking for land. They were all in a hurry to get to their destinations before the rains really fell—the *siyam-siyam* that would
transform the plain into a vast rimless ocean of brown and the
giant river, the Agno, into a rampaging sea.

At night when they bivouacked, sometimes with other settlers, while cooking their meals or just drinking an occasional
coconut bowl of *basi*, Istak came across wisps of his recent past.
A squad of Guardia Civil was stalking the caravans, asking questions about those who had come from Cabugaw. He told his
brothers and uncles to avoid the other settlers, not to talk with
them unless necessary. They now camped by themselves, away
from other groups, even though they had also come from the
north.

In the mornings, when they started out, there was always
something uplifting about the land, the cascade of light everywhere, the brilliant glaze on the leaves of bamboo, on the aca-
cias. Even the razor grass seemed greener in the plain. Indeed,
the rains had begun.

There was more variety in their food now. The saluyot
shrubs had started growing in the fields and alongside the roads
more catuday trees had bloomed, and they gathered the pink
and white flowers and cooked them.

Once they encamped along a long, sandy stretch of land
near a creek. The place was overgrown with tough ledda grass.
Shortly before nightfall, the air was suddenly alive with huge insects. Some clung to Istak's clothes while others just buzzed

about. Dalin called happily from where she was cooking the rice. These are May beetles, she cried, and like a madwoman, she started flailing and catching them, storing them in a fish basket. She called to them to do as she did, and they set about catching as many as they could.

They were northerners and though they ate everything, even the small white larvae of the big red ants and the young green leaves of mangoes—food that was unusual to Dalin then—they had never tasted these beetles. And that evening, they sat down to their first supper of May beetles cooked in cane vinegar and coconut oil. They were not queasy eating it, and they liked the bottom best, the milky, juicy taste of it.

That night, Istak wandered off to the line of shrubs beyond which was the trail that they would follow in the morning. In the distance, the lights of bull carts proceeding on their journey flickered until they dimmed and disappeared completely.

He sat on a tree stump and pondered the riddle of what awaited them, and the pursuers they must elude. Maybe, after they crossed the Agno, they could come upon some anonymous corner where no one had been before.

Others had done it, escaped the clutches of the Spaniards, who called them *remontados*. They left the security of the towns and sought refuge in the forest, where they cleared land and raised their food, far away from their tormentors. Some were changed, though; they became brigands as well, preying on the poor who could not defend themselves, who would rather have the peace and security "under the bell." Perhaps, in the new land, they would be left alone without the past rising out of the ashes to threaten them again.

Istak envied the young Igorot friends he had made in the Cordilleras, half-naked, their arms and chests tattooed, their teeth blackened with betel nut. They had listened to Padre Jose's exhortations, they were even baptized, but they had reverted to their ancient worship once the priest had gone. Up there in the mountains, their lives were complete. But then Istak remembered, too, the skulls which adorned their houses. Any one of those skulls could have been his if he had not gone to them with Padre Jose and his gifts of salt and tobacco and his promises of salvation.

There is no escape, then, from this prison that is living, just as there was no escape from his unquenchable yearning for knowledge.

How did it all start, really? Did it start with his father? With his being in church? It had come to him before, though not as clearly as it did now. It was the harsh living in Po-on, really, more than anything, which had drawn him to the Church, to seek not salvation but a future that was not limned by hunger. It was really for this reason that he would have become a priest, as did most of the Indios who came from the lowest stations. They would overcome the hazards of peasant birth and become teachers if not priests, and thus bring not just comfort to themselves and their families, but a bit of the respectability such as that which Capitán Berong had.

Padre Jose had taught him how to worship, to hold on to the rosary as if it were a sturdy rope which drew him up from the black pit of creation. And this rope gave him a strength that others from Cabugaw or those born like him would never have. It would draw him not only out of the pit but from the putrefaction of the poverty and villainy of the village—out and into a world of abundance and a surfeit of ease which the Church gave only to a chosen few. He saw this in Padre Jose and in the other priests—resplendent in their vestments, gorging on the food that people had worked so hard to produce.

Would he transform this rope into a leash?

It was the priest who ruled, who enacted the laws of the Church and of man, and added to such laws the lash of prejudice, for power was always white, Castilian, and not brown like the good earth.

It seemed so long ago now, but even when he was in Cabugaw it was often talked about in whispers, like the dusty whiff of age that whirls up from cupboards and cabinets long shut—the death of those three mestizo priests, Gomez, Burgos, and Zamora—why were they killed? Could they have managed to weaken the Church—just the three of them? The very Church to which they belonged and which they served?

Did the Spanish priests really believe that the Indios—even if they were mestizos—could be equal to the Spaniards, that they could be the highest officials of the Church?

There were always excuses, there was no escaping them, for the power to disagree was not with the Indios, just as it would never be with him. So the Church, then, was Castilian. The Church was not interested in justice, or in the abolition of inequality. The temple, then, was just another pit, and the rosary he held offered no salvation. No God can haul men like him up from the abyss of perdition.

But God, I don't doubt You. I can see You in the morning, in the dew on the grass. Should I worship You in silence, without the obeisance and obedience to Your ministers? Should I stop singing and, within me, let my deeds speak of my gratitude and belief in Your greatness?

The men who taught us of Your presence, who opened the doors of Your temple that we might see the light—they are white like You. Are You, then, the god of white people, and if we who are brown worship You, do we receive Your blessings as white men do?

I pray that You be not white, that You be without color and

that You be in all men because goodness cannot be encased only in white.

I should worship, then, not a white god but someone brown like me. Pride tells me only one thing: that we are more than equal to those who rule us. Pride tells me that this land is mine, that they should leave me to my destiny, and if they will not leave, pride tells me that I should push them away, and should they refuse this, I should vanquish them, kill them. I knew long ago that their blood is the same as mine. No stranger can come battering down my door and say he brings me light. This I have within me.

H E returned to the cart to find Dalin already asleep. She woke up as he lay quietly beside her. Rain pattered lightly on the palm roof and she drew the old blanket over her legs. He turned on his side and fondled her flat stomach, feeling its smoothness, its warmth.

"Where have you gone?"

"I was by the trail, by myself . . ."

He had never asked her before, and they had never talked about it, although he had always known that, in her own way, she was religious, crossing herself every morning when she woke up and again when she went to sleep.

"Do you believe in God?"

Though he could not see her face clearly, he could make out her eyes and they were wide open.

"What kind of question is that?" she said, then quietly: "Surely, I believe in God. We are together—this is God's will."

He lay on his back again. He wanted to tell her then, but there were things he could not reveal to others; he was not sure now that he still believed.

CHAPTER

9

THEY WERE up early in the morning. Two merchants from Abra with a dozen horses trailing them trotted up to where they were brewing the corn coffee. The men traveled very light; they carried their provisions in packs on two horses. They were going all the way to Manila and may they just cook their meal with them? They had dried meat and leftover rice which needed to be fried. Both were in their early thirties, dark-skinned, and obviously well traveled. While Dalin waited for the pot to boil, the younger man talked about the horses. They were for the races in Manila. After retiring from the races, the horses would be used to pull the carriages of the rich. Then, casually, he asked where they came from.

"From Ilokos Sur," Istak said with some hesitation.

"What town?"

"Cabugaw," Istak said.

The man shook his head and dug his bare toe into the soft earth. "Two towns away," he said, "in Binalonan, there are Guardias with a Spanish officer."

"What does he look like?" Istak said.

"White like all Kastilas," the man said. "He has short hair." There flashed in his mind the image of Capitán Gualberto.

"The Guardia are searching all the caravans from the north. There is a one-armed man from Cabugaw they are looking for. They have been beating up people, particularly those who come from Sur, to get information from them—even if they are not from Cabugaw. But they did not bother us—he knows how to deal with them." The man thrust a chin to the older horse merchant, obviously his employer, busy turning the dried meat roasting on the coals.

"There is no one-armed man here, as you can see," Istak said.

"Even so," the man said. "You are from Cabugaw, aren't you? If I were you, I would put as much distance as I could from them immediately . . ."

Dalin had heard everything.

The other man spoke softly. "Yes—after you eat, you should leave. You never know what they will do. I hope all your papers are with you."

Dalin turned to Istak. She did not speak; her eyes told him of her fear. He turned around to the morning activity, children playing in the sun, wives preparing breakfast, and men checking on the work animals, giving them their ration of hay.

Their visitors would ride all the way to Tarlak, and from there, they would put the beautiful animals on the train to Manila. Finished with their breakfast, they mounted and were on their way.

Istak did not want to distress the others. He let them brew

their coffee and roast the dried python meat on the open fire.

It was best that only he and Dalin know that the Guardia were closing in on them again. They must leave now. Already the Caraballo range loomed ahead. A few more miles and they would cross the Agno, and from then on, the promise of eastern Pangasinan.

Now, they struck out onto trails even Dalin did not know. A pelting rain by midafternoon hid almost everything from view, but they moved on, the water seeping through the walls of the carts. The wheels soggy with mud, they sloshed through villages enveloped with rain and as evening finally shrouded the land, still they moved on. By now, the uncles from Candon understood only too well why they must not pause. For supper, they ate cold chunks of rice and the dried python that was roasted in the morning; the cold rice stuck to their throats and had to be washed down with water.

The men who went ahead of the caravan were wet and they shivered but they, too, marched on, stopping only once in a while to ask from an isolated farmhouse the general direction of the ferry which they would have to board to cross the Agno. Shortly before daybreak, the rain finally lifted and the east was bathed with the mellow light of a new day.

They were back on the old road, muddy and impassable in many places. They had to detour through fields and indentations that were made firm by banana trunks laid over them. An-no, who was ahead of the caravan, rushed back to them eagerly shouting: "The river, the river—it is ahead."

It was finally before them—the life-giving artery whose delta was so fertile and wide it could swallow all the settlers with nowhere to go. They could not settle permanently in any place, however, for anytime during the year when the rains came, the waters changed course and laced the delta with rivulets, rising no higher than a woman's ankle.

They stopped at the river's bank. Indeed, exactly as Dalin had described it, the river was wide and swift. In the middle and close to the bank were whirlpools. The current carried trunks and branches of trees from the mountains and islands of water lilies.

They should make their crossing immediately. At the landing below, people were gathered. But there was no ferry, no raft, and there was none on the other side either.

It started to drizzle again, and in a while the drizzle turned into sheets of lashing rain. Under the canopies, almost everything inside the carts was dry. Out where he sat holding the reins, Istak was thoroughly drenched. The palm leaf helmet and cape were no protection. But just as quickly as the rain started it petered out.

Istak went down the incline to where people were gathered, farmers with goats and chickens which they wanted to transport to the other side, and women carrying baskets filled with greens.

"How do we cross?" Istak asked no one in particular. A farmer turned to him and shook his head.

"You could swim," he said lightly.

When Istak did not speak, the farmer went on. "The ferry— it broke from its mooring in the night when the water rose. It must be far downstream now with the ferryman, who perhaps had fallen asleep."

"Is there no other ferry?" Istak was anxious.

The other farmers who were listening shook their heads. No other ferry but this one. Maybe, if you go downriver to Alcala— but that is very far from here. And in Bayambang, there is a ferry there because they are building a bridge.

"And upriver?"

Again, a collective shaking of heads.

"There must be a shallow place where we can cross."

"Yes, there is," a farmer said, pointing to the line of carts up the incline of the bank. "But it will be dangerous."

There was no time to think. As leader, he must now decide. "We are in a hurry," he said. "God will take care."

During the dry season, when the river was shallow, the ferrymen had built a roadway along which carts and people could pass. Where the river was shallowest, they piled the stones; they stretched across the shallow water several coconut trunks on top of which they spread cogon grass, then a layer of gravel. They did not use the ferry anymore. With this bridge, they charged a cheaper rate.

"The bridge is there." The man pointed it out to him. "You can cross but don't stray from the embankment because it will be deep now on both sides. And as for the coconut bridge, you must go ahead of the carts and feel for it with your feet. It should still be there."

The carts came down the gully. The men had dismounted and were holding the animals by their reins so that they would not go down too fast.

An-no took the lead *carabao*. The road to the small bridge had not been washed away by the rain, though the water had risen. The stone embankment still showed through the brown water.

The uncles from Tagudin were reluctant to cross. Blas suggested that they could very well settle in this wide and fertile plain—surely there were still forests they could clear, where they would not be hounded.

"It is a distance we need," Istak said, "distance from those chasing us. They will ask people and so many have seen us—they will know where to find us. The farther we go, the more difficult it will be for them to follow. And after we cross the river, no one would really know where we headed."

And because he was learned, they finally agreed.

The bridge had to be tested first, and Bit-tik, who was a

good swimmer, went ahead, following the embankment. It was still secure, as the men at the riverbank had assured them. He moved slowly in the brown moving waters which never got higher than his waist, feeling with his feet the boulders that had remained. The carts could go over them. Then the line of boulders ended and he was on the bridge itself. The coconut trunks had not been dislodged—they were intact all the way, but the current had become swift and Bit-tik had difficulty steadying himself.

Once across, on the embankment again, he turned to the waiting carts across the expanse of water and shouted: "The bridge is still here. You can cross."

The *carabaos* were used to water; every day during the journey, they had to look for some stream or well so that the animals could be bathed. The bull might be scared, but Dalin was sure it would be all right; she led it steadily into the line. Istak went onward to the middle of the river, and realized that he was not yet all that strong and could be swept away by the current.

The *carabaos* were not too sure of their footing, and the carts jerked and swayed with every boulder; then the wheels tumbled across.

Istak could feel the current, at first slight and then a steady pushing against his legs. As he moved deeper toward the middle of the river, it came as a powerful force that could easily have swept away the children if they had not been in the carts, holding on to their mothers. An-no in the lead kept screaming at them to go straight for the middle and not to stray and fall into the depths and be washed away. The ten carts were now well into midstream. There was no turning back.

An-no finally hit the bridge. "I am here," he yelled at them, his voice carrying through the rush. He was waist-deep now in the brown swirling waters.

Then Istak saw the big branches of trees, huge swatches of grass and reeds that must have been torn away upstream, and they rushed toward the carts, sometimes pushing them danger-ously close to the edge of the embankment.

One of the men went toward the left to push away the branches that had gathered on the side of a cart. They moved on, swaying and jerking as they went over the coconut bridge, the water pushing steadily against the solid wooden wheels.

Within the carts, some of the children were shouting, enjoy-ing the sight of the swirling waters, unaware of the danger they were in. The first cart was now over the bridge. An-no was going up and was shouting again, telling them to keep a straight line, that the bridge was not that long, and it was still solid under-foot. As he went up, he saw it. He shouted, fright in his voice, for in the middle of the river, hurtling toward them with the cur-rent, was a huge uprooted tree.

The men shouted and pulled at the leashes of their *carabaos*. The women and the children peered out of the carts, at the mountain of leaves and branches racing toward them. On its downward rush the tree had also amassed reeds and water lilies.

Istak led the last cart with Mayang and their seed rice. If he tarried, the tree might sweep away the coconut trunks underfoot. He was now in the middle of the river, directly in the path of the oncoming tree. He shouted at the animal to hurry. It was then that the cart refused to budge, its wheels stuck between the co-conut trunks. No matter how he pulled at the poor beast, the cart would not move. He shouted at his mother to get out quickly, but Mayang, perhaps too tired to move, did not hear, or if she heard, she acted too late. The tree was upon them like an avenging hand.

It towered over the cart, swallowing it. Istak felt the trunks under him give way. He let go of the leash and ran to the other side, the leaves, branches, and island of reeds engulfing him. For a moment, the green mass seemed to smother him. His legs, his body, were being pushed toward the rim of the embankment. But his feet touched a boulder, solid and secure, and the mountain of branches and leaves swept by. He emerged in time to see the *carabao* slip into the water, the wheels of the cart bob up briefly, then disappear altogether. It was but an instant, but like a lightning flash in the darkened sky, fate passed before him. He witnessed it all and did not move, the current eddying around him, while the men who were on the shallow side of the river raced past him and, screaming at one another, dove into the river. And when they surfaced, they were already downstream. They swam back toward the shallow rim of the river, then to the embankment, and dove again and again. The *carabao,* which had broken free from its harness, was recovered; it was no stranger to water. Some of the men who were waiting for the ferry at the other side saw what had happened and they, too, joined in the search.

Not once did Istak dive. He prayed that his mother might finally be granted the peace she never had in life.

Far into the afternoon, they ranged along the river, but found no trace of the cart.

AT SUNDOWN, they stopped and set up camp for the night. Beyond the river were newly opened fields and Carmay—a solitary village on the fringes of a forest being cleared. The great trees that had not yet been felled were burned; they stood around like huge black skeletons. The caravan found refuge from the rain in the houses, and the women, who had no dry firewood, cooked the evening meal in the stoves of kindly villagers.

Early in the evening, the three brothers sat down together for the first time in weeks to a meal prepared by Dalin. They had barely spoken to one another the whole day, and though words were not uttered, Istak knew that his brothers resented him; perhaps they even blamed him for their mother's death. Why did he not dive at all—he, the eldest son—when even men who were strangers helped? Why did he give up too soon?

The vegetable broth warmed their insides, and the salted fish with crushed tamarind tasted good. Istak had no appetite; he put into words the thoughts that rankled An-no. "Do not blame me, my brother, for our mother's fate. Do you think I wanted her dead? Who is the son who would wish this on his mother? I would not have been able to save her. The hands of fate are stronger than mine. I prayed."

"You did not even try." An-no's words were like prongs that dug into his flesh.

Istak bowed, then stood up and walked away, down the muddy path toward the river, the dusk thickening around him, the insects noisy in the grass. Dalin, who was serving them, followed, but Istak waved her back: "Let me be alone," he mumbled.

What was it, really, that had happened to him on that submerged bridge? Why did he not dive after the cart? It all came back—how it was when Ba-ac was nowhere to be found. In his mind, it had quickly formed—this knowledge, this certainty that the old man was dead. And again, at the river, it had flashed through his mind clearly, that there was nothing he could do, as if something stronger than the current had held him back, telling him he could do nothing, nothing. He was not a coward, he reassured himself; when he decided to stay behind in Po-on, he was fully aware of the risk. What was this in him that seemed to guide him in his deepest thoughts? Was it some supreme intelligence that he had gleaned from the *kumbento* in Cabugaw? If only he could explain this to his brothers, if only he could put into words these fears and feelings, inchoate and yet so real. It was not just Mayang they had lost. Lost, too, were the sacks of seed rice which must have pinned her down when the cart overturned. Now they would have nothing to plant and little to eat. But at least they were alive; they could subsist on weeds and insects. Ilokanos can eat what other people cannot. And most of all, with the bridge gone, for the moment, at least, they were farther away from Capitán Gualberto and his Guardia.

The rain resumed the following morning and the fields around them were flooded. The road to the valley, Dalin said, would be a quagmire. Istak and his brothers left Carmay early and paced the riverbank, asking the few settlers who lived nearby if they had seen the cart or Mayang, but no one had. The water was higher, with more islands of water lilies and reeds, occasional logs and small uprooted trees that drifted with the current.

All through the journey, Istak was amazed at the kindness of villagers, how readily they were invited to sleep in kitchens, in sheds, or under the houses if there was no space upstairs. He understood then how Dalin and her family could go so far with a cart loaded with more goods to sell than what the family needed to live.

He asked them to please bury his mother if her body ever surfaced; he would surely come back to find out and to express his gratitude to whomever had done the Christian thing.

At noon, Istak asked his brothers and everyone in the caravan to join him at the riverbank to pray. Dalin had gathered a basket of white rosal flowers in the village, and these she made into a wreath which she then tied onto a small raft made of banana trunks.

Rest in peace, Istak intoned as An-no and Bit-tik lowered the wreath into the water. Bit-tik pushed it toward the middle, where the current was strong, and silently they watched it drift down the river. It was caught in a whirlpool briefly, then bobbed up and swiftly floated down the vast brown expanse. They watched it grow smaller, till it was no longer visible, hidden as it was by the flotsam from the mountains.

"We are orphans now," Istak said, turning to his brothers. "Whatever may rile us, whatever differences we may have, we must be closer together. We have no one else."

THE FARMERS who gave them shelter in Carmay told Istak that in the town of Rosales they could get some help.

"You must go to Don Jacinto. Everyone knows him, for his big house is by the big balete tree. He is good—he will help you . . ."

They left Carmay at midday; the rain had eased somewhat. The sky was scabbed with gray clouds that scudded away and the sun came out in short shifts, full and bright upon a land now laved in green.

To their right, a straggle of trees and beyond the trees, farther in the distance, was the heavily forested mountain called Balungaw. Dalin told Istak of a village with the same name near the mountain, of a hot spring there where the sick often went. To their left was another creek which emptied into the Agno, and like the Agno, it was also swollen.

SHORTLY before nightfall, thatch-roofed houses with buri palm walls appeared on both sides of the narrow road. Pigs wallowed in side ditches. From under the houses, mangy dogs appeared and trailed and barked at the slow-moving *carabaos*. People went to the windows to look at the caravan, the palm-leaf canopies of the carts dark with rain, the solid wooden wheels caked with mud, and the new settlers walking beside their carts while inside were their women and children. They were in Rosales at last.

It was one of those new towns carved out of cogonal wastes and forests by settlers like them. As in most of the new towns that lined the road to the valley, its leading citizens were mestizos who were the favorites of the friars. Some took advantage of the recent opening of the colleges in Manila for Indios and went to the University of Santo Tomás to study law and medicine, and became infected, too, with the ideas of liberalism, that deadly contagion which the friars detested and ranted against. Large tracts of land toward the east, all the way to that prosperous village of Balungaw, to the very foothills of Mount Balungaw, were claimed by the first Spanish settler in this part of the country, but there were also equally large areas titled to the *principalia*—the educated men like Don Jacinto.

Since most of the settlers in this wild part of the country were Ilokanos, their new settlements were named after the towns they came from—Casanicolasan, Cabalawangan—or after the vegetation that abounded in the new land—Cabaletcan (balete trees) or even Rosales itself, after the rosal bush which lined the roads and with the start of the rainy season had started to bloom with puffy white flowers. They brought with them not just implements from their old villages, but the attitudes of hard work and perseverance that had made them endure.

From Rosales, if they pushed onward to the south, it was to the towns of Nueva Ecija—Cuyapo, Gapan—most of them still surrounded by forests; and to the north, Santa Maria, Tayug; and onward to the Caraballo range, the new settlements of San Nicolas and Natividad. And to the east, Umingan, Lupao, then San

José, the big town that was also a gateway to the valley, for beyond San José, up to the first mountain range that was a barrier
to the valley, was the narrow trough of Santa Fe.

Like most of the new towns, Rosales had no municipal
building except a ramshackle shed near the open market, where,
sometimes, the health inspector conducted what little official
duties he had. There was no telegraph as yet in this part of the
country, no Spanish official. The priest in the new church was
Indio, for the Spanish friars usually stayed in the bigger com-
munities where their quarters were more comfortable and their
meals more nourishing. Civic order was imposed traditionally
by a member of the *principalia,* and in Rosales, this authority
was vested in Don Jacinto, who was not only rich but also educated.

His house stood prominently in the middle of the town, and
from there he dispensed patronage, and like the Indio priest,
was revered for his many acts of kindness to his tenants and
those wayfaring strangers passing through. It was a big house
roofed with tile, and its wide yard was dominated by a balete
tree, massive and brooding, a perpetual abode of spirits and endowed with an awesome talisman. Its trunk was three, even four
times the size of a cartwheel, larger than any of the forest trees
they had passed. The thick veins coiled around it, fat as pythons,
thrust upward and merged with each other, forming a mantle, a
pall, of vivid green.

Across the plaza was the small wooden church with a grass
roof. Istak could put on the soutane and say Mass now for
Ba-ac, for Mayang, but he was not a priest, he was not going to
be a priest. It was getting on toward evening and the Angelus
should soon be tolled. The Indio priest who was pacing
the churchyard walked to where the carts were unhitched in the
shade of the balete tree and asked where they had come from.
The Ilokos, An-no replied politely.

They were Ilokanos; they did not have to be told about the balete tree. In the evening before eating, they would make an offering of food to the spirits. In the old country and here, there were many things that could not be explained. One had to accept them without question, just as one welcomed the morning and recognized God.

Istak would go to Don Jacinto in the morning, tell him what had happened. The work animals were their most precious possessions; he would leave one of the *carabaos* if necessary so that they would not starve.

In the onrushing dusk, he glanced at his arms; they were sunburned. His palms were no longer soft—the few days' work in Po-on, gathering firewood, feeding the *carabaos*, all that had callused his hands. And there would be harder work now that he would really be the farmer he was not meant to be.

No one but he could talk to Don Jacinto. There was not much that the Carmay farmers could tell him except that Don Jacinto had studied in Manila, and that he was rich—as all the few educated people were. He wondered how it would be when he would finally ask for help. Else they would have to eat banana pith and all those weeds meant for pigs.

He pitied Dalin most. She had known only tragedy, and she would be hungry, too. And only because she had elected to cast her lot with them. What more could a man want from a woman but this loyalty?

MORNING stole into Rosales during the rainy season with little sun, but there was the pleasant odor of cooking fires, and the stirring of work animals. The farmers had to go to the sodden fields early to plow, to plant, to watch the seedlings. Then the sun rose, and the grass in the plaza shone; beyond the edge of the plaza were green hedges of rosal in bloom. Dalin had risen earlier and she had again gathered a few of the white blossoms and now, with the flowers in an empty pot, Istak drank the fragrance. She had taken a piece of black cloth, cut it into strips, and pinned it on the sleeves of the menfolk and on the blouses of the women. They could not afford black dresses to wear as emblems of their grief. They would wear these ribbons for a year, after which there would be a *bakas,* the ritual end of mourning.

Istak put on his best trousers and the white shirt that Mayang had woven. His clothes were now tight, but they were all he had.

He was asked by a servant to go up the staircase, so polished that the reddish narra grains shone. The house, though made of stone, was not as big as the houses in Vigan, nor as old; the brick sidings were new and no weeds sprouted from the tile roof as yet. The walls were painted with a lime wash, but with the oncoming rains, the wash had turned a dirty brown.

Inside the house, all the sash windows were wide open, and the waxed floors were solid, thick, and wide, as they were cut from huge tree trunks. The furniture had probably been made in Manila, for the pieces were sturdy but not as well made as some of the furniture in the *kumbento* in Cabugaw, which had come from Europe and was finely crafted, resplendent with gold and silver paint.

He stood in the middle of the *sala,* waiting. Then the rich man came out from one of the rooms.

He was about forty, with patrician features—a thin nose and a wide forehead. He was fair, like most mestizos. It could have been his grandfather—perhaps a Dominican friar? perhaps a Spanish officer? But there was nothing haughty about him. Warmth, welcome lit his eyes, and at once he asked Istak to sit on the wooden chair by the window which opened to the plaza where the carts waited.

"Good morning, Apo," Istak began in greeting. "I am Eustaquio Sal—" He hastily corrected himself. "Eustaquio Samson, Apo. We arrived yesterday and those are our carts."

"Yes," Don Jacinto said. "I saw you when you arrived." He did not waste words. "What is it that you want?"

"We are from Cabugaw, Apo." Istak paused. Did the rich man know? There was no question in his face. "We are planning to go to the valley. But the other day—" He paused again. His lips trembled and his eyes misted. "The other day, when we were crossing the Agno, one of our carts overturned—then it got carried away by a tree that rushed down with the current. My mother—she drowned, Apo."

The rich man's face softened, and immediately Istak saw sympathy in his eyes.

"We also lost all our seed rice in that cart and some of our provisions. It is the rainy season now but we have nothing to plant. And we will be hungry, Apo."

Don Jacinto had listened attentively, then quickly asked, "What do you want now?"

"We would like to borrow grain from you, Don Jacinto. And pay for it with a *carabao* or some of the tobacco that we have."

Don Jacinto stared out of the window at a plaza washed with morning sun and glinting on the new grass. "It is a still a long way to the valley, you know. Rotten trails all the way now that the rains have come. And I am sure, the pass across the mountains in San José would be impassable in parts, very muddy, if not washed away. You can stay here, you know . . ."

Istak looked at the handsome profile. There was kindness and compassion in the man, and Istak knew at once that he could be trusted, mestizo though he was.

"We have to hurry, Don Jacinto," he said evenly. "Even now, I know we have but little time. When the ferry is back . . ."

"Are you fleeing from anyone?" Don Jacinto asked. How quickly the man had guessed their plight! "If you are, you don't have to run anymore. You can hide here, in the forest close to the mountain, in the cogonal near the delta. You must work hard."

Istak did not speak. "My father, they are looking for him, Apo, but he is dead . . ."

Don Jacinto waved a hand and smiled. "Do not tell me why. I can guess the reason. After all, you are not the only ones running away. There are so many of you, and I understand."

"We have no *cédulas,* Apo," Istak said plainly.

Again, the low, pleasant laugh. "Pieces of paper," Don Jacinto said. "You can get new ones here. I'll help you. And if you are worried about having new names—no one need know about this."

Istak was silent. He had said more than he should have but, again, almost instinctively, he knew this man, this rich mestizo, was not like Capitán Berong or any of the mestizos in the Ilokos who flourished because they pandered to the friars. Don Jacinto would not betray them, though he may on occasion have pandered, too.

"I can help you," he continued. "You must help me, too. I have land which I cannot clear or plant because there are not enough hands for it. You can work there . . ." Then he turned to Istak. "There is plenty of land here—across the creek are more cogonals, mounds, many, many trees. They are yours if you can clear them. So why don't you work for me and I will give you all the seed rice you need? There is still time—if you want to stay— to prepare some of the fallow land for planting."

Already, Istak could envision fields of ripening grain, all theirs, and no priest telling them to leave. Already, he could imagine himself building a house, and asking Dalin to live with him.

THE RICH MAN told them to sleep in the large *bodega* roofed with iron sheets beyond the house should the rains come strong in the evening. They could store their things there while they built their houses.

After they had eaten breakfast, all the men went with Don Jacinto beyond the town, onward to the still unplowed farmlands spread on both sides. They reached a small creek, brown and full.

"It dries easily after the rainy season," Don Jacinto explained. "Since this is all rainwater, when it stops raining, the creek becomes shallow and there are places where you can cross on foot, although a simple bamboo bridge would help. You can build a better one when the dry season comes."

A bamboo raft was tethered to a sapling near the bank and they pushed it to the other side; the creek was not really wide, no more than a length of bamboo, and it was not swift the way the Agno was.

Across the creek, more cogon wastes dotted with mounds as far as the eye could see. Don Jacinto described an arc to the right: "All this is my land," he explained. "And beyond the cogonal are swamps—you will see, they never really dry up, even when it does not rain anymore. There are a lot of mudfish there—as big as your legs—and you will always have snails and frogs—if you have the patience to look for them—even in the dry season."

In the horizon, to the west, an uneven line of trees. "When he was a boy, my father planted those to mark where his father had said the land was theirs. It is all recorded in the titles I keep. How can I farm all of this?" He spread out his hands in a gesture of futility. Istak was surprised; Don Jacinto's hands were rough like any farmer's. The rich man knew what he was talking about. More cogonals to the left, and within the near distance, all the way to the foothills of Balungaw mountain, the forest began—a thick, green canopy upon the land, brooding and secret.

"The forest belongs to no one—it is yours to clear if you want. Mark the land you clear. I told you, you don't have to go to the valley. Here there is land for everyone who wants to sweat for it." Turning to Istak, Don Jacinto whispered warmly, "It is also a good place to hide."

Then, as if dragged into some deep misgivings, the rich man's countenance changed. He shook his head, mumbled, then inhaled deeply. The lines in his brow deepened. "I hope I am not giving you false hopes," he said softly, as if in apology. "The most powerful people in this part of the country are the Asperris; they are Spanish, they own whole villages, all the way to Balungaw to the east and Santa Maria to the north. They own the biggest house in this region—you will see it on the way to San Pedro—a castle of a house, with many, many rooms, and a tower—a massive building of brick. They came here much earlier than my grandfather and only God knows if they have title to the mountain, too. I am sure that this land that I am showing you, which I tell you is mine, is really mine. Help me, too, if you can."

They left Don Jacinto by the creek, then they headed toward the forest, beating a path through the high grass, disturbing pigeons in their nests, and gathering their eggs in their palm-leaf hats. Although the rains had come, new cogon shoots had not sprouted yet. If only the sun would shine the whole day and tomorrow, they could set fire to large tracts to make them easier to plow.

They reached the forest before midday, first the primary growth of trees, and as they went deeper, the forest thickened, tall trees blotting out the sun, vines clambering everywhere, the earth damp and wet, smelling of rot and the decaying veneer of the land. When Padre Jose and Istak went to the Bagos, the forest they passed was a fearful domain whose recesses could never be reached, where death could waylay those who did not treat the forest with respect. It was a haven for the Bagos, who knew how to live from its surfeit, a sanctuary to the *remontados* who had escaped the wrath of the Spanish. It was neither haven nor threat—it was an enemy to be vanquished, and the conquest must be complete—not a single tree must stand so that the good earth would yield its blessings at last. Grimly, Istak recalled what the old men of Po-on had said, how they, too, had cleared the lands below the Cordillera. They had poured their sweat, even their blood, into each patch. And how did it all end for them? For Ba-ac? The land belonged to the King of Spain—all of it, and the King's ministers were the friars—it was they who benefited from the land for which they had shed not a drop of sweat.

But he was not here to question, no matter how painful the memory. There was power which was man's, and there was power which was God's alone.

At Vespers that evening, Istak went to the church. Like most of the churches of the new towns which they had passed, the church in Rosales was quite small, unlike the stone churches in the Ilokos. The floor was hardened earth—it would be some time before the town would be prosperous enough to have a church of brick. How would he ever thank God for their new fortune? Dalin, most of all? He owed her his life. What, after all, was belief or faith? It was easy for Jesus to want to live, not die, but He died. Did He know He would rise from the dead? His agony was real. So, then, perhaps it is faith that is tested, not by those who will kill for it but by those who will die for it. I have not lost faith, Istak cried within himself. I will always be under this holy roof, but not under the bell.

Yet now, more than at any other time, this implacable sorrow hounded him—the knowledge that they were forced to leave the warm womb of home that had nourished them. If they had not left, if they had not been ordered to depart immediately, surely Ba-ac and Mayang would still be alive. Was all this part of a divine plan which no man, least of all himself, could sunder?

I have always worshipped You according to Your rules, given You proper obeisance, and still You were unmindful of Your son in his hour of need. Where, then, did they all go—my hours of penance? Were they lost in the ether? But You are wise and ever-present like the air I breathe. You snatched me from Death once, and perhaps will again, and still again. And each time Your gift of life is renewed, I stray further from You. What really was my suffering? How could it ever compare with what You suffered on the cross? You have tested me and though I have faltered many times, still I have been true. There must be some deeper reason why I am this way, why men commit themselves to something they cannot touch or see. If You are the God of my people, how could You also be the God of those who oppress us?

He had not cried when his mother died, and now Istak wept, the tears burning in his eyes. All the bruises that had hurt in the last few days became this vise clamped upon his chest.

His mother. His father. They had paid dearly. Their flight had come to an end.

IT DID NOT rain that night, so they did not go to Don Jacinto's storehouse to sleep; it was wide and empty until the next harvest season, when it would be full again with the rich man's share of the harvest.

After supper, they gathered around Dalin's cart, now Istak's as well. Above it, from a low branch of the balete tree, a lamp dangled and lighted up their faces, work-weary—yet alight with hope. The children had all been put to bed, but the older ones were awake, trying to listen to what was being said.

"You have seen the forest," Istak said. "It will take us years before we can clear it."

"We will burn the trees during the dry season," Kardo, the youngest brother of Ba-ac, said. He had some experience clearing the forest beyond Cabugaw.

"We will plant whatever we can in the land we clear," An-no said. "We will trap the wild pigs and deer that will come to destroy the crops, and we will raise our families here," he continued, his eyes touching Orang, beside Dalin at the other end of the circle. She had overcome her shame and no longer kept to herself. Dalin had drawn her out slowly. In the tawny light of the lamp, her long hair shone.

Orang's voluble father did not say much this time. "Though we did not start with you in Cabugaw, we have shared many things—we traveled as one family. I think we should continue this way. When we start building our houses, we should all be neighbors."

"What shall we call our village? Shall we name it after a saint? Or after a flower the way this town is named?" Bit-tik spoke eagerly.

"I should not have brought posts from the old house," Blas continued. "They remind me of where I came from."

Indeed, there was enough mature bamboo for posts. There were the trees in the forest to use as timber. And cogon for roofs. They would just build huts now; the planting was more important, and after the harvest, they would build their permanent homes.

"Our village should be close to the creek. We could bathe our work animals there. We should have a street which we hope will someday be wide enough and long enough to lead to town. We have to sell what we cannot eat or use," Istak said.

Kardo added: "We will dig a well in the middle of the village, and when we have enough money, we will line it with brick so that it will not cave in."

"And we will have a fiesta, too, don't forget that." Blas started to gush. "And we will have a patron saint, just like Rosales has San Antonio de Padua. This is Istak's choice—I will sing the *dal-lot* and compose new poems. I will celebrate our journey, retell vicissitudes we suffered and how we surmounted them all, no matter how sad and painful. This, after all, is our own calvary, is it not so, Istak? And during the Holy Week, I will sing the *pasyon* in a way you have never heard before. Orang—daughter of mine, are you listening? She has the best voice in all Candon and she can sing very well. I have taught her well . . ."

"But what will we *call* our barrio?" Bit-tik was insistent.

"Cabugawan," Istak said simply.

Part

TWO

A ND SO the rains came, and the typhoons and the floods as well, and after the rains, the drought—a cycle blessed with God's bounty and damned by His negligence.

They persevered. In the evenings, the cogonal distances crackled with huge bursts of fire which quickly died, for that was the way the wild grass burned. That was the way—so the Spaniards said—the Indios also behaved, with rash and easily spent enthusiasms. The cogonals they cleared yielded to their will. These lands had never been plowed before—the roots of the wild cogon had bored deep and wide into the soil and many a time a plowshare would snap as it lost in the constant wrestling with the stubborn mesh. All of them also worked parcels in Don Jacinto's land, and here they did not have too many difficulties; the land had been planted before and had merely lain fallow; the soil yielded smoothly to the plow.

The rats did not multiply as fast as they were warned would happen. For one, the rats were herded into bamboo traps—lured there with grain and beaten to death. They were as big as cats, and were skinned carefully, dried in the sun or broiled in open fires, their fat sizzling on the coals. Like chicken, they all said.

They rose earlier than the sun and, having vanquished the wild grass, pushed the forest farther. What they could not cut they burned, leaving some trees as markers of their property.

Snakes lurked in the mounds which dotted the plain. Some of these mounds were spared as markers, too, and the others were leveled after the appropriate prayers so that there would be more land to till.

At night, if there was a moon, they plowed or harrowed, and dug the ditches that would bring water to the fields. In the flooded paddies, frogs were plentiful and they filled the night with their croaking. It was easy to catch them—they seemed mesmerized by the light of the lanterns and they were brought back in strings for the women to skin.

Even in a year of bad weather, the harvest was abundant in the lands of Don Jacinto; half was theirs, which was good. The harvest was niggardly in the newer land, but all of it was theirs, which was even better.

With Istak, time hardly mattered anymore, only work. The blisters in his palms had long since hardened into calluses. He had ceased wearing slippers after he left the sacristy; his soles had thickened and could no longer be easily punctured by thorns. His muscles became hard as stone and he sometimes marveled at his strength, how he could now lift the wooden mortar all by himself and how long he could endure the sun or the continuous rain that sent the other farmers home shivering, their skin wrinkled by the cold. He liked the cold more than the heat;

the water dripped through his palm-leaf hat and palm-leaf cloak, his lips lost their color, but he worked on, sometimes thinking of what awaited him at home, steaming ginger broth flavored with cane sugar. And Dalin—the sweet peace with which she always welcomed him.

As in the planting and harvesting, they helped one another build their permanent homes near the creek. The houses were bigger than their first huts, with posts of sagat, some of which they dragged down from the foothills of Balungaw. They fenced their yards with split bamboo and planted fruit trees in them. Farmers in Carmay whom they befriended helped in the harvest. They gathered the ripening gelatinous grain and roasted it over slow-burning strips of old bamboo that had rotted and dried.

Istak and Dalin were married the month they arrived in Rosales, and a year after, An-no and Orang. There would have been no wedding feast, for Istak had nothing, but Don Jacinto, who was their godfather, gave them a goat to butcher.

An-no was better prepared. Not only had he built a new house by then, he had also raised two pigs for the wedding feast.

Orang's father declaimed, his rich, loud voice drowning the babble of children and women, and they paused to listen to his exultation:

I have raised this tender plant, lavished it with care
Now, the plant is as beautiful as the morning,
Now, it is in bloom, and someday will bear fruit
This is the rich reward of parenthood—
To see the young plants grow, then give them away
When the time comes, just as I give you away,
Fair Leonora, to a man worthy of you
Strong provider and brave protector. May you, Mariano,

Remember we love her more than you ever will
And someday, soon, may we see the fruits of your love
May they grow into beautiful plants . . . our grandchildren.

The women wept.

MORE LAND waited for those who were willing to go to the east
toward Balungaw mountain, but that land belonged to the Asperris, who had come to Rosales way back when most of it was
wilderness still. The family lived in Manila, although at the eastern end of the town they maintained a massive stone house that
was more of a *bodega* than a residence. Spanish friars and officers visited the house sometimes, but no one was known to stay
there permanently. When the Manila landlord came, bright
lights bloomed from within, raucous laughter rang out, and at
the landing stood a line of black carriages drawn by handsome
Abra ponies. When Istak passed it, he was reminded of Capitán
Berong, his tremendous wealth and his three daughters, and yes,
Carmencita—she must have children by now, maybe a dozen
handsome bastards, and again the ancient feelings were recalled.

How fortunate that they came upon the free land Don Jacinto had shown to them. Istak had studied it before they started
clearing—the limits to what was flat, a slow rise of ground with
three huge mounds overgrown with grass. He must be generous
to his brothers, his cousins, his uncles. When they parceled out
the land the lots with mounds went to him.

"This portion I could make into a *bangcag*," he explained.
"Plant vegetables, fruit trees. Bit-tik and An-no are tired of working on such land; with level fields they could grow rice."

Dalin helped in the clearing. By the second year, the bamboo which Istak had planted as boundary to his *bangcag* had

taken root and soon there would be shoots to harvest for food. He had planted three species—kiling for fences; siitan, which was thorny, for size and strength; and bayog, which when cut into strips while still tender would make good twine, but once mature it made good house posts, so thick and sturdy bugs could not destroy it.

SILVESTRE, otherwise known as Bit-tik, was taller and hand-somer than his two brothers. His brow was wide, his shoulders broad, and he walked straight. He seemed strong enough to lift a water buffalo, but with all his attributes he was not really in-terested in farming. He worked his plot of rice land poorly, let-ting weeds grow and the water escape from gaps in the dikes he did not repair, so that his harvest was often the poorest in all Cabugawan. He was fond of traveling and had gone beyond the nearby villages and well into the other towns—Alcala, Villasis, Balungaw—not so much in search of adventure or opportunities as simply because the spell of new places, new people, attracted him. It was logical for his relatives to assume that he would be paired off with Sabel, Orang's younger sister, and Istak and his uncle Blas had talked all too often of this possibility in the near future. But Bit-tik seldom paid attention to the young woman, who had now blossomed as handsomely as Orang.

There was enough to eat in Cabugawan and Bit-tik had no family, so they let him wander where he pleased and be their eyes to the strange new dimension beyond Rosales. After three or four days he would return with a few things, dried fish or dried meat, a basket, and most important for Istak, news about their neighboring towns and villages, if the Guardia was on the prowl, and if there were better places where they could flee.

Dalin and Orang often cooked his ration, usually gelatinous

rice boiled in coconut milk—it would keep for three days—dried meat already roasted, and a cake of cane sugar.

On this trip, Bit-tik started in the deep, deep dawn. By late afternoon he was in Tayug, a town as decrepit as Rosales but much closer to the Caraballo mountains, which were a high green wall to the east. It was his first visit to the place. It was Sunday, a market day, but this late in the day, all the people from the nearby villages had gone, and the merchants had already loaded their bolts of cloth, mosquito netting, salted fish, soap, and other goods into their carts.

A few shops near the plaza were open, selling sugar cane, vinegar, *basi*, salted fish, cigarettes, and *galletas*. He met the two young men in one of the shops. They were looking for matches but it was one of those times when the supply had run out. As it often was in the villages, the farmers had to have a log in their stoves smoldering the whole day if there were no matches. The two men were poorly garbed, their *carzoncillos* brown with dirt, their hair in need of trimming. Both carried spears, which were their walking sticks. Obviously, they came from the mountain. Though neither could have been more than twenty, their faces looked old, disfigured by smallpox craters that seemed to merge into one another. Even their lips were pocked.

Having heard them, Bit-tik gladly offered the extra box of matches he always carried. They had little money; they had come to Tayug to sell dried meat and mountain fish preserved in fermented rice, and the big jars which they carried slung by a rattan net on their shoulders were filled with salt which they would bring back to their village.

"You don't have to pay me for this," Bit-tik said as they walked out of the store. Bit-tik was planning to sleep that evening in one of the sheds by the church.

"Where do you come from?" he asked. "I have no place for the night, and I have to heat roasted meat for supper."

The two men looked at each other. Their Ilokano was accented—they could be from the big valley, Bit-tik surmised. He had heard that accent before from the people in the valley who had gone down to buy salt in Pangasinan.

"Come with us and share our humble home," the taller of the two said with downcast eyes. He seemed shy facing people; with that kind of face, Bit-tik understood.

The afternoon was now cool, the plaza where the merchants had finished packing their goods was empty but for the scraps of trash they had left. "It is a long walk, but perhaps you will want to visit with us . . ."

And why not? Bit-tik had never been apprehensive about going with strangers; there was in his manner a disarming friendliness. Besides, what did he have to lose? Pieces of dried meat, *suman*, and the shabby clothes on his back? He was not a profitable prey for any *bandido*.

"I will go with you," Bit-tik said quickly.

He was not rested yet after the long hike from Rosales and he was going on another long walk. They headed toward the Caraballo range—the mountains loomed so near but they were still a distance away. "There, there." One of the newfound friends pointed his spear to a foothill; behind it the mountains burned with the gold of the setting sun. "Beyond that is where we live. Are you really sure you would like to come? We want you to come—and know this, not many have visited us, even the people in Tayug. You must have noticed how they regarded us as Bagos. We are not . . ."

"Forgive those who are ignorant," Bit-tik said.

It was already dark when they started climbing, first through cogonals along frequented paths that were distinct in the afterglow.

He marveled at their strength. They had carried those jars strapped to their backs for a long time. Even empty, they could weigh a man down and drive welts on the shoulders where the rattan web was strapped. In a while, the stars swarmed out of the sky; there was no moon and the mountain became alive with the call of night birds, the celebration of insects. He had done much walking on level ground and he realized that though he was as strong as a water buffalo, he would tire after every brief but steep ascent while his two companions, even with their heavy loads of salt, seemed to glide easily up the incline. The trail vanished altogether and the forest dropped on them like a giant pall, forbidding and black. The stars that once glimmered above had disappeared. Sometimes there would be a spot of greenish glow—ghostly yet ethereal, the sudden shrieks of birds disturbed in their roosts. They shook him and sent a quiver to his heart. His new friends seemed to sense his apprehension, for they started a familiar song which he knew, although the words as he remembered them were all earthy and impolite: *Pamuli-nawen . . . pamulinawen . . .*

The forest was drenched with the odor of moss, dead leaves, and rot, and he wondered if there would be pythons hiding, too, waiting to strike. The two did not seem worried—they knew the uncharted way as if by instinct and as they told him afterward, the warm, delicious smell of home guided them.

Toward midnight, he asked them if he could rest once again, for his legs were already numb. And God, he was thirsty. One of them left, then returned with what seemed like a short length of bamboo cut on one end. He raised it to his lips and the water was sweet, almost like the water of a young coconut. They let him sleep briefly, then he was awakened, refreshed, and ready to challenge the mountain again.

They knew their way through the densest gloom. It was as if at every turn an emerald swamp opened up to swallow them and they had become the foliage itself, alive in the moss-covered trunks, in the roots entwined with one another, in the giant ferns that brooded around them.

The east started to glimmer, and the tiny patches of sky turned into bronze, the lofty trees took shape, their leaves started to glisten as morning poured upon the range. It was then, too, that they broke through the last curtain of trees. Before them spread a wide valley, a stream running through, and in the middle, a village, the smoke of cooking fires curling above the grass roofs. Coming as he did from the bowels of night, he could feel mist gathering in his eyes; before him, the glorious beauty of creation, all that he would have wanted to live with if Cabugawan did not have a claim on him.

They raced down the mountain, through fields of young rice plants watered by springs and well-groomed plots being prepared for planting. At the edge of the fields were pits covered with leaves. Bit-tik was warned about them—they were traps for wild pigs and deer which ravaged the ripening grain.

They passed houses, heard the laughter of children but there was no one at the windows. Sometimes a figure would dart way ahead into a house, a woman in a skirt, her hair shining in the sun, or a boy, half naked, but no one came out to greet them. They took him to the biggest house at the far end of the village, apart from the other dwellings.

"This is where Apo Diego lives," he was told. "We will leave you here so you can eat and rest."

He went up the bamboo stair into a wide room floored with solid planks that were roughly hewn. The grass roof was so thick, Bit-tik was sure it could last a hundred years. On the low eating table, as if it had just been placed there, was a plate of steaming rice, pieces of dried meat, slices of tomato, and yes, real coffee—its aroma seducing him. Surely the food was for him. He sat down and started to eat. He didn't stop till he was full, yet no one came out to meet him. "They must be asleep still," he told himself, and reclining on the floor, he gazed out of the open doorway at the fields slumbering in the morning sun, heard again the happy voices of children, although he couldn't see them. A sweet, dreamlike peace came over him like a deluge and he was soon asleep.

IT WAS LATE in the afternoon when he woke. Close by, squatting on the wooden floor, was an old man whose hair was white and long; it flowed past his nape and down his back. The old man's face was lined with deep furrows. His clothes were coarse, almost like sackcloth, but they were neat and seemed newly washed.

"You must be rested now," he said, smiling. His voice was almost like a woman's, soft and warm, not gravelly or raspy.

The old man rose and turned to the open doorway. Beyond, the valley basked in the last light of day.

"Thank you very much, Apo," Bit-tik said, "for the good breakfast, the sleep that I needed."

The old man told him how they, too, descended from the Ilokos a long time ago; no one in the original caravan was left— just him. At first, the Bagos made war on them, and many on both sides were killed. In time, the settlers made peace and learned to live with the Bagos, but by then it was difficult for complete mutual trust to develop. There was much suffering— although there was enough for everyone, the Igorots worried that their lands were being snatched, and the settlers, who believed they had finally fled Spanish tyranny, had simply found another vicious enemy.

They had wanted to go into the deepest jungle, where the Spaniards could not reach them, nor could the big men in the

towns who made them work without pay. They could go no farther. Life was difficult. They worked hard enlarging their clearings, and the forest became a benefactor, a provider of meat, and
most important, a sanctuary, finally.

"Why did you leave the Ilokos, Apo?" It was a question he
should not have asked. Perhaps the old man had killed a priest
or a Spanish officer as his father had.

"I am Diego Silang," the old man replied quietly, firmly.

From the deepest recesses of his mind, Bit-tik dredged up
the name. As a boy, he had heard it spoken with awe, this brazen
Ilokano who dared oppose the Spaniards and set up a fragile
Indio government with Ilokano laws and an Ilokano army to replace the bulwarks of stone the friars had built. But Diego Silang
was betrayed and killed, and his followers were disbanded, persecuted, and slaughtered.

To Bit-tik's incredulous look, the old man had an answer:
"You're thinking, I am an old fool. How can I be Diego Silang,
when he died long ago? But his spirit lives and it came to me,
became me. How old do you think I really am? They are all gone
who joined me in the beginning. I am alone now and the young
people—they are our grandchildren and great-grandchildren. I
worshipped Diego Silang's memory, just as I worshipped all the
men who fought for our freedom. What Diego Silang believed I
also believe with all my soul. I believe that this land, this water,
this air we breathe—they are God's gift to all men and cannot
belong to just a few merely because they are white or wear the
cloth. So we honor all those who have died for this belief. Here,
we prepare for the day when we will be ready and strong to
strike again. We are not alone. Beyond this mountain are people
like us and still more people like us in the valleys beyond. They
may not recognize their poor, oppressed brothers elsewhere.
Someday they will. Then we will leave this valley and with our

prayers, we will defeat the ones who despoiled our land and robbed us."

DUSK AGAIN, thirst and hunger again. In the dimness that was quietly descending upon the valley, they now came out—the children and women, and in the yard of Apo Diego's house, they built a bonfire and gathered around it to share its warmth, for a chill breeze had come with the night.

"You have seen how fecund the land is," Apo Diego said softly. "Let me convince you to remain here, to live with us and share our sorrows, our joys."

From the rear of the house, a group of women emerged. They set the low eating table again with roasted meat, a bowl of steaming rice, and roasted green peppers. There was also a plate of greens. It tasted like saluyot but was not slippery. The women who served him turned their faces away. While he gazed at the bonfire as the children and people gathered around it, he realized why they hid themselves when he arrived, just as the women now, even in the faint light, could not face him. All their faces were horribly scarred by smallpox, the scourge leaving craters so deep and large.

"You will not be lonely here," the old man was saying. "We have so few men left. Then came this terrible plague. We have more women now than men . . ."

In the golden glow of the bonfire, he could see them clearly. Those girls, how they must have looked before the dreaded disease had swept over their valley.

"The women are industrious," the old man said. "They know how to weave, to care for plants, and to raise children. . . . I can see in your face that you are a seeker, that you will travel distances to find happiness. Stay with us. Every day brings something new. You need not search further for your fate, or for God."

For a long while, Bit-tik did not speak.

In his mind's eye, the Agno again—so wide and harsh—how they crossed this last barrier to Cabugawan, his brothers, the land they had cleared together, the kindly neighbors. He belonged to Cabugawan now. Bit-tik talked about his village, his brother who spoke Spanish and Latin, who cured the sick with his herbs and prayers. Did anyone in the valley speak Spanish or Latin at all?

The old man nodded. "Diego Silang does," he said simply. Then he asked Bit-tik if he could read and write, and Bit-tik proudly said he could.

"That is very good." The old man was enthusiastic. "We will need wisdom to defeat our enemies. Even now, they are plotting against us, seeking to dislodge us from this land which we carved from the forest. Two more hands here can do so much."

Bit-tik could only think of Cabugawan, and yes—Sabel, who he knew would always be there when he needed her. That was ordained by the stars.

"I am thinking of a woman I left in Cabugawan," Bit-tik said, feeling uncomfortable that he could not give the old man a better reason.

The old man brought in a jar covered with dried banana leaves and told him to drink his fill of *basi*. The *basi* tasted so good, unlike any he had had in the past. It was slightly bitter but it must be a special brew. He reminisced and felt completely at ease telling the old man about his father's searing hatred for the friars and why they had to flee Po-on.

His eyes began to sink, the bonfire in the yard seemed to grow smaller and dimmer, the voices of people became muted. He was feeling drowsy, so he lay down on the floor, yet struggled to keep his eyes open. Through the blur of oncoming sleep, he saw six women surround him just as the light from the oil lamp on the low eating table flickered and died. He did not object when they started to undress him. He remembered embracing each one, though he was already half asleep. Six of them, and to each he gave his seed. Then all was blissful ignorance, the deep, deep quietude of dreamless sleep.

HE WOKE UP; his head had become a heavy rock, his eyes blinded by dazzling light. He closed his eyes quickly and in the red orb before him, he remembered what had transpired. He opened his eyes again. He was in the shade of a giant narra tree and when he rose in what seemed to be unfamiliar surroundings, he saw the spire of the church of Tayug in the near distance. To his right, the green of the Caraballo range. It was late afternoon and the sun shone fully on his face. Beside him was their parting gift, an earthen pot filled with mountain fish in fermented rice.

His legs were wobbly, but he regained his balance after the first few steps. The heaviness in his head disappeared. He walked toward the town, wondering if it was all a dream. And for the first time, he realized that he wanted to go back to Apo Diego, to the valley and its beautiful peace. He gazed at the mountains where they had started on the long hike and quickly realized that he would not be able to retrace the way through the labyrinthine maze. With a sense of elation he remembered the women who had caressed him. Did it happen at all? It was his first time ever, and there were six he had embraced, not just one. It could not be real! It was one of those grand illusions that only *basi* could inflict upon the mind. He untied the cotton string of his long *carzoncillo* and looked at his limp penis. He smiled to himself—it was no dream at all.

ALL THE WAY to Cabugawan, through a humid, cloudless night, he thought of things to say to Sabel, for he would really pay court to her, build a house for her, and not live with his brother. He was man enough now to settle down. And all he had to do was ask his uncle Blas.

It was about Sabel that Orang spoke first that morning when he arrived to share their breakfast. Sabel was gone—she had eloped the day previous with a farmer from Carmay. The wedding would be next week.

"It was not a dream, Manong," Bit-tik told Istak. He showed the small jar of fish in fermented rice which they left beside him. It was the best Dalin ever had.

"Could a spirit enter another human being and give it a purpose?" Bit-tik was anxious to know.

"Yes, it is possible," Istak said after a while, "for a man to welcome into his mind and heart any spirit, a belief, a faith that was expressed in thought and deed by another man. If the receptacle is clean, I think wonders can be achieved. Is this what you are looking for?"

Bit-tik shook his head, "I don't know, Manong."

"You must not wander too often now," Istak advised.

He valued Istak's advice, so he made plans to build himself a house, and in the next few weeks, he roamed the forest beyond the farm looking for sagat trees for posts. He found them, cut them, and waited for them to dry. It was not difficult to gather cogon for the roof, buri palm leaves for the walls, and bamboo for the floors. And when anyone built a house, the neighbors always helped, and their only pay was the day's meal.

Bit-tik did not build his house. The small first hut that he built looked like a beggar's hut beside the new and bigger homes. A gust of wind could blow it down. An-no added a large room to his house, then told his brother to move in with them.

Bit-tik continued his wandering and journeyed to Tayug again in the hope that he would meet once more the young men who had taken him to their distant valley. He asked the people in the marketplace if they had ever come down again. No one knew—in fact, the people of Tayug knew little of what was beyond the mountains except that it was forbidding and hostile, and the only people who lived there were the Bagos and those who had become savages.

He returned to Cabugawan more subdued than ever. If Dalin and Istak asked him the usual question about when he would finally bring a woman home, he had the same answer, "Maybe when the crow turns white."

As Orang surmised, he truly loved Sabel and could not find someone to replace her.

THERE WERE occasions when thoughts of the past crowded Istak's mind. During Holy Week in the year Bit-tik told him about the valley high up in the Caraballo range, he remembered the journal he had left in Cabugaw and what his uncle Blas had said about how he would compose a poem about their journey. Hearing the *pasyon* sung by Orang, listening to her relate the suffering of Christ at the hands of His own brethren, and His betrayal, he relived the past, its sorrow and fear. Listening to Orang, tears burned in his eyes.

Yet, there was comfort in the convent, the certitude not only of God's presence and the beneficence that Padre Jose had selflessly given. The church was once a redoubt against the violence of Muslim raids, so why could it not be a haven from injustice itself?

IT FINALLY CAME during their fourth year in the new land. First, it was just some rumor brought by Blas, who went to town on Sundays—the market day—to look at farm implements, gossip, and get a little drunk in the *tienda* there. They were idling in the village yard—the evening was young and a full moon adorned the sky. The children were playing, and their shouts and laughter decorated the vast stillness of the night.

They were talking softly; the planting season would soon be upon them. Though there were still wilds to clear, life already had a distinct, well-ordered pattern that could be rent only by nature's vagaries.

"In the market this morning," Blas said, pausing to spit out the wad of tobacco he had been chewing since after supper, "I heard this salted-fish merchant from Dagupan say there is a plague in the south—and it is spreading to the north. Some towns in Cavite already have it. People die in just two days—they vomit and defecate continuously until there is no more body to them."

Istak tensed; it was the dreaded cholera, for which there was no cure, just as it had been with the pox which infected all Cabugaw when he was still a boy just starting out as an acolyte. His family had survived it; would they survive cholera? Always, like some thorn embedded in the flesh that hurt when memory stirred, he would remember the weeping of people, the bodies with ripe, red sores, the pus oozing out of them. At first it was just three or four deaths in a day, then it was ten or twenty, then fifty—and all had to be buried hastily. "The cholera is worse," Padre Jose had said, tears streaming down his craggy face. "Perhaps we have not been Christian enough." And again and again, he heard the old priest intone sadly, dully: "It is the hand of God."

The very night Blas told them about the plague, Istak had a dream.

He was harvesting the grain, but every time he stooped with the scythe, the stalks in his hands turned to ash and the whole field became an expanse of black.

He was now running away from it, and someone was chasing him, the footfalls behind him growing louder and louder although he was already faster than the deer. Then, on his head a huge hand rested. He stopped and turned to look at what he knew was a giant behind him, but there was no one there and no matter how quickly he turned around, he could not see who was behind him, although he could hear the gusty breathing and feel the great hand clamped on his head.

He ran again, his limbs racing the wind, but still the hand rested on his head, and behind him, the laughing, mocking voice: You cannot run away from destiny.

His legs began to feel like logs. You are not destiny, Istak shouted.

Then who am I?

The devil!

And if I am the devil, what am I trying to do?

You know that I have wavered in my faith, you want me on your side.

Istak slowed into a wearied walk. More derisive laughter behind him, and again he turned abruptly to confront his tormentor, but whoever he was, he was quicker and was behind Istak again.

I am not the devil, the booming voice said. And I will prove to you I am not. Tomorrow, when you waken, there will be a guava branch in your yard. Boil its leaves—the broth can heal the sick. Its fruits though sour can fill the stomach. Plant it in your *bangcag*. You have three mounds there. You will know which mound to select—dig a hole before it. There will be a treasure there and the guardian of this treasure will test your courage. I do not know if you will pass. If you do, plant the twig close by. It will prove to you that I am neither the devil nor his disciple. I am God's messenger and you will use all His gifts when the time comes.

Liar! Istak screamed, and again he twisted around. The hand was no longer on his head but there was no one behind him either. The voice!

He remembered it then; it was old Padre Jose's.

MORNING CAME to Cabugawan with the splendor of May; mayas chirping on the grass roof, and beyond the open window, the bamboo bending to a breeze, the chicken cackling in the yard. It all came back with the urgency of birth or death or whatever could shake the world, for there on the ground was the guava twig that he had seen in his dream, only it seemed bigger, its leaves fuller and greener.

He rushed down and picked it up with trembling hands, raised it to the sun, bent it. Yes, it was real, and to Bit-tik, who was then starting out, he asked if there was anyone who had come that morning to the village to visit, any of the children . . .

The children? But they were all still asleep; they had not breakfasted yet.

This cannot be, this cannot be; this is reality and what I saw was a dream.

He hurried back to the house and to Dalin, who stirred from their mat, he said, "I must do some digging in the *bangcag*." He wanted to explain to her what had happened, but anxiety prodded him. He wanted to know the verity of what lurked in the depths of his mind, what sorcery it was that placed the twig in his yard, for surely it would now reveal itself in the hole he would dig.

The farm was but a short distance from the village. The saplings he had planted here—catuday, marunggay, sineguelas, pomelo—they were bigger now. The mound to which instinct guided him relentlessly was the farthest of the three; twice as tall as he, and crowned with tough ledda grass.

He had brought a spade and a crowbar to loosen the tough earth. He was so intent with his digging he was unconscious to all the world until a sharp hissing shocked him to attention. He breathed deeply, stood erect, and looked for the source of the sound. Then he saw it, close to the base of the mound, but almost as tall as he, this cobra, its shining body almost as big as his leg, its hood now spread—so big, remembering it afterward convinced him it was as wide as a winnowing basket, its eyes glaring at him, its fangs bared.

The guardian of the treasure! And briefly he felt that instant of emptiness within him when he faced the gun of the Spanish officer. It was not quite the same feeling, though, and knowing that he was defenseless, that the doom which stared at him with beady eyes could strike before he could move, he remembered the dream, the courage that he must show. He stood motionless. The liturgy! Padre Jose repeating solemnly, *Kyrie eleison, Christe eleison*—his heart thumping wildly now, his arms nerveless now. *Christe eleison* again, this time the words taking shape, a hoarse whisper. *Christe eleison*—this time loud enough for him to hear himself. Then, it happened. The hood which had expanded to the breadth of a winnowing basket started to contract, the head started to sway sideways, the fangs withdrew and the huge snake sank to the earth then slithered into the hole from whence it had come.

Istak breathed deeply, drawing in huge drafts of the good, sweet air; he started to sweat, and his legs felt watery. He wanted to run but could not move, his whole body was numb. The air that had rushed to his lungs reminded him that he was alive, with no venom clotting his arteries, stopping his heart.

The guardian had tested him and he had passed.

In a while, his strength and command of his senses returned. But doubts tugged at him, told him he should leave im-

mediately, forget the dream, the treasure, and even his farm itself. What if there was gold beneath his feet? Or some talisman
which was reserved for him alone? Think of your wife, your relatives, and how their lives could be made better. Think.

He grabbed the crowbar and started to dig, scooping up the
hard crust of earth which he had loosened. Already, he had dug
up to his knees and still there was nothing solid to stop him. The
earth began to get soft, then wet, and it was soon muddy. Still,
he persisted; he was down to his waist when the mud erupted
into a bubbling spring. He had cracked the casement open and
water gushed upward so that the hole started to fill.

Water! Life! Istak turned skyward to a sun which now
burned in the cloudless sky, and thanked God for this gift. The
farm would not be infertile, then. About ten feet from the spring,
he dug another hole and stuck the guava twig into it. Then, with
the spade, he filled the hole with mud from the spring. The twig
would not grow, he told himself; but after what had happened,
he knew that here in Cabugawan, in this new Po-on, anything
was possible.

CHAPTER

11

T HE FIRST TIME—there is always the first time when recognition and discovery come. The knowledge brings the inner vision with which even the blind can see, and reality is no longer something to touch but to covet. Here it was, then, the first time that Istak realized that he could heal, and with it, the exaltation that he had become not a destroyer but what he had always hoped to be, a giver of life.

In November, on the day of the dead, the three brothers journeyed to the Agno. The river was no longer swollen, for the rains had dwindled and the sun came out steady and strong. The few plots planted to the three-month rice had already been harvested, and along the way, they came across Ilokanos who had come down from the north to help in the main harvest. They would stay on to glean the fields.

Every November Istak went to the river, and again he carried a length of siitan which he would cut and make into a small raft when he reached the riverbank. Dalin had prepared the usual offering—a coconut bowl of soft sticky rice cooked in coconut milk. A shelled hard-boiled egg was embedded in the middle, and beside the coconut bowl Istak would place a hand-rolled cigar and a betel nut; then he would put a lighted candle atop the raft and its offering, pray the Rosary, and let the raft float down with the current. Somewhere, amid the reeds or deep in the murk and loam of the great river, Mayang's spirit would know she was remembered.

They had done all this and now it was high noon—time for the lunch of rice with strips of dried deer meat which Dalin had wrapped in banana leaves, time to dive again for those sticks of pine washed down from the mountain. Thrice a year they went to this river for kindling wood to ease the kitchen chores through the soggy days of the rainy season. When the winds were gusty and the oil lamps would flicker, then dim, the lighted pine splinter gave a steady, sooty flame.

The river was clearer. It eddied slowly—a green and living thing. There was hardly any spot now where the water was higher than a man's head and they could explore the bottom with their feet. It was easy to recognize the driftwood they were after. With a bolo Bit-tik skimmed off the veneer. Pine wood was always scented and yellowish.

By midafternoon they had gathered enough kindling pine and the bull cart was half full with driftwood as well. The sun blazed down, and beyond Carmay they rested in the shade of an acacia tree.

An-no was in the cart, holding the reins of the *carabao*. He turned to Istak suddenly and shook his head. "There is something wrong with me," he said. "I feel dizzy, and my head seems to be splitting apart."

Istak felt his brother's temple—indeed, it was hot, although they were in the shade. And his pulse was beating very fast. "It must have been the coldness of the river," Istak said. "Or it must have been something you ate this morning." What could his brother have eaten in Cabugawan that he himself had not?

He made An-no lie down on the floor of the cart and over his face he laid a banana leaf to shield him from the afternoon sun. Then An-no rose quickly and retched.

That night, back in Cabugawan, An-no could not sleep. Orang and the two small children gathered around him, watching him vomit and defecate in the *batalan*. Toward early dawn, when his vomit was nothing more than water, chills shook him. They called Istak, who told them to cover him with blankets until the chills subsided. In the morning, An-no was as pale as a cadaver, and seeing him thus, Istak told them all to leave the house so that he could minister to his brother alone.

All that he had learned in Cabugaw came to mind—the medicinal plants, the human body, even astronomy—all the minutiae that Padre Jose had taught him. But of what use were these if it was the spirit of the river that had been displeased?

Then he remembered the guava which he had planted near the spring, the spring which he had dug by the mound and which was now funneled by a series of bamboo tubes to irrigate his farm and to water the tuber pond.

He rushed down and ran to the *bangcag* with an earthen jar which he filled with water. And from the guava tree which had grown he gathered a handful of young leaves, and with these he went back, told An-no's wife to boil the leaves, and have him drink as much of the brew as his stomach could hold.

A weak, almost lifeless man—his head held up by his wife—An-no took short drafts of the brew, then lay down. Squatting on the bamboo floor beside him, Istak closed his eyes in prayer. And in that small damp room smelling of tobacco and sweat and imminent death, he was catapulted to another time and place, to a vast white void where he was surrounded by luminous unearthly shapes as if he were within a cloud, and he was stretching his arms, beseeching, asking the unknown around him for his brother's life.

When he opened his eyes again, they were all in the room—Bit-tik, the children, Orang, even Dalin—all staring at him as if he were some apparition. And beside him, An-no—the color returned to his skin, his eyes open, too, as if he had just wakened. He asked softly if there was food in the kitchen.

The following day they brought a four-year-old boy to Istak—the son of his own cousin. His belly was swollen. Istak knew at once it was not air, worms, or food, but a boil that must be lanced.

He looked within himself, at the new life he had obtained for An-no; it was not just the guava leaves and his brew that had helped. It was his prayer, his faith in the Almighty ever present in the very air he breathed, watching and helping him! Of this he was now sure when he raised his hand—it was as if the hand were no longer his, no longer subject to his will. His right hand calmly pressing the swollen side of the boy had become an instrument, a knife. Where his forefinger had pointed, there spurted thick, greenish pus. It spilled on the bamboo floor and down to the earth below. He pressed the belly until no more pus oozed from it. He had merely wished the child's belly to open, to drain it of its poison, and that was what had happened. Where the wound should have been, there was just this slight indention, the skin untouched and whole. They had all seen it—the children, the women, the men—their eyes wide in supreme awe. Eustaquio, their cousin, their uncle, their neighbor, was blessed with faith. He would be the true light that would lead them.

Within him, Istak cried in humility and wonder: I am no different from you! We come from the same Po-on and here we are cast together by fate. So it is only I who know so much, but you have knowledge, too, which I do not have—the knowledge that each of us retains, as experience has given it to us, that which is ours and ours alone.

THE AFFLICTION that had almost taken the life of An-no was not confined to Cabugawan. Soon enough, there spread stories of how people were dying in the south, not by the dozens but by the hundreds. Manila, where there were many *médicos titulados,* was not spared by the plague; the whole city was engulfed for days by smoke from fires that were stoked constantly so that the plague would be fumigated away.

As the hot season dried up the rivers into stagnant pools, as the heat festered and Apo Init bore down upon the land like an avenging ball of fire, the plague took more victims in Rosales and in the villages that ringed it.

"Do not go to town," Istak told his relatives, at the same time wondering when it would strike the village in full force. "We are self-sufficient here, we will keep our village free."

He could not stop, however, those who sought his help, the sick in the neighboring villages who had heard of his healing powers.

It was shortly before the Angelus on a particularly hot and humid day that Istak himself finally became afflicted. It came as a hot flush of fever which engulfed him totally, enervating him, fogging his senses. Then he was defecating and vomiting as well.

By nightfall, he knew that cholera had gotten into his system. He told Dalin to leave the house, to stay away from him until death claimed him, and that when it happened, they should not touch him or anything he had used, for surely the contagion in his body would strike her, too.

"This cannot be, my husband," Dalin wailed.

"Do as I tell you, Old Woman," he said weakly.

Dalin did not leave him. She brought him instead plenty of water to drink, water from the spring and brewed from the guava leaves. And she washed him with the same water when he could no longer move.

Tearfully, she walked into the night assisted by An-no and Bit-tik and made the brew in an open fire in the yard, not just for Istak, but for everyone.

While there was still a little sense to his mind and he could still pray, softly Istak intoned: *Ave María purísima, sin pecado concebida. Santo Dios, Santo Fuerte, líbranos, Señor de la peste y de todo mal . . . por vuestras llagas, por vuestra líbranos de la peste, O divino Jesús . . .*

DAYS AFTERWARD, Dalin told him how his body had grown cold, how he sought the life-giving brew from the spring almost by instinct when he could no longer speak. Sometimes, in the night, he would mumble prayers, then lapse again into silence, while beside him, Dalin braved the pestilence and watched.

On the third day, Dalin said, they thought he had become mad, for he suddenly started talking to someone whom they could not see, someone in the room.

He was damning the invisible visitor, telling him that he was paying too heavy a price for all that he was doing, that he wanted to be no more than what he had always been, a farmer like all of them, to live in peace, undisturbed by hallucinations and disordered dreams. He had gone back to sleep, froth in his mouth. And they were all afraid until he began to snore.

Late in the night, he woke up, his body taut as a bowstring. The oil lamp was burning low on the wooden table at his feet. He turned fitfully and saw Dalin sitting upright by the window.

A shouting in the yard had wakened him; he wanted to rise, but it seemed as if his whole being were tied to the floor.

It was not he who did it; it was my father, but he is dead. What do you want of us? Haven't you sought us long enough? Did you not leave me for dead? I have a new life, I am no longer the man you left in Po-on with a hole in his chest, he wanted to shout. But no word escaped his mouth.

His ears picked up the minutest sound, the snap of house lizards on the beams, the shuffling of horses' hooves in the yard, even their slow breathing, and most of all, he now recognized that voice, rasping and almost effeminate, could almost see the man speaking; how could he ever forget the last words that he had heard from him? Or that blaze of red that had exploded in his face before he was lost to the world?

"Do you think you can run away from Spanish justice? To the highest mountain? The deepest jungle? There is no running away!"

Yes, Capitán Gualberto had caught up with them.

He lifted his arms, but they did not respond; a shout erupted from his lips, but he heard no sound; more shouts in the yard, and as he struggled with words that would not be freed, a sudden weakness came over him—his body had withered; he could feel it shrink smaller and smaller until all memory and all feeling were stilled.

MORNING. On the brink of this lightless day, the beating of his heart was a faint echo in his ears. He realized that he was breathing and could hear his lungs sucking in air. He wanted to lift his arms again, but they were numb. It all came back, the voice of Capitán Gualberto in the yard, the scuffling there, and yes, Dalin had whispered to him: "They are taking An-no! They will not bring him back!"

Fools! He is my brother, yes, but he is an ignorant farmer who can hardly write his name. What did he ever do to you? It is I who did everything, who sent my father on an errand of death. It is I who should pay . . .

There was no more scuffling in the yard. He would remember it all clearly later, but now his mind was clouded and all that he could perceive was this narrow room, this sad-eyed woman bending over him.

He lifted his eyes to the grass roof, where a house lizard clung motionless to a bamboo rafter, and then at Dalin again. Tears gathered in her eyes. "Thank God," she murmured.

His strength was returning slowly; he raised his hands— they were not his and he recoiled at the sight, the bones kept together by brown, withered skin. And his palms, when he turned them, were white and bloodless.

What happened to me? he wanted to ask, but all he could hear was a meaningless rasp, not his own.

"You are alive," Dalin murmured in his ear.

He lifted the coarse Ilokano blanket and saw the big bones that were his knees. His thighs, his legs—they were withered, too. Shocked, frightened, how did all this happen? It was only last night that he had gone to sleep.

Dalin had hurried to the kitchen and returned with a bowl which she set on the floor. Then, propping his head against the buri wall, she fed him a spoonful. The soft-boiled rice was spiced with strips of onion but the aroma escaped him and so did its taste. It scalded his mouth and tongue. The gritty gruel sank quickly and brought a warm glow all over his middle. It brought, too, a new kind of throbbing to his head, and he was conscious now of the nearness, the soft nudging of Dalin's breast against his shoulder. His hand had become sweaty and, trembling, he sought the cool, smooth touch of the bamboo floor and the breeze that came up through the house from beneath it.

"Eat now," Dalin said, dipping the spoon again into the bowl. "It has been a month—a month that you were very ill, that you knew nothing."

"A month? It cannot be—just seven days, just seven days . . ." He sighed, then with eyes closed so that he would not see the house suddenly turning over, he sank back onto the floor.

"My husband," Dalin said huskily. "You have to live—not for me, but for the child I am carrying . . ."

This was the moment of revelation, and he would have wanted to see her in her full splendor, drink her very essence, wallow in her tenderness, but he did not dare open his eyes for fear that he would be suspended in midair, that she would not be within the frame of his vision but would be mist, as even now, with his eyes closed, he was sinking into a vast hollow, the world was whirling, and he could not stop it.

CHAPTER

12

THINK, remember how it was, the very beginning when the fever suffused you. Is there ever a beginning with no end? We have always been here and shall pass as all others have, leaving nothing behind.

The dizziness ebbed, he dozed off into a limbo, and when he woke, it was already light—not dark as he remembered; the sun splashed on the buri wall. He tried to rise but could not. His head had become a leaden ball. He lay still, all sense of direction dulled, and the small house itself seemed to be falling into an abyss.

It was Dalin again who stopped the fall; she came in and by her very presence steadied him. She placed a bamboo chair before the window, then returned to him, went down on her knees—so close that he could smell the sun on her skin, the honey in her breath.

"You can sit there," she said.

He tried to rise but to his amazement there was no strength in either his arms or legs. "I am not strong," he said. She bent still closer to him and held him in the crook of his legs and shoulders so that he snuggled to her, and as a mother would take a baby from the crib, she lifted him and gently propped him on the chair.

He saw what the new world was—the sun a white flood upon the plain, so green and shiny he could feel the earth throb. In the sky, clouds billowed in masses of kapok white. This was creation itself and Istak began to cry.

It came back—the dim voices in the night, his brother An-no shouting in the yard, the scuffle there, the curses, and Dalin, her face taut with despair.

"What happened to An-no?"

His words were clear but she merely looked at him and did not speak.

"Tell me," he insisted, turning away from the window and the new life framed there.

"They took him away," she said sadly. "He claimed as his what your father did. They wanted to get you but he said it was he. You were very ill. We understood."

"That his life was not worth as much as mine?"

She looked at him and did not reply.

"They showed us his body—they wanted us to know. Then they gave it to us. He had a good funeral."

For a long time he did not speak; head bowed, he closed his eyes and brought to mind how it was, the journey that brought them to this land and to the beginning which was Po-on. Again, those days when An-no, Bit-tik, and he were small, roaming the green fields in May, searching for the first growths of saluyot that their mother cooked with grasshoppers which they had caught to eat as well, three brothers swimming in the river, gathering the fruits of camantres and lomboy that grew wild there. What did these years engender? He had been away from them for ten years and yet, though there were enmities among them, the bond had endured—reaffirmed by a supreme act of love. Why did An-no do it when he could just have remained silent and they would have taken him instead? Why did he do it and in doing so gamble as well? Istak was ill and dying—how could An-no have known that he would survive the fever? He turned all these questions over, remembering only what was good to remember of a past that he wanted to forget. Did he not even have a new name? He started to cry again, the tears scalding his eyes, trickling down his cheeks, and he shuddered, his thin frame shaking with the immensity of his grief.

Dalin embraced him.

ONE EVENING, when Istak was already well and could stand and walk around the house but not venture into the yard as yet, Bit-tik and Orang came with a big bowl of wild-pig meat stewed in vinegar. Bit-tik had trapped the animal that had been destroying the peanut patch at one end of his farm.

Istak could eat his fill and would soon be strong enough to work in the *bangcag,* and teach and heal again. They ate in the kitchen, savoring the meat, Orang hardly speaking. Sadness still lingered in her face, but neither grief nor motherhood had destroyed her handsome features.

"I want to ask you a question, Manong," Bit-tik said when they were finished. Dusk was descending quickly, and in a while, Dalin would light the earthen oil lamp that dangled from a rafter, then join them squatting around the low table.

"When was it that you could not ask me anything?" Istak asked.

He could see Orang nudge Bit-tik on the side, and Bit-tik

looked at her briefly, then spoke again: "It has been three months now that Manong An-no has gone. I live in his house."

"It is also your house," Orang said softly.

Bit-tik glanced at her, then went on. "The year of mourning is not over. Is it a sin, Manong? In my heart, I know it is not."

Istak knew at once what his brother would say next; he did not let him. "Orang needs someone to look after the farm An-no left behind. And her two very young children—they hardly knew their father. You will now be father to them. And you can truly love them, for your blood is also in them. And now, you have two farms to work, not just one. But when will you stop wandering, and be tied to a house? Orang keeps a good house, and she knows how to cook very well—look at this *adobo*. Where can you get something as good as this except in a rich man's house?"

Dalin sat beside Orang; she was older by at least five years and since that time when Capitán Gualberto had ravaged her, there had existed between the two a bond stronger than that which welds two sisters together.

"I am very happy it will be this way, Orang," Dalin said.

THE RAINS came and in early July a typhoon blew across the land and bowled over many farmers' homes. But not the houses of Istak and An-no. With the typhoon came the nine-day rain which flooded the fields and swelled the rivers to overflowing, and with the land washed fresh, the pestilence disappeared. As Dalin's belly grew, Istak regained strength. He had not brought any books from Cabugaw and had yearned so much for something to read, particularly in those times when, weak and emaciated, he could not leave the house. He tried recalling the important though tiny bits of knowledge taught him, and formulated a chronology wherein he could recall events, people, fragments of the past that must be resuscitated so that the present could yield some meaning or, at least, be explained.

With his improved health, he started to heal others again and news of his healing touch reached the nearby villages. They came seeking cures for stomach pains, late menstrual periods, fevers, and they left thinking he wrought miracles with his Latin *oraciónes*, which were really just the prayers that he had recited in church.

He attended to everyone, and in some instances knew he could do nothing as in that deep pit of his vision no light prevailed, just the blackest of black. It was at such moments that he prayed silently, asking God to have mercy on this human being, that the end be painless and quick.

Istak did not accept payment; he was not a *medíco titulado*— and what he did offer was but water brewed from guava leaves.

They usually came early in the morning, sometimes even before sunrise, for it was at this time of day that Istak felt he was best prepared. Those whom he cured recounted how it was when he "touched" them, the unseen force emanating from his hand which ended the pain, the warmth that flowed from his touch inundating the body and, finally, the feeling of being lifted from the mundane self for an instant into a state of well-being, if not of grace. When someone told him this, Istak would not believe it was his doing. It was the Divine who inhabited these parts, not he who was mortal, who sinned. Why had he not had this "touch" before, why now was he endowed with it, and in this particular corner of the world? Could it be that here, perhaps more than in Cabugaw or anywhere else, was where the kindly spirits dwelled?

What they did not know was that every time he "touched" the sick, he was drained of strength, and by midmorning, although there were still people waiting, he could no longer attend to them. He had become so weak, at times he had difficulty stumbling up to his own house.

He did not want anyone in the village to remain illiterate like his parents, so he gathered the children and taught them the *cartilla* and a little arithmetic. They did not have books and almost no paper and pencils, so they used banana leaves and charcoal from their stoves, and wrote on smooth bamboo boards or on the ground. He taught them a little Spanish, too, enough to understand some conversation, told them never to speak the language when Spaniards were within hearing, that whatever they knew of the language they should keep to themselves.

The produce from the farm sufficed and there was the additional grain, pork, chickens, and eggs his teaching earned for him. At first, it was just the children in Cabugawan who came to learn, but soon children and even adults from the nearby villages also came. A shed was built at the end of the lane close to his house, its earthen floor hardened with *carabao* dung. The roof was cogon and the walls were palm leaves. One side was completely open. At one end was a small table, and above it, close to the rafters, dangled a wooden crucifix. Aside from being a schoolhouse, it was also here where he ministered to the sick.

He also built a small shed in his *bangcag* near the mound where the huge snake had appeared. This mound was never touched, as were most of the mounds that dotted the fields. It was now surrounded with orange trees.

Down the shallow incline to the ground were the neat vegetable rows of ampalaya, eggplant, winged beans, watered constantly by the spring. This hut was his and his alone. He would lie on the bamboo floor and shut off everything—even the whisper of the wind on the grass roof. It was here where he replenished his strength, for after every healing he felt like a hollow length of bamboo—inert and useless, his innards spilled out, his veins and arteries drained. He stayed in the shed sometimes well into the night, when the whole village was already asleep, and would return to Dalin's side shortly after the cock had crowed. Lying there, he could feel his spirit leave his body slowly, like an essence floating away from a bottle, or smoke which rises from the kitchen stove to disappear in the air, and from there, he could see everything clearly, himself weightless on the floor. He could feel himself soaring over the fields, over Cabugawan. Then that blinding light that seemed to wash over everything, a brilliant wave cascading down on him, and still more light so intense he dared not open his eyes. I have seen another world without the hard crust of earth. I have gone beyond passion and craving; I have seen the spirit, an invocation beyond understanding . . .

When he was in his shed in the *bangcag,* Dalin, who understood, did not have to dissuade people from bothering him. It was not necessary, not after what happened to those who had trespassed.

At one time in the early part of the dry season when the watermelon and pomelo were ripening, two interlopers tipsy with *basi* thought they could simply snatch a few fruits. They were taught a fearsome lesson they would not forget, a lesson which soon got whispered about in the villages. One had seen the fat pomelos dangling from the trees, and without asking permission, simply walked through the uneven fence of thicket and bamboo and started to reach for the fruits. His story was frightening.

The watermelon thief had come upon this length of big bamboo stretched between the leafy rows. Only it turned out not to be bamboo, but a giant snake suddenly come alive, hissing and staring at him with beady eyes. As for the orange thief, he was about to reach for the fruit when he saw a fat vine coiled around the tree trunk. Only it was not a vine, but the long body of a snake with its fangs bared. Both could have been killed and they thanked the spirits that the snake did not strike them. They understood only later: it had merely warned them.

THERE WERE eight houses in Cabugawan in the beginning; soon there were more as other settlers from the Ilokos joined them. There was land for everyone who dared challenge the forest and the wild cogonals that bordered the swamps to the south. The lane between the new houses widened, planted on both sides with marunggay trees, and another gully to the creek where the *carabaos* bathed was carved out.

Dalin was a good wife and mother but memory was her implacable enemy and at night when they were in their small sleeping room, she would remain awake, badgered by thoughts of what was, wondering if Istak truly loved her in spite of all that had happened.

She was very glad when the baby came—a boy—for she knew that with him they would be brought closer. He was baptized Antonio, in honor of her father, and this truly made her happy, and happier yet when, in a couple of years, the second baby came—also a boy—and was named Pedro, in honor of her grandfather. She had hoped for a girl, so they would have her to depend on in their old age—but no girl—in fact, no more babies came after the birth of the second child. Her life was ordered, comfortable, and she had no complaints. Istak provided well, he was esteemed and everyone regarded him as the repository of wisdom, although he was not the eldest. His uncle Blas was certainly much older, and was better with words.

In times like this, when the world was still and their

thoughts were distinct and whole, it seemed as if they were completely one, their bodies merging, their spirits entwined as well, and the days ahead seemed clear and without shadows. Still, when she spoke her thoughts, it was as if this ancient sorrow never could be assuaged, not by her two boys, not by this man who had sworn to serve her to the very end.

"Old Man, when will you no longer want to have me lie beside you?"

"Old Man, will there ever be a time when I will forget what happened years ago, and remember only that I live for our children and tomorrow?"

"Old Man, who will take you away from me?"

He would hug her closer, feel the beating of her heart against his chest, smell the sun and earth on her skin and wonder why, after all these years, the old wound had not healed. He was a healer, but this was one wound he could not close no matter how much he reassured her, no matter how much he showed her by deeds that he loved her.

"I know it," she said, holding him tight. "Someday you will leave us."

Neither one was allowed to forget that they were running away and that even in Cabugawan they were not spared the omens of events to come. The news which reached them was of troubled times, of men being killed by the Spaniards in the north and the south. They did not hear the gunfire, so Istak consoled himself with the hope that perhaps they would no longer be hunted. What he had read convinced him that the tides rise and ebb. Though they could erode the shore, the sea itself remained constant, just as the land will be and they who work it, inseparable and perhaps indestructible.

"Whatever ill wind blows, we should not run anymore," he told Bit-tik, Orang, and his cousins. "We will work as before. If there are men who believe so much in themselves that they can drive away the Spaniards, let them think that way; let them shout themselves hoarse. Our duty is to our families."

As talk about the wildfire spreading in the south, particularly in Manila, heightened, they looked at the house of the Spanish landlord in Rosales for signs. The house stood there, quiet and impregnable, and the Spaniard's many tenants continued to leave his mountain share in the *bodega* behind the house. Could it be that he had the unblemished loyalty of his tenants and was not worried about any Indio recalcitrance? Or could it be that he, like Padre Jose, was unsparing in his criticism of the Indios yet loved them as only a father could?

The harvest that year was very good and the sacks which Istak and the new tenants brought to Don Jacinto were fat and heavy. Their benefactor received them, however, not with great joy but with a face overcast by gloom. Once, as they were about to leave, Don Jacinto took Istak aside to the shade of the balete tree in his yard and presented him with a bottle of new *basi*. Then, the serious talk. Don Jacinto, *gobernadorcillo*, the authority of office imprinted all over him, was now merely another Indio in a moment of mourning. "Rizal is dead, Eustaquio. You may never have heard of him, but he is known to many of us who believe in justice. The Spaniards executed him last week at the Luneta . . ."

Above, the January sky was swept clean and a breeze that careened by brought to them the scent of harvest. A time for rejoicing, and because he loved Don Jacinto, he must now show that one man's passing had touched him, too, although he did not really know who Rizal was.

"Tell me, Apo, about him."

"He was a good man, Eustaquio. I think it is about time that I showed you some of the things he wrote—I have them, you know. His novels, copies of *La Solidaridad* . . ." Don Jacinto spoke softly. "I am telling you this because I know you are an educated man. But more than this, I know that I can trust you."

"I hope I deserve that trust, Apo," Eustaquio said humbly.

"Promise me—do not show them to anyone, and don't tell anyone they came from me. And when you are through, give them back to me."

"As you will it, Apo," Istak said. They took a drink from the bottle. The *basi* was sweet—it had not fermented long enough and was fit for women only.

"Come," Don Jacinto said, motioning to Istak to follow him to his house.

Istak had, of course, been in the house a few times but had never been in the bedroom of his benefactor. The house was not as old as the house of the Spanish landlord, but it was of immense proportions, and the bedroom with its giant four-poster bed was bigger than Istak's whole house. It was not just a bedroom—it was a library as well, and Istak immediately felt comfortable in it. The books lined one wall, but the novels of Rizal were not there. From a wooden trunk under the bed Don Jacinto took two books and a thick envelope with folded newspapers within. He carefully bundled them, then placed them in a sack.

"Be careful," Don Jacinto said. "And when you are through, let us discuss them all. Maybe it is time we went to Manila together."

Manila—Royal City, was another world, unreachable, although once upon a time he had dreamed of walking its splendid streets and watching those big boats set sail for distant and exotic ports. Most of all, he would have loved visiting the university, listening to all those venerable men who had amassed wisdom from different lands and who, possessed with goodwill, would impart their knowledge to him.

Now the dream beckoned again. All the way back to Cabugawan, Istak thought of Don Jacinto, why he would talk of bringing a farmer like him to the city.

The trip to Manila, however, was never made. In a few weeks the country was in turmoil. It was then, too, that Istak fully realized what Don Jacinto was.

THERE was little confusion in Rosales. Life continued on its even course. Even the Spanish landlord, who had all the while stayed in Manila, was not harmed. It had seemed that he was one of the few of his countrymen who had sided with the Indios.

How strange it all was that even when Don Jacinto had revealed himself, Istak still felt nothing but affection for old Padre Jose, who must be dead by now. If not, they must have spared him physical pain. Did not everyone know how good he was? Istak had read Rizal's novels by then. Though he was profoundly touched by them, he could not damn Padre Jose. There was in the language he learned from the old priest a nobility that affirmed man's worth. Spain was the personification of granite pride, for how else could the Spaniards, coming as they did from an arid peninsula, build such an empire and still spread the faith? Surely, it was more than gold, exploitation, or superior arms which had moved them. Why did they lose their bearings? Why did they weaken?

CHAPTER

13

I N ANOTHER YEAR, a new ruler—and a new enemy—had come. The Americans had defeated the Spaniards and were now battling the republic's poorly equipped army. General Aguinaldo had none of the giant horses and the big guns that enabled the Americans to move with speed and overwhelm the puny units that faced them. They were also a ruthless enemy who defiled women and bayoneted children. In a few months, they had taken most of Luzon and were soon advancing to the north. Rosales was not on the main road. In Cabugawan, Istak and his kinfolk waited, wondering if they should flee to the forest.

Well ahead of the Americans, together with the monsoon in July, there came to Rosales in secret a man whom they all held in awe. Only a few saw him, but everyone knew he was in the safest, most comfortable place in Rosales—the house of Don Jacinto. Apolinario Mabini, the famous thinker and ideologue of the revolution, was a cripple. He arrived in the night in a hammock carried by bearers who left as quickly as they had come. As a leader of the new republic, he was a hunted man and surely the Americans would soon track him there.

Istak was faintly curious. The revolution had never really mattered much to him. He had gone over the copies of *La Solidaridad* and returned them; when his benefactor had asked him what he had found in them that impressed him, he had said quickly that there was great truth in what the *ilustrados* wrote about being rooted in the land. This truth was self-evident to those who worked the land themselves.

Don Jacinto did not reply; perhaps he understood that there was no measure for love of country except in sacrifice, and why ask the poor for more sacrifices? It was the comfortable, the rich like himself—although Istak did not put it this way—who should express it with their wealth. The poor had only their lives to give.

ON THIS day, Istak had gone to the delta, to Sipnget, to attend to a sick boy whose father had come to him begging with an offering of two live chickens. Istak always helped even if there was no gift. More than a decade had passed since they had crossed the Agno for the first time and always, upon reaching the river, he prayed for the soul of his mother.

It was late in the afternoon when he returned to Cabugawan. The rains had paused and the sky was clear. As he entered the arbor of bamboo which shaded the village lane, he saw Kimat, Don Jacinto's horse, tethered to the gatepost.

The rich man was waiting in the yard, talking with Dalin.

Soon it would be dark; the leaves of the acacia had closed and cicadas announced themselves in the trees. From the distance that was Rosales, the Angelus was tolling, and after Istak had greeted Don Jacinto, they stood still in silent prayer.

The rich man did not come often to Cabugawan, not even during the harvesttime; he had entrusted his share to the honesty of men like Istak, and the settlers had not failed him. He was burdened with having to run the town at a time when chaos and lawlessness prevailed. He had done this well, relying not on force but on the respect that the people had given him. He was, after all, the only one from Rosales who had gone to Manila to study.

"I have been waiting for some time now, Eustaquio," he said, smiling. In the dimming light, his face was drawn and pale, even stern. "Your Dalin and your two boys have been very good company. I even had a taste of *suman* and a cup of your new *basi*. I say it is ready, although Dalin says it is not."

"You are a better judge of that than I, Apo," Istak said.

"I came here to take you to town," he said. "Now—if you have nothing else to do. I have a guest . . . you know that, don't you?"

Istak nodded. "It cannot be hidden, Apo. Not in the way he arrived. Most of all, because he is with you."

Dalin wanted them to eat supper first. She had broiled a big mudfish and the pot of rice on the stove was already bubbling. Don Jacinto demurred; they must hurry and they could very well eat in his house.

On both sides of the darkening trail, the fields spread out, deep green in the fading light. Soon they would turn yellow and golden with harvest. Istak walked beside Don Jacinto, who was astride his horse, mosquitoes and moths around them, the frogs tuning up in the shallow paddies.

"What do you know of my visitor, Eustaquio?"

"Nothing much, Apo. That he is your old friend."

"Nothing can really be hidden in this town," Don Jacinto said. "Still, you must remember that there are spies, people brown like you, and we must make his presence as secret as possible. The Americans are no different from the Spaniards. Do you think it matters that we are destroyed as long as they get what they want?"

Istak did not speak. He had always been circumspect before those who wore shoes and jackets. He had long believed that only by listening would he be able to acquire more knowledge.

Don Jacinto noted his silence. "I did not get you so that we could discuss the politics of acquiescence," he said. Then he explained what had happened—both the Cripple's* manservant and secretary were ill and had left. And now, the Cripple himself was not well. He was always perspiring. Something was wrong with his urine—it was darker than usual and pains were shooting up his sides. The mention of pain in his sides alerted and alarmed Istak, but he could not be sure until he had seen the sick man.

It was already night when they reached Don Jacinto's house. Like most of the people of Rosales, Don Jacinto's father came from the north. He had done the *cartilla* in Rosales and then went on to Manila, and upon returning, he acquired more land. His father was an enterprising trader and knew how to please the friars as well. More than that, he had his son learn not just the intricacies of the law but how to deal with officials. No

---

*The Filipinos usually coin nicknames (often terms of endearment) from a person's physical attributes. "Kalbo" ("bald") is the name given to a man by people who know him. President Ramos is called "Tabaco" because of the unlit cigar always clamped in his mouth. A fat boss will be called "Taba" ("fat") by everyone in his office, although not to his face.

one in Rosales had suspected that the man who was very friendly with the friars and the *capitán* of the Guardia in Urdaneta, who often played chess and drank sherry with him, was actually a member of the northern revolutionary junta. They did not know that when studying in Manila, he had met other young *ilustrados* who were to lead the uprising against Spain.

Now, he was *cabeza*, and though there was not a single soldier in town, Rosales was peaceful. The town fiesta in June, which should not have been held anymore if only to protest against the friars who instituted it, was held just the same with the *comedia* and all the delightful entertainment that he arranged.

The oil lamps in the big house were all lighted and frames of yellow glimmered from the shell windows. The dogs in the yard howled, and out of the open gate, a man on a horse galloped into the night.

Don Jacinto reined in his mount. "I hope he did not bring bad news from Tarlak," he said softly, more to himself than to Istak, as he cantered into the yard.

Up at the great house, in the sallow glow of the lamps, the red floor shone, the porcelain pedestals stood serene in corners, the carved wooden chairs with crocheted covers were all in place as if the house were not intended to be lived in. Istak followed Don Jacinto across the polished hall to the *azotea* beyond, and to an open door which led to a large room. It was better lighted than the hall itself—a new Aladdin lamp dangled from the ceiling, ablaze with light, and at both ends of the massive table, two other lamps were perched. Don Jacinto's visitor was seated at the table, a sheaf of newspapers before him. The Great Man wore a white cotton shirt that hung loosely about him as if it were too big. Though young, he looked wasted and had a sickly pallor. He was poring over papers, shaking his head and cursing under his breath. Istak could make out the *"sin vergüenzas"* as they erupted in an almost steady stream.

"I hope it is not bad news, Apolinario," Don Jacinto said in Spanish.

The Cripple did not even look up from what he was reading. "It is always bad news now, Jacinto," he said, also in Spanish. "We are facing a superior enemy, as you very well know, with far more resources than the Spaniards. And still we haven't learned. Our generals quarreling. No discipline! And these Americans, they also have the means to tell the world how righteous they are . . ."

He finally turned to them, flailing a sheet of paper. "Here is the latest outrage by their correspondent, this wretched Thomas Collins—calling our soldiers cowards who refuse to fight in the daytime—that when we fight at all, we are always running."

"But wasn't that what you wanted, and General Luna, too?"

"Of course, of course!" the Cripple exclaimed and drew back, sitting straight. Beside him was a reclining chair and with great effort he eased himself into it. Don Jacinto strode forward to help him, but the Cripple waved him away, saying, "I told you, I told you . . ."

The Cripple drew a shawl over his wasted legs. "A guerrilla war—that is what we must now wage. But General Aguinaldo—forgive me for saying this—he is selfish and stupid. He is envious of generals like Luna who tried to put some discipline into the army. Luna is dead, killed by the same people he sought to discipline. We lost a good leader, one who could build a fighting force from the rabble . . . and yet, much as I loathe Aguinaldo and disagree with him, he is now the symbol of resistance against the enemy. My personal feelings—" He paused and looked upward to the ceiling adorned by an unlighted chandelier. The soft, warm voice continued: "How can I reply to their charges, show that we are ready to rule ourselves? And when are a people ever ready? Should another race determine that for them? Our constitution—it embodies our national sentiments and can stand as a document of freedom with any other free constitution in the world." He dropped the sheet of paper on the floor.

"These Americans, this Thomas Collins, they do not understand. Or perhaps they don't want to understand because what they really want is to subdue us. Still, I have to reply to such lies so that the world will know we are not cowards or immature children. Do you know that in one of his dispatches he said all Filipinos are thieves? Their soldiers camped in Manila told him this—that unless their supplies were well guarded, they would all be stolen by Filipinos. If so, then let it be! It is not thievery to steal from them—it is an act of war, and may Filipinos bleed them to death . . ."

"How long did the courier travel from Tarlak this time?" Don Jacinto asked.

"Less than a day's ride," the Cripple said. "So I really am not too late with the news—" The Cripple stopped and looked at Istak, who remained standing by the door, hearing everything.

"You can trust him, Apolinario," Don Jacinto said quietly. "This is Eustaquio. He understood everything we said."

Istak bowed and fumbled for words: "Good evening, Apo." The familiar Spanish words flowed out finally.

Don Jacinto continued: "There is no doctor anywhere near but Eustaquio is very good. He has taken care of many people. If we have to have a doctor, we have to go to Tarlak."

The Cripple shook his head. "The Americans will soon be there," he said wanly.

Don Jacinto nodded. "Give him a chance to help you."

"I do not have a choice," the Cripple said, suddenly laugh-

ing, the pallid face instantly transformed. He was homely and
dusky, with a narrow forehead, but the severity of his countenance was banished. He was just another man still in his youth,
brimming with humor.

Don Jacinto left to arrange for their supper.

"I hope that my humble self can be of service to you, Apo,"
Istak said in very polite Spanish and in the same obeisant tone
with which he had always addressed Padre Jose.

The Cripple looked at him, then shook his head. "Do not
speak to me in such a manner, Eustaquio. I am not old or venerable. Besides, I am really at your mercy." He pointed to one of
the rattan chairs close by. "And don't stand there. Sit down."

Istak took the proffered chair. Beside him was a porcelain
washstand with a polished mirror, and close to the Cripple's bed
was another table piled with books, an inkstand, and sheets of
paper. The man had been writing and Istak could see the careful
script. Istak could still write as well as that, perhaps even better.
He had taken pride in his penmanship but had not held a pen
in a long time and had done whatever writing he had to do with
a pencil.

"Tell me, Eustaquio," the Cripple asked. "How is it that you
speak Spanish so well?"

"I was an acolyte in the church of Cabugaw, señor. In the
Ilokos."

"Jacinto says you are a healer. How long have you been
one?"

"About ten years now, Apo," Istak said. "I learned a little
from an old priest about medicinal plants. And, of course, with
prayer and God's help there is always hope."

Silence. Then the Cripple spoke again: "I have been suffering
for some time now. I have pains here," he said, pressing his
sides. "You cannot see it now because the pan has been emptied,

but when I urinate it is very milky. And I perspire so much, as you can see." He wiped his brow, which was moist even in the cool September evening.

His meal came in—the new rice still steaming and fragrant, salted eggs, a small dish with salted fish and sliced tomatoes, and dried meat which was fried.

Istak shook his head. The Cripple wanted to share the food with him but Istak demurred; he would take his meal with the servants in the kitchen after Don Jacinto and his family had eaten. He stood up; he had confirmed what he suspected. "I will go now, Apo," he said. "I will come back shortly with your medicine."

In the dining room, Don Jacinto had already sat down with his family to eat and a servant hovered by the table waving a paper wand to keep the flies away. "I will return in a short while, Apo," Istak said.

He hurried down the deserted street, disturbing the stray dogs lying there. At the edge of the town, he looked at the saplings, then crossed the creek to the other side until he came to a young banaba tree. He could make out the blossoms; they would be a pretty violet in the sunlight. He reached out to a low branch and plucked a lot of them together with the young leaves. With the bundle under his arm, he returned to Don Jacinto's house and told the cook to boil some of the flowers and the leaves immediately.

His dinner was ready; Don Jacinto was indeed a good man—the food that his servants ate was the same as his honored guest's.

He let the concoction cool a little, then took it to the Cripple. He was now propped up by pillows before the table and was writing in his journal, the Aladdin lamp bluish and brilliant above him.

"You must drink this, señor," Istak told him, placing the pitcher and a glass on the table. "It is slightly bitter, but I hope it will do you good. And don't drink anything else but this. I ask you not to eat salty food. In fact, it would be best if you had no salt at all."

"And what is this?" the Cripple asked, raising the glass and examining it in the light.

Istak showed him the flowers and the leaves. The Cripple knew them. "There are many of these here," Istak said. "And if there aren't any, I can make another equally good remedy for you."

As the Cripple took the cup and raised it to his lips, Istak recited, "*Dominus Jesus Christus apud te sit, ut te defendat et te curet . . .*"

The Cripple paused, and laid the cup on the table, his eyes wide open in surprise. "Do you know what you just said?"

Istak smiled. "Yes, Apo. The ritual prayer."

"Translate what you said, word for word."

Istak made the translation into Spanish. "May the Lord Jesus Christ be with you, that He may defend you and cure you . . ."

"You surprise me!" the Cripple exclaimed, a wide grin spreading across his homely face. Then he took the cup and emptied it with a grimace.

"Now you condemn me to hell as well. Perhaps it is better that I starve. Food without salt! What else did that old priest teach you?"

"What is perhaps taught in a seminary, señor," Istak said.

The Cripple seemed pensive for a while, as if he were savoring what he drank, as if he could not quite believe what he had heard. "The world is full of surprises," he finally said. "Here I am, a stranger to this place, to the language, and yet I feel so safe because I know I am among people I can trust." He glanced around the room, then at the *herbolario*. "Jacinto and I were classmates in Manila, Eustaquio. I have entrusted my life to him—just as I have done to you."

"Thank you, Apo," Istak said. There was nothing for him to do.

"Will you return tomorrow? Early? And have breakfast with me? If your medicine is good, I will wake up healthy!"

Istak fidgeted. He would be imposing on Don Jacinto, at whose table he had never eaten before, and now, with this awesome company. The Cripple seemed to divine his thoughts. "Eustaquio, I come from a poor family in Batangas. We must stop thinking of ourselves as inferior before those who we think have more knowledge than we do, or who are taller or fairer of skin. How many mestizos or Kastilas can speak Latin as well as you? You are very rich, Eustaquio, and your wealth is yours and yours alone. No one can take it from you. I will tell Jacinto that you will come shortly after sunrise."

DALIN had cooked the new rice and its scent filled the house. She had also fried some dried pork, and the low eating table was already set. She waited for him to tell her how his visit was; she never asked what he did. In the warm glow of the oil lamp that dangled from the rafter, her eyes came alive with curiosity. Even after the birth of the two boys, she still retained her pleasant features, the mouth that was quick to laughter, the eyes that sparkled. Her coarse blouse seemed fine only because she wore it. But her hands were not soft like the hands of Carmencita, and her legs were dark, the soles of her feet as thick as any peasant woman's. He must banish her unspoken anxiety.

The boys were busy with their food; Antonio, who was older, however, would turn to his father often, as if he shared his mother's inquisitiveness.

"There is a new lamp in the big house," Istak said. "It has a large wick and is fed by a different kind of oil. It is very bright, ten times brighter than candles and our own lamp."

This was not what Dalin wanted to know.

"He is a kindly man," Istak finally said. With his hand he shaped a ball of rice and then dipped it in a dish with fish sauce and sliced lemon. "He is ill—and I will see him again tomorrow. And you know, Old Woman, he wants me to have breakfast with him. This farmer Istak, having breakfast with such a noble person. I cannot believe it."

Dalin smiled, pleased at the honor given her husband.

Istak seldom had Po-on on his mind now; still, there were instances out there in the soggy fields when he remembered. Memories no longer wrenched from him the ancient sorrow. His granary was always full, the *bangcag* and the guardian that watched over it had been kind, too; the bamboo thrived, the orange trees bore sweet fruit, vegetables grew even during the dry season—all he shared with relatives and neighbors who were too lazy to plant. He was a good provider; he was a better teacher.

Night came swiftly to Cabugawan. After supper, Dalin cleared the low eating table, then leaned it against the palm-leaf wall. She placed the leftovers into a coconut shell which Pedro, the younger boy, took below the house for his dog, Lightning. Dalin drew up the bamboo ladder.

The two boys slept in the kitchen while Dalin and Istak slept in the small *sipi* which adjoined the living room. Below the house were the plows and the harrow, a couple of hoes, and the loom Dalin used for weaving.

The small window would stay open till they were ready to sleep. Dalin had closed the other windows and slung a pole across them so that they could not be opened from the outside. The two *carabaos* and a calf were in their corral by the granary; there had been some cattle rustling in Carmay and Sipnget, but none so far in Cabugawan. Any stranger wandering in the neighborhood would be announced by the barking of dogs. One rainy night, a howling roused Dalin from sleep. She gripped the arm of her husband, who was then wide awake, too. He crept to a crack in the buri wall and peered outside to see shadows moving toward the corral. He opened the small window slowly. He kept a basket of stones ready for such a time. He started pitching with all his strength at the forms in the dark. Thuds, a scream of pain, men rushing, and soon the shouts of neighbors who had also been wakened. Not one of the *carabaos* in the village was taken. How would it be if the rustlers had guns? So much uncertainty and violence threatened them now, and those who plundered the countryside often did so in the name of the revolution.

Again, the thought came swiftly—if only he and his family could flee to some deeper forest where they could clear and work the land without being badgered by other men. This was what so many had done—the fugitives from Spanish forced labor and the lash, the *mal vivir,* who had challenged the wilderness or sought community with the mountain peoples—the Aetas, the Balogas, the Bagos—and became one with them. He could do this with confidence born out of the sweat, the agony of having tried. He knew how to pit his intelligence against animals, even against some of nature's whims. In fact, nature was no enemy but a friend. There was tight kinship here, all his neighbors shared with him this beginning. Would they all be driven away again and be estranged from one another? Everywhere there was no peace such as he might have found had he become a priest. And again, old Padre Jose came to mind.

Time had dulled Istak's earlier enthusiasms, and even his

preoccupation with faith and liturgy now seemed a precious memory. How was it ever possible for him to believe in the seeming omnipotence of prayer? Of Padre Jose's missionary courage? Did he delude himself in believing completely what he had learned in the sacristy? It was what he learned from there, after all, which had made him what he was. Would it have been better if he had had the open mind to accept all there was to accept, even the unexplainable such as those things which he witnessed? There were those aspects of living that need not be questioned anymore, the futility of it all, the dying, this night that covered the land, those distant stars that Galileo was troubled about.

In the kitchen, one of the boys was already snoring. Beside Istak, the softness of Dalin. Lifting the rough blanket which covered her, his hand slid up from her smooth, flat belly to her breasts. They were firm still in spite of two breastfed babies. She turned onto her side, breathing on his face, and laid an arm around his chest. Outside, in the corral the calf was mooing and a night breeze stirred in the bamboo grove beyond the house. The air smelled of harvest, of the good earth.

"I wonder what he wants," Istak said softly.

"It is an honor," Dalin said, "when someone like him needs you. It could be dangerous, too."

"He told me that." He quickly remembered.

"And we are small people, Old Man," she reminded him.

Istak did not speak. Long ago he had learned how to live with his smallness. This woman beside him made him strong, his fate more bearable.

IN THE MORNING, at her urging, he had a breakfast of coffee, fried rice, and roasted dried venison. Dalin told him he would be uncomfortable before the Cripple; he would be so self-conscious of his manners that he would not be able to take two mouthfuls.

Don Jacinto met him in the wide *sala*. The sun was already up, yet the house seemed dark but for the shine of the hardwood floor and the mirrors on the walls.

"Apolinario is really impressed, Eustaquio," the *cabeza* said, beaming. "And I did not know you could speak Latin." He slapped Istak affectionately on the shoulder.

He was ushered into the room of the guest. The Cripple was not there; he had been transported to the nearby *azotea*, which was now flooded with the morning sun, brilliant on the potted palmettos, on the red tile floor.

The Cripple was still pale. Beads of perspiration clung to his brow. The cook came with their breakfast in trays and Don Jacinto left them. The Cripple's food—upon Istak's order—was now almost without salt, and he grimaced as he ate the broiled fish and fried rice.

"As you can see, Eustaquio," he said, "I am a very good patient." He took the glass of light brown liquid and drank all of it.

"I feel better," he continued. "And my urine, it was clearer this morning. I drank four glasses last night."

The Cripple turned and picked up two lead pencils and a beautiful new notebook beside the food tray. "I hear you don't accept payment—so take these. You are a teacher. You need them."

As Dalin had said, Istak had difficulty eating even with the Cripple's continued urging. He had never used table napkins before or the silver that the Cripple was using, although he had seen them in the sacristy.

"It is your kidneys, I suspect, Apo," Istak said. "They are

probably not working well and what you are drinking merely helps clean them. I am not sure it can do everything if the damage is serious. I am not a doctor, Apo."

"In the absence of one, you are heaven-sent," the Cripple said. "And since you are my doctor now, I will tell you frankly what I fear." The Cripple beckoned to him to come close so that he could listen better. Now his voice became softer, as if revealing a horrendous secret. "You must keep this to yourself. Will you promise that, Eustaquio?"

"Yes, Apo." He had emptied his cup and felt invigorated; the coffee was real.

"When I was young"—the Cripple's face was now dark with gloom—"I had this terrible fever. I was so weak, I could hardly move. It lasted but a few days and when it left, I thought I was finally well, except for my legs. They felt numb. I tried to rise but couldn't. After I had eaten, I thought I would be stronger. When I finally had sufficient strength, my legs could not support me. I was so surprised and sad—I cried when I fully realized that I had become a cripple. But not here!" He laid a hand on his breast. "And here"—he gestured to his head. "I had medical care, of course, but I think I went to the doctor too late and so I am like this. Which is just as well. You see, the Spaniards found it too much of a bother to imprison a cripple. They thought that I would not be able to do them any harm. They let me live, but my friends—well, they were all shot at the Luneta."

Istak listened intently. He had heard so many of these stories in the past, he bore witness to what was done to him and his father. Then they took his brother, too, as if his brother's life were forfeit and his more important, reserved for some design that was not for him to know, just as the Cripple was saved from the firing squad.

"I am happy that you are here with us, Apo," Istak said.

"But you pity me because I cannot walk," the Cripple said,

his face brightening. "Let me tell you a secret—while these two legs are useless, the third leg is still sturdy but unused!" Istak looked at the thin wasted legs. Yes, it would be a miracle if the Cripple could walk again. Istak grinned; the Cripple was not made of stone; he knew how to laugh. But then, the Cripple suddenly raised his hand and brought it down hard on the table, rattling the silver and the plates. "Oh, that I were not like this, imprisoned in this damaged body. If only I could use my legs!"

The sudden irruption vanished quickly. "It would be a miracle, Eustaquio, if I walked again?"

Istak did not answer. He tried to recall what was in the medical encyclopedia that Padre Jose had in the library and which he often read.

"I am not optimistic anymore. But then—" A scowl came over the Cripple's face, his eyes suddenly blazed. "¡Sin vergüenza!" he cursed softly. "And do you know what my enemies spread about me? Those wealthy mestizos who ingratiated themselves with the president? To destroy me, who exposed their perfidy and stood in their path, they spread the rumor that I had syphilis. Syphilis—it damages not just the body but the brain! No, they did not say it bluntly, to my face and hearing. They insinuated it, hinted at it. In this, I couldn't confront them, fight them. The people close to me, they knew it was a lie. That behind this is nothing more than greed and, perhaps, envy. I never aspired to wealth, Eustaquio. So I can look any man in the eye. Remember this, Eustaquio. Remember this."

ISTAK had finished the hard-boiled egg, the fried rice from Don Jacinto's kitchen much tastier than what he had at home; it was fried with pork fat and had bits of onion and garlic.

"I would have peace of mind if I were you, Apo," Istak said. "Just use less salt." He leaned forward and pressed the flesh in the Cripple's forearm. The indentation left by his thumb lingered.

"You have a little edema," Istak said. "I really think it is your kidneys."

The Cripple grinned again—the happiness spreading across his pinched, pallid face. It was the first time Istak had seen him so pleased, the melancholy eyes dancing with laughter.

"What else can you do, Eustaquio? You speak Spanish, Latin—both very well. And you are a healer like no *herbolario* I have ever seen. What are you really or what do you want to be?"

"I am a poor farmer, Apo," Istak said.

"No, you are not just a farmer," the Cripple said. "In the past, surely, you must have wanted to be something else."

So it was; Cabugaw again, the old church, the stone belfry and the bats that roosted in the eaves, the booming clap of bells in his ears and old Padre Jose telling him to read as much as he could, for the world was open only to those who could read and this skill was the most precious gift that any teacher could give.

"I had a teacher, Apo," Istak said with a touch of sadness. "I wanted to be a priest, to be like him, knowing so much and imparting it all to others."

"And why did you not become one?"

Istak turned away. "I am an Indio, Apo," he said simply.

The Cripple leaned forward, his eyes ablaze. "You can still be one if you want to, Eustaquio. Bishop Aglipay has founded the Filipino Church. It is very strong and it is all ours. No Spanish friars ordering us. And we are not subservient to Rome. We must build this church not only because it is ours but because we must have a continuing faith in God. My mother wanted me to be a priest, too. So you are not really alone.

"Do you really believe in God?" the Cripple asked after some silence. "This was a belief you got from the Spaniards, no matter how kindly they may have looked upon you."

For some time, Istak could not speak, although it would have been so easy to affirm his faith. He had prayed as a matter of habit when he ministered to the sick, a prayer which those who were healed thought had curative powers in itself. He had not tried to correct the impression, for who really knew what prayer could do? There was this power he held, power which was not really his but Someone else's. Yet, there were times when he doubted the existence of a just and merciful God, and now that it was put to him bluntly, now that he must open up his own mind to himself, he realized with some sorrow and apprehension that his belief was not as steadfast as it once had been and that if given the chance he would not now want to be a priest. Was it all Dalin's doing?

"I do what I think is right, Apo," Istak said.

"You are not answering my question."

"I doubt, Apo," he said quickly. "And I am ashamed that I do."

"No, no, Eustaquio!" The Cripple shook his head emphatically. "You doubt, you think—have you forgotten the old injunction? What did the Spaniards say about us? That we are children, without minds, that we can easily be led. This is what the Americans are saying, too. This is what they are telling the world. That we cannot manage our affairs, that we do not deserve to be free. A nation which has people who can think, that nation already has strength. It is the mind which rules, Eustaquio—not instinct or habit."

LONG AFTER they had parted, the Cripple's words burned in Istak's mind. In their next encounter, he would have more reasoned-out replies not only to his inquisitor but—he now realized—to himself. He went to his *bangcag*, the life-giving well, to the guardian of the earth, to draw from them the knowledge that seemed to have ebbed. It had pleased him, of course, to use Spanish, and a bit of Latin again, to argue in a language that was not his and find that desuetude had not dulled his mind, that he could still express himself fully in it, although, at times, the words shaped slowly. He brought to mind how he once told Padre Jose that he was tormented by doubts and the old priest had tweaked his ears, reminding him that there are questions of faith which have no answers, for the ways of God are immutable and imponderable. Istak had believed; he had wakened in the mornings, smelling real coffee brewing in the kitchen. He had lingered, too, at the belfry when he tolled the Angelus and from that pinnacle, watched the west burn with the dying day, the whole rim of the world ablaze with dazzling reds that turned to purples, voluptuous forms or ogre shapes obscured with the onrushing night. Only God could paint these.

The guava tree had borne fruit and the well was full and flowing ceaselessly into the bamboo conduits that carried the gift of life to the seed. He would bring some of the fruits to his patient and boil some of the young leaves in water from the well. Mushrooms had also sprouted in the pit where he had stacked the dead trunks of bananas and hay, and he filled his fish basket with them. The Cripple would like a tasty meal even if there was no salt in it.

He had never taken care of anyone before with whom he was as involved as he was now. Although it had given him immense satisfaction to hear the Cripple tell of his improvement, Istak was not sure that he was doing right, he was not even sure that the Cripple's old ailment was completely cured. It was in moments like this that uncertainty badgered him, that the hunger for more knowledge became more acute.

Would he raise his sons, for instance, the way he was—full of questions? This early, the older boy, Antonio, had already shown intelligence and a questioning spirit. He had taught the boy the *cartilla* and he could read just enough Spanish for a nine-year-old to absorb. Istak regretted most that he had no books here; in Cabugaw, there had been the Augustinian texts, the literature and science of Europe. Now that he had shared the rich man's food, perhaps, Don Jacinto could lend him some of his books.

All this was in his mind the evening he returned to town with his medications. This time, however, the Cripple did not bother him with questions; he offered Istak a job instead.

In the *azotea* again. Across the wide expanse of grass the balete tree was ignited by a thousand fireflies, and beyond the old tree, the orange lights of several homes flickered. The evening was cool; it would be December soon and the bracing winds from the mountains would veer down to the plain.

The Cripple had finished his supper. He had also drunk the concoction which Istak had brought in a bamboo tube but that was now in a glass pitcher. The Aladdin lamp was lighted and its luminous glow reached out to them.

The Cripple was pensive, his eyes on the far distance, the pith of darkness. "I have difficult days ahead, Eustaquio. I am depressed by the way the war is being fought, and now, all these personal problems, too. As you very well know, Cayo, my secretary, is not well. He is in Balungaw with my servant, in the hot springs there, recuperating from this fever and I don't know how long he will be there. Thank God, it is not the pox. I need someone to transcribe what I have written, to remember the things that I say. Your Spanish is polished—as if you grew up with the language. Do you have difficulty recalling it?"

"Yes, Apo," Istak said.

"You will do. And as for Tagalog, it does not matter that you don't speak it. You can learn enough so that you will understand what I automatically say sometimes."

This kind of work was beyond his expectations. He should forget the dream but in his heart he was glad that the Cripple saw value in him still. But what was this votive flame that was drawing him closer to this cause that led men to their graves? Would he eventually be singed by it, would it scorch all the allegiances of the blood?

"What are your feelings toward the language of our masters, which we have learned? Does it give you a sense of pride? Of being equal to them?" the Cripple suddenly asked.

It had never occurred to him this way. Language was a window through which he could see—as Padre Jose had said, and indeed, he saw so much, learned so much. But how was he to explain this now? He turned to the side of the room where the bookshelves were. All those books were in Spanish, and perhaps, a couple or so in Ilokano.

"I have made their language mine, Apo," Istak said finally. "And with it, I am able to speak with you, to Don Jacinto—but to my relatives, my wife, I have to speak in my own tongue, which I love no less."

The Cripple smiled, that cryptic smile that could be mistaken for cynicism. "And I have to write in Spanish, and this then will have to be translated into English by our friends in Hong Kong. English, the language of our enemy—so that it can then be spread to many corners of the earth. To reach our own people, we have to use the language of foreigners. But someday we will be able to talk with everyone in a language that is our own. Yes, Eustaquio—there is so much the world does not know, how the Americans have tortured our people, committed the most brutal crimes against humanity. And yet, read their own constitution—how civilized and humanitarian it is. Yes, we have so much to tell everyone."

The Cripple paused as if a heavy cloak of weariness had descended upon him. "And Luna is dead. Only he really understood how the war should be fought by men lacking arms but not spirit. Everyone can help in this war, Eustaquio. Do you understand?"

Istak bowed. "I am just a poor farmer, Apo." His voice did not rise above a whisper.

Perhaps, had the Cripple been able to, he would have risen quickly. He jolted himself upright, instead, his voice leaping, his eyes burning: "You are not a poor farmer! You are Eustaquio Samson—is that not your name? And you are a Filipino with a good head—this I recognize as you should recognize it, too. And this is what has always been wrong with us—yes, the Spaniards have succeeded in humiliating us, always they are the superior teachers—we the inferior pupils! Whatever we do that is honest and good, we must be proud of it. We must not be subservient to anyone, not you to me, as I have never been to anyone. In me, in you—in all of us is dignity. We should stand bravely because we are citizens of a sovereign nation no matter how weak that nation. We are Filipinos now, do you understand, Eustaquio?"

Istak did not move. The words swirled around him, engulfed him, lifted him off his feet. No one had ever spoken to him like this before; his parents had always stressed obedience, hard work, and Padre Jose—for all his goodness, what did he din into him but piety, love, respect, duty—how they differed from Mabini's thralling call to pride.

"Yes, Apo," Istak said.

"You do not know it," the Cripple continued equably. "I am no longer an official in our government. What I do now I do as a duty, not to the president but to Filipinas. Our motherland, she is bigger than any of us, and we must serve her, and serving her means serving you and everyone who is Filipino. Even now, President Aguinaldo is fleeing from the Americans, just as I am hiding here, unable to run. He has a weak, undisciplined army—what is left of it—led by General Tinio. He will be safe. But the Americans will surely capture me—I don't know when they will come or when I will be betrayed, just as I don't know when they will catch up with the president. Some say that everything is lost, that all we can do now is run and hide, but we can still wage war from the mountains, from the swamps, where they cannot reach us. We know the folds of the hills, the depths of the muck—they don't. But even if the war is lost, even if there is an American pointing a gun at each one of us, we must continue to oppose this new master till Filipinas is free."

A long pause, then the Cripple continued sadly: "But when will Filipinas ever be free from its leaders who are wealthy and crooked, in whom we have put so much trust?"

To Istak's questioning look, the man sighed. "I am voicing thoughts that I should keep to myself. But I have always mistrusted the wealthy men who have joined the revolution. I know that great wealth is always accumulated by foul means, by exploiting other people. If we have wealthy men at the helm, we can be sure that they will enrich themselves further. Virtue and wealth seldom go together. The greatest criminals are also the wealthiest men."

Istak looked at his bare feet, at the shiny wooden floor. Was he the epitome of virtue because he was poor? How had it been in the village? There was foul gossip and cussedness anywhere in the world where small men had to think of their stomachs first before thinking about others. "The poor are not always virtuous, Apo," he mumbled.

"Ah, but I did not say they are." The Cripple became vibrant again. "What I do say is this: it is more difficult for the poor to be virtuous. When you are hungry and you steal a *ganta* of rice, that is not a crime; but when you are rich and you steal gold, is that not despicable? In this war, hundreds have died with honor, but I also know that some have already profited by their professions of patriotism. When this is all over, we will know who among the *ilustrados* have enriched themselves with the funds that should have gone for the purchase of guns, food, medicine for our soldiers. We will know who betrayed the revolution to the Americans. And because we are Filipinos, we may even proclaim these thieves as patriots. Patriots don't become rich, Eustaquio." The Cripple raised his hand in a gesture of futility and for the first time, Istak pitied him, his infirmity, his incapacity to express himself beyond words, in deeds that would bespeak iron physical courage as well.

What could a farmer like him do? Had the lives of people really changed during all the years that salvation was offered by the priests? If the revolution succeeded, what assurance was there that his life would change? Would brown rulers be different from the Spaniards? Would it not be worth waiting to find out what kind of rulers the Americans would be? He did not know much about America, but he had read about Lincoln and how he had freed the slaves. Surely, there must be some redeeming virtue in a nation which produced such a man.

"I don't want to make you angry, Apo," Istak said clearly. "All that I can look after is my own farm, serve those who seek me when they are sick. I have my children to look after so that they will not know what hunger is."

The Cripple bowed as if enveloped in thought and for some time he did not speak. Darkness deepened, dishes clattered in the nearby kitchen, mice scurried in the attic, a dog howled somewhere in the vastness of the night. The Cripple spoke again. "I understand only too well what you are trying to say. That you are a farmer? Or that you are Ilokano? And if I ask you, what is under your skin, inside your skull, do not tell me it is blood and flesh and brains!" His gaze turned to the sky studded with stars and as if he had reached out for one and held it out to the farmer, his words took shape again, crystal-clear, lucid. "Don't ever be a patriot, Eustaquio. Those who think they are or will be delude themselves. Patriotism is selfless. And it is not the generals who are the bravest—they usually have the means to stay away from the battle and thereby lengthen their lives. The bravest are usually those whom we do not know or hear about, those anonymous men who dig the trenches, who produce the food. They are the corpus—you understand that word—the body and also the soul of a nation. Eustaquio, my words are just words, but all through history—and you have studied it—it has always been the many faceless men, those foot soldiers, who have suffered most, who have died. It is they who make a nation."

CHAPTER

14

MY CONCERN is here in this land that I have cleared. Yes, my house is small—a typhoon can destroy it. I have no weapons to defend it against the Americans, who have everything. I will welcome them to partake of my food, and if they will command me to serve them, what choice do I have? The little people have always been like this—they die, but then they can bring on a plague. All that I want is to be left alone.

Amami adda ca sadi langit—

Dalin and the two boys intoned the Lord's Prayer. Always in the hush of dusk before they supped, they prayed with the words that the Augustinians had shaped for them, and with the end of the novena, they now sang softly, their voices blending together with what Istak had taught and explained to them:

Tantum ergo sacramentum
Veneremur cernui
Et antiquum documentum
Novo cedat ritui . . .

So be it, the old giving way to the new. Where the senses cannot confirm, let faith be the unswerving guide, the final and only answer. Faith made them persevere so that they could reach Rosales. His two boys, his wife—they looked up to him with more than faith; Dalin could only write her name before; now she could read and knew a lot more than woman's work. Still she had not changed really—she was still the same woman who took that desolate trail to Po-on. What is it, then, that makes people endure? To remain steadfast? Surely they must be imbued with more than courage.

And now, the Cripple was asking him to face the enemy, fling stones at him, and bare his chest to him. No, courage is also the capacity to use wisdom so that we, not he, will prevail, to learn how the enemy can be destroyed, to have the patience to wait, to search for his weakness, to attack when he does not expect it.

Istak could not sleep. The gecko called from the dalipawen tree beyond the house, and the cocks crowed from their roosts in the nearby branches. Dalin was quietly asleep beside him. In the morning, he would have to return to town with answers that had been thought out, dredged from his deepest being. It was only at night when he was home lying wide-awake that the big thoughts—as he called them—came but did not linger. A body that was tired succumbed easily to sleep; he waited for it but it was a long time coming.

Daylight again, Dalin preparing breakfast in the kitchen, the smell of corn coffee, of dried fish frying in coconut oil. Outside, the boys already shouting, the dogs yelping, the world alive and pulsing, and here he was, though rested, still disturbed, still unsure.

At the low eating table, the two boys ate noisily. He nibbled at the dried fish, the fried rice almost untouched on his plate.

"Whatever it is that the Cripple is asking you to do," Dalin said, "do it. He is a man you respect and honor; he will not ask you to do work which will dishonor you or leave you without reward. And reward does not mean silver."

She seemed fairer in the morning light of the open doorway. It must have been her blouse as well, its long sleeves rolled up. Her hair, neatly combed, hung down her shoulders. Every so often, she washed her hair with the ash water from the stalks of palay that she burned—now it shone lustrous in the light.

"I am not going to be involved with his violence," Istak said quickly. "My duty is to them." He thrust a chin at the boys, who continued eating. "And to you."

Dalin shook her head. "How quickly you have forgotten." She sighed. "You have tried to run away from it, but it seeks you just the same."

"We have had peace for years now," he said, shaken a little by what she said.

"We cannot escape our fate," she said softly, reaching out to touch his hand.

DON JACINTO gave him a corner in the cavernous storeroom beneath the house. The windows were wide, the sun flooded in, and it was bright even till late in the afternoon. Then, a maid would come with a candle or a pair of oil lamps and he would continue writing till the work was done. If needed upstairs, he would go up the stone flight of the *azotea* without having to pass the main hall. The Cripple merely thumped on the wooden floor with a cane and the dust of many years would drift down, threatening to smother him. But soon, no matter how loudly the Cripple thumped, no more dust descended on him.

The work was not difficult; most of the time, it was simply copying neatly what the Cripple had written and corrected. Istak had some difficulty at first—he had not written with a pen for a long time, and the nib often flattened out as he pressed on it too hard. After two days it all came back—the old agility, the smoothness. Though his back ached from the hours hunched before the writing table, it was not the body that was really fatigued but the mind, for everything that the Cripple wrote, he absorbed. Writing provoked thinking as well, and it had been a long, long time since Istak was made to think as he was doing now. He marveled at the Cripple's tenacity and how, despite his infirmity, he could still write so much, even now that he was no longer in power and the war was being lost. The Americans were getting closer and very soon they would reach Pangasinan.

It was the Cripple's view on the Church, on Bishop Aglipay, whom he wanted to be the undisputed leader of the Filipino priests, that bothered Istak most. Mabini's belief in God was formidable and steadfast, but he thought little of the Roman Church as an institution. The Cripple's letters and resolutions asked instead for the creation of a Filipino Church, serving not Rome but the Filipino people.

Shadowy figures stole into the house and talked with Don Jacinto, who then took them to the Cripple's room. They did not tarry. Their faces were grim and melancholy when they arrived, but when they left it seemed as if they were recipients of indescribable grace, their gait quicker, the sorrow banished from their faces. Surely, the Cripple held some secret talisman as well.

Istak was justly proud of his penmanship, which he had developed through the years. Though he no longer gave his capital letters fancy loops, he still decorated them with a curl or two. It was, after all, with this penmanship that the trained writer was recognized; the more elegant the calligraphy, the better it spoke of the writer's skill.

The Cripple was meticulous; he said the loops occupied too much space and interfered with the reading because they were distractive; the penmanship drew attention to itself and not to what was being said.

"Remember, Eustaquio, these are curtains to a window. And the words are themselves the window. First, the writing must be neat but not ornate, for if I wanted beautiful letters, then I would have nothing but a page of the alphabet in ornate lettering. The Chinese consider calligraphy an art form and it can be beautiful, but attention, as tradition demands, is drawn to the shape of the characters themselves. Great calligraphers are, therefore, great poets, too. But you are not Chinese. Words should not hinder the expression of thought unless one is expressing poetry. I am not writing poetry; I am writing to convince people of the validity of our struggle, its righteousness, and the utter fallacy and hypocrisy of the Americans in saying we are not capable of self-government."

For all his wisdom, Padre Jose had never spoken to him like this and with such lucidity. How he would have rewritten now that pompous journal which he had started in Cabugaw, influenced as he was by the classics and the Latin poets; he was but twenty-one then, and Padre Jose—bless him—had said that even one so young as he had already shown wisdom by being concerned not only with living but with what made life bearable. How apt, how beautiful it had all sounded. He was shut up in the convent, assured of his meals and safe from conscription in the public works in Vigan and elsewhere, yet he could see the inequities heaped upon his people, the drudgery that warped the lives of his own kin in Po-on. He saw, but could not bring himself to loathe the old priest, just as he could not hate the Americans the way the Cripple did. He had heard in frightened whispers what they had done to Filipino soldiers, the women they chanced upon, these big men with red hair and red beards, pillaging the villages, but he had seen not a drop of blood nor heard one gunshot.

"They have done all these, Eustaquio."

He brought to mind what had happened to Po-on, how he was shot and left to die, but there was a reason.

"There is no need for reason in war," the Cripple said with a sneer. "Passion rules. And yet, for those of us who can and should think, we must always remind ourselves that if we lose, it will not be only our lives—which have become inconsequential—but those of our future generations. We have so many structures to build so that we will be strong—for one, a church that is truly ours. We are a divided citizenry. We have ambitious leaders who think only of themselves, and an army in retreat. But not everything is lost. Our men can continue fighting even though they may no longer be in uniform. They will be indistinguishable from the village people in the daytime and at night, whenever the opportunity comes, they will strike. Every Filipino becomes suspect then."

IN A MONTH, the Cripple had regained his health and Istak returned to his *bangcag*. The rains lengthened, the rice grew, and by October, the first harvest was in. Now, the rains no longer came in nine-day torrents; the sun shone and the air was thick with the scent of newly cut hay. The moon came out silvery and full. It was on nights like this, lying on the sled in the yard, listening to the children play in the moonlight, their eager voices lifting his spirit, that thoughts bedeviled him. The Cripple still believed in God, but not God as the source of all good. Men could be morally upright not because an omnipresent God meted out punishment to those who strayed, but because men possessed reason. Where did this reason, this conscience come from? Man did not sprout from some empty seed by himself, but through a Supreme Will. And the city which this man builds is the City of God as well; shall it have blood as its foundation—as the native belief held and thus struck fear in the young—so that it will last for centuries, longer than Rome, for all eternity even? How long can this city last if it is not God who keeps watch over it?

AN UNBLEMISHED November day, the fields caparisoned with gold. He was starting out for his *bangcag* when Don Jacinto arrived. Had the Cripple's condition worsened? He had prayed for him more than he had ever done for any of the sick who sought him.

"It is not his health," Don Jacinto said. "He wants you to go on an errand—something only you can do."

AS HE ENTERED the room, the Cripple turned to him, grinning. "Thank you for coming, Eustaquio."

"At Don Jacinto's bidding, Apo," Istak said. The Cripple pointed to a chair. What errand could he do for this man who, with his pen, could squeeze water from stone?

"Have you ever gone back to the Ilokos since you left it, Eustaquio?"

"No, Apo," Istak said with a shake of the head.

"You told me you know your way across those mountains to

the valley. Through the land of the Igorots. You said you were there every year with this old priest. That you even made some friends among the Bagos . . ."

How well the Cripple remembered! In the late afternoons when he asked Istak up to the *azotea* to have a *merienda* of cocoa and *galletas,* he had asked Istak about his boyhood, how he had learned so much without formal schooling. Istak had reminisced, sometimes with reluctance, for he was uneasy recalling his Spanish mentor.

The Cripple's mind was a cavernous repository not just of ideas but of facts. He asked Istak about the Igorots—how they reacted to the missionary priests, how he himself felt about the savages that they were, whose homes were decorated with the skulls of their enemies, who regarded the Christian Ilokanos with hatred. Istak was frightened of them at first and that fright had not really left him, even afterward when he saw them again and remembered many of them, not just their villages perched on mountainsides or their well-groomed fields but also their names. There came to mind how the Bagos had attacked their bull-cart train. Would they ever change, would they ever be brothers to us?

"Yes, Apo," Istak said. "I was with them. Perhaps they still have no guns, so they cannot fight those who are armed. But they know their land—they rain stones from the mountaintops, they ambush those who are not wary or who cross their territory without their permission."

"They were a splendid sight in Malolos when the republic was inaugurated," the Cripple said quietly. "They paraded in their loincloths, armed with axes and spears. Like the Moros in the south, they are our brothers. We must recognize their belonging to Filipinas, their willingness to fight for her."

He turned to Don Jacinto briefly, then to Istak. "Some months ago when the war already seemed lost—yes, Eustaquio, we always prepared for the worst—Bishop Aglipay and General Luna went north to look for our last redoubt. Now I am going to ask you, Eustaquio, to do a favor not only for Don Jacinto and for me—but for yourself, your family, though you may not think of it this way. In time, I know you will. It is a very dangerous job, and you must do it with great caution and secrecy. You will surely go through territory already occupied by the Americans and if you are caught, you will most probably be tortured before you are shot. Remember, the enemy has spies who are brown like us, the opportunist Chinese and mestizos in Manila whom the Americans have enlisted to work for them, and those bastard Macabebes."

"Please don't tell me what you don't have to, Apo," Istak said. "Just tell me what the job is, if I can do it."

"You can," Don Jacinto said, smiling benignly. "We have been discussing this since yesterday. You are the man to do it."

"You know the land of the Bagos. The Ilokos is your own country," the Cripple said. "You speak excellent Spanish, and even Latin, and it is just as well, for the people you are going to meet cannot speak your language, nor you theirs."

Istak sat still, taking in every word. He recalled now how they had talked about the many languages in Filipinas, how necessary it was to have but one with which the people could reach one another. For the time being, it would have to be Spanish, but in the future, it would be a language wholly theirs, expressive of their souls and rooted in their lives.

The Cripple continued: "You will not attract attention—this is one reason why we have chosen you. Forgive me, Eustaquio— but you don't look like a soldier or the *ilustrado* that you are. You are a farmer . . . the way I was."

How well he had put it! The praise burned in Istak's face. An *ilustrado*—so that was what he had become.

"The most important thing, Eustaquio," the Cripple emphasized, "is not that we are not farmers anymore, but that we should never, never forget that we were." He paused and looked at his old friend. Don Jacinto nodded.

The Cripple now told him what he was to do:

"Ride to Bayambang—that is where they will be tomorrow. They are moving very fast at night, with the Americans pursuing them. I should not tell you, but this knowledge should never leave you, not even if they torture you, that the president is headed for the Ilokos. He will cross the mountains into Cagayan. This is as much as I know and I cannot tell you more although I wish I could. There is no other way, Eustaquio. The Americans have landed in San Fabián and their cavalry has advanced already to San José, to the towns near here, San Quintín and Umingan. The escape route is sealed."

"You don't have to tell me everything, Apo," Istak said, wondering when the Americans would backtrack to Rosales itself.

"I trust you," the Cripple exclaimed. "If only we could learn to trust one another—Tagalogs trusting Ilokanos, Pampangos trusting Tagalogs. An Ilokano showed the way—more than a hundred years ago, Diego Silang trusted his neighbors. The people of Pangasinan became his allies. His rebellion was defeated, yes—but it was a beginning, the cooperation among the peoples of the north. More of this and, Eustaquio, we have a nation! Not this, not this . . ." The Cripple sighed and shook his head. From a folder on his desk, he withdrew a sheaf of papers. He picked out a few and began to read. "The defeat of the insurgents is inevitable; not only are they disunited and disorganized—they are also hated by the natives . . ." He paused, looked at Don Jacinto and Istak and asked: "Does it not sound familiar? It is this chauvinist Thomas Collins again, and his report tells of how bands and cheering crowds have welcomed them in the towns they have entered. Yes, this could all be true, maybe it is also true that there are many Filipinos who do not like war and want peace at any cost. But this . . . this!" The Cripple's lips were compressed and anger flashed in his eyes. He returned to the paper he was reading and quietly continued: "Our forces are assisted by Macabebes—native scouts from Pampanga—who know the terrain and are familiar with insurgent methods. Like our Indian scouts in the Indian campaign, they are absolutely loyal to us . . ." The Cripple stopped, his head dropped, silence.

"There is truth in what this Collins says," he finally said in a small, defeated voice. "How can we build trust among our own people? How can we make them confident of themselves and their countrymen so that they will not sell their souls for a few silver dollars? We need more leaders like Diego Silang." He raised his thin arms in a gesture of futility, then dropped them on the table. "There is so much that the past can teach us," he continued softly, as if he were talking more to himself than to anyone else. "Diego Silang—more than a hundred years ago, what did he prove? That with a brilliant and selfless leader, we can be united the way he united the north. And united, we can then make Filipinas strong, formidable . . .

"We have no time for remonstrances, fault-finding, self-scrutiny. We must only think of how we can survive. No, not us, but the republic. The president must not be captured."

"They must flee quickly," Don Jacinto said. "And to escape their pursuers, they need a very good guide, someone who knows those mountains. I have not forgotten what you have told me, Eustaquio."

The Cripple opened the drawer on his desk and brought out a small brown envelope. "You must give this letter to the president, Eustaquio," he said quickly. "If it is lost or if you have to destroy it, remember that this is what I have written in this letter, and you must repeat this to no one but him. No one, remember that. I believe that the war is lost, but not the struggle. The mistakes that were committed, we learn from them. We cannot fight an enemy as powerful as America in the manner with which they are slaughtering our men—with cavalry and cannon. We will fight them—I am simply reiterating this—in a guerrilla war everywhere. A long, costly war, not set battles and frontal attacks. They are well trained, well supplied. We should never stop and I—I will continue what I am doing—trying to reach the councils of the world, speaking of our rights. I will wage this campaign in their own newspapers, in the chambers of their own government. I will do this with the pen. Whatever we do, in whatever battlefield we fight, we must be united. The president is a just man. Tell him what I have told you—that this is not a Tagalog war, but a war involving all of us."

One last question was burning in Istak's mind; the Cripple, the president, all of them—surely they must know that the revolution had failed. And it had failed because the leaders could not see themselves as Filipinos. Always, they were men of Cavite, of Bulacan, and now, he was Ilokano. How could anyone rise from his origins? Everything starts from there just as with him everything started in Po-on. But he asked it anyhow:

"Why do you persevere, Apo, if everything is lost?"

The question was lightning, perhaps, or thunder. Don Jacinto, who was listening to everything, head bowed, jerked up. The Cripple, immobile in his chair, leaned forward and raised his hands in an angry gesture, but slowly brought them down. In the morning light, his face had seemed solemn and at peace but suddenly the fire in his eyes banished all this. He breathed deeply, then spoke: "You say then that we must leave the leader to his fate? He has committed mistakes . . . but until he is captured or killed, he is not just a leader, he is a symbol of our struggle, of our will. Yes, we have already lost the war. This is true.

Even an unlettered man can see this. This land belongs to us, Eustaquio, and someday, we will win. We lose now, but we will fight again, each one of us, until they tire, until they are bloodied and wearied, until we are free and justice triumphs."

ISTAK HAD NOT ridden in years, but Don Jacinto assured him that Kimat, his beautiful chico-colored horse, was not a difficult animal. He should not forget to give the horse a piece of sugar cake every afternoon, together with the grass. Don Jacinto gave him fifty pesos—the largest sum Istak had ever had. The letter in a leather pouch was sewn into the jute mat that was to be his saddle. Farmers could not afford the leather saddle Kimat was used to. At the gate, Don Jacinto embraced him, reminding him what the Cripple had said: "Eustaquio, you are no longer Ilokano, you are Filipino."

How would he tell Dalin what he was to do, where he was going? There were just the three of them who knew. Remembering the stories of torture the Americans had inflicted upon his people, he wondered about his capacity to be silent if his flesh was torn, or if his boys or his wife would be forfeit for what was entrusted to him. He had kept a few secrets to himself. Not even to the old priest from whom he had learned so much or to Dalin had he revealed how he had been aroused by Capitán Berong's daughter. That was, of course, a trifling matter, important only to himself. What he knew involved not just the two friends who shared the secret with him, but, perhaps, a thousand others whose lives depended on how well he could keep the secret, then lead the president to the valley.

Don Jacinto held the reins for a while and patted his favorite horse on the head. Before he let go, he whispered to Istak: "Do not worry about your family."

A chill wave collapsed on him. He might never return; how would he tell Dalin this? She had understood why he had to work for the Cripple for days. And how exhilarating it had been—to have the mind soar again, to speak again with someone who could scale those ethereal heights. He had forgotten the feeling, although on occasion something akin to it would lift him from his mundane self, when he brought back color to faces already marked by Death, when a bony arm still and numb responded to his touch. *Kyrie Eleison! Christe Eleison!* Would Dalin understand? For all her intelligence, she had never really thought much beyond what was circumscribed by Cabugawan. Nights he would lie awake, his arm laid across her breast, and they would talk not about what the Cripple had said but about the ripening corn, the sick, and why he had to see all who came to him as if a compulsion possessed him. How would he explain to her the sickness which he had survived, which ordained him to do what he was doing? And now, no dream hastened him, nothing but a cripple's words—yet they were all that mattered.

Even without Istak's telling her, Dalin knew how much he had enjoyed writing again. The time would come when the words he shaped would spring to life, and these same words would claim him—not as words but as a promise, as Vigan in the past had been, and perhaps, someday, Manila—all the evocations that the Cripple had made. Manila, where people could appreciate better what he did with words and prayers; Manila, where there were more men like the Cripple. But it was not to that Queen City he was headed. He was going back to the north, to the beginning.

LATER: How would he tell his sons? Antonio was not even ten and though the boy already knew how to plow straight furrows and control the plowshare so that it did not sink too deep, still he was just a boy. And Pedro, who could help in the transplanting of rice, in the pasturing of the *carabaos*, who was as proficient as his older brother at reading and writing—what would happen to them? They would not starve as long as Dalin was alive, that was true. He regretted that he had spent so little time with them.

Kimat cantered through the narrow lane bordered with flowering madre de cacao trees. The jute-mat saddle held the letter sewn within, the silver pesos were in his pocket. Slung across the horse's back was the bag with cakes of cane sugar. He would add to his pack rice, salt, and dried beef. It would suffice. With money, he could always buy provisions on the way.

Antonio's dog, Kebaan, barked in greeting when he approached; the barking frightened the horse, which reared, but only for an instant. Kimat became still as soon as Istak smoothed his mane and said a few soothing words. All the boys in the neighborhood who had heard the neighing rushed out of their homes to look at the beautiful beast, bigger than the ponies which pulled the *calesas*. Though Don Jacinto had been to Cabugawan a few times, Kimat always drew attention from the children. Their own uncle astride the steed impressed upon them all of their uncle's importance, that something unknown, exciting, was happening.

Dalin came down the stairs. Through the open door, the kitchen fire reached out to them with its warm glow. Istak, tying Kimat to a gatepost, could discern at once the anxiety in her face as she approached. He held her by the waist and drew her up to the house, leaving the boys in the yard to admire the horse.

"That is Don Jacinto's mount," she said. "Where are you going?"

He did not reply; instead, he kissed her softly on the brow. It was moist with perspiration. "Do not be angry, Old Woman," he said affectionately. "Just do not forget that you are precious to me and that I will always treasure you in my mind and heart."

The concern in her face deepened. He told her everything without any embellishment, and when he was through, she embraced him and cried, "I may not see you again. I have waited for this day, I knew it would come."

She had always been brave. Like the house posts uprooted from the Ilokos, she was also sturdy. She would be able to withstand the long wait, the uncertainty, he assured himself as he held her, feeling the quiver in her body, the trickle of her tears against his cheek. "I will return, just wait," he whispered.

He left her so she could finish her cooking, the smell of the vegetable stew clinging to his nostrils. This was the pleasure of home he would certainly miss, and briefly, he wondered where he would have his breakfast; the road to Bayambang was not within his compass and he did not know of a single eating place along the way.

At his instruction, his older son had gone quickly to the neighbors, to Bit-tik first. Now the men, the women, and children were gathered in the yard, sitting on their haunches, on the long wooden mortar where the sheaves of rice were pounded.

To them, he entrusted his family. He was leaving, he said, on a journey to the north. They knew of the Cripple's presence in Rosales, this great man whose wisdom they could not fathom. He was tempted to tell them he would go across the Cordilleras and that he would probably try and see Po-on again. Po-on where they came from and where it all began. Po-on which clung to them tenaciously as memory.

In the afterglow, he recognized all the faces raised to him. The soft light hid the lines of care and hard work just as it hid from them, too, the glaze of tears in his eyes.

He was valuable to them—teacher, healer, patriarch; now he

realized with searing sharpness that they were valuable to him not only as cousins and neighbors—they were the earth, the water, the air which sustained him.

He asked Bit-tik to stay after they had gone; he would have a last word with him. They stood in the yard talking, while above, the stars swarmed and the cool harvest air filled the lungs. He wrapped an arm around his brother's shoulder. "How do you think the weather will turn out in the next few days?"

"You are the one who knows more about the ways of God, Manong," Bit-tik said. "I hope that it will be good, not because the harvest season is upon us—but because you will be going on a long journey."

"Yes," he murmured. "It is a long trip. And the boys—you know, they cannot yet take care of the farm or of their mother."

"Do not insult me," Bit-tik said. "If we eat, they will eat."

Istak did not speak again. Before he turned to leave, he tightened his arm around the broad, strong shoulders of his younger brother.

Supper was waiting in the house; the stew was steaming on the low eating table, on top of it a big black mudfish which had been broiled. The new rice in the open pot was red and fragrant. A small coconut bowl was beside the rice pot; it was half filled with salted fish sauce flavored with lime juice and roasted red pepper. A plate of boiled camote tops completed the meal. The two boys ate quickly with their hands; they were growing and they always seemed famished. He watched them—Antonio, who was older, who had already handled the plow, whose brow was wide like his; and Pedro the younger, who had inherited his mother's handsome features. He had delivered them himself—held them up to his wife, their umbilical cords still uncut, their bodies still wet and shining with the juices of the womb. They were such tiny, wailing things then, and now they were big.

Three more harvests, just three more short years and Antonio would be circumcised, and Pedro after him. Would they be able to take care of their mother? Would they stay in Cabugawan, or would the call of far and exotic distances bewitch them as once he himself had hearkened, had longed for the distances he would traverse? Now, there was this long and perhaps perilous journey. What new wisdom would he extract from it?

"Take me with you, Father," Antonio pleaded, looking eagerly at him. "I can ride behind you, I know. I will take care of the horse, gather the grass for him."

"No, son," Istak said softly. "This is a journey I must take alone. Maybe, when I return—we can go on a long, long ride. You in the back, Pedro in the front because he is smaller."

They continued eating, Dalin wordless now. Outside, the darkness was complete.

They all went down to the yard, the night alive with the soughing of the wind, the whispering of insects. He held his two boys close to his chest, half kneeling, smelling the day on their young bodies. Antonio—he had learned some reading, writing, a little arithmetic, and Pedro—only eight years old—alert of eye and swift with his hands and legs. Again—how would they fare when he was gone? But Don Jacinto had promised to help them if by some awry turn of fate he did not return. And they were among relatives here.

He stood up and held Dalin, felt her heart thump against his chest. The hard work in the fields, the pounding of rice, the weaving, and the cooking had roughened her palms. With the pain in her face was this grace, this luster which he had always loved. He could say nothing except look at her and hope to God that whatever might happen, she would always be safe. He wanted most to remember her as he saw her, the starlight in her eyes, the silence of her prayer. He held her tight, then let go.

His provisions were light—the sack that was half full, a clean shirt and trousers, a thick blanket which Dalin herself had woven, a length of saluyot twine, his old bolo, and a pencil and his journal. He tied them into a bundle which he slung over his shoulder. It would be his pillow for the night.

As he mounted the horse, Dalin finally broke into a plaintive cry. Tears burned in Istak's eyes. The boys followed him beyond the gate, where they were joined by their cousins. It was too early for them to sleep; soon the moon would be out in all its sheen. They would have gone with him beyond the arbor of bamboo at the end of the village, but Istak told them this was as far as they should go.

The night was all around, fireflies winking in the air. Bayambang was two towns away to the west. The president would be there in a day. If Istak did not tarry, he would be there ahead of them. He had all that time to plan.

CHAPTER

15

I STAK took the road to Santo Tomás. Times were perilous and brigands who preyed on travelers would covet his horse. Kimat was well trained and amiable, and he responded quickly to every nudge and snap of the reins. The night was cool; the shadowed, even fields, some still heavy with grain, were perfumed with the scent of harvest and newly mown hay. From underneath some of the farmhouses along the road, a dog would stir and sometimes rush out to snap at the horse's legs. But Kimat did not frighten easily. Istak rode at a canter, almost in a walk. He did not want to tire the animal needlessly—there were many miles to go. Before he reached Alcala, after Santo Tomás, the moon sailed out of a cloud bank. He found a spot beyond the road with a stand of tall grass behind it; he dismounted, took a long sip from his water bottle. His eyes had become heavy and the hide of the horse was wet with perspiration.

"A pity, Kimat," he whispered into the animal's ear. "This is just the beginning. We still have many rivers to cross, mountains to climb. Patience, my friend. Patience."

He tied to his own leg a length of saluyot twine and attached it to the reins so that if Kimat strayed too far, he would wake up. With his jute-sack saddle unrolled into a mat and his knapsack for a pillow, he lay down.

Above, the moon had disappeared into a cloud bank. How vast were the heavens and here he was, a puny man with a puny life. He had tried to give this life meaning by being a healer, by hoping that he would leave his tiny imprint at least in Cabugawan. But all men die—as anonymously as they have lived, no matter what their achievements.

While the horse grazed, he closed his eyes and imagined Dalin, her smile, her eyes.

He must have fallen asleep; he was awakened by the crunch of cartwheels on the dirt road. He rose quickly. There, on the road beyond the screen of grass was a column of men, some of them on horseback, moving toward Bayambang. In the waning moonlight, it seemed their horses were much, much bigger than his mount and the men seemed bigger, too. They marched with stolid yet easy strides; they did not seem tired. Yet they did not talk—they would have come upon him with the stealth of a cat had it not been for the creak of the carts drawn by horses and the shuffle of feet on the dirt.

They did not see him, nor did they see Kimat, who had now raised his head but did not neigh or make a sound. How fortunate that he had dismounted a distance from the road, and had a grass screen to hide him. He was sure now that they were not Filipinos—they were Americans, and the shorter men behind them were probably their Pampango scouts. They were going to close in on Bayambang, where President Aguinaldo was!

The last sound of the column had barely died when Istak

mounted Kimat and cut across the fields—it was now all plain all the way to Bayambang. He must detour around Alcala, and though he did not know the way, at least he knew the general direction of Bayambang—the Ilokano farmers would show him the way through pockets of scrub and new clearings if he strayed.

Near the town of Alcala, just as light was about to break, intermittent gunfire erupted from across the expanse of ripening grain. Then silence again, the crowing of cocks. Now, a sallow light upon a land rimmed by flounces of bamboo, woods, and farmers' homes. Close to the right was a village. The people there would no longer be Ilokanos but Pangasiñenses. He had learned a little of their language from Dalin, so he would be able to ask directions. How would they greet him, a stranger with a beautiful horse?

He rode swiftly through a line of trees to the village. He was wrong—it was still Ilokano, and at the well, a group of women were filling their earthen jars. They looked at him passively as he approached. Why had he come this early? And not through the village road but across the field?

"I was lost," he lied, allaying their suspicions immediately. "My horse needs a drink, and so do I . . ."

One of the women filled a wooden tub and Istak led the horse to it. Kimat took long drafts, and shook his mane after he was full.

"I am on my way to Bayambang," he said. "And on the way, I saw the Americans—I did not want them to take my horse, so I cut across the fields."

"Were you the one they fired at?" one of them asked, her eyes wide with expectation. "We were wakened by the shooting."

"No," he said with a smile. "It seems God is very kind to me. They did not see me at all."

A farmer and his sons appeared with sickles; they were on their way to harvest before the sun came out in full force.

"Follow the village road," the man said, "then turn right at the fork till you reach the river. From there, just follow the river to the west. You will be in Bayambang."

He was hungry; he wanted to cook his breakfast and roast the dried beef. But the man's wife, who was among those by the well, said there was still enough rice, coffee, and fried fish waiting in their kitchen.

BEYOND the fork of the road, as the man had said, Istak came upon the Agno and its wide delta. He was familiar with the delta in Carmay, how the waters came cascading down the mountains and every year wrought new channels upon it. But the river, giver of life, was also cruel. Again memories—how his mother was swept away and he was unable to help her. Where in its long and uneven course did she finally surface? Or had her body sunk to the bottom? Through the years, all through the length of the river that he could reach, he asked so that there would be one spot at least where he and his children could pray, where they could light the votive candles when the Day of the Dead came. He never found out; the whole river, then, was Mayang's burial ground, each drop sacred.

Alcala was now behind him; would he be too late? But the president did not travel alone, unguarded or without arms. And the men who had passed him in the night could not have been more than a hundred.

Beyond the narrow strip of delta was the ferry, a huge raft made of three tiers of bamboo strapped together by rattan. At one end of the big raft was a hut where the ferryman stayed when it rained or when it was hot. It was the start of the dry season and the Agno was no longer wild and deep. One man with a pole could push the raft to the other side. But during the typhoon season when the river swelled and giant whirlpools sucked away in the current, four men would have difficulty guiding the raft across.

Istak dismounted at the river's edge where the ferry was moored. The ferryman, like the drivers of the carriages and the bull carts that carried commerce between the towns, would be a rich source of information. He was small, dressed in loose, tattered clothes that seemed to hang from a frame about to collapse. He was eating a breakfast of dried fish and freshly cooked rice, and a couple of fish were still roasting over the coals in the stove by the hut. The strong aroma reached out to Istak.

"Let us eat," the ferryman said in greeting.

Istak said he had already eaten, then asked the ferryman if he had heard the gunfire early that morning. The ferryman nodded between mouthfuls. "It must be the rear guard of the president," he said.

The president had been able to escape, then. "Three days ago," the ferryman said. He had finished eating and was dipping the tin plate into the calm brownish water to wash it.

"Did they cross here?" Istak asked.

"No," the man replied. "There were so many of them, I would have had to make a lot of trips. Farther up the river—in Bayambang. They crossed over the bridge. Hundreds of them, with guns, big bundles, and women and children."

The man gazed at the broad spread of water. "Still, there were those who crossed here." He turned to Istak. "Years ago, we had that ferry in Bayambang—but then they built the railroad and that bridge, and we earn so little."

"Can you take me across?" Istak asked. There was no need for him to proceed to Bayambang.

"Are you a soldier?"

Istak shook his head. "Just a farmer in a hurry to see my dying father."

The man continued: "It was three days ago that they left Bayambang—that is what my passengers told me."

Three days—if they marched every day, they would already be far, far away, well into La Union. There was not one moment to squander.

"Will you take me across?" he said.

"You are alone," the ferryman said. "You must wait for the others. There should be more in a short while."

"I am in a hurry," Istak said.

The ferryman grumbled.

"You just had a very good breakfast," Istak said.

"If you are alone, you have to pay *benting*. And your horse, that is another *benting*. That is *salapi*. A man's wage for two days. Are you sure you want to cross alone? Wait till there are at least five of you so you will pay only *micol*."

Istak shook his head. "*Benting* it will be," he said, and proceeded to the shallow rim of the river, Kimat in tow.

The man strained at the bamboo pole, and slowly the raft floated toward the deeper reaches. It was quite placid, unlike the last time he had crossed, when it was a massive tide of brown. Again, an ancient grief swept over him. How many lives had this river taken?

"There are portions which are not deep," Istak said. "At this time, it is possible to wade across."

The ferryman laughed. "If I told you where it is shallow, what would happen to me? Everyone would wade across. I should really tell you that it is dangerous to travel alone."

"My horse is swift," Istak said.

The ferryman looked at Kimat; the horse was erect, undaunted by the waters eddying around the raft.

"The Americans," the ferryman said. "I have heard so many

bad things about them, how they tortured and killed. And you have a horse which they might take."

"But I am not going to Bayambang," Istak said.

"Yes, but they have already crossed the river, too. Yesterday, in large numbers. That was what I was told."

"They can have my horse," Istak said. "What can they do to me? Just a poor farmer . . . the horse is not even mine."

The sun now blazed down, burnishing the delta with brilliant white. In midstream, the current was hardly discernible and the ferryman guided the raft deftly. On the other bank, a row of trees and the deep gully through which he must pass. Where the raft would be moored, a couple of women were waiting, their bamboo baskets filled with greens.

"The roads are not safe at night," the ferryman warned.

"And the Americans? What advice can you give if I should meet them?"

"They don't bother us little people," the ferryman said.

UP THE INCLINE, more ripening fields shimmered in the morning sun. To his right, several women were already harvesting the grain with hand scythes. There would always be a few stalks left for gleaners and those who would glean would most probably be Ilokanos, just like the first settlers in this part of Pangasinan.

He mounted again.

At noon, when he would rest, he would bring out his journal and write about his crossing and the gunfire that ripped the quiet dawn. There were still many rivers to cross but they would be narrower and he could ford them on horseback.

He rode through villages already stirring. Dogs sprang from under the houses to snarl at him. He varied the pace of his ride. No animal could run indefinitely without tiring, but it was as if Kimat anticipated his every move. He trotted, slowed down to a walk, or gathered speed in a gallop without waiting for Istak to snap the reins on his flanks.

He had ridden most of the night and all morning. His buttocks began to throb with a dull, raw pain. So this was how it was with Padre Jose when they toiled up the hillocks of the Cordilleras. The old priest had always complained of how much his buttocks had been mashed, but only on the second day did the old priest moan. He was on a horse, of course, but Istak, his favorite sacristan, always followed on foot.

He was not tired but his eyes grew heavy. Unharvested fields all around; in another week, they would be bereft of grain. He sought the shade of a low butterfly tree away from the road and dismounted, tied the length of twine to the reins and to his leg, and brought down his knapsack for a pillow and lay down. Kimat could wander as far as the length of rope would permit. Above, the noonday sky was swept clean of clouds. From the knapsack, he brought out his journal.

The Cripple had given him the journal but it was seldom that he had used it. He had made only four notations, one about the Cripple himself, how quick his wit and how he had compared the wanderlust of the Batangueños, his kinsmen, with that of the Ilokanos, and how clannish both people were. Both were also proud and steadfast in their personal honor. How quickly they defended it with their lives, the Batangueños with their folding knives, the Ilokanos with their bolos. How does the old Ilokano saying go? *Inlayat, intagbat.* If you raise the bolo, you must strike.

Yet, he had always detested violence; he was patient, he was industrious. These virtues were instilled in him as a boy; his two sons would be no different, although they had Pangasinan blood.

Dalin came to mind, and for a while he could imagine her— her long tresses shiny with coconut oil, her face, her radiance.

How well she had raised the children and, most important, she had stood by him and supported him when he wavered.

He took the pencil out and started to write, this time in Ilokano, for he wanted Dalin to read it someday:

> My Dearest Wife—I am now far away resting in an open field, but it seems you are near and I can even imagine hearing your voice. We have gone through ten years together yet it seems as if all these happened only yesterday, only because when I am with you time stops. Thank you for having shared my sorrows, the times when the harvest was niggardly, when there was little rice in the bin. Thank you for having taken care of me and grabbed me before I could fall into that black, bottomless pit. I will still have many distances to travel, but even now, I feel like I could fly, only because I want this journey to end so that I can hurry back to you. I have asked myself so many times why I am doing this and while I am not yet sure of the reason why—of one thing I am sure: Cabugawan is where I am headed, for that is where you are.

Words are never really enough to express love, and words having failed him, he closed his eyes and dreamed.

It was the sun, warm on his face, which woke him. Kimat was close by, grazing on the grass. He had not looked around closely before. To his left, he saw the village—some eight thatch-roofed houses. It must be an hour before sundown and the afternoon had become cool. He started to rise and it was then that a bolt of pain shot down his spine as if someone had lanced him—his whole being was aflame. He felt that if he so much as made one slight move, he would die. He fell back on the ground, gasping. He remembered then that he had never ridden far before. After a while, he rose again—the pain no longer throbbed. He reined Kimat in and, with some difficulty, placed the saddle and the twin sacks on the animal's back. Leading the horse close to a low dike, he mounted the dike, then the horse, the pain coursing through him quickly again.

In the village, he looked for a *calesa* driver. There was always one who provided the village with its transport. He needed some grass and rice bran for Kimat. The villagers were Ilokanos; he was close to San Fabián now. The sea lay ahead to the left, the low hills of the Ilokos loomed to the right, and ahead rose the blue-green ranges of the Cordilleras.

The driver had just come in for the day; he had a new *calesa*, with the floral designs on the sides still bright and the tinwork on the harness still shiny. The grass and the bran would cost Istak five centavos.

"Tell me about the road from San Fabián to Rosario—the road along the coast to the north. Are Americans already there? Surely, you must have heard."

The driver was a farmer, perhaps in his early twenties. He had not traveled far, he said, but was sure the Americans were not yet there.

"They are already in Bayambang," Istak said.

"Maybe just a few," the *calesa* driver said. The bran that Istak wanted was already mixed with molasses in a wooden trough, and Kimat had started eating.

"I am going north," Istak said. "And I don't want to cross their path."

If the president had crossed the river from Bayambang, he would probably have gone on to Dagupan by train and from there onward to San Fabián. The people here would be Pangasiñenses; they would probably understand Istak if he spoke in

Ilokano. He could always speak in Spanish but he did not want to appear to be an *ilustrado*. The people of the north had always regarded the Pangasiñenses with condescension, for they were considered self-indulgent and lazy, they waited for their co-conuts to fall rather than climbing the palms to harvest them. And their women—he smiled in remembrance of the tattered concepts of his own womenfolk—they are lazy like their men, and worse, they are filthy. He had teased Dalin about this when they finally dismantled their makeshift hut and built a better dwelling with hardwood posts, but Dalin had always kept her pots clean and the yard well swept. She even bathed the two pigs she raised as if they were human beings. It was not right—attributing inborn faults and virtues to people, but if he felt comfortable anywhere, it was among his own people.

The Cripple had decried the treachery of the Macabebes. Perhaps it was money which made them join the Spaniards. With American silver they were now fighting their own kin. Why do people betray their brothers and eventually themselves? Do not trust anyone, not even your own instincts, the Cripple had warned; you are alone, you must always be on guard not only against those who will harm you but those who will take the message and stop you from doing your job.

He had talked with the boatman as he was now talking with this stranger—freely. They were little people like himself, far removed from the battlefield or the cares of high office. He knew his instructions, but he must also trust people. Still . . .

The driver was inquisitive. Istak was just another traveler—one of the hundreds that had crossed the river. He must now tell a longer story, with a semblance of truth to it.

"I am going to Cabugaw," he said. "My father is dying. We have a small piece of land there—and maybe, with the share, we can go back to the Ilokos—my family and I. There is nothing like living where you were born, where you know everyone. You know what I am trying to say."

The driver turned away. He stirred the molasses and added water and bran in the trough where Kimat was feeding. In the thatch-roofed house beyond them, a stove fire had been kindled and the driver's wife was preparing the evening meal. To her, the man said aloud: "Be sure you include an additional plate for our visitor," to which Istak said quickly: "No, you have already been very kind. I must be on my way."

"You cannot travel in the dark," the driver said.

Istak did wait, though, for a plate of hot rice and a piece of roasted dried meat. While he waited, the rig driver told him about the village, how his villagers had come down, too, from the north—Paoay—and how they had claimed the forest. Large patches of jungle still covered Pangasinan, and the natives were too lazy to clear them. And there were no more tributes or excessive taxes to pay. Surely, the future was better here.

ISTAK MOUNTED Kimat again. The November wind was balmy and he felt so refreshed he was sure he could travel the whole night. The pain in his buttocks and at the base of his spine was no longer as sharp as it had been earlier in the day. Now, he was familiar with the rhythm of the horse, its even pace. He rarely used his heels to prod the animal. He had learned, too, of Kimat's signals, how his head drooped when he was tired, how he raised his head when he tensed to alien sounds. Kimat seemed almost human in his expression of gratitude—he would nudge Istak after being given a piece of sugar cake or merely patted on the neck.

Still no trace of the Americans. Soon he would reach the sea. How quickly he had traveled, unlike the time when they came down the Ilokos in a caravan. Kimat made all the difference. The mountains were closer, the wooded hills and long stretches of vacant land that were cattle ranches. In the coming dusk, the mountains were caparisoned with the soft luster of gold and blue, and high up in the ranges toward the land of the Igorots, clouds of deepening purple were impaled by peaks. He was sure he would find the trail and overtake them—they were such a big group, they would not be able to travel as fast as he. Indeed, the strongest man is the solitary man.

In the late afternoon of the fourth day, he saw the coast. He was up in the hills. Tension tightened the air. He knew this by the manner in which the people of these shallow valleys responded to his questions. Anytime now, he should cross the path of the president—or the Americans. The coast was still far away, and the towns along them were a good half day's ride.

It was evening when he reached the village where the road branched from Pangasinan—a narrow road flanked by weeds and bananas. He entered it at a walk, hoping there would be someone who could lend him a pot and a stove to cook his supper.

No dog growling from the houses, no poultry disturbed in the roost—just sepulchral quiet. The village was empty; either the Americans had just passed or were coming. He must move on.

The road entered the open fields, which had already been harvested, and the harvest was spread in the fields to dry.

Kimat was tired, so he dismounted and again led the horse farther up and away from the road. He laid his saddle on the stubble of hay and promptly went to sleep.

He thought it was Kimat who woke him up with his grunting. The animal stood still—his head raised in the air, his ears pointed upward. Then Istak heard not just the grunting of horses but the creaking of wheels. He turned to the left and there, outlined against the night sky was a column—men on big horses, bigger than Kimat, cannon trailing their huge wagons, men with packs on their backs. Americans.

His feet grew cold and his throat went dry. He crouched and held the animal tightly lest it make a sound. But Kimat did not move.

It seemed as if the column would march on forever—the shuffling of feet, the strain of wagons, of gear. But in time the column ended. There must have been five hundred men. Istak mounted his horse and cut swiftly across the fields. He must outrace them in a wide arc, through clumps of bamboo and along irrigation ditches. Kimat seemed to understand and he ran faster than before. Istak crouched, the wind rushing toward him, cold and swift as a whiplash. He paused briefly to let Kimat drink when they forded a stream.

It was dawn when he reached Bauang. He remembered the town: nothing had changed. He rode slowly; he had left the Americans behind. It was quiet and at first, until he got to the church, Istak thought the people were still asleep. There, hanging from the branches of the acacia tree were three men. In the early light, there was no mistaking them—Filipino soldiers in their *rayadillo* uniforms, their bare feet tied with wire, as were their hands. The church, the whole town was empty. He must get out quickly. He backtracked to a narrow sidestreet, and it was then that, from his right, he heard a loud command: "Halt!"

He did not have to turn; that was an American voice. Digging his heels into the sides of Kimat, he dashed through an empty yard onward to the road beyond it. Kimat responded with a great surge of strength.

The shot sundered the morning quiet and for an instant, he thought: I am dead—but he felt no searing impact against his flesh, no blackness claiming him. Kimat ran on, across open fields, through a barrier of madre de cacao trees, and behind it, more fields, and beyond that, a *sitio* of some five or six huts.

By then, Kimat had slowed and though Istak prodded the animal, he would no longer run. His canter turned into a slow walk, and just as they entered the village, the animal stopped, shuddered, and collapsed.

Istak scrambled down and looked at Kimat. The horse had been hit—the rump was bleeding and blood trickled down the leg of the poor horse. Istak fondled his head; Kimat's breath come slow, then he lay still.

Istak turned to the houses before him. People had seen him for they now came forward.

"The Americans," he told them quietly, "they shot my horse. It is dead. You can have it for meat." He patted the animal.

They gave him food and asked where he came from and where he was going. He told them the usual story, then asked why there were no people in town. He knew the reason but he wanted them to explain. The president had passed through that afternoon with his party and the people had come out in the streets, rejoicing. Surely, the Americans were closing in.

He had missed the president by a day, a few hours at the most. He thanked them for the meal and wanted to know if there was a horse he could buy. There was none. He must not waste time; now he must continue on foot.

THE QUICKEST, shortest way was through the towns. When his legs felt numb and he could no longer run, he walked. Dogs followed and snapped at him, but they remained quiet after he had recited his *oración* for dogs. Always, he asked in each village for a horse he could buy, but there was none and the *calesa* drivers whom he hired could take him only as far as the next town. At times, he left the road, which was rutted with the deep imprint of bull-cart wheels during the rainy season, and went to the beach, where the sand was firm. Walking there was easier but the beaches were not always sandy. The shoreline was often rocky and it sometimes dropped, rugged and sharp, to the sea. He returned to the road, parts of which were not cobbled for carriages. If only he did not tire or go hungry! He had to pause for naps, then walk on, half asleep.

Toward midafternoon, having slept so little the previous night, he paused again for a nap, hoping it would not last too long. An acacia tree at the edge of a village shaded him from the unrelenting sun. When he woke up, children were around him, waiting.

They laughed when he stirred. He asked them where he was. Close to the town of Bangar, they said. Did they see the president and his party pass? Yes, they said, the other day. Were the Americans coming?

Yes. The older people had fled the village, but they were children and they said the children were not harmed. As a matter of fact, the children were given candies. They were waiting for those candies.

He felt relieved; surely he could reach the president before the Americans did. He asked for a drink of water and they brought him a small pot from which he drank, savoring each sip.

The sun was once again a brilliant flood on the land. To his right, beyond the town, the hills were ramparts he must climb, and beyond, the mountains that fenced the Ilokos from Cagayan Valley—formidable ranges one after the other, and in the center Mount Tirad, straight and sharp. The pass was below this peak.

It would be a three-day hike—and already his legs stung where the thorns of bamboo had slashed, and his arms and face were hot with sunburn. He had not changed his clothes—they had been wet with perspiration and dried and they smelled.

IT WAS DARK at last and he had not eaten anything save the sugar cake that was for Kimat; he had slaked his thirst in the first stream that he crossed and his stomach was full. But God, he was tired. He could go no farther, and how his muscles ached! Wearily, he brought his knapsack and saddle down by a rock and the moment his head rested on it, sleep came like a balm banishing the day's fever and fret.

MORNING laves the shore towns of the Ilokos with the rich smell of harvest commingled with the salty tang of the sea. Though the nights were cold, the sun creeping up the Cordilleras brought warmth quickly. The day was clear, dew still sparkled on the grass, and in the yards of the houses, trash fires burned. He must be barely a day ahead of the Americans. Near Candon, at the first house where he went for a drink, he asked if they were near.

The owner of the house was a music teacher and his three young pupils, interrupted in the solfeggio lessons, sat idly by. Brass instruments—a battered trombone and a couple of trumpets—lay on the table in the kitchen, where he was taken for his drink. Istak always felt comfortable talking in his own language with his own people. If he were going to Cabugaw instead, it would take just two more days.

"I came from Cabugaw, Apo," he said in deference to the man who was older and did not do manual labor. "I just want to know where the Americans are so that I can avoid them. They move quickly and without warning. In Bauang, I did not know they were already there. They hanged three soldiers right there in the plaza. And they shot my horse."

The music teacher took him to the tiny living room. The house was not a farmer's house, but it was not a rich man's house either. Its walls were split bamboo, the roof was thatch, and only the wooden floor attested to the man's more prosperous means.

"They will not find the people of Candon cheering them—if what they will bring are torture and vile words," the man said evenly. He was past forty and had gray hair. "How long have you lived in Pangasinan?"

"More than ten years, Apo," Istak said. He had finished the second glass of water, and had stopped perspiring.

"Only recently, did you know that we fought the Spaniards? We were overwhelmed, but we had proven we were not afraid of white men—Spaniards then, Americans now. Haven't you heard about Candon and how the people here fought for freedom?"

He decided to be honest. "No, Apo. But I am glad to hear of it."

The man took him down the road, telling him perhaps he had a better chance of getting a horse in Candon—if he could afford it.

Candon was one of the biggest towns in Sur, with a tall church majestically spired. To his right, the blue ridges of the Cordilleras beckoned with more urgency. There it was—unmistakable in the distance, the sharp and pointed outline of Tirad. The narrow trough to the left beneath it was where the president would go through. The trail up the mountain was flanked by huge trees, and the pass itself had been widened with forced labor by the Spaniards so that they could cross to the other side on horses.

The road from Candon led through ripening farmland, and

farmers had started to harvest the bearded rice, which the Ilokanos preferred. It was a tedious chore—separating each stalk, then snipping each off with the hand scythe. The sheaves were piled in mounds in the fields to dry.

By midday, he had started to ascend the foothills toward Baugen. There were no more extensive farmlands up the hilly and forested terrain. The trees had been cut and there were cattle—he was in ranching country, for which Baugen was noted. It was here where dried meat was cheapest, and draft animals and horses were brought all day down to the plain.

It was hot. The dew on the grass and the morning mists that draped the low hills had vanished. The last creek which he crossed was warm, and warm, too, was the earth under his feet. Sometimes, a pigeon—gray and streaked with blue and red— would suddenly flutter ahead of him to seek a new canopy of green. He had rested and was suffused with his sense of well-being. Above him loomed Tirad—no longer as sharp and pointed as it first appeared from Candon. Now, it was a jagged summit.

SHORTLY after noon, he approached the fringes of Baugen. Down the ridge, in the narrow valley, the barrio was a huddle of thatch-roofed houses with a single street through them. Experience in the last few days had taught him to be so cautious on entering any town that it was often necessary to skirt it. He surveyed the approach and decided he should go to the left, parallel to the small stream that originated from the mountain and ran through a slice of rice fields and jackfruit trees.

The cogon was tall and he walked leisurely. He told himself later how lucky he was that he had followed his instincts. He was about to emerge from a stand of bamboo when he heard laughter. They were not Ilokanos laughing.

He dropped to his knees and peered through the thin veil of trunks and leaves. Close to the river was an American soldier in blue, his rifle resting in the crook of his arm, while below him, down the shallow incline, were a pile of blue-and-gray uniforms, rifles stacked, and beyond, in the clear waters, six soldiers were naked and washing themselves, their white bodies shining in the sun like newly washed radishes. They were huge men, hirsute and heavily muscled, with legs as thick as posts and such long penises which, upon scrutiny, he saw were not circumcised.

Beyond the creek were a dozen giant horses grazing on hay, four soldiers eating. His heart thumped so hard he thought it would break out of his chest.

He realized with quiet deliberation that he was not really afraid. Now he knew what the enemy looked like, and there came this exhilarating feeling that they were not gods, that they were like him, with soft flesh that could easily be pierced and their blood spilled.

He turned around to find out if there were other sentries like the man he saw at the bank. He listened for movement but there was none, merely the wind creaking in the bamboo around him, the rasp of his own breathing, and the thumping in his chest.

Did they know where the president was headed or were they just a patrol scouting a way through unfamiliar terrain? He did not tarry to find out. He crawled away from the protective wall of bamboo, crouched low, then circled in a wide arc, seeking the cover of high grass and thickets, all senses working, waiting for the crack of a rifle shot that would mark his doom. But after some distance, when no shot came, he knew he was safe from them. It was then that he realized he was in a cold sweat, his brow was wet and his shirt, and again the old fear was a reality that dried his throat and transformed his legs into heavy stumps of wood.

But he was safe, safe, and briefly, too, relief akin to pleasure welled in him and at the turn of the hill, his legs were his again, and he started to run toward Tirad.

He paused to look at it—it was as if he could touch the green, green peak although it was still very far. God, he prayed, give me strength, this is all I ask. They have wings and I have but two aching feet. Surely, they must have a guide who knows this place, the recesses in these mountains. How else could they have known the way? You are right, honorable Cripple, we have been betrayed again. This is the changeless way of the world; will it never end?

The tough mountain grass, sharp and pointed, lashed at him and boulders rose to block his way. Beside him, the gullies yawned and he stumbled but always rose and ran onward, not wanting to look back for fear that he might see giant horses thundering after him.

CHAPTER

16

THE DRIED *CARABAO* MEAT and the rice were long gone, so when hunger struck, he gathered a few green guavas along the trail. His legs were blistered. Where the thickets were high and thorny, they had lashed at his arms as well.

He stopped once to drink from a small stream that forked from the Buaya River, then rested his back against a mossy boulder, facing the turn of the stream and the trail which he had just taken. In a short while, he would be in Baugen and he hoped there were people there who could tell him how long ago the president had passed. There were reports he could not quite believe, how the Americans were welcomed with brass bands and cheers in some of the towns of Sur. What was it that made his own people greet their conquerors and regard their own countrymen with ridicule if not hostility?

He brought out the notebook from the knapsack.

I am now very tired. My feet are sore. My chest is ever tightening and a weariness like a fat sack of grain weighs me down. At night, before I sleep in the open, the mosquitoes buzzing in my ears and keeping me awake, I wonder if I will wake up to a morning blessed with sunlight. I wonder why I am here, so far away from home. Is it because I cannot say no to the Cripple? Just as I couldn't say no to Padre Jose? The Cripple, Don Jacinto—they did not say it, but I know they love Filipinas and this I cannot say for myself because I am not sure. How can I love a thousand islands, a million people speaking not my language but their very own which I cannot understand? Who, then, do I love?

Tomorrow, when I wake up, I will no longer be surrounded by rice fields. I will most probably rise with the sun as it climbs from the east, first like a big winnowing basket of orange, then a blinding presence which brings green to the leaf, fruit to the trees, and yes, blue to the sky. It is the same sky above Cabugawan, a kindly roof to the people there, my kin, my loved ones.

O Apo Dios who sees everything, knows everything, am I wrong? I feel no affection for these mountains, these people whose fates are not my concern. I feel only for Cabugawan, my people waiting for my return, waiting perhaps in vain.

THE TIREDNESS in his bones disappeared, and once again he was alive to the sounds and scents around him and to the peace that the forest seemed to exude, comforting him with its somber stillness. He rose quickly, making sure the sack was slung securely on his shoulder. He always examined the twine with which it was tied—it was not loose even after all that climbing and straining. In fact, the sack had given him comfort, as he also used it for a pillow.

One more hill, then Baugen. He recalled what he knew of it, a village with a dozen or so thatch-roofed houses, farmers who worked the narrow valley and looked after the ranches of cattle that were now sparse. They were all Ilokanos, and braver than most, for it was in these hills where the Igorots often rampaged. Baugen was also a way station for those who went up the pass at Tirad. How often had Padre Jose and he stopped here for a bath at the village well, for provisions, sometimes dried meat and dry-season fruits, a restful night in one of the houses, an early-morning Mass, perhaps a baptism and confirmation, then onward to the pass by noon.

He breasted the hill, no longer keeping to the trail which he knew the Americans would take; he walked behind stands of grass as he cautiously approached the village.

It finally came into view. There were more houses now, more fruit trees. Then a shot rang out. He dropped onto his stomach; no, the shot was not for him. Blue-shirted American soldiers dashed into the village, shouting, firing. The screams of pain and fear were not only of men and women but of children. He crawled away to the edge of the forest bordered by butterfly trees and though he could not see the village now, he could still hear the screams, the guttural shouts, and the neighing of frightened horses.

When the firing stopped, he slithered close to the village again; the big men walked about the village. They had gathered in small sheaves portions of a roof and were igniting them and tossing them onto the houses. How easily the grass caught fire— first a grayish trail of smoke, then the flames in a crackling, swirling rage. Sparks burst from the roofs and landed on the

other roofs which were already burning, too. A dozen houses—
and not one was spared.

Po-on all over again, the toil of years vanishing in an
hour. So this is how a house burns; how quickly the fire devours
everything—the palm-leaf sidings, the floors of bamboo, all the
familiar implements, the remembered corners, a bamboo post
where some coins were kept in its hollow, an eating table, a battered chair, a chest. In a while, everything was ash but for the
sturdy posts of wood which still stood, blackened and red,
slowly burning, smoking.

The soldiers did not leave immediately; it seemed as if they
wanted to be sure that nothing was spared, nothing lived. They
had bivouacked in a gully beyond the village, and they came
back to look at their handiwork. They had mounted their
horses, their packs in their saddles. He counted carefully—there
were twenty-three soldiers, and the twenty-fourth did not sit
upright; he was slumped like a sack across his horse instead.
Perhaps the soldier was dead, for his body was tied to the saddle.

Were they all the Americans who had come to this village?
They rode easily and they seemed to be in no hurry as they
headed toward Tirad.

Istak looked keenly around him, wondering if there was
someone left behind, a rear guard, perhaps, or the main force
following this patrol. There was none.

He ran to the village, no longer cautious, wanting to know
if there would be someone, anyone, who had lived through this
hell. Not a moan, not a whimper from the bloodied bodies
sprawled in the yards; to each he went looking for a breath of
life. Who would bury them? There was nothing he could do, no
one he could save. He moved away from the human pyre, the
bodies with indistinct features. Toward the other end of the vil-

lage was an old brick-lined well and there, a youth slumped on the wet ground, a spot of red on his back.

Istak bent over him—he was not even seventeen. His pulse was still beating, though faintly. Istak turned him over carefully and the glazed eyes beseeched him. He tore open the shirt. The bullet had pierced his chest. Only a miracle could help and when Istak closed his eyes to pray, the path ahead of him was filled not with light but with darkness.

"Tell me, what happened?"

The lips opened, a gurgling sound. There was no need for him to know. Had he not seen what was done? The gurgling ceased, blood had foamed in the young man's lips and some of it had dried. Then the words came softly, disjointed. "My sister— she was taking a bath at the well . . . one of them started forcing her, I cut his skull in two . . ." The eyes closed.

Istak could feel the life leak away as if from a broken pot. He could not put back the blood which had soaked the ground around him; it was not just this boy's blood—it was an American's as well.

Wearily, he rose and walked down the trail toward Tirad, where the butchers had gone. He saw her lying on her back in the sun, the girl who was taking a bath at the well, the piece of blue Ilokano cloth she had wrapped around her body already dry and in a heap beside her. She was so young, so very young— perhaps not even fourteen. Those small breasts were just starting to grow; below the waist, the pubic hair that was barely discernible was covered with blood. A little wound above the navel no longer bled. A line of blood had trickled right on the grassy trail and dried. He stifled a sob, remembering Dalin, what was done to her and how she had survived it. And Orang, too, how a Spaniard had defiled her. He picked up the cloth and covered her with it.

He must say a prayer. He knelt, and as he started to pray, he heard a thunder of hooves behind him. He turned, but not quickly enough, and the last thing he saw was a blue shirt.

CONSCIOUSNESS returned, his head throbbing as if it would split. He passed a hand over it, and at the back of his head was a huge lump now pulpy and soft. He withdrew his hand to look at what had stuck to it—clotted blood that had not yet dried. For a while, his vision dimmed and even in the blur, he saw again the girl prostrate on the grass. He stumbled, reached out to her and held her hand—it was still warm but limp. The face was calm, the eyes closed. Go to sleep, young one, and in this sleep, forgotten is the past, the anguish and the pain. Go to sleep, young one, and rest in peace.

Overhead, the sun was still high. When he tried to rise, it seemed as if the earth heaved and the sky was suddenly so close he could touch it. He let the dizziness pass without moving, afraid that if he stirred the sky would fall on him. It was no longer darkening; all around him the land was bathed with light—the edge of the dark forest, the slope of grass.

He rose slowly, feeling his bones, wondering if there was any other wound in his body that had numbed, but there was none. He was not yet up on his feet when he realized that the bundle slung over his shoulder was no longer there; it had been cut loose. A pang of anxiety gripped him. He looked around quickly. It was nowhere, not on the grass, not on the rise of ground before him. His hands went to the pocket of his loose trousers; the notebook was still there—it had not been taken—and so was the nub of a pencil.

What would he do now? Without the letter, who would believe this peasant? It was all there—the reason for his being here, his purpose, his measure as a man. But he knew what was in the letter. No, he must not stop. He must go on, convince them he was sent by the Cripple not just with a message but to help them through these mountains. He must tell them, too, of Baugen.

CHAPTER
17

DECEMBER was at hand and the air was already crisp, the valleys scented with harvest. He needed to rest—his lungs were caving in, his legs were like logs. Though his throat was parched, he did not approach any of the few isolated houses along the way to ask for a drink. Time was precious, and it must not be wasted on his simple needs.

At times he tried to run, his failing breath permitting it. How he wished Kimat were with him now. But in this tortuous region, anyone on horseback would be easily spotted by the Americans.

The Cripple was right; the Americans were no different from the Spaniards—they were here to humiliate, to deny life. The three *insurrectos* who were hanged in the plaza in Bauang—they had been dead for more than a day and still they were not cut down and buried decently. The people must see the fearsome handiwork and be coerced into betraying Aguinaldo.

The trail that clung to the hillside was darkening and in the night it was not the marauding wild boar or the snake that he was afraid of. It was the occasional brigand whose face he could not see and the treacherous crevices hidden by weeds and caved earth at the side of the trail.

The Buaya River was no longer swift and bloated the way it was during the rainy season. It whispered through boulders and pools, placid in the starlight, the trees and reeds alongside it like a black margin to the river's course.

There was no habitation along the trail, even in those narrow valleys. Once or twice, he went down the river to drink, and put to flight a couple of deer as thirsty as he was.

Often, as he walked in patches clear of foliage, he would see the silhouette of Tirad—lofty and serene against the sky. Around him spread this quietude as if the earth breathed, muted sounds of crickets in the grass, night birds in the trees.

And again, thoughts of Cabugawan! He drew his strength from the earth and the earth meant peace. It was all changed now; he brought to mind the horrors that had been described so many times, they were vivid and real—how the Americans pumped water into the mouths of their prisoners, then stomped on their stomachs to pump out not just the water but information as well. Surely, they must have given him up for dead, as in Po-on. Otherwise, with the letter from the Cripple, they would have tortured him and he would then have brought harm not just to himself and to the president, but to the courageous Cripple he had left in Rosales.

He was in a narrow valley, small rice fields close by, the mooing of cattle, some farmer boy calling his water buffalo, a mother shouting to a wandering child to hurry with the firewood—the sounds of home that were all too familiar.

Then in the soft dark, a village suddenly stood before him. The thatch-roofed houses were indistinct. Some oil lamps were lighted, and cooking fires glimmered through the cracks of split-bamboo walls. He knew the village—the last before the ascent to Tirad. How many times had he been here with Padre Jose, and beyond, to the forbidding country of the Igorots. If he had to go deep into their land, he hoped that the men he knew—Kuriat, Ippig, and all the others—would still be in their villages and remember him. He had in the dim past brought them sugar, salt, and tobacco, and they in return had given him baskets, spearheads, and most important—protection.

He had not even reached the first house when from out of the darkness, the shout "¡Alto!" The command did not have to be repeated. He stopped and waited. From the shadows, two soldiers, their rifles pointed at him, approached, and a feeling of relief came over him, so pleasurable that he was smiling when the soldiers were upon him. He did not wait for them to speak. He addressed them in Spanish. "I have a message for the president," he said.

One of the soldiers pointed a gun at him while the other frisked him carefully. He had nothing, of course, but the sack with the empty water bottle, the notebook, and the pencil.

"With your kindness," he said with some exasperation. "There is so little time. I have an important message."

The frisking over, but with their Mausers still pointed at him, they told him to walk in front to the far end of the narrow road. One of the soldiers went into a house beneath which were other soldiers getting ready to sleep. He could make out, beyond the fence, out in the fields, the figures of men standing sentry.

Another soldier came out with a candle and Istak recognized at once the boots, the *rayadillo* uniform, the sword. The Cripple had told him about this brave young man, how well he had fought. In the faint light, how boyish General del Pilar looked, how self-confident.

"Good evening, Señor General," Istak said.

General del Pilar, impassive, raised the candle to have a better look.

"I had a letter for you, Señor General, from Don Apolinario. As you perhaps already know, he is in Rosales. You must believe me. It was taken away from me. Below, in Baugen. They—the Americans struck me on the head. Here," he turned to show the clotted wound on his head. "I know these mountains, Señor. Don Apolinario said I could help. And that is why I followed you all the way from Rosales, to guide you to your destination."

He must tell the general, too, grapple with words too painful to use, describe what he saw in Baugen. "The children, the women, the men—they were all dead, their houses burned. And a boy—I tried to help him but it was too late. He died, whispering to me, 'Americano, Americano.' And there was a young girl—so very young." He choked and was soon sobbing.

The general was quiet. He finally spoke. "This is nothing new."

"But why the children and the women?" Istak asked in anguish.

"Do not ask explanations for what happens in war," the general said. "We just have to give it to them double when we can."

The youthful face gleamed and in the sallow light, the young eyes seemed to tease him. "So you are going to be the president's guide. Surely, you must be tired and hungry."

"No, Señor General," Istak said. "There is no time to eat. You must get out of here quickly. I don't think they saw me—I circled around the village. They could still be there—in Baugen. I did not count, but there must be two dozen of them, with horses. There is no time, Señor General . . ."

The young Bulakeño put an arm around Istak's shoulder. "Run away from a few whites?" He laughed softly. "We cannot run on an empty stomach, can we?"

They did not go into the house; there was a table by the

bamboo stairs, and the food was placed there in a battered tin plate—cold chunks of rice and pieces of dried *carabao* meat that had been roasted and burnt in places. There was also a glass of water and to Istak it all never tasted as good as it did now.

They let him eat alone, which he did, swallowing the hard lumps of rice quickly. Then the general called for him in the yard, beyond the hearing of any of the men who were either asleep or seated on their haunches, talking softly under the stars.

Now they would be able to talk; now he would be able to tell the general everything that the Cripple wanted him to relay to the president.

"*Sigue*," Del Pilar urged him quietly. "What is it that you really want to say?"

"It is for the president's ears, my general," Istak said. "I was told to tell only him," he caught himself quickly—he was not going to hide anything from this young man, "but since he is not here . . ."

"He is not here, he is far from here," the general said curtly. "Continue."

"Don Apolinario said that we should continue to fight, that the president must be safe always, for he is not just a leader but the symbol of our nation . . ."

Silence, and a slow nodding of the head.

"Don Jacinto and Don Apolinario—they think that since I know these mountains well, I should be your guide to wherever you want to go. They did not tell me where—all that I know, my general, is that I should guide you through these ranges."

Istak did not expect the next question: "Where did you say Don Apolinario is now?"

"I already told you, Apo. In Rosales, where I came from."

"And who is taking care of him there?"

"His former classmate and friend, Don Jacinto. I also told

you this. Don Apolinario was ill. His secretary, Cayo Alzona, and his servant were also ill. Don Apolinario's kidneys weren't functioning properly, so I gave him medicine to drink—boiled flowers and young leaves of banaba. He is better now."

"You speak good Spanish," the general said. "Where did you learn it?"

"In Cabugaw—here in Sur, Señor General. I was born here. I was an acolyte for many years. I know this part of the country very well. Padre Jose, the priest in Cabugaw—we used to go this way and beyond, to the land of the Bagos, where he preached."

The general was silent, as if he were measuring carefully everything he was told.

"And how is Don Apolinario now? And what is he doing?"

"Writing, Señor General," Istak said. "Always writing. I copied his drafts because he gets tired and he wants to write so much, to send them all to Hong Kong, and from there, to the world."

More questions, some of them repetitive. Then it occurred to Istak—like a bludgeon it struck him, filled him with sadness and a dismal sense of futility—that for all the distance he had traversed, the hardships that he had undergone, the general did not believe him. The general was waiting for one mistake with which he could be trapped and then declared a spy.

He remembered what Don Apolinario had said, and it came to him in gleaming clarity. "We must learn to trust our own people, their judgment, if we are to build a nation. There will always be traitors, for it is the wretched who are often the most ambitious, but for every traitor there are a dozen who are true. We are going to build a nation—not of Tagalogs, Batangueños, or Caviteños—we are going to build a nation which includes all our brothers and sisters from the far south to the far north. Do you understand, Eustaquio, why I am here? I could hide much

290 + F. SIONIL JOSÉ

easier in the villages or in the mountains of my own province, among my people, and I would probably be safer there."

"My general," Istak said sadly, softly. "You have not really heard any of what I have told you. What do I have to do so that you will believe me?"

Del Pilar stepped back; perhaps he did not expect this farmer to talk like this. He raised his right hand, but the hand did not cut across Istak's face—it just loomed there, then dropped slowly. In the soft dark, he could see the young face, the earnest but mocking eyes.

"Eustaquio," he said finally, "no one speaks to me like this." Then he turned and marched toward the house.

IN A WHILE, everyone was stirring, and the yard was soon alive with men, their voices harried and tense. The general finally believed him, but how much he would never know.

They marched out in single file, the horses in the rear and the general himself in the lead, and headed toward the mountain—an endless curtain of darkness across the length of the land.

Although they did not tie him up or hinder his movements, two soldiers never left him. Soon, they entered a fold of land neither cultivated nor inhabited. They seemed to know where they were going. Certainly, the general had a map, a compass. At this time of the year, the mountain streams were shallow and could be crossed on foot.

Once there was a commotion in the middle of the column, for a boar had charged out of the darkness. Though it did not hurt anyone, it had caused some excitement and it was just as well, for they had, perhaps, become sleepy; Istak himself had started to drowse.

It was close to midnight when the column paused. Someone from the front came down the line. Istak thought his guards were to be relieved, for he could not understand their Tagalog. It became clear to him when the men beside him moved on, and he was told in Spanish not to move. It was here where he should stop and he was not to follow them.

He watched them plod on, swallowed by the night, the sound of their marching muffled till it was quiet again. Frustration, massive and overwhelming, swept over him; anger, too, beyond words. His chest tightened and only when he broke down and cried silently, the tears streaming down his face, was he able to breathe easily again.

He wanted to shout, but no one would hear, no one would care. It was all wasted then—the days of racing against the final hour, and it came in one, swift blur—the lowland dangers that he had passed, the patrol which almost trampled him. He knew the way, but he was not trusted, so they left him to go back. At least he was not shot. Did he not convince the general with all he knew about the Cripple? Or was it difficult for the general to believe that a peasant like him, speaking Spanish, could be just a peasant?

He wanted desperately to rationalize, to absolve the general. He was young, and because of his youth he was a poor judge of men.

HE WOKE UP in the chill dawn, the grass at his feet wet with dew. The trail was near the river. The sharp rise of hillside was studded with butterfly trees in bloom. Quickly, he remembered again with some relief that the general did not order him shot—just left behind to find his way back. He rose and turned around—the cool majesty of the mountains before him and below, more of the low hills which they had passed in the night. In a while, sunrise—the mountains were blue, the peaks covered with mist and beyond the haze, the pointed ridge below which the pass cut through.

They must be over the pass, the soldiers who emerged faceless out of the darkness. A new day, perhaps a new life. Why should an impetuous young man and this fleeing president of a country riven by jealousies and personal hatreds matter to him?

Yes, just as he had told the Cripple, why should I care for others who are not members of my family, who have not done anything for me? I have this piece of land which I have cleared. My duty is not to this nameless mass you call Filipinas. No country can claim my time, my loyalty. And as for God—I served Him well by doing my fellowmen no harm, but instead brought them health when they came to me with their bodies racked with pain. And for all these, my father was punished, I was punished. I am not going to test fate again.

The Cripple had looked sadly at him, then spoke, the words taking shape like jewels shining, glittering, impinging into his consciousness how easily he had been seduced by self-preservation: "If there is no country as such or as you know and recognize, then in your mind you must give it its boundaries. Do this because without this country you are nothing. This land where you stand, from which you draw sustenance, is the mother you deny. It's to her where your thoughts will go even if you refuse to think so, for it is here where you were born, where your loved ones live, and where in all probability you will all die. We will love her, protect her, all of us—Bisaya, Tagalog, Ilokano, so many islands, so many tribes—because if we act as one, we will be strong and so will she be. Alone, you will fall prey to every marauder that passes by. I am not asking that you love Filipinas. I am asking that you do what is right, what is duty . . ."

"And in the end I will be betrayed as others have been?"

"There will always be betrayals because we are men, not angels. They who betray—no pile of money, no shining title or other forms of adulation by which they were bought can assuage the self-hate, the sense of inferiority and sickening weakness which will corrode their very bones. They know this and there is no greater punishment than this self-knowledge. They cannot end it with suicide, for they know that such an act is the final push that bogs them into the slime of their own creation."

Was he rejected because he was Ilokano, or was it simply because the general did not know him? He had given all the incontrovertible proofs of his identity—not things that one could touch, or feel, but the account of what he had seen, what he knew. Had he been a spy, he would not have ventured this far, and alone. Again, the Cripple came to mind. He would understand.

IT WOULD be a long walk back to the plain, to Cabugawan. He had slept soundly and the tiredness in his legs seemed to have gone. He felt hungry again; it should not be difficult to calm that hunger and in the first stream that he had passed, he drank his fill. Nearby were papayas with fruit. The birds had eaten into the very ripe ones; he did not like them too ripe, for these often harbored tiny worms. He picked two and walked on; along the way, there would be guavas, too, or tree mushrooms.

He slept briefly, then woke up, the mountain breeze caressing his face. He brought out the journal—stained in places—and looked at his notations; it was ten days since he had left Cabugawan—it was now December, the first day of the month, and tomorrow would be Saturday.

He wet the pencil tip with his tongue, a habit that never left him, and wrote:

Duty comes in many forms; at times duty to country may conflict with duty to family. Yet, with a lucid mind the guises can be torn away and in the end, duty becomes but one, and that is duty to value justice above everything—to do what is right not because someone ordains it, but because the heart, which is the seat of truth, decrees it so.

Duty. Justice. All his life he had never really given much thought to these, or to the possibility of his being really free. He was concerned with being secure, with being part of the structure that the friars had built, because wherever he went, he saw that they did not even have guns. Their being white marked them as superior beings, for how else could they have conquered this land, how else could they have written all those books and understood the mysteries of God? For as long as he was brown and Indio, he was marked an inferior man, destined to be no more than an acolyte.

All this ignominy had been wiped away—the Indio had fought the white man and won, but how fragile, how short-lived that victory had been.

It would be a hellish trek out of the Ilokos, and ahead of him, now, was a long march out of this towering ring of mountains. Closing his eyes, in the black pit of memory, his past came instantly alive, ever present and bright, as if it were only yesterday that he had left Po-on. God forgive me for this one conceit; I am not just a healer, but in a way, I was Moses, too. He had read the Bible and seen the world in the Magnificat: "He hath put down the mighty from their seats, and exalted them of low degree. He hath filled the hungry with good things and the rich He hath sent away empty . . ."

He closed the journal and turned to the narrow plain below,

and there, in the last light of day—the pursuers in even file. He started counting quickly those that he could clearly see. A hundred, two hundred. Perhaps five hundred men, their horses loaded with provisions. By nightfall, they would be at the pass. How could they have marched so fast? They would get to Del Pilar before morning if they marched through the night.

He should no longer care, why should he? He had come to warn them, help them, and the general had rejected him. Let him and his men and even the president suffer the fate they had fashioned for themselves. He could save himself easily—he knew where to detour to a distance away from their line of march, and he would then be free to return to Cabugawan. There was all the time to do that in the safety of the night.

O Apo Dios, You who know everything and see everything. You will not begrudge me if I seek safety so that I can be with my loved ones. I have tried to give these soldiers all that this humble self can give but they did not trust me. Surely, I will do no wrong to the Cripple, to Don Jacinto, and most of all, to my own self-respect if I leave them to their fate. Surely, O Apo Dios, You will understand.

He turned to the darkening and disheveled landscape around him, the mountains that bore down on him with their silence and their gloom. He listened to his hurried breathing, to the thunder in his heart, to the depths of himself crying, yes, I do no wrong, but I must prove in flesh and in spirit that I am Indio, I am one of them!

CHAPTER

18

THE NIGHT came quickly, and though he was already up the incline, following the trail which laced the mountainside, still the pass seemed as distant as the stars that glimmered above. What sublime obstinacy was it that demanded he should now persist? He consoled himself; at night, the Americans might not march, not in this jumble of trees and rocks where they could be ambushed easily, that they were—like the Spaniards and the Guardia—afraid of the dark and the Indio phantoms that lurked in it.

He had raced the wind, propelled by a strength that did not flag. He climbed the trail, now shrouded by tall trees, quiet and sepulchral, and dark as men's minds. What was it that urged him on?

Duty—the thought was emblazoned in his mind, a torch

over the trail, food to his stomach, the rich, fresh air in his lungs, and yes, the bone to his tender flesh. Duty, and this meant Dalin as well, his two sons, and oh, my father, I can see you now with your one good arm reaching out, and Mother—you who had prayed that I be able to vault the distance from Po-on to a pinnacle where I could draw you up, where you would no longer know the cares of living.

And remembering them, tears stung his eyes, blurring briefly what was ahead, the brambles that tore at his legs, the huge boulders that blocked his way.

Then someone shouted the familiar *¡Alto!* He did not stop; he ran forward instead, shouting: "The Americans! They are coming. With horses. Hundreds of them. The Americans—they are coming!" A commotion ahead, a mad whirl of bodies. Arms seized him, clamped his mouth, pinioned him, bade him keep quiet. Around him figures moved quietly.

They knew who he was, and he was thankful that he had reached them safely. They left him by the side of the trail while a soldier went up toward the pass. He sat quietly, letting the coolness of the mountain seep into his being, quieting down the tremor in his heart. And it was then that a tiredness crept into his limbs, his body, and with it, a heaviness of the eyelids, the diminishing awareness of everything around him, and finally, sleep—deep and dreamless.

HE WOKE up with the whole world grown still; even the insects seemed to have gone to sleep. Then, the sound of digging, low Tagalog voices, brisk commands. Above him, the night arched beautiful and dusted with stars. It had become cold; he missed the familiar warmth of Dalin, the contours of her body, and the smell of their narrow *sipi*. Dalin—how she had changed through the years, from the headstrong woman that she was when they first met, into this wife and mother who knew how to persevere, to wait for the good times that might never come.

His mind remained sharp; it encompassed in one sweep again how it was in Po-on, those seemingly wasted years in the convent in Cabugaw. If he were there still, perhaps at this time he would still be reading, or writing, putting into pompous words the thoughts that came: he was so presumptuous then. Now, he was no longer afflicted with verbosity; he had discipline, detachment, maturity.

A soldier approached him.

"Yes," he mumbled, "I am rested now."

In a while, another soldier came with a cup. It was hot coffee sweetened with cane sugar, and it warmed his insides quickly. Then another came with a plate; he could see the pieces of dried meat, the white chunks of rice. He ate gladly, thankfully.

The air smelled so clean, spiced with the scent of grass. The crickets came alive again and they filled the night with their music. Thoughts of his boys crowded his mind. And Dalin most of all, the sound of her voice calling him Old Man. What was he doing up here, on this lonely roof of the Ilokos?

A soldier jarred him from his reverie. The general wanted to see him. He rose and followed him to the dark turn of the trail, and there the general sat, reclining against a boulder.

"Good evening, Apo," Istak said.

"You came back to tell us the news, Eustaquio," the general said quietly. "Have you rested?"

"Yes, Apo," he said. "I am grateful."

"Do you know how many they are? Surely a thousand."

"I did not count, Señor General. I couldn't go near—I was afraid—" He paused. That was the truth, he had been afraid. "They were in a very long line. With many horses. More than a hundred. Maybe three."

"Sleep now," the general said after a while. "We have plenty of work when it is light."

The stone upon which he rested his head was hard, and the grass pierced the blanket in places and pricked his arms, his legs, but sleep did come again, this time fitfully.

He woke up long before daybreak, birdcalls echoing from the forested slopes below them. In the first flush of light he viewed the sweep of mountain and sky, the summit grassy in places. He knew the turns of the pass very well; every year he and Padre Jose, old, portly—beads of sweat on his ruddy face and even on the smooth dome of his bald head—had taken this route on the way to the village of Angaki and the other Igorot settlements beyond.

All around, these young Tagalogs barely out of puberty, the milk of their mothers not yet dry on their lips, pausing in their labor, appraising the earthwork they had made on sections of the pass. Among them, he felt old and tattered in spirit. He was not equal to them in strength, but he knew this land better than any of them, the secret crevices of these mountains, the labyrinthine ways to the valley—and the Igorot villagers that might attack them. He could lead them to wherever they wanted to go. This was, after all, what he was here for. And if it was their decision to make a stand here, they could do it better with ambushes farther down. They should also secure the mountainside at the right, for there was a steep trail there which overlooked the pass.

He turned again to the young men around him, sardonic indifference on their faces. It was not only their youth which saddened him—it was the casualness with which they waited in their trenches. Would these also be their graves? How many funerals had he attended, how many open graves had he seen, watched the coffins eased down, or sometimes just a frayed mat in which the corpse was bundled, the feet sticking out, the soles white and sometimes still specked with dirt if the man had been a farmer and could not afford slippers, let alone shoes. He wanted to strangle the thought but he saw with horror that, indeed, many of the soldiers were barefoot like him. They were farmers, too, but they were all Tagalogs; they would not trust him, they would not want him by their side when the hour came.

The wind swooped down bringing with it again the scent of grass and earth. It was harvesttime in the plains below, in Cabugawan as well. In his mind's eye, his boys were romping around, trying to help although they could do but little, trailing behind their mother to see if she had missed any stalk with her hand sickle. There would be nothing missed, of course, and in a week the field would be bare and the sheaves would be laid out, spread like flowers to dry in the sun before they were neatly piled in the granary behind their house. How wonderful it was—the smell, the taste of new rice, the steam rising from it, even with just a dash of salted fish and lemon.

Istak did not speak with the soldiers. He doubted if any could speak Spanish. In fact, they could be wondering how it was possible for a farmer like him to know the language of their former rulers. He was much older, too, and he realized with some discomfort that he was not young anymore.

Morning rode over the hills, gleaming on the narrow valleys below, shimmering on the trees, its song of praise reflected on the shale and on the smooth surfaces of red rock. It came to him with a sudden twinge of remembrance that it was Saturday and if he were in Cabugaw now, he would be about through with the offertory of the morning Mass. He must not think about that, he was here in the splendor of morning, the hillsides burnished with light. If only this would last!

From around the curve of the pass above, the general appeared on his white horse. He came down at a slow canter, his

spurs reflecting bits of sun. He was handsome—Istak saw that;
no wonder then that the women in Pangasinan and wherever he
went had swooned over him. He had a yellow scarf about his
neck, and though they had climbed trails and muddy gullies, his
rayadillo uniform was clean and his boots neatly polished. He
was examining the earthworks, pointing out here and there what
needed to be done. Their positions gave them a clear sweep of
the terrain below.

The general rode to where Istak sat on a shoulder of the narrow pass. His gold epaulets shone. He had been viewing the sur-
rounding flanks with his field glasses and he seemed satisfied
with what he saw. "Do you think they marched in the night, Eustaquio?"

"I do not know, Señor General," Istak said. "I am not sure. It
seems they are afraid to fight at night."

Istak could see better now; the trenches were rimmed with
earthworks. On both sides of the pass, soldiers were stationed
behind boulders, but instinct told him at once—although he
was no soldier—that there should have been trenches way up to
his left, up to the peak of Tirad itself. It would be a difficult climb
for the enemy to make, to crawl up that cliff and cross the ravine
now covered with grass, but anyone who persevered could do it.

Would it do to tell the general, this imperious young man,
what he had missed? He had had so much experience, he had
lived through battles, and he, Istak, had never been in one.

Still, there was time to do it. He went to the solitary figure
at the crest of the pass. The general was seated on a boulder,
looking down in the direction of Angaki on the opposite side.
What were the thoughts rankling him? He had but a handful of
men to block the oncoming horde.

"My general," Istak said. "Please do not be angry with me—
but I know this pass. I have crossed it several times."

Del Pilar looked up from his perch and there was a brief flash of kindness in the young eyes.

"Yes, Ilokano," he said. "What do you want to tell me?"

"That side to your left, there is a trail there—maybe you think it cannot be scaled, but it can—"

The general smiled. "I have thought of that," he said coolly. "But the Americans—they are not all that persevering. They don't have the patience. There are so many of them, and so well-equipped—they will not do it the difficult way. They will do it the easy way—like it has always been . . ."

Istak bowed. Why was this boy so sure of himself? What bravado was this? Or courage?

A shout erupted from below; the air tensed quickly. A soldier raced up to the general. "They are here, my general. We wait no more!"

The general turned to where the soldier had pointed. A line of blue ants was clambering up the slope, dodging behind boulders disappearing in the tall grass, perhaps two hundred of them, five hundred even—and more farther down.

The general turned to him and spoke curtly. "I have been generous—perhaps, you can see that. You can save your life now by going down the mountain and joining the Americans. You will carry a white flag so they will not shoot you. This is the only way out for you. And you have my word that you will not have a bullet in your back. So go, Eustaquio—while there is still time."

Istak listened, his chest tightening, his whole being aflame. A soldier had flung disdainfully before him a bamboo pole and to it was tied a big white kerchief. He looked at it, but he must not be angry, he must suppress all the emotion that sought to erupt in him as it had once, the anger at the Guardia, at what he saw in Baugen, and now, toward this dumb, unfeeling dolt of a boy, so very much like the new priest who had replaced Padre

Jose, so full of life and yet so distrustful and vicious. But the general was doing what he thought was right, he was a soldier who commanded the loyalty of all these men, all of them older than himself. He had turned and marched away, he was down the pass, and Istak could hear him exhorting the men, though he did not understand Tagalog too well.

He was rejected, then. But there was no one who could reject what he would do, and he would do it not because he wanted to prove them wrong; he would do it because now, there could be no denial, not after Po-on, not after Baugen.

He looked disdainfully at the white flag and detached it from the pole. Rising, he flung the pole away in the direction of the enemy, then folded the kerchief neatly and laid it on the grass. He would stay, he would care for the wounded, for surely there would be many.

He turned to his left, to the soldier posted there; he was dark, with very grave features, but the man was smiling at him.

"Cover, cover," the soldier said, thrusting a chin toward the boulders on the shoulder of the rise.

Istak nodded, and said thank you in Tagalog, but did not go to the boulders. He walked, instead, to the trenches down the pass. That was where most of the men were positioned and that was where he would be needed. There was no firing still, just this waiting that tightened the nerves and parched the mouth. He could still run, as the general had said, toward the enemy and live. He had chosen to stay. Alive, he could still follow, convince the president, run errands, aid the wounded, or simply help them through the hostile Igorot lands. But there was a wearying tiredness in his bones, a gasping for breath, a deadening in his flesh—perhaps he should not run anymore.

It was such a beautiful Saturday morning; the sky was pale blue, and clouds white as newly harvested cotton floated along the far horizon. Mountains, mountains all around—it did not seem that he had traveled so far and he would still have so many mountains to cross; he should stop here now, so that his flesh, his blood, could blend inexorably with this land. Rain on parched earth, benediction.

His gaze wandered to the distance below; they were still very far off, but he could see them clearly, shapes moving up the steep curves of the trail, shirts vivid blue against the bright green grass.

Is this then the final flood? And who can escape it when even this mountainside would surely be submerged by it? There came to mind quickly again, *Si Dominus custodierit civitatem frustra vigilat qui custodit eam.*

I do not watch in vain, and it is not God who is fighting against my city. I am a man of peace, I will not throw a single stone. My words, my thoughts may be hostile, but my deeds will speak of love. I will try to give love and light to those who need them . . .

But would he do this now? Those were no brutal illusions—the anguish, the death he had seen in Baugen, and in remembering, Istak shuddered. The nightmare would not pass—it was living blood which he had touched, it was a dead girl he had cradled in his arms, and the homes that went up in flames were homes of living people, just like Po-on had been, just like Cabugawan was now.

It is for Dalin, then, for my boys, for my neighbors who do not know of the struggle for this lonely summit. The few of us who are here waiting—we can hold back the flood, and even if it were to immerse us all, it would have to ebb and we could raise our heads again.

All around was stillness, strained breathing. All around was this clearness, not of doom but of life. Men defying steel—they were not like him, they were trained to kill, and he had never held a gun; he did not know how to load one, much less aim one and play God.

The general had dismounted; he marched up the pass, telling his men in Tagalog, and now in Spanish as well, that they should wait till they had those blue shirts clear in their sights. Then and only then, he was telling them, although he himself perhaps was trembling, not to be afraid, that since they would not get out of this alive anyway, they should die like men. "Like men—understand? How many men are left in the world? You there, Kulas, you have no beard and no beard will ever grow on that face. But I know you have testicles. You are a man, are you not, Kulas?"

Laughter.

"Maybe, my general."

More laughter.

It was eerie, the laughter that welled from them on this early morning.

The general mounted his horse again and rode to the edge of the pass, to the promontory where from down below he could be seen.

Volleys from below, bullets whistling, pinging on rocks, but none touched him.

He was taunting death with a boyish infidelity to life. No, this was not courage—this was madness with no explanation to it, as Istak could easily explain the raw fear which gripped him, made his legs heavy, immobile, as if they had been roots implanted deep in the land itself.

"Oy there, Simeon," the general was saying now. "You have fought in Calumpit, in Tarlak. They are not good fighters, my brothers. They are cowards and they waste their ammunition. Do you remember how they fired without looking at us, without raising their heads? They are white like milkfish and just as ill-trained."

Now, the Krags resounded below and the bullets whined above him, thudding against the earthwork and cutting the leaves of grass. In the trench to his right, one had fallen and the blot of red quickly spread on the soldier's back.

"*¡Fuego!* Fire!," the general barked and their Mausers thundered as one. "*¡Fuego!*"

Istak raised his head and saw three men collapse way down the grassy sweep below. They did not rise—the blue distinct on the green.

"First squad," the general was shouting now in Spanish. "I know you have testicles. But why do you shoot like women? They are coming now to your right—and you are missing them, although you can already smell their baby breath. You must like these barbarians who raped your sisters and your mothers. Are you my brothers? Or my sisters? *¡Fuego!*"

The Mausers roared and the Krags below replied.

The numbness in his legs and the pounding in his breast had subsided. Now, Istak could think clearly, could feel keenly, as if he could trace every gulp of cool air that rushed to his lungs. Every touch of grass upon his skin reminded him that he was alive although death was in the air, in the shrill whistling of bullets above him, around him. He held his palms to the sun—they were as rough as they had always been. He crouched, blood rushing to his legs, then he raced to the trench at his right where the soldier had fallen. He crawled to the prostrate form; the *rayadillo* uniform was soiled with the green of leaves and branches and the rich brown of the mountain earth. The blot on the man's back was like a gumamela blossom. *Hibiscus rosa sinensis.* He got the rifle and knelt by the fallen soldier—his pulse was still.

Why do you falter, why do you hesitate? These few moments are your last, you know that. What does life mean to you now?

NOW, NOW, NOW!

All my life, I have tried to be a man of peace and You have rewarded me amply by entrusting me with Your healing gift. I have served You well, my God, and though at times I wavered, though at times I questioned You, always I was true. Every time I healed, I knew it was not I but You who did this, and having been Your willing and happy instrument, I have given some substance to this empty life.

NOW, NOW, NOW!

I will give up this power, this gift entrusted to me—will I give You up, too, now that I have decided? Tell me, my one true God, assure me I do no wrong if I kill my enemy; it is not the question of my life or his that is impelling enough. It is right against wrong—good against evil—and my God, You are not blind—YOU know!

He was not a healer anymore. He was a destroyer and the gun which he now grasped seemed a part of himself. Feeling its weight, its cold steel, it was indeed a part of his arm, his very flesh. He had seen them take the bullets from their leather canisters and load their rifles—it was not difficult to do the same.

Then, from his right, the general greeted him in Spanish: "Oy, there, Eustaquio! Are you sure you want to die here? I told you to flee but you chose to remain. Oy, there, Ilokano, learn how to shoot, then."

The soldier at his left lifted his rifle and ejected the spent cartridge then rammed another into it. It was easy—he did not need a lesson on how to load. And it was even easier to aim.

Istak lifted the gun and steadied it on the rock before him. Through the sights, the patches of green on the mountainside below, the dead Americans lying on the grass, blue on green. The soldiers were still far, but they stood out clearly in his sights as they flitted about looking for cover or for a way to charge up the pass. Something moved behind a screen of cogon to the right; he aimed at it and fired, the report ringing in his ears, his shoulder jolted back so hard he thought it would be wrenched away. From behind the sprout of grass, a dash of blue sprang then fell.

Joy coursed through him like lightning. But was it really joy? He did not know; he was sure only of its intensity as it inflamed his whole being. He had finally killed a man.

And the exultation—if it was that—which had lifted him, dashed him back to the earth, saddened him. He had taken a life. This was war, this was righteous. What right have these white men to be here, millions of arm's lengths away from their own land? He should have done this years ago when they were driven out of Po-on, when his village was burned.

He glanced fitfully upward; the sky—how blue it was, how serene and peaceful, even with the gunfire that rattled around him. The soldier who had taught him how to put a bullet in the belly of the gun now shouted at him to load again. The soldier— he was just a boy!—smiled at him. They were all strangers to him only a while ago. Not anymore; he was now one of them. In death, all men are brothers.

How clear his thoughts were now: here on this mountaintop, there is meaning to all this, bigger than life. None will thank me for this, nor will anyone remember. I have worshipped God. Is my salvation in my suffering? Or will suffering teach me of its necessity? I have become a new man. I have seen what can be seen only on top of a mountain.

He inhaled deeply, and turned to his back, toward the east bathed with luminous, early light.

I have been blinded, as many of us have been blinded by our

needs. I had thought only of my family—this was the limit to my responsibility, and therefore, my vision. On this pinnacle I can see much more now. I am no longer Eustaquio Salvador. So then I will pit this tender flesh against the steel of a new master. I can do this because my pulse is quicker, because I am free. Listen to the wind in the grass.

Who are they who come to us promising to teach us what we already know, who will give us a new god to worship? God is in all of us. Who are they to say that we are children, that they should be our teachers? Their defecation is foul, they are flesh who will be ripped apart by bullet or blade. But why are they strong and why are we weak? Can it be that their faith has made them more capable than we, more enduring, more brilliant? And even nearer to God?

There came to mind again old Padre Jose, sweating beneath his black cassock in the April heat, doggedly toiling up these mountains, braving a malignant land and an equally malignant people about whom he knew little yet was willing to meet and risk so much in his desire to learn more, and having learned more, would then convert and conquer. Conquer with what? With knowledge, more than anything, for what are guns? They will rust and fail, but not knowledge, which is strength. This was what Padre Jose had told him, and this was what he had learned to believe. Knowledge was just the instrument—there had to be a will to put spirit into the flesh, and move even old and creaking bones so that the hands may shape new churches and the tongue will utter the words that will touch men's hearts.

When you know you will die, you accept Death. The thought is no longer fearful. It was thinking about Dalin, and his two sons, that pained him; they did not even know he would be here on this desolate mountaintop haloed with light and churned by the whirlwind. He prayed that they would grow strong, that the land they would inherit would always be theirs, and most of all, that their mother would know no more travail.

They are coming now—more of them, down there below the gorge where they have left their horses; there are so many of them and there are so few of us. I am thirsty—sweat creeps down my back.

Why aren't you coming up? Are you afraid?

Have we really stopped them? The president—he must be far away now with the time that we have bought for him. This is our gift not to him but to Filipinas. Honorable Cripple, I am not a patriot. But how do you measure the sacrifice this poor man beside me has made? He lies still, his hands no longer feel. He is so young, so very young—what had life promised to hold for him? Who is the woman he would have made happy, who would have borne his children? Honorable Cripple, you know the answers. And God—do I take Your name in vain? I don't even know why I am here when I could have run away. It must be pride, or stubbornness, of which men of the north have plenty. If it is pride, what, then, can I be proud of? I have nothing to show, nothing which I have built by myself. Why then am I here? I will search the depths and will find nothing there. Nothing but

Duty,
Duty,
Duty.

Epilogue

Dear Jim,

Thank you very much for your comments on my dispatch on the battle at Mount Tirad. It takes such a long time for my letters to get to you, and I cannot send messages by cable unless they are absolutely necessary. You must content yourself with letters, then.

I must tell you that I am not altogether happy about your decision to come here and teach school. I made this obvious, I hope, in my dispatches describing conditions here. But I will not try to dissuade you because I know your mind is made up and, certainly, you can do much in a territory like the Philippine Islands. In a sense, therefore, I am quite pleased that my brother has found a noble motive, to bring our civilization to this bleak corner of the world.

I just want to be sure that you know what is in store for you. Remember that Manila is not Boise, Idaho, and knowing of your adventurous spirit and your earlier desire to go to China, you will probably want to leave Manila for someplace in the mountains that is more interesting and challenging.

You have asked me to describe the Philippine Islands in some detail.

First, Manila. I must warn you that it is an Asiatic city, inconvenient and filthy. By steamer, you will go up the Pasig River, which empties into the bay. It is a very dirty river, with blobs of green water plants which have pretty purple blossoms. There are many native boats in the river; some are carved from whole trunks of trees, and cascos—boats with flat bottoms—which are pushed by the Tagalogs on the riverbanks. About these Tagalogs—they usually wear their shirts out, a custom which the Spaniards imposed on them to set them apart from us Occidentals, who always tuck in our shirts. You will disembark near the Puente de la España—or Bridge of Spain—a brick bridge which spans the river, then you will be taken to your hotel on a horse-drawn carriage with two wheels. For a more elegant ride, take the two-horse carriage.

The natives eat a lot of onions and garlic but the food—I have had a bit of it—is not as spicy as in India. You can feast on a variety of tropical fruits, and my favorite is the mango, which is tastier than our peach. And bananas and papayas—they are big and luscious. Keep away from pork, particularly outside Manila, for the pigs feed on human excrement. The water buffalo meat is tougher than beef, but it is certainly cleaner. Goat, chicken, and duck are also available.

At night, you will sleep in a giant four-poster bed with curtains, even. Sleep under a mosquito net—it is an absolute necessity. The mosquitoes are big and vicious and you may get malaria, which will give you constant fevers and chills. There will be no mattress on the bed but you will get used to the woven cane, which is also used for the seats of chairs.

Manila has a population of about one hundred fifty thousand, mostly natives. You will find many Chinese, Creoles, and a sprinkling of Europeans. Most of the Spaniards have left.

Almost all the Europeans—you can recognize them in the streets—wear white suits, as do the wealthy natives. The Chinese wear their own costume. It is really ridiculous seeing mestizos and natives suffering the heat attired in European suits with pointed leather shoes and, yes, black English derby hats. But the women dress sensibly, if elegantly, with blouses that seem to flower at the wrist, a folded kerchief around their necks, and billowy skirts which sometimes trail behind them. Their blouses are made from pineapple fiber and they are gauzy and very delicate. The women wear their hair long and they keep it glossy with coconut oil. It may not smell right, though, and you need not ask how I came to know.

There are very few big buildings here other than the churches, which are small compared to the churches of Europe. They have been constantly rebuilt, for this is also a land of earthquakes. The wooden houses are often roofed with tile. For windows they use seashells which permit light to filter in. The houses are really very airy. The lower portions are reserved for animals, carriages, and servants.

Yes, there are streetcars in Manila, but they are drawn by pathetic-looking little ponies. Escolta, the main shopping street, is stocked with all sorts of goods from the Continent. The Chinese shops are on a nearby street called Rosario.

Beyond this street, to the north, is a district called Tondo. The natives live here in tiny bamboo houses with palm-leaf roofs. The land is swampy and the whole place is foul; under the houses feces and rotting garbage collect in stagnant water. This is where the Katipunan—the secret society that ignited the revolution against Spain—was founded.

Intramuros—the old Walled City built in the sixteenth and

seventeenth centuries—is surrounded by a moat fed by the Pasig River. It is an ugly and filthy moat spanned by eight bridges. The walls of Intramuros are thick—a squad can march on its ramparts. But the walls were never a defense against our naval artillery. There are many churches here, including the palace of the Archbishop. The streets are cobbled and the houses of stone are really old.

Beyond the Walled City is the Luneta—a promenade which is very popular, specially at dusk. There are a couple of bandstands and regular concerts are held.

In Manila, or anywhere in the Islands, I advise you to boil your drinking water else you will catch cholera or the pox. The latter is a horrible disease which scars the face with many small holes—I have seen this in children and in women who otherwise would be beautiful.

Manila has electricity, but it's not very reliable, so always be ready with a match and candle.

The newspapers are all in Spanish, so you must learn the language if you want to reach the educated Filipinos. English must be taught here and I am glad that this will be one of your duties.

Transportation to the other islands is by boat and on the major island of Luzon where I am, you can go by train to Dagupan in the north. Otherwise, you go by carriage on poor and narrow roads. I would like to visit the south, where the Muhammadans are, and the mountains in the north inhabited by the head-hunting Igorots. There is gold up there.

You ask what the natives are really like. There are many tribes and dialects. In Manila are the Tagalogs; they are like most of the natives, a small people with black hair. They are very grace-

ful, particularly the women. They have dark eyes and since there has been some intermarriage with the Chinese and Spaniards, there are many half-breeds. They are wily, passionate, irresponsible, and cannot be trusted. Our men say they steal anything they can lay their hands on.

Some have been educated in Europe, like the insurgent leaders we are now chasing. They revere a man named Jose Rizal who was also a novelist, a doctor, a poet, and God knows what else. Naturally, the Spaniards executed him in the Luneta, which I described earlier.

You want to know how the war is going. You have read my dispatch on the battle at Mount Tirad. I did not exaggerate. It was such a heroic stand by a small band against our superior Texas Rangers. We must respect courage wherever we encounter it.

There will be those of us already here who will perhaps want to remain. Opportunities are abundant. Farming, mining, and business are possibilities.

Although you have not asked, you will perhaps want to know about our future with the Philippine people. This expensive little war is almost over. Except for some guerrilla activity in the Visayan Islands and in Southern Luzon, I am sure that we will secure the territory very soon. General Aguinaldo's days are numbered; sooner or later, General Funston will get him.

And after that, we will have to stay and build.

I agree with you that we have a God-given responsibility to the world. We have worked very hard to make a great and prosperous nation and we must extend our influence beyond the two oceans. Spain is corrupt and it is right that we defeated her and took over these poor islands which have long been mired in igno-

rance and poverty. We will teach the Philippine people the values of our institutions, prepare them for self-government, impart to them the virtues of self-reliance and freedom. Above all, we must teach them dignity, show to them those shining pillars of democracy we have built for ourselves. These are righteous causes for which American blood has been spilled.

You will, therefore, have a splendid opportunity to do what has been ordained by destiny for us. Our future in this part of the world will be enhanced by what we will do in these Islands.

I had not meant to denigrate the natives in describing them earlier in the words of our men. I have written glowingly of their heroism at Mount Tirad; I think I should also mention here their capacity for learning, or for mimicry, if we want to condescend.

I was very surprised to find in one of the dead insurgents— he was barefoot like the rest and not in uniform, so many of the guerrillas are like this—a journal which, at first, I thought were instructions entrusted to a courier. The notations were in Spanish and Latin; my knowledge of Spanish, as you know, is excellent and my Latin, though rusty, is still good. The dead man—his name was Eustaquio Samson—had a pencil on his person; it was he who wrote in that diary as he journeyed from a place called Cabugawan to this mountain pass. He writes in awe of Mabini, the insurgent leader who was captured recently. I have a good mind to see him and tell him about Samson and, perhaps, visit as well the Samson family in Rosales. So hearken now to the last notation this barefoot soldier made about his enemy—us:

"Conquest by force is not sanctioned by God. The Americans

have no right to be here. We will defeat them in the end because we believe this land they usurp is ours; God created it for us. The whole history of mankind has shown how faith endures while steel rusts."

Think it over.

Yours,
Tom

GLOSSARY

anahau: Short palm tree, no taller than a man. Its leaves are made into fans, rain capes, and the like.

Apo: Respectful form of address.

Apo Init: The sun.

azotea: Area attached to the rear of large homes, lacking a roof (Sp.).

bakas: Ilokano ritual to mark the end of mourning, when Ilokanos stop wearing black.

banaba: A tree with medicinal leaves and purple flowers.

bangcag: A plot of land not suitable for rice. It is planted with vegetables, root crops, and/or sugarcane.

basi: Sugarcane wine.

batalan: Same as *azotea,* but on farmhouses, where water jars and some potted plants are placed.

benting: A 25-centavo coin (no longer used).

bodega: Store or house (Sp.).

calesa: Buggy (Sp.).

carabao: Water buffalo. The animal does not perspire, which is why it needs to soak in water or mud every day to cool off.

cartilla (literally "primer"): The alphabet (Sp.).

carzoncillo: Shorts for men, tied with a string around the waist, usually made of cotton, often knee-length.

catón: Primer; a reader for children (Sp.); a teacher.

catuday: Tree with white or pink flowers that can be eaten.

cédula: Residence certificate (Sp.).

culibambang: Tree with leaves like green butterflies, hence its name. It grows wild, usually on hillsides.

dalipawen: A very tall tree, like a palm, that draws fireflies.

dal-lot: Traditional Ilokano poetry, usually chanted.

galletas: Biscuits (Sp.).

ganta:	Measure of grain; term no longer used, as grain is measured in kilos.
gobernadorcillo:	Town mayor.
herbolario:	Native healer, who usually uses herbs.
ilustrados:	The first Filipinos, usually of means, who studied in Europe (beginning in the 1880s) in order to become "enlightened"; literally, "learned" or "well-informed" (Sp.).
inang:	Ilokano equivalent of "mama."
ipil:	Tree usually used for firewood.
kumbento:	Part of the sacristy where the priest lives.
kusing:	Smallest monetary unit, even less than a penny (no longer used).
lomboy:	Edible fruit, like purple grapes, but with a big seed.
madre de cacao:	A shrub planted as fencing, with beautiful cherrylike flowers in dry season.
mal vivir:	Spanish name for Filipinos who fled from Spanish tyranny.
Manong:	Affectionate, respectful form of address for older brother or man. Ilokanos do not call older relatives by their given names alone.
marunggay:	Its leaves and young fruit are cooked as vegetables.
médico titulado:	Officially licensed doctor (Sp.).
micol:	Five-centavo coin (no longer used).
municipio:	Town hall (Sp.).

oración:	Prayer, usually in Latin (Sp.).
pañuelo:	A scarf worn by women, usually with the national dress (Sp.).
parunapin:	Hardwood tree.
pasyon:	The Holy Week story of the crucifixion, usually sung in verse form.
patintero:	A game usually played in the moonlight.
pomelo:	Tropical orange, often as big as a soccer ball.
principalia:	The provincial elite, usually landlords (Sp.).
rayadillo:	Seersucker design of the revolutionary army; tiny blue lines on white.
remontados:	Spanish name for Filipinos who fled from Spanish tyranny.
sagat:	Hardwood tree. Sagat is the hardest Philippine wood, used for house posts or railroad ties.
sala:	The living room in large houses (Sp.).
salapi:	Fifty centavos; also denotes money, lucre.
saluyot:	A wild-growing shrub with leaves that are the best-known Ilokano vegetable, slippery like okra.
sineguelas:	Tree bearing a green fruit no larger than a Ping-Pong ball.
sipi:	A small room attached to the farmer's house, where pillows and the rice bin are stored.

sitio:	A group of houses smaller than a village.
siyam-siyam	(literally "nine-nine"): Nine days of constant rain.
sopa boba:	(literally "fool's soup"): Small consolation (Sp.).
suman:	Gelatinous rice cooked in coconut milk, usually wrapped in banana leaves or young palm leaves.
Tatang:	Ilokano term for father or affectionate address for an older male.
tinto dulce:	Sweet wine (Sp.).
tulisanes:	Thieves.

ABOUT THE AUTHOR

With the publication of *Three Filipino Women* by Random House in 1992, the work of F. SIONIL JOSÉ began appearing in the United States. He is one of the major literary voices of Asia and the Pacific, but (after encouragement by Malcolm Cowley and others) his novels and stories are only now gradually being published in the country that figures in much of his work as both a shadow and yet a very real presence.

José (widely known as "Frankie") runs a leading bookshop in Manila, was the founding president of the Philippines PEN Center, publishes the journal *Solidarity*, and is best known for the five novels comprising the highly regarded Rosales Saga (*Dusk* [*Po-on*]; *Tree; My Brother, My Executioner; The Pretenders;* and *Mass*). He is widely published around the world and travels steadily.